Advance Praise for *The Concrete*

"*The Concrete*, Daniel Abbott's searing debut novel, marks the introduction of a fresh, exciting, and important voice to the American literary landscape. Filled with uncommon insights into the human heart, this gritty, brave, redemptive novel tells truths we all need to hear."

—**Connie May Fowler**, author of *Before Women* and *Wings* and *The Problem with Murmur Lee*

"*The Concrete* grabbed me, shook me, and didn't let go. Abbott's characters are all fighters because they have to be: their neighborhood doesn't offer any easy lives, or easy wins. The triumphs here are hard fought and hard won— and often, painfully, hard lost. This is a fearless, unflinching debut."

—**Caitlin Horrocks**, author of the story collection *This Is Not Your City*

"Two brothers search for peace and light in a world with no map or meaningful navigation. The truth they find is hard, abrasive, and necessary. Daniel Abbott leads the reader down a path that turns into a gentle maze that becomes a jarring labyrinth of pain, peace, and discovery."

—**Jimi Izrael**, author of *The Denzel Principle*

"Daniel Abbott's novel has more body and soul, more swagger and sin, more beauty and brokenness, more pain and more love than another dozen brilliant debuts put together. To borrow a phrase from hoops, Abbott leaves it all on the floor—which is to say, the concrete. He's written this gorgeous, dark, healing book like someone's life might depend on it."

—**Ellen Lesser**, author of *The Shoplifter's Apprentice*, *The Other Woman*, and *The Blue Streak*

"Daniel Abbott writes with authority about the hardscrabble realities of inner city life. With unflinching honesty he explores those souls trapped in darkness and their sometimes heroic struggle to recapture the light. In this strong and gritty novel, Abbott establishes himself as a striking new voice in American fiction." —**Clint McCown**, author of *Haints*

"How many times has someone written about a 'stunning debut novel by a dynamic writer'? Enough times that those words never need to be written again. And, yet, I am writing them right now. Why? Because this book, *The Concrete*, truly is a stunning debut novel, one that takes readers through countless lives lived in Grand Rapids, Michigan, and threads together all these lives into one driving story. Only a dynamic writer like Daniel Abbott can control this larger of a world, but Abbott does exactly that! Read *The Concrete*."

—**Sean Prentiss**, author of *Finding Abbey:*
The Search for Edward Abbey and His Hidden Desert Grave

"Daniel Abbott mines the underbelly of an inner-city Michigan neighborhood, sifting through the love and casualties of its inhabitants to find the light and hope that persists in the darkness. *The Concrete* is a striking and extraordinary debut."

—**Sophfronia Scott**, author of *All I Need to Get By*
and *Unforgivable Love*

THE CONCRETE

A Novel

Daniel Abbott

PUBLISHING

New York, NY

Printed in the United States
First Edition
10 9 8 7 6 5 4 3 2 1

Ig Publishing
Box 2547
New York, NY 10163
www.igpub.com

ISBN: 978-1-63246-070-7 (Paperback)

This book is dedicated to my brother Dennis.
For over twenty-five years of unwavering love and support.

CONTENTS

THE CONCRETE

Francis Street

2007

A U-HAUL TRUCK STUMBLES DOWN FRANCIS STREET. Winter has melted into spring. The cold Michigan air takes its last few icy breaths. Joey Cane lights a Camel. His eight-year-old daughter, Lyric, rests her head on his lap, buckled loosely, the seat belt dangling across her hip. Four teenage boys play tips in the middle of the road with a rubber basketball. Joey honks and motions with his hand for them to move. One boy aims a finger gun at Joey then fires an air bullet through the windshield. He blows invisible smoke from the barrel before stepping away from the truck. The U-Haul trudges on.

Joey inhales deep and exhales slow. Cigarette nestled between his lips. His left palm controls the steering wheel. He places his right hand on Lyric's head and twists his long bony fingers through her frizzy curls. He parks the U-Haul in front of the house, leaves Lyric sleeping on the seat, and steps outside. Across the street two men sit on a porch drinking beer out of paper bags. They eyeball Joey and speak in low tones. Joey runs his hand across his clipper-buzzed head. He cracks his knuckles, his neck. He loosens his shoulders.

Joey's girlfriend Tara pulls up in his burgundy Oldsmobile Delta 88, both hands on the steering wheel, seat pushed up too far, smiling the same smile she's been smiling this past month, since her Section 8 went through, a smile like life could get no better, a smile like she's "made it."

3

While Joey doesn't share Tara's enthusiasm, he does have to admit, the house on Francis Street is better than Miss Netta James's basement. He was laid off twice last year and unemployment couldn't cover the bills and the rent at the two-bedroom apartment in Kentwood. Late became too late became evicted and they landed at Tara's mother's house a few blocks from here on Franklin, a street with teeth in a neighborhood with claws, and that's when Joey stopped being Joey and started being White Boy, and that $200 per month rent went from a good way to get on their feet to getting old real fast.

Tara parks the car against the curb and kills the engine. Across the street one of the men stands and takes a swig of his beer. "That ass though, Lorenzo!" says the man standing. Tara's out of the car now. The other man laughs. The trunk is open. "Hey yo, Thunderbooty!" yells the man standing. Tara ignores him. Joey just stands there watching the man, glancing at Tara, then at Lyric, who's still asleep on the seat of the UHaul.

"Thunderbooty," says Joey to the wind. "That's a new one."

Joey respects the burden of having that much ass. A magnet for tactless eyes, inspiring *damns* and *aw shits,* grabbing hands and smacking palms. She has a body built for sex. No denying it. A 'hood Helen of Troy. Like Tara James was sculpted by the hand of God himself for the sole purpose of dragging the minds of men into the gutter.

But when your girl has a body like Tara has, and she's black, and you live in the southeast side of Grand Rapids, Michigan, the tone they use when they call you white boy. is something between spite and respect. You have no choice but to eat some shit. But if you eat too much they'll think you're soft. And if you're too eager to fight you'll wind up dead. Finessing that balance is the key to surviving this place.

"Baby," Tara shouts. "Help me with these boxes."

"Miss Thunderbooty!" says the man across the street. The one called Lorenzo sits sipping his beer, watching Joey. "Can I be your baby?" says the man standing.

Joey walks up to Tara and pulls her close, wraps his arms around her, and smiles at the man across the street. He nods his head in a way he hopes conveys, "You've had your fun but Miss Thunderbooty's mine."

"Alright then," the man says. "I see you, white boy."

"New street. Same shit," says Joey.

"Forget him, baby," Tara says.

Across the street the man has finally shut up and sat down. The one called Lorenzo is talking into his ear. A black Cutlass cruises past, the driver leaning as he drives, bass so loud it's knocking rust off the wheel well, the gold rims probably more expensive than the car. A heavy-set Hispanic woman walks down the sidewalk holding a child's hand. She's braless in a large Michigan sweatshirt. Her enormous breasts rest on a pregnant stomach. At the house to the right a door slams. A couple argue on a lawn. The woman screams at the man. The man screams back. Two small children stand behind their mother, a bead-headed girl wearing nothing but a diaper—snotty nosed and crying—her six, maybe seven-year-old brother standing with crossed arms, looking at his father, like, leave.

Joey lets Tara go. He watches her walk up the porch and unlock the front door. "New street. Same shit," says Joey.

Nelly's rusty white Dodge Shadow rattles into the driveway. A U-Haul truck is parked next door. A tall white man with a buzz cut stands on the porch smoking a cigarette. He wears baggy shorts, sandals, and a hoodie two sizes too big. He might be twenty; he might be thirty. Nelly can't tell. She puts her key in the lock and turns it. The new neighbor looks over. She steps into the house not bothering with polite introductions.

A pale blue breath of light spills into the living room. The static hum of a left-on television. Her son Isaac is asleep on the couch. He's ten and all limbs. His legs sprawled about, his left arm resting on his chest, his right arm hanging off the edge, his fingers kissing a social studies book that peeks out of an unzipped backpack. She peels a throw from the back of the couch and covers him with it. "Mom," says Isaac, but that's all. He hugs the throw and turns. Nelly watches him sleep, considering time and how it moves, trying to pinpoint the moment Isaac stopped being her baby boy, those first signs—the Mead notebooks he's always writing in, or sitting in the dark watching the world from a window—and started being a boy drawn to seclusion, accustomed to this neighborhood, but unwilling to engage with it.

Nelly slips out of the living room and climbs the stairs. The hallway light is on. Her husband Frank is snoring in the bedroom. She shuts and locks the door. Strips out of her clothes. Finds a bedside lamp and turns it on. Frank sleeps in the fetal position, wearing nothing but boxers, this large man, wrapped around himself. She touches his shoulder. "Frankie," she says.

Frank swats her hand away and rolls onto his back. The Cock falls out of the boxers. The infamous Cock. The dumb, useless, novelty Cock of Frank Page. Or Big Frank Page. Or Long Dong Page. Or Frankie Baby if you're some curious twat like Nelly was, wondering if the legend was true. And at nineteen Nelly Terpstra most certainly was a curious twat. Bosnian born and abandoned. Raised by Dutch-Christian missionaries old enough to be her grandparents, Nelly spent her childhood in church and private schools, getting A's and silently applauding God. She appeased the Terpstras by attending Calvin College until February of her freshman year, when she was expelled for "having an inappropriate relationship" with a professor. The Terpstras, in their natural embarrassment as alumni, board of trustee members, and Christian ambassadors of the school, threatened to disown Nelly, and then did, when with a smile on her face Nelly told them there was a second professor, dozens of boys, and even a couple of girls, that she had (and she held up quotations when she said it) "inappropriate relationships with."

So Nelly landed at Grand Rapids Community College, a small urban campus in the heart of the city, not because she had a plan, but because she didn't. And there she met "Frankie Baby," who worked nights as a janitor at the school, always holding, but never really pushing a broom. The kind of man who liked to lean on walls and watch girl's asses. His navy blue uniform bulging everywhere. He was something between a Flintstone and a Fonzie. Almost handsome; almost asshole. Not quite either. Expression on his face like he was trapped inside of a thought he didn't understand.

People talk and walls whisper. Nelly learned that lesson at Calvin College. At Grand Rapids Community College, The Cock of Frank Page was legend. And Frank's behavior was certainly some code of conduct violation. Funny how Nelly was punished for her indiscretions, given the Calvin College equivalent to a scarlet letter, sent packing, banned from the land of The Elect while Long Dong Page was allowed to lean on his wall in the Main Building at GRCC fishing for pussy, being idol-worshipped by pimply-faced boys.

But Nelly wasn't bitter. She was curious. Curious and bored. And for the first time in her life she was free, entirely free, away from the watchful gaze of the Terpstras, loosed from the Dutch-Conservative-Republican thumb, liberated and reckless, so when Frank asked for Nelly's number, she gave it to him. And when Frank asked her over for a movie, she said yes. And when the opportunity presented itself that very first night to confirm the legend, she did, and boy-oh-boy was Big Frank Page as advertised.

It was The Cock she fell in love with, not the man. She learned that when the morning sickness came. When the oaf paced the living room of his apartment repeating nothing but, "Oh shit, oh shit, oh shit," over and over. Months later they were married at the courthouse. Then Nelly dropped out of Grand Rapids Community College, and Frank was looking for a better job, and they were trying to figure out what it meant to be a family.

She touches it. The Cock. Again Frank swats her hand away. He rolls onto his side, turning his back to her. It's been weeks since they've been intimate. The hornball and hound, the youthful and virile Frank Page is gone. He works days and Nelly works nights and weekends. Their marriage, this family has become a space they occupy together, but rarely at the same time. The nights are getting longer and lonelier. This bedroom is shrinking. She comes home from her shift at Meijer, the local grocery superstore, and for hours she stares at the ceiling, the itch in her body left unscratched, surrounded by this man's snoring and the rot of stale beer on his breath.

She needs to breathe. Nelly switches off the lamp and opens the window. The chill of the air makes her nipples stand. The neighbor has gone inside. Across the driveway the blinds are drawn but a window's cracked open. A sliver of light and quiet conversation. The laugh of a woman. Nelly tries to remember the face of the neighbor. Tries to invent a face for the woman. A face to match the laugh. But Nelly only sees herself. Herself and Frank. Back when they smiled sometimes. When life was a thing happening and not a thing that happened.

The sliver of light has been swallowed by darkness. The neighbor's blinds sing a metallic twang against the breeze. Bedsprings moan. Nelly closes her eyes and touches a nipple. Frank has the slow jams playing. He has candles lit and he's naked with a farmer's tan. His large clumsy hands can't figure out her bra strap. He snaps it off and throws it across the room. Nelly drops to one knee and her fingers creep lower. The scene is gone. There are only sounds. The rhythm of the bedsprings. The muffled pleasure of the woman next door. The heat between Nelly's thighs. The wet. The rush. The throb.

Then it's finished. Nelly sits on the floor and leans against the wall. She listens to the night. There are no crickets on the southeast side. Just the occasional car. Loud laughter from a porch a few houses down. Shattered glass. A beer bottle probably tossed into the street. And then the noise is gone. There is no sound but Frank's snoring.

The block has finally gone to sleep.

Little Floyd's fighting De La Hoya tonight. It's Cinco De Mayo. The southeast side is buzzing with love or hate for one of its own. Floyd used to run through these same streets. Before the Olympics. Before he won his first world title. Before he was considered the best pound-for-pound boxer on the planet. Before he got filthy rich and moved to Vegas. Before Grand Rapids became his past, nothing more than an asterisk next to his name. Frank Page didn't know Floyd back then, but Frank knows people that knew him. The consensus is that back then Little Floyd was a little shit.

Frank has the queso dip slow cooking in the kitchen. The kid's watching the pre-fight, gathering statistics in one of his notebooks, watching highlights of both fighters—Isaac's "expert" opinion will come moments before the opening bell, if he can stay awake that long. Frank's rolling with Floyd. He always rolls with Floyd. It's not a loyalty thing, a Grand Rapids thing. Frank's just a logical man—Floyd Mayweather Jr. is simply the best in the business.

Frank gives the house a once-over. The kitchen's clean. The living room's vacuumed. Snacks are staged on the countertop island. "Alright. Alright," says Frank. He opens the refrigerator and finds a can of Coke and a bottle of Bud Light. "Isaac," he says. He tosses his son the Coke and Isaac takes his eyes off the TV just in time to snatch it out the air. Frank sits on a stool, twists the cap off his beer, and sips.

"Mayweather's never really been hit, Dad," says Isaac. "What happens when De La Hoya hits him?" Isaac looks up from his notebook. He's staring at Frank with that intense unsettling gaze that he gets sometimes. That boy. His mind always churning. One time Frank picked up one of Isaac's journals, curiosity getting the best of him, and found words he didn't even know, page after page, a description of a woman breastfeeding a baby, or the house across the street, shit, a crack in the sidewalk, and Frank couldn't help but be both proud and somehow ashamed, Isaac ten years old and is seeing things, saying things deeper than his own father can comprehend.

"If," says Frank. "If he hits him."

"Yeah," says Isaac. "If." His expression changes to one of concern. His eyes shift back to the TV.

Frank sips his beer and watches his son. He knows he needs to do a better job of being a dad, knows he needs to get Isaac out of the house more often. But the kid's always saying no thanks. No thanks to fishing. No thanks to camping. Isaac's world has become this house, these notebooks, or the handful of books he reads over and over. What does a man like Frank have to offer a boy like Isaac?

"I got De La Hoya," says Nelly. Frank can smell the shower on her. Strawberry shampoo and Irish Spring soap. Her hair is still wet but it's pulled into a pony tail.

"He is the bigger man," says Isaac. "But they're saying Mayweather's too fast for him."

"Only a matter of time," says Nelly. "That cocky little shit can't run forever. Somebody's fist is gonna find him. Then we'll find out what he's made of. Then we'll find out if he's man or mouth." Nelly touches Frank's shoulder when she walks past him, opens the refrigerator, and grabs a beer.

"My wife is so cool," Frank says. He means it. Frank takes Nelly's beer and twists the cap off for her. "You're so cool," he says when he hands the beer back to her. He squeezes her butt when she walks past him into the living room and sits on the couch with Isaac. He feels a tinge of guilt when he watches Nelly ruffle Isaac's hair and smile. He wonders how long it'll be before she accuses him of cheating. And how could he blame her if she did. When a man stops touching his wife the natural inclination is that he's touching someone else. What lie could he muster if she calls him on it? Or how could he twist the truth so it wouldn't slap her right across the face?

"Terrell still coming?" asks Nelly.

"Yeah."

"What time?"

"Don't know, babe. Depends on if he got permission. If his wife gave him shit he'll have to sneak out while she's sleeping." Frank laughs. In the beginning Frank couldn't keep his hands off Nelly. She had this attitude about her. This, what was it? A rebellious sexual appetite—or craving—or some kind of nymphomania that had Nelly asking for it all the time. And those were the dick-throwing days. Back when all Frank did was work and see women. Lots of women. When he met Nelly he let the other women go. Her appetite seemed to never be quenched. And the challenge of that unattainable goal filled Frank with such excitement and lust. Nelly became all he desired. But the pregnancy changed that. The excitement, the lust, it all began to wane. When his son started moving around in her stomach, when Frank felt Isaac kicking, when Nelly took on that glow—everything changed when he realized he loved her.

They settled into this life. The comfort of a family. And for Frank his own sexual appetite simmered down. It's like the beast he once was had been tamed. And lately Nelly's been hot. Hot like she used to be. Her hands wandering in the night when she thinks Frank's sleeping. It's like she wants the beast back. And that feeling, when she's rubbing on him, trying to coerce him—it's like being poked at or prodded. How could he tell her that? What version of that truth wouldn't have her in tears?

Terrell's at the door now and the undercard fights are beginning. Frank lets Terrell in and he comes in loud. He smells like weed and beer and cheap cologne. "What's with the neighbor?" asks Terrell. He stops on his way to the couch and stands in the path of the TV. "He was over there on his porch staring me down, Frankie. Like Jeffrey Dahmer or something. Like me saying what's up was gonna land me in a skillet."

"Who's Jeffrey Dahmer?" asks Isaac.

"One twisted motherfucker, little man," says Terrell. "One twisted motherfucker." Terrell smiles. Frank's always thought Terrell looks like Theo's friend on *The Cosby Show*. That chipmunky looking guy that was always comparing girls to burgers. They met back in the Grand Rapids Community College days, back in the janitor days, both of them young and neither of them married. They used to party together. Terrell stayed on at the school when Frank took the job at the foundry, and for years they'd been out of touch. Then one morning a few months ago, Terrell showed up at the foundry with a small group of temps, saying he lost his job at GRCC, but not saying why, asking Frank to put in a good word with the foreman, saying temp-money was no good, saying he had a wife and two sons, a family to feed.

"Tell you what though," says Terrell. "I'm all about diversity. It's nice to see another white face around here. But don't worry, Frankie Baby. You're still my favorite white boy. You're THE white boy. I know for damn sure I ain't gonna end up in a skillet over here!" Terrell finally realizes he's standing in front of the TV. He moves and sits on the small green sofa flanking the couch.

Nelly hasn't actually said so, but Frank can tell she doesn't like Terrell. He'd been over twice before tonight and each time he stayed too late and got too drunk. And the man's loud. The volume of his voice fluctuates with his level of excitement. Nelly does this thing when she gets annoyed. Her forehead kind of crinkles, her lips get tight, she's doing it now, and then she gets real quiet. Nelly's never been the type to yell, or confront you with what she's really thinking. Instead she asks questions: *Terrell's wife doesn't mind him being out this late?* She asked Frank that the last time Terrell was here, when Nelly came downstairs and asked to speak to Frank alone. *Why don't you ever hang out at Terrell's house?* She asked that yesterday, when Frank told her he was buying the Mayweather fight on pay-per-view, and that Terrell had invited himself over.

"What time do you think the fight will be over?" asks Nelly.

Frank goes to answer, but Terrell cuts him off. "Late," says Terrell. "Floyd's bitch ass'll keep you waiting until those wee hours. We'll be watching that motherfucker dance until morning."

Nelly smiles but doesn't show her teeth. "Okay, boys," she says. "I think I'll go to bed and read. You won't be *too* loud, will you?"

When Nelly walks away Terrell says, "Your wife, Frankie. She's cool. Tami wouldn't have it. She'd never let a guy's night happen at my crib."

"Yeah," says Frank, feeling a bit dickish. "Nelly's real cool."

Isaac's already nodding off. The notebook still on his lap, he's leaning on the arm of the couch, fighting to keep his eyes open. He still hasn't made his fight prediction.

"Isaac," says Frank.

"Huh?" he says. Startled.

"Who you got?"

"Mayweather," answers Isaac. "Mayweather by decision." Then he closes his eyes.

"Frankie," Terrell whispers. "He a heavy sleeper?"

"Yeah," says Frank. "When the kid's out, he's out."

"We got a couple hours before the main event. You want to step outside for a bit?"

"For what?"

"I got some recreational," says Terrell.

Frank's thinking he means weed. He's already feeling a little guilty. Terrell reminds Frank of his youth, those Frankie Baby days, when every night was a party, every night was a new high, or a new chick, a new experience. It's not that that life was better because it wasn't. It's just now, everything feels more routine. He works, he eats, he has a couple beers. He sleeps. Then he does it again. It's not that he's bored, or maybe it is? Maybe that's what it is. Frank's original plan was to buy the fight and watch it with his family. To bring some kind of excitement to the monotony. Now Nelly's off to bed and Isaac's knocked out. Terrell wasn't part of the original plan and he's the only one left. "I don't know, T," says Frank.

"C'mon, Man. The fam's going to sleep. Let them sleep."

For Terrell, it seems, the party never stopped. Marriage, kids—the party bus keeps rolling, and Frank would never admit it to Nelly, but sometimes Frank wants to climb aboard. It's not that he wants to go back to that life, no, he just wants to relive it from time to time. Not the women, but the party part of it, people disproportionately happy and euphoric off substances. A few laughs and a few bad choices. A break from all the responsibilities. A break from the daily grind.

"Frankie Baby," says Terrell. "The fam's off to bed."

Frank follows Terrell out the house and into the night.

"You remember Leslie Chambers?" asks Terrell. He pushes a button on his key ring and chirps open his Dodge Caravan.

Frank climbs in through the passenger side door. He waits for Terrell to join him in the van. "Leslie Chambers? From GRCC?" Frank asks.

"That's right. Big ass titties. Kinda cute, kinda chunky."

"Yeah. Yeah. Old Leslie. Decent piece of ass," says Frank.

"I bumped into her the other day at the liquor store."

"Really? How's she looking?"

"Not bad," says Terrell. "She asked about you, Long Dong. She wanted me to give you her number. She tried to slide it to me even after I told her you were married." Terrell shakes his head and laughs.

"What?"

"We're standing there in the liquor store, Frankie . . . Leslie gets to talking about The Cock. I mean right there in the store, people standing in line, Leslie's going on and on about Long Dong Page."

"Shit, T."

"What? Don't act all embarrassed."

"Don't we got better things to talk about than my dick?"

Terrell laughs. "Anyway, Leslie got me thinking . . . You remember a few years back when those Joy Green flicks came out."

"Joy Green?"

"Joy GREEN, Frankie. That RnB singer. She had that hit song back in the day, *Boys* or some shit."

"Sounds vaguely familiar."

"One hit wonder," says Terrell. "But she's from G-Rap. Anyways, this cat Cesar Bolden found her stripping at Iggy's Place and talked her into shooting a few porn flicks."

"The drug dealer, Cesar Bolden?"

"One and the same. You know him?"

"No," says Frank. "Just know the name."

"But you never heard of the movies?"

Frank shrugs.

"Well shit, you're white. I guess I shouldn't be surprised. In the black community these movies were a big deal. I mean a BIG deal.

Cesar, that motherfucker made a killing off those movies. Some cold shit, though, Frankie. For real. What happened to Joy Green was riches to rags, feel me? Cesar Bolden got it all on film."

"Okay."

"Rumor has it he's shooting another Joy Green flick."

"And?"

"Fuck you mean *and*? You got that pornstar dick, Frankie."

"Shut up, T."

"I'm serious. Get you a few thousand dollars. Give your boy Terrell a finder's fee." Terrell reaches into his pocket and pulls out a glass pipe and a sandwich baggie. He empties a small, pissy-white colored rock in his palm. "What?" he says. "Don't look at me like that, Frankie."

"What's that, Terrell?"

"You know what it is," Terrell says. "Don't look at me like that, Frank. It's for recreational use only. This ain't a habit."

"Recreational?"

"That's right."

"Crack?"

"That's right."

"Really, T? *Crack*?"

"You can say it a million times, Frankie, it won't make it be nothing else. Man, you watch too many afterschool specials. This shit here, get you high as a kite for like fifteen minutes, then you come back down like you never left. Those motherfuckers you see walking around here like zombies, trying to suck dick for cash, stealing shit, trying to get your quarters and pennies—they ain't no different than alcoholics, or anything else. You toy with substances you need a strong mind. You use the drugs, you get what you want from them, then you get out of there, dig?"

"Yeah?"

"Yeah, Man. I'm what you might call a vacationer. One hit every now and then. My daily's: my weed, my beer, that's what gets me through my week. A hit on this shit though, that's only for special occasions. This shit here: Don't pass go, take you straight to Wonderland."

"What's the high like? Like weed?"

"Naw. Nothing like weed."

"What's it like?"

"Only one way to know that, Frankie."

Frank watches Terrell put the pipe between his lips, pull out a black Bic lighter. Terrell sparks the flint and cuts Frank a sideways look. He brings the flame to the open mouth of the glass vessel, sucks, chokes, turns to Frank, and coughs out, "You want to hit this shit?"

Frank watches Terrell lean back in his seat, his pupils draining into his coffee-colored eyes. He looks angelic beneath the pale yellow streetlight that stretches into the van. Terrell looks so peaceful it's moving. How could something that makes you look that beautiful be bad? Frank reaches for the pipe and the lighter. The quiet voice of his conscience or God speaks to him. It gives him an out. But Frank's lost in the moment. He takes the word *crack* and he sets it aside. He wants nothing but to look like Terrell looks. To feel what Terrell is feeling. You get one life, Frank Page tells himself. Just one. He works hard. He takes care of his family. Why can't he have a little fun? Why can't he ride the party bus every once in a moon? Frank brings the pipe to his lips. Brings the lighter to the pipe. The flame to the rock.

When he exhales he hears bells. A tranquil sensation begins in his legs, moves to his stomach, and then his entire body is numb. He feels like . . . he feels like he's falling in love for the first time. It's like a first kiss, the sensations running through his system, the possibilities endless. And when he hits that peak, that perfection, when his body feels better than he knew a body could feel—Frank is consumed by a fatal sadness, an awareness.

He will never feel this way again.

Keep telling yourself, Nelly. With the rent due and Frank's job calling the house asking where he's been. With the bank account emptied and your rainy-day stash discovered and stolen. With Isaac asking questions. Keep telling yourself, Nelly. Keep believing everything is going to be okay. Sit in your car and smoke another cigarette. Don't cry, Nelly, you're stronger than that. Ignore the empty space in the driveway where Frank's truck should be. Smoke another cigarette.

She pulls a Marlboro out of the pack lying open on the passenger side seat. She lights it and leans back, looking at the neighbor's porch, empty tonight, which is rare. How she's feeling, tonight—if that man were on his porch, maybe she'd go over and introduce herself, not because she gives a shit, but because at least she'd have someone to talk to, or listen to, she's not quite sure what she needs. Three houses down Lorenzo's porch light is on. She doesn't know him well, but Frank buys weed from Lorenzo sometimes. Maybe she should cop a bag of weed. Maybe she should smoke until her thoughts are floating around in her head. Smoke until her worries aren't worries. Until her worries aren't real. But it's late. She was off at 11:00 and she's been sitting out here for at least an hour. What would Lorenzo think, her coming down there at this time of night? And how many young girls has Nelly seen coming in and out of his house? Maybe it's not weed she needs? Maybe it's something else. Sleepless, restless, fingers wandering—a pink dildo hidden in a shoebox in her closet—the one perk of Frank being gone, she can lock the door and light the candles and behave how she wants to behave, behave with no shame.

Nelly finds a ten in her purse and leaves the purse in the car. She can't tell if the stars are brighter tonight or the sky is blacker. And it's quiet. She walks past Brenda's house. Brenda has four children by two different fathers. Both men love her. Neither man can stay out of jail for long. There are usually no problems when only one man is free. But let them both be out of jail at the same time, like they were last night—when one man almost killed the other, when he had the other on his back with a knife raised to stab him, all four of Brenda's kids and half the neighborhood watching, when Brenda cracked open his head with a Louisville Slugger, and all three of them: Brenda, and both men went to jail.

Francis Street is a soap opera. An R-rated one. If each house was made of glass, if all deeds were exposed—you'd see fucking and fighting, kids watching cartoons or playing their video games—it's all normal: the domestic noise, the violence, the cheating—it's all part of life around here. What does that mean for Isaac? Watching this place from a window. Writing in his notebooks—what if Nelly's hunch about Frank is true? What if it's drugs? Not this petty shit, this weed. What if it's worse? Eight years on this street and they've avoided the drama. What now, if Nelly's right? What now if bad things are coming?

"Who's that?" asks Lorenzo as Nelly approaches.

"Nelly Page."

"Frank's lady?"

"Yeah."

"It's late," says Lorenzo. He sits in the dark corner opposite the porch light. Nelly can't see his face but she can feel his smile.

"I know, look, I'm sorry . . . I have ten dollars."

"I see," Lorenzo says. "C'mon up here, Frank's Lady. Have a seat while I get you together."

Nelly climbs the porch and sits beside Lorenzo.

"Thirsty?" he asks, handing her a bottle.

Nelly doesn't answer. She sips. It tastes dark and spicy. It bites her tongue, burns her chest. "Have you seen Frank?" she asks.

"Naw." Lorenzo appears to be rolling a joint. "Way I hear it, Frank's moved on from weed."

The sweet stinky smell of weed fills the porch. Nelly sips again. It's too dark to get a full-view of Lorenzo's face. He is a voice and an image. The image: forty-something with his pants sagging, one of those convict tethers, the kind that beep when you stray too far from your house. But he is man. He is bravado. And tonight he's a warm body, blood coursing through his veins. Lorenzo passes Nelly the biggest blunt she's ever seen. "I call that a dickhead," he says. "Don't hit it too hard or you'll choke."

Nelly takes a small hit and chokes anyway. When she stops

coughing she finds Lorenzo's hand resting high on her thigh. It's been eleven years since anyone but Frank has touched her that way and she likes how it feels. Her marriage means something. It does. But lately . . . Lorenzo's hand creeps a little higher. Damn. Lately she been feeling so . . . Nelly waits for the guilt to come, but it doesn't. Her conscience seems to give her the green light. Guilt is speechless. It's not even clearing its throat. Nelly and Lorenzo have the street to themselves, the night to themselves. Nelly takes another pull on the blunt and passes it to Lorenzo.

"How you feel?" Lorenzo asks.

It's been so long. Would she brag about it? Would she confess it, even with a gun to her head? The weed's put a gentle hex on her mind. Who knows where Frank is. Who knows who Frank's with and what he's doing. And tonight. Tonight the pink dildo is staying in the shoebox. "You want to know how I feel?"

"I asked."

"I feel like going inside," says Nelly. "That's how I feel."

She follows Lorenzo into the house and up a set of stairs. He leads her into a bedroom and turns on the light. There's nothing in the room but a twin-sized bed and a rickety brown dresser. A framed photograph of a young girl with beaded braids sits atop the dresser. There is nothing on the walls. Nelly sits on the bed. She runs her hand across a green scratchy military blanket. There are two pillows on the bed, neither with a pillowcase.

Lorenzo closes the door and leaves on the light. He takes off his shirt. His body is a shrine of bad tattoos. He is not a handsome man, but his smile almost takes the edge of the ugly. He drops his pants. He has a nice cock. Not long like Frank's is long, but nice, and he wears it with confidence. Which Nelly finds sexy.

What surprises her is how tender Lorenzo is. How soft his lips are against her own. His patience—his tongue touching every crevice, the way his head stays between her thighs, a place Frank refuses to go. And then he takes her from behind. She lay flat on her stomach while

Lorenzo grabs a fist full of her hair, his lips on her neck while he strokes deep and hard. Nelly's mind slows down. There is no Frank, no Isaac, no southeast side of Grand Rapids. She is a girl in the moment. She is young again. She is youth. She is coming. Lord have mercy! For the first time in years Nelly Page is coming. She's falling right back in love . . . with coming.

Nelly leaves Lorenzo sitting on the bed when it's over. A *Vibe* magazine balanced on his thighs, rolling a blunt. He watches her dress. She doesn't feel like an adulterer. She doesn't feel like she's betrayed Frank, or her marriage, or herself. She feels nothing but a tinge of giddiness in the wreckage of good sex. But then she wonders what Lorenzo's thinking. Was this a one-time thing or is he going to cause problems? She thinks of Brenda's house and those two men fighting, fighting for Brenda, her heart, her love.

"Lorenzo," says Nelly. She's dressed now. "You won't say anything, will you?"

Lorenzo laughs. He sets the magazine aside and licks the blunt. This one's not as big as the Dickhead.

"You won't, will you?" Nelly asks again.

"You smoking or leaving?" Lorenzo asks.

"I'm serious, Lorenzo. You won't say anything, right?"

"Your secret is safe with me, Frank's Lady," he says. "One condition, though."

"Okay."

"You bring that pretty little pussy of yours down here anytime you get the itch."

With that the deal is sealed, thinks Nelly. Excited by the prospect of these late-night rendezvous. Frank or no Frank. It's like some primitive rebellious gene has come alive in her. Okay, Long Dong Page, you want to lay there in the bed and ignore me? You want to leave without warning, no conversation, no note, and stay gone—the bank account emptied, the Folgers jar emptied—no word, not even a hint of your whereabouts? You want to leave me with your son asking questions? Fine! Nelly is going to do Nelly. "I better go," says Nelly. "My son's at home."

"Suit yourself," Lorenzo says. But lock that door on your way out.

They are in a shithole motel that rents by the hour. Terrell shakes in his sleep. Frank sits in the corner of the room, hugging his legs, crying into his knees, scratching his arms. A woman beats on the door, screaming, "Terrell, you motherfucker, let me in!" Terrell doesn't budge. Frank doesn't know what day it is. Doesn't care. All he knows is he has to go home. There's a skinny mixed girl named Erica lying naked on her back next to Terrell. She has small breasts and big nipples. Her pubic hair is overgrown. They met the girl behind a dumpster on Division. Early last week when they still had money, when time was still moving how it's supposed to move, she said she was tired of tricking. Erica was hugging her legs much like Frank is now. A rose tattoo wrapped around her thigh.

Terrell looked at Frank. Frank looked at Terrell. They both looked at Erica. For three, maybe four days, Frank can't remember, they smoked and fucked and smoked some more. Then the money ran out and Erica split. Frank had already emptied his savings. Terrell's wife had already wised up and cancelled the joint account Terrell's name was on. Then Frank remembered the Folgers can that Nelly keeps stashed in the freezer. He idled his truck down the street from his house. His own house. Watching. Waiting for Isaac to go off to school, waiting for Nelly's Dodge Shadow to sputter off to work. Frank snuck into the house and stole it all. Erica found them an hour after they copped. Then they smoked and fucked and smoked some more.

"Frankie." Terrell is awake. The screaming and knocking has stopped. Frank hadn't noticed until now. Terrell sits on the bed leaning against the headboard. Erica rolls over onto her side. A tattoo that says Alex begins on her hip and curls around her left ass cheek. "What we gonna do, Frankie?" Terrell asks.

"I'm going home, T. I gotta go home."

"I'm in a bad way, Frankie. Give me one more chase. Just one more."

"I'm going home, T. You should do the same."

"It's too late for home, Frankie." Terrell reaches for a pack of Winston's. He pulls a small lighter out of the open pack and an upside down cigarette. "My lucky," says Terrell. The cigarette is bent, almost broken. His hands shake when he tries to light it. After a few tries the lighter spews a flame. "Give me one more chase, Frankie. Don't make me beg."

"There's no more money, Terrell."

"The Cock, Frankie."

"I'm not doing porn, T. Period."

"Why?"

"I'm married."

Terrell takes a drag on his cigarette and glances at Erica. Then he looks at Frank like, motherfuckerplease. "Yeah," says Terrell. "You're *married.*"

"I don't get it," says Frank. A couple days ago he saw Joy Green tricking down on Division. There was nothing "porn" about her. Whatever she used to be, she wasn't. "I mean, who wants to watch a junkie fuck on film?"

"Joy Green back in the day, Frankie. She was like a Grand Rapids Janet Jackson. I mean, she was on the map, dig? MTV. BET. I think she might have done Oprah too . . . I'm just saying, any black man in the city would have given their left nut to fuck Joy Green."

"Yeah," says Frank. "Now anybody with ten bucks can fuck her."

"You still don't get it, do you? Those Joy Green flicks, Frankie— Cesar Bolden ain't selling sex. Cesar's documenting a downfall."

"That's sick."

"No shit, that's sick. That's sick, Cesar's sick . . . we're sick. And we're going to be real sick if we don't get some money soon, Frankie."

•

When Nelly sees Frank's truck in the driveway, guilt finally makes an appearance. Or maybe it's fear. She smells like sex. She looks like sex. She still feels the texture of the green military blanket on Lorenzo's bed. No, this isn't guilt, this is definitely fear. Ten minutes removed from adultery, buzzed off bliss and sobering quickly when she opens the door to find Frank and Isaac sitting at the dining room table.

Frank's got a forty-ounce beer half-drank and sweating on a coaster. He smells awful. Like cigarettes and ass. Like death. Isaac is wearing Batman pajamas, working on a *Return of the Jedi* puzzle. He has it halfway finished. Frank stares at the box like he's remembering the eighties, rubbing Isaac's shoulder with the hand not babysitting the beer.

"Hey, Mom," says Isaac looking up from the puzzle. He's awake. Why is he awake? How long was Nelly down at Lorenzo's? Is she paranoid or does Isaac know something? Did he hear her car pull up earlier? Was Isaac watching out the window when she walked down to Lorenzo's house? Did he say something to Frank?

"Hey, Baby." Nelly kisses her son on the forehead.

Frank still hasn't spoken. He's changed. A man home from war. PTSD. He'll need counseling and medication and patience. He'll need love. He is a veteran. He is Vietnam. He is Desert Storm. He has lost ten pounds. Has he lost twenty pounds?

"We got any money?" asks Frank. He doesn't look at Nelly when he says it. Doesn't question where she was. Frank doesn't offer any explanation for his absence the last few weeks.

"What?"

"I'm sick."

"Frank, where have you been?"

"You don't want to know."

"Jesus, Frankie, where the fuck have you been?"

"I need money, Nelly."

"Baby," Nelly says. "The rent's late. We can't afford to . . ."

"We can't spare ten?" Frank finally looks at her. His expression is dark, rabid, gone. He's scratching his arms. Nelly remembers she left her purse in the car. Thank God. "Where's the money, Nelly?"

"There's no money."

"You're lying."

Isaac stares at his puzzle. He's stopped looking for pieces.

"Ten, Nelly. All I need is ten."

"Isaac," says Nelly. "Go to bed."

"Ten," says Frank. "Ten motherfucking dollars!" He flips the table over and stands. The forty doesn't break. It rolls across the floor soaking the carpet with beer in three spots before settling against a wall with the Colt 45 label staring at the ceiling. The coaster it was resting on is nowhere to be seen. Isaac hasn't moved from his chair. Most of the puzzle is somehow still intact, laying facedown at Frank's feet. Frank checks the freezer for the Folgers can. He pulls a Frosted Flakes box from the cupboard and pours its contents on the counter.

Outside there are gunshots. Three of them. Or fireworks. There is no chaos that follows. No sirens chasing the noise. Then Frank looks at Nelly. She backs against the wall as he approaches. "I need money," says Frank. His anger has simmered. His voice is calm. "I just need money." Tears in his words, but not his eyes. His eyes hold something else—a desperate kind of finality—a look like Frank will stop at nothing to get whatever he's after.

"Baby," says Nelly. "We need to get you some help."

Nelly thinks he's coming to hug her at first. But then his hug becomes a meaty fist that she sees briefly before the lights go out. Then Isaac is kneeling beside her. His breath smells like Doritos. His mouth is moving but his voice throbs inaudible words. Her left cheekbone is tender. A cool breeze moves across the room through the open front door. The ten in her pocket is missing—the ten Lorenzo never asked for. She remembers her purse—she has a couple hundred dollars in it and can't remember if she locked her car.

"Mom," says Isaac. "Are you okay?"

•

Joey Cane sits under a flickering porch light, gutting a Swisher, emptying stale tobacco on dew-damp grass. He blows excess fragments off the thin shell and drags his tongue across its brown skin. From a plastic sandwich baggie, he empties a trail of weed and then rolls it into a blunt. He snaps open a Detroit Lions Zippo. Its flame chews the air. Joey inhales smoke and listens to the city breathe.

Nighttime in the southeast side of Grand Rapids is a symphony of sirens and squealing tires, domestic altercations, the occasional gunshot. And Joey's trained ear knows the noise of bad choices. Felonies succeeding or failing—criminals running free or leaving handcuffed in patrol cars—victims filing police reports or leaving the 'hood in body bags.

Beneath a haze of smoke, Joey watches the neighbor boy, Isaac Page, who's sitting on the couch writing in a notebook. The neighbors have no blinds covering their living room window, and when the night hits its darkest hour, and the lights are still on next door, the window looks like a television, and Joey can't help but watch sometimes. Though nothing ever happens. It's summertime now and the boy never comes outside. He reads, he writes, he paces. The boy's father Frank, rumor has it, is cracked out and gone. And Nelly, Isaac's mother, has never spoken a word to Joey, always with a curious stare, but never so much as a smile in his direction.

"Shit," whispers Joey, when he sees Lorenzo. The man is dragging down the sidewalk, baggy jeans hanging past his ass, a thick, black belt clinging thigh high. He looks like he left his house fat and then shrunk in his clothes. And Joey swears the motherfucker has a weed detector. It seems like whenever Joey lights up, lo and behold: here comes Lorenzo.

"Let me smoke with you, yo." It's never a question with Lorenzo, always a statement.

He got paroled to his mother's house, who lives two houses down, after doing time in Jackson State Penitentiary for armed robbery. Lorenzo can be seen daily with a forty-ounce Mickey's, walking up and down the street bullying teens for cigs, or slanging his own weed off his mother's porch while she works double shifts driving the city bus, pay-ing the mortgage while her dead-beat son small-time hustles for cash.

"When we gonna smoke *your* weed, Lorenzo?"

"Rules is," says Lorenzo. He's five-eight, a buck eighty. Has a chipped tooth, skeptical eyes, and a head that stays on a swivel. "You don't get high off your own supply."

"No," says Joey, "you get high off mine." He grabs a lawn chair and sets it beside him. Lorenzo sits and adjusts himself so he can see the street. Relaxes into the chair like he owns the porch.

"You got balls smoking with that tether on, Man," says Joey. "You ain't careful they're gonna send your ass back to Jackson."

"State of Michigan got bigger things to worry about than me get-ting high." Lorenzo reaches for the blunt.

Joey nods at the plastic cuff wrapped around Lorenzo's ankle. "What kind of range does that thing have?"

"I get around." They sit in silence for a moment. Lorenzo leans back in the chair watching the smoke float over his head and gather around the sputtering porch light. "What's up with Miss Thunderbooty, yo?"

"Sleeping," says Joey.

"And you out here?"

"What can I say?" says Joey. "I'm a child of the night."

"You's a goddamn fool, white boy." Lorenzo's half-laughing, half-choking on smoke. "If I was you I'd be in there waxing that ass."

"If you were me," says Joey, reaching for the blunt, hitting it, blow-ing smoke toward Lorenzo, "I'd be smoking your weed." He hits it again and hands the blunt back to him. "Not that it's your business, but she likes it when I wake her up." Joey's tired of the inquiries. Lorenzo always asking his slick questions, or sitting on the porch across the street with loudmouth Panko laughing and drinking beer. Always looking like he's plotting to rob you. "Thunderbooty," says Joey, "knows she's gonna get it when I get inside."

"Okay, white boy," says Lorenzo. His swivel head cocked sideways, aimed at the street.

Joey has the urge to slap him across his mouth, but knows better. He doesn't look like much, but Lorenzo Williams isn't someone you fuck with. Known to lose it over nothing, over a misconstrued glance, Lorenzo stepping up, saying, "Fuck you looking at?" ending the conversation by stomping some victim bloody with the heel of his boot. A few days ago he shorted this kid, Darnell, on an ounce of weed and Darnell called him on it. That conversation ended with Lorenzo's nine millimeter Glock in the kid's mouth.

"You know the concrete's been talking about you, white boy," says Lorenzo.

"Is that right? What's it been saying?"

"Saying you were Mr. Basketball in '99. Saying you had a ride to Duke on the table and turned it down cold."

"That's right." Joey had heard the concrete talk too, saying Tara was poking holes in his condoms with a sewing needle back then. Eighteen and digging for gold, setting a trap for the white boy with the sweet jumper. He doesn't know if the story is true, but he remembers how Tara's face dropped when he told her he was staying home, taking a job at Grand Rapids Plastics, that he wanted to concentrate on being a dad, taking the road less travelled while the block shook its head, thinking *dumb motherfucker.* Joey gave his childhood to the concrete. Now he's twenty-six years old with arthritic knees and ankles. Instead of playing shooting guard for the Detroit Pistons he's stuck here in the southeast side of Grand Rapids. In this life. This shit.

"All that for Thunderbooty?"

"No," says Joey, "for Lyric."

Joey has plenty of regrets, but Lyric isn't one of them. The highlight of his day is coming home from the factory and finding his eight-year-old daughter waiting at the door, wrapping around his leg, saying, "Walk like a giant, Daddy!" her brown frizzy curls bouncing as he stomps through the house beating on his chest like an ape. Or sitting on the couch watching Spongebob, drinking chocolate milk, Lyric cuddled up with him.

The blunt is down to ash. It hisses on the damp grass when Lorenzo flicks it and stands. "Give Miss Thunderbooty my best," Lorenzo says, gripping an invisible waist with his left hand, and slapping an invisible ass with his right. "Dumb muh fucka," Lorenzo whispers as he walks away, tugging at his pants while his boots scuff along the sidewalk.

"Loser," says Joey, after Lorenzo is out of earshot.

Maybe Lorenzo had gotten under his skin a little last night, bringing up the past, the possibilities of a bigger, brighter life. Or maybe he just ached for it: the sound of the basketball echoing off the concrete. The snap of the net. The deafening silence of the world around him. But this morning Joey dug through the boxes stacked in the garage, unpacked his childhood, and found his dusty, worn-to-peach-fuzz Spalding with the initials G.H. markered on the ball. He remembered the words of George Hessler, an eighth-grade history teacher who told Joey he would never make it to the NBA, never leave the city, never amount to shit.

Joey runs a finger over the initials and his lips curl into a nostalgic smile, remembering the hours he invested honing his skills, the sweat he'd given the concrete, picturing the face of his bitter-for-some-reason history teacher, dribbling until the initials faded from the ball, freshening them with a Sharpie when they did. Shooting before school, the court barely lit by the rising sun; after dark when the moon hardly sufficed as a floodlight; in summer covered in sweat, a farmer's tan in sleeveless shirts and sockless Chuck Taylor's; in winter shoveling off the court and shooting with stiff fingers, the ball frozen and bouncing with a heavy and hollow thunk.

But George Hessler was right. Joey has gone nowhere. As far as the world is concerned Joey Cane isn't shit. You don't get a Purple Heart for sacrificing your life to love a frizzy-haired girl. You get no accolades for being a father. The ball is a loud heartbeat thumping against the driveway. Francis Street is sleeping. The sun rising. Joey threads the ball between his legs, around his back. It goes where he guides it. After all these years the ball still goes where he guides it. He remembers something his father once told him about talent and God. About everyone being blessed with one thing. One talent. And it's up to the individual to nurture that talent. And when the individual works hard enough and that talent blooms, that individual is in a perfect relationship with God.

In one smooth motion Joey scoops the ball off the dribble, flicks his wrist, and watches the ball spin through the air, watches it travel across its arc and snap the net. "Look at me now, Pop. Look at me now," he says. The ball rolls off into the patch of grass flanking the driveway. Joey finds his Camels in his pocket and lights one. He leans against the house. Across the driveway, in an upstairs window, young Isaac Page stands watching him. Joey waves. Isaac presses his hand against the window. Then his mother's in the window with him, arm around Isaac, watching Joey. Joey looks away. He takes a deep pull on the Camel. When he glances back at the window both of them are gone.

Frank's dressed in a shirt and tie, sitting on a wooden bench, in something like a dressing room. There's a chill in the air and the emptiness of the room seems to crank up the volume of the cold. He can't stop thinking of Nelly. He sees his fist crashing against her face, Isaac trying to wrestle him to the ground, Frank backhanding Isaac across the room. The boy sprawled about in his Batman pajamas. Frank closes his eyes. He takes these images and he moves them out the way. He sees himself scooping dirt with the mouth of a Bobcat, rotating the machine ninety degrees, and accelerating toward an open garage door. He sees slow-moving union men working around him, the cold foundry loud with the quiet hum of machinery, the laughter of bandannad middle-aged men sitting on crates. He sees himself working the pits with Terrell, shoveling burnt black sand, the air thick and dank, they're wearing cheap white masks and still sucking in some of the dust, so much dust, it clings to their sweat, their white Haynes T-shirts have turned gray.

"You ain't looking too good, Frankie," says Terrell.

A crack rock-bottom is beneath rock-bottom. It's a slab ceiling in every direction. A concrete box filled with guilt. During the chase you're focused. The only thing that exists is the fix. Your mind is lost in the now, in the journey. Your life, everyone you're hurting, everything you left behind, it all quiets down until you find this bottom, this moment of clarity. And when you find it the guilt is upon you. There's nowhere to go. Not until the fix frees you.

"I gotta get clean," Frank says.

The door to the dressing room opens. Cesar Bolden stands cool in a pale yellow button-down shirt and kakis. He wears a white Kangol hat and glasses. He could be an English professor or a poet. He doesn't look at all like the scumbag reputation that precedes him. His gray eyes are exotic and mean, but they have an educated wisdom that seems to Frank to extend far beyond the streets. Cesar is both beautiful and terrifying. He doesn't have to raise his voice when his gaze finds Terrell. "Get your dirtball ass out of my sight," he says. Terrell leaves immediately, giving Frank one last desperate glance before walking out the door.

"Big Frank," Cesar says. "You are a white business man who wants to pay for black pussy. You are an actor. On the other side of that door you will find a real-life crackhead. A real-life prostitute who has lived this scene a thousand times. She is not Joy Green. You don't know who she is, or was. You're nothing more than a horny customer. She's nothing more than a whore. I'm paying you for authenticity. I can't have you all shaking and jittery. I can't have you scratching at your arms like you're doing now.

For a moment Frank thinks Cesar's going to smile. He measures Frank with thoughtful eyes. "You think I'm a monster, don't you? I see how you're looking at me. Your mind's racing, right? Trying to figure out what's rumor and what's fact. I'll tell you what, Big Frank. How about you focus on your job and let me focus on facts. Cause that ain't Joy Green on the other side of the door. Not anymore. And your job is simple. Go get paid."

Frank stands. He's a half-a-head taller than Cesar yet still feels like the smaller man.

Cesar hands Frank a ten-dollar bill. "Walk through the door and show this to her. She'll do the rest."

Frank follows Cesar across the room and through the door. Frank expects a swank set with bright lights, other men standing around in robes waiting for their scene. What he finds instead is a room with no drywall, no flooring. Grafitti tagged on cement walls. A newspaper spilled from a plastic bag, wet, smelling like it was pissed on. A makeshift ally. The lighting is dim. A cameraman lurks about, saying nothing, his footsteps making no sound. Joy Green leans against a wall smoking a cigarette. She wears a red skirt and a white blouse with a brown stain on the collar. Frank looks into her eyes and sees himself. Just another chaser. This chick will get paid and hit the block, just like he will. Cesar will pay them. Then they'll both give Cesar his money back and get high.

"What, Motherfucker?" asks Joy.

Her eyes are the scary kind of gone. Like she's lost somewhere between the real and the chase. That place you won't ever admit that you arrived at. You see others there and they are the lost ones, lives forfeit, the past not even the past anymore. Their life never happened. It's not even a dream. Frank shows her the ten and she smiles, tosses the cigarette on the floor. She has beautiful teeth. Somehow she still has beautiful teeth. She motions with her head for Frank to join her at the wall. Joy plucks the ten from Frank's hand and in one quick motion the money disappears. She unbuttons her blouse and out fall her tits. Sagging, sad, the only flesh left on her fragile frame. But at least it's something to look at besides those eyes. "Fuck the bitch. Get paid," Frank thinks. Or maybe he says it. Joy's on her knees now failing with his zipper. He tries to imagine what she looked like back in the day but can't muster an image.

Joy has finally freed The Cock and now it's filling with blood. Frank reaches down and finds a nipple. He strokes it with a finger and thumb.

The camera man is inches away, but Frank doesn't care. He grabs Joy under the armpit and lifts her to her feet, turns her around, pins her wrists to the wall. Joy widens her stance. Frank hikes her skirt up over her ass. She wears no panties. He spits into his palm twice then rubs The Cock. He thrusts upward and it finds its home. Joy lets out one deep moan, but that's all, her head pressed against the wall, and then the only sound in the room is skin slapping skin and both of them breathing.

The facts no longer matter. That Frank's cheating on his wife. That it's a junkie he's fucking. That Joy Green looks bad. That they're both going through withdrawals. That the images don't stop coming. That Frank sees Nelly and Isaac clear as if they're watching. He sees them smiling, moving on, Frank hovering over the southeast side of Grand Rapids like some kind of phantom, some Ebenezer Scrooge. Because the fix has set him free. Nelly and Isaac are incidental, figments of some other place Frank used to be. The concrete walls have come crumbling down.

"Cardboard!" shouts the cameraman.

Joy Green twists around and moves to the left. A box has been unfolded and pressed down on the floor. Frank's never liked the feel of cardboard. Never liked the scraping sound it makes when it moves across cement. Joy lies on her back on the broken-down box. She fingers herself. The gentle vibration of her breasts reminds Frank of rippling water. Her nipples are erect and thick as thimbles.

Frank straddles her. He puts The Cock between her breasts and spits on it. Joy pushes her breasts together and looks up at him. They both know they're close. So close to the money, to the fix. Maybe they'll go together. Maybe they'll put on their clothes, get paid, and hit the block. Maybe they'll get high and fuck some more. Maybe. Frank watches The Cock stab in and out of her breasts, its pale-purple head popping against her chin. Frank feels the pull, the pulse of an approaching climax. Joy can feel it too. She takes The Cock in her hands. She strokes three or four times and Frank comes hard, and his mind goes blank, and the cameraman yells, "Cut!"

•

That morning in the driveway, that slip into the past, had awakened a forgotten longing in Joey Cane. For some other life, another option. Something besides the drudgery of a day's work. Something more than a marijuana sedated what if, that late-night dreaming, that cruel nostalgia, the life he could have lived and can't seem to let go of. That spotlight he used to swagger in, seventeen and signing autographs, the world spinning on his middle finger, George Hessler on the cusp of being wrong.

Joey leans back in the lawn chair and watches weed smoke swirl against the finally-dead porch light. He imagines that life. A couple years at Duke. Drafted by the Pistons. Sending Tara money. Spending time with Lyric during the off-season. But the thought of not being with his daughter stings him. It makes him feel soft. Weak for love. Lyric with those frizzy curls and her pretty little voice. Always singing with her mother on that cheap karaoke machine Joey bought her for Christmas last year.

Nelly Page has stepped onto her porch and is walking toward him. Joey drops the blunt and hides it under his shoe. Joey sees Isaac propped against the arm of a couch through the next-door window, one socked foot crossed over the other, scribbling in a journal. His mother walking toward Joey, an aura of mystery thickening around this woman with each forward step.

"Got a smoke?" Nelly asks. She's wearing a Michigan State hoodie.

"Sure." Joey thumbs a Camel out of its package, lights it, and passes it to Nelly. She has wild green eyes and a sensual mouth—thin black hair falling out the hood of her sweatshirt like some kind of anime ninja kid. She's probably five or six years older than Joey, but she looks young, like a wanton teen playing at adult.

Nelly takes a hit on the Camel. "My son wants to know if he can use your basketball hoop."

Joey glances back into Nelly's living room window. Isaac is in the same position, leaning, feet crossed, scribbling away. "Why didn't he come over himself?"

"He's shy." Nelly sees Joey looking toward her house, glances where he was looking, sees what Joey sees, what he has been seeing. "That's a pretty nice view of my life," she says. "Is that what you're doing out here every night? Peeping in my window?"

"You don't have curtains." He remembers the other morning, Nelly and Isaac watching him from their window. He starts to call her on it then stoppers his tongue. He has a soft spot for the boy. For Nelly too. What happens to a household when a man disappears? A son has a father and then one day he's gone. What does his mother tell him? What excuse does she make?

Nelly takes a pull on the cigarette, tilts back her head, and puffs two loose rings into the air. "I bought Isaac a basketball."

Joey says nothing, just watches Nelly Page watching her son through the window. He imagines himself leaving. Imagines Lyric standing by the door waiting for her daddy to get home from work, she's waiting for hours, Tara calling around, trying to track Joey down.

"It would be good for him to get outside. Used to be you couldn't shut the kid up. Now you can't get two words out of him," Nelly says.

"That's cool," says Joey. "I mean it's cool, Isaac can use the hoop."

"Thanks," says Nelly. She breaks her cigarette in half and drops it off the porch. "Isaac is only ten," says Nelly. "He doesn't deserve this shit." She waves her hand in a small fan motion, as if taking in the entire block with her gesture.

•

Joey wakes to the echo of the ball bouncing off of the concrete. It's five o'clock in the morning. Tara stands in front of the bedroom window, peeking outside through the blinds, naked besides a red thong, thunder booty hanging like an anchor from the small of her back. "You know anything about this?" She turns, whispering, as if Isaac Page is a deer that might run away if he hears her voice through the screen of the open window.

Joey nods. "I didn't think he'd be out there this early."

"He reminds me of you," says Tara, still whispering. She eases shut the window and walks toward him. A tattoo of his name is scribbled on her swaying left hip. Joey scoots up against the headboard. They'd been dating for years and there had been no talk of marriage, no talk of love. But there is some version of love between them. There is commitment. They are family. There is a physical attraction that still hasn't simmered after all these years. Maybe Joey just doesn't know what love is? He'd never been in anything serious before Tara. His priority was always basketball until he met her that summer at Garfield Park, with her booty shorts and tank tops, with her grown-woman curves. It was lust that drew him in. It was sex that took him under.

Even now there are these moments during sex where they get lost, they slip out of this world, and Joey feels like he's falling. The Earth stops spinning. The life noise is gone. In that space it feels like love, almost, and Joey goes looking for it. But it never fails. When he comes that feeling slips through his fingers. That's when he questions everything. It's like he's living the wrong life, that he's settling, that in his relationship with Tara there is something missing, some need or purpose Joey has that she simply cannot satisfy.

"Baby," Tara says. She twists her nails through his chest curls, across the tattoo of Lyric's baby picture on his right shoulder, free-handed by Watson, a former biker turned ink-artist, who studied a framed picture of Lyric at four months old, put the photograph away, and somehow made the tattoo look more real than the picture itself. "Lyric won't be up for at least an hour," she says. She kisses him, and that's all it takes, a flick of her tongue, her hand moving down his chest to his stomach and into his boxers. He can still hear the ball bouncing off the concrete. He wants to go outside and check on Isaac Page. But first . . . Joey closes his eyes and lets himself fall. He lets himself feel for however long he can.

•

Isaac Page is a sad sight with a basketball in his hands. Slapping at the thing when he dribbles, using both hands when he shoots, ball clanging off the front of the rim or the backboard, shooting it like he is trying to break something, like he's pissed off at the world.

"Hey, little man." Joey approaches, cigarette nestled between his lips, smoke hovering eye-level, rocking a white wife-beater and black Nike shorts, wearing sandals and white socks.

Isaac turns and looks at him. The kid has fierce eyes, ancient eyes, eyes a thousand years older than the rest of him, eyes burning blue like butane flames. He's an intense ball of anger. Joey wonders what Isaac writes in those notebooks he's always scratching away at, imagines what Isaac has seen that Joey hasn't observed through the window.

"Mind if I shoot with you?"

Isaac tosses Joey the ball and Joey dribbles twice, then flicks his wrist. The ball arcs through the air. The net snaps inside out.

"Change," says Joey. He gives Isaac a once over. Joey knows he hasn't been through or seen half the shit the kid has. Growing up in East Grand Rapids, getting dropped off at Garfield Park by his lawyer father on his way to work. Isaac Page was born in this shit. Joey Cane had tossed himself off of a building and landed in it.

Isaac retrieves the ball and tosses it back. "It's in the wrist," says Joey. "See?" Flick. Snap. "You try . . . Wait," says Joey, "get closer to the basket, little man. We have to fix your form before you step out here." Joey asks for the ball. "The most important thing is balance. Feet shoulder width apart, right foot forward—do what I do."

Isaac mimics Joey. He stands ready to shoot.

"Okay," says Joey, "It starts with the toes of your right foot. Make sure they're pointed toward the rim. Bend your knees. Good. Your right knee should line up with your right toes. Now line your right hand up, fingers along the seams. When you shoot it, you'll lead with your pointer finger. Yeah, nice, you're getting it. The left hand is only used to balance the ball. You want that off to the side, your right thumb angled toward your left. Good. Now, when you shoot it, your right elbow should line up with your right knee, which should still be lined up with your right toes. The shooting motion isn't a push, it's kind of a half-toss, half-flick. Go ahead, try it."

Isaac's ball travels feet short of the rim.

"Nice."

"I missed," says Isaac, the first words he's spoken.

"Doesn't matter," says Joey. "You kept your elbow straight and you flicked your wrist. Keep practicing and you'll start making shots."

Joey Cane stands in the driveway and Nelly sits in the grass watching. He has a black bandanna tied around his head like a headband, soaked in sweat, white wife beater clinging to his wiry frame. This man's sad blue eyes, long girlish lashes, pulling on a cigarette, like it's the last one he's ever going to smoke. Always looking like his mind is in another world. Tugging on his earlobe when he's deep in thought, or rubbing his buzzed head, or staring into the ash end of a cigarette like he's staring into Hell.

Joey Cane is no Messiah, but he's the closest thing Isaac has to a father anymore. For that Nelly is grateful. Joey gives her hope. Maybe he can lift Isaac above this shit, this life, this street, this block. Maybe through Joey Isaac has a chance. How many nights this summer, Nelly up pacing in her bedroom, or walking home from Lorenzo's, or sitting in the morning drinking coffee and watching Isaac sleep—how often has Nelly thought of leaving, of giving Francis Street the middle finger and moving on. The bills getting further and further behind. Frank becoming more and more gone. But the thing about leaving . . . leaving's not an option when there's nowhere to go.

Should Frank come back clean, should he come correct, really come correct—Nelly would forgive him. She would. Those late-night rendezvous with Lorenzo, creeping up and down Francis from streetlight to streetlight, lurking in the shadows, hiding from the eyes of the block—the adultery would stop. Nelly would fight those late-night urges, the temptation, and she'd be a good wife. She would.

Nelly knows the truth though. She feels it in her bones and the bones don't lie. Frank's not ever coming home. Not like he was. And Lorenzo's not an option. Even if she wanted something more than sex,

Lorenzo wouldn't want her back. She's meat; he's meat. Nothing more. And this feeling she's feeling for Joey, this lust gone love gone something in between, it's just too much to burden right now. There's no space for this feeling, no place to put it. Joey has a woman and Joey's woman sees all. Tara caught Nelly watching Joey from her bedroom window the other day and cut her a warning glance, a cut-the-bullshit-bitch-I KNOW look, a keep-sniffing-around-my-man-and-I'm-gonna-fuck-you-up look.

Nelly took notice with a swallow of fear. But fear's not enough to stop Nelly from fanning the longing inside her. She can't stop her imagination from making her crazy, putting her mind on escape, fantasizing of Joey Cane taking her and Isaac away from this place, packing a few bags and leaving everything else behind, Tara, Frank, Lorenzo, Francis Street.

She hasn't fucked Lorenzo in a week. She hasn't had the urge to. Lorenzo hasn't asked about it either. "You bring that pretty little pussy of yours down here anytime you get the itch," he said. Like he knew what Nelly's sexual craving meant. Like he knew she'd be back. Nelly was easy. She delivered the pussy to his doorstep. Delivered the pussy to a felon on house arrest almost every night this summer. Every time she got the itch. Just like he told her to.

Today Tara is gone in Joey's car. Lyric is gone with her. Isaac's shooting the basketball and getting really good at it, looking less awkward, the ball seems to pause for a moment and hover over the rim. It seems to breathe, to inhale and then exhale before it snaps through the net. Joey's been acting funny today. He won't look at her square, he's nervous almost, or preoccupied—glancing at the street from time to time—is Joey feeling the same way Nelly is? Is he worried what his woman might think? Joey, Nelly, and Isaac—it sounds nice in her head: Joey, Nelly, and Isaac. And Lyric. Joey's daughter can come too. Four southeast side refugees packed into a burgundy Oldsmobile, full tank of gas, destination Green Pastures.

Tires screech when Tara pulls up in Joey's car. A car door slams. Joey shakes his head and holds his hands in the air as if to say, "What did

I do now?" Maybe Joey doesn't see it—this thing Nelly's feeling. But Tara does. She sees it, smells it; a woman always knows when another bitch is crazy for her man. Tara says nothing. She stops halfway down the driveway like she can't go any further. Like she's come to the edge of a cliff. Isaac shoots and misses and the ball bounces hard off the rim, rolls past Isaac down the driveway. Tara stops the ball with an all-white Air Force 1. She smiles at Isaac, but her eyes aren't smiling. She has straight white teeth and a beautiful brown complexion. She's all curves: firm tits, hips and ass. No gut. Body like she never had a child. Even Nelly has to admit, the girl is a fox.

"Hi, Isaac." Lyric breaks the silence. She stands behind her mother.

"Hey." Isaac puts his hands in the pockets of his jean shorts.

Nelly's too scared to move, like one word, one sound, any motion at all and Tara will lose it, and Nelly will get her ass kicked all up and down Francis Street. It's like Tara can feel it too—the threshold no more than a glance, one look at Nelly and Nelly knows Tara is coming for her. No kind of clawing and hair pulling would save her either. Nelly's barely five-foot-tall and only a hundred fifteen pounds. Never been in a fight. And that time Frank punched her he knocked her out cold.

"Joey," says Tara, her eyes piercing her target. "I need to talk to you inside."

Nelly exhales when they walk away. She'd probably cry if the kids weren't around. Lyric's now sitting in the grass a few feet from Nelly, watching Isaac shoot the ball, oblivious to the screaming going on inside her house.

Joey's feet are propped on the porch rail; he's pulling on a Camel, enjoying a melancholy marijuana buzz, solo, no Lorenzo to cramp his high. He glances down the street toward Lorenzo's house. Dead but the porch light. A couple nights ago Joey and Tara were out here enjoying the night. Lyric was asleep and Tara had popped open a bottle of Grey Goose and was drinking it mixed with cranberry juice. And when Tara drinks she gets real friendly. So when Lorenzo was making his rounds that night she fixed him a drink. Lorenzo sat on their porch for hours, talking, laughing. The more Lorenzo talked, the more Tara laughed. And Joey might have smoked too much weed. He might have been too high, or a little paranoid, but while laughing, Tara touched Lorenzo's thigh, and the two of them exchanged a look, a look that maybe Joey was translating wrong, because he was too high and maybe a little paranoid, but the look seemed to say this wasn't the first time they'd hung out socially.

Then Joey's mind started fucking with him. He imagined Lorenzo sitting on his porch smoking a cigarette, watching Joey drive off to work. Imagined Lorenzo creeping down the sidewalk, knocking on his door, swivel head double-checking the street for Joey's Delta 88.

Joey pictured Lorenzo ascending the steps to his bedroom, tugging at his pants, watching Tara's ass as she leads him up the stairs while Lyric slept in the other room, Tara leaning against the bed with her ass up in the air, the stupid smirk on Lorenzo's face when he drops his pants and mounts her. It was probably all irrational. The hand on the thigh, innocent, incidental. Joey's never suspected Tara to be a cheater—she's always gotten attention from men, but she's always deflected it, made Joey feel secure. But since Isaac Page has entered Joey's life it's been Tara who's felt insecure.

"Hey, You." Nelly has appeared suddenly. It's as if she crept through a fold in the night. She stands in front of Joey's porch, her arms crossed, hair thrown into a ponytail. It's the wrong night for Nelly to swing by. "Can I get one?" Her head tilts toward Joey's open box of Camels napping next to his Zippo.

"Help yourself," says Joey.

Nelly Page has never crossed the line. She's never said anything offhand or insinuated anything sexual. But Tara's convinced she's after something, with Nelly always lurking about. And Lorenzo, that night he was over here drinking, told them he heard Nelly was a nympho. He called her a gotta-have-it girl. When he said it, Tara gave

Joey an accusatory glance. There's always some truth in the word on the street. There's always some truth in women's intuition. But how much of that is truth and how much of that is bullshit, how much is in Tara's head?

Nelly grabs the cigarette pack and the Zippo. "I just want to say." Nelly pulls out a Camel, sparks the lighter, and inhales deep. Exhales slow. "I appreciate what you're doing for my boy."

Tonight Joey just wants Nelly to smoke and leave. Any moment Tara will open the door and be on the porch. Tonight she's going out. She made the announcement an hour ago, after Lyric fell asleep. She said it with a payback tone and pursed lips. Does she really believe he's cheating? Does she know him that little? "It's nothing," says Joey. He glances at the door.

"No, it's something. Isaac's crazy about you, Joey."

"He's a good kid."

Nelly measures Joey with sly eyes, sneaky greens canopied by thick black lashes. She has pouty lips and a series of diamond piercings in the cartilage of both ears, glowing in the night like two half-moons. She's slight in her baggy sweatpants and hoodie. For the first time Joey tries to imagine her naked, but his mind can't imagine any substantial curves, instead he summons an image of a siren, singing, angelic, seducing him away from his family and then growing fangs and horns.

Okay. With Nelly always on the edge of their life. With the time Joey spends with Isaac. Joey's seen Nelly in her bedroom window, hiding behind the blinds, watching. Okay. "Listen," says Joey. He has to flat out ask her. Nelly, is there something happening here? He has to nip it right now. Because this look Nelly's giving him. This love or lust look. Either way it's bad. "Listen, Nelly," he says.

Then Tara opens the door and steps onto the porch. She wears skimpy denim shorts and a Pepsi T-shirt. She rolls her eyes when she sees Nelly. Nelly steps away. Tonight Tara's empowered. She's too large to be jealous. The sidewalk is her runway. The Olds is her chariot. She's a Badmammajamma. Too bad for a chauffeur. Southeast side beware!

Miss Thunderbooty is on the prowl! Joey Cane has never felt more insignificant. Tara moves with no noise, but her ass seems to growl. He's forgotten Nelly Page is there.

"Tara!" yells Joey.

"I'll be back when I get here." She doesn't look at Joey when she climbs into the car, revs the engine, and peels off into the night.

•

For a while Joey paces the bedroom. It's hot and humid tonight and not even a breath of a breeze. No AC. The screen has a small tear in it. Rogue mosquitoes have found their way into the room. They have no plants. There are no pictures on the wall. There's no TV. He and Tara's shared dresser inherited from Tara's childhood home. "Tee loves so-in-so etched in the flawed wood finishing, the boy's name concealed beneath permanent black marker.

He considers asking Nelly to watch Lyric so he can soldier the southeast side on foot, or catch a cab. But fuck that. Tara's not going to make him jump off that ledge. Instead, he walks into Lyric's bedroom and wipes drool from her cheek. He kisses her and tightens the bedding around her.

His stomach turns at the thought of leaving this house. To tuck his tail between his legs and go back to East Grand Rapids, back to his childhood home and start over. That option has always been there. But something about the way his mother looked at his baby girl, with her brown skin and her frizzy locks—Joey's mother with that judgmental smile, those phony eyes—*We're not racist people, Joey. We're not. There are African-American lawyers at your father's firm, guys your father depends on, trusts, makes money with. We're not the type of people who see color, Joey. It's just . . . there's educated and uneducated. There's rich and there's poor. The name Cane means something in this city. And that girl—Her name's Tara, Mom—That girl, does she even know who her father is, Joey?*

Joey could never go back; not to that life. Lyric deserves to be loved, not tolerated. His mother, with her talk of privilege—what she really meant was White Privilege. Whatever white privilege Joey once had he lost when he fathered a biracial child.

Tara comes home late. Early-morning late. She tiptoes up the stairs. She stands on the threshold of the bedroom fidgeting with her purse before she enters. Joey sits on the bed, leaning against the headboard. "Where were you, Tara?"

"I met some girlfriends at a bar." She looks away. Closes and locks the door. Tara walks over to the dresser and sets her purse on it.

"Which bar?" Joey pictures Tara with Lorenzo in some vague semblance of a dive bar, but remembers Lorenzo's tether. He imagines Lorenzo there anyway, cops showing up with guns drawn, the bartender pointing to the restroom, Tara bent over a sink, thunder booty bouncing against his thighs, Lorenzo's pants at his ankles.

"It's not important," says Tara.

"Who were you with?" It comes out a lot louder than he had intended. But he's feeling so much. Anger, betrayal—he feels like a fool—like everything he stands for, the life, the path he chose was for nothing. He takes pride in being a Martyr. Saint Joey who had it all and chose to stay home, to be a father, to handle his responsibilities like a man. And it all blows up in his face.

"Baby," says Tara. She's crying. "I'm so sorry."

"Sorry? What did you do?"

Tara doesn't answer. She peeks out of the blinds at the house next door. "Promise me you're not fucking her, Joey."

"Shhh," says Joey. "You'll wake Lyric."

"You promise me, Joey."

"Don't question my loyalty. I gave you my word, Tara. I promised to be faithful. This life, this shit . . . that's all I have left, you understand me? All I have left is my word."

"Is our life that bad? Is it really that bad?"

"It's not you . . ."

"Don't give me that it's not you it's me shit, Joey."

"That's not what I was going to say . . ."

"What? What were you going to say?"

"It's just, sometimes I feel like I'm not living the life I was supposed to live."

"That was your choice. I didn't tell you to turn down that scholarship. If you remember, I was the one that called you a fool."

Joey doesn't respond. She's right. Maybe his honor was misguided. How many young men would have made that choice? The blame is his own. Maybe that choice was self-righteous. Maybe Tara was just along for the ride. And now, now that ride is coming to an end.

"I love you, Joey. Do you understand me? Do understand what that means?" She'd never actually said the words. All of these years. Not once. "Why don't you love me, Joey?"

If he knew, he'd tell her. He'd give her a truth that would hurt her, a truth that would set her free. But his truth won't break her heart, it'll only bruise it some more. The truth is he's tried to love her—the truth is he's searched for that allusive, missing thing—in this contract, this agreement, this domestic partnership or whatever the world might call it—this babydaddy/babymomma situation, this real-stakes game of House—and now more than ever he's convinced there's nothing there, there is nothing to find, that he and Tara are no more than two humans spinning their tires. "I don't know," says Joey.

Tara wipes her eyes. "Of course you don't know," she says. The crying is done. The moment is gone. Joey wants to question her some more. He wants to accuse her. He wants to ask her why she came home crying. He saw her, he wants to say, he saw her touch Lorenzo's thigh! What she was apologizing for? He wants to ask her what she was doing tonight and who she was with. He wants to interrogate her. But Tara's taking off her clothes. The Pepsi shirt, the jean shorts, they're on the floor now. The bra is unclamped and being tossed across the room. "Lie to me, Joey. Tell me you love me."

"What?"

She's crawling across the bed now. Pulling off his shorts, his boxers, taking him in her mouth. Joey's following her spine with his index finger.

He's admiring the beauty of her curves, the arch of her back, the angle of her waist before it becomes her ass. That big beautiful ass. She's after his soul. And he wants her to have it. She could have it all. If he only knew how to give it to her. Joey takes off his T-shirt and drops it on the floor.

Tara straddles him. "Say it, Joey. Lie to me," she says. "Tell me you love me. I want to hear the words. Say it. Cause I'm not going anywhere you motherfucker. So you better lie to me. You better make me believe it."

"I love you," says Joey.

This night no more words need be exchanged.

The Shadow's life is coming to an end. It's stalling now when it wants to, when Nelly's idling at a stop sign, or when she's trying to leave work. She can hear the muffler scrapping against the street, like its dangling by its last rusty thread, one pothole away from being left where it lands. The car is loud. The muffler, the engine—it rattles and sighs and complains—a grumpy old terminally ill machine begging her, Please Nelly, please just leave me laying on the side of the road.

Tonight she's got this sinking feeling inside her. Like Frank's dead, or on his way to being dead. Or maybe he's in trouble, in jail? God knows what Frank's been into this summer. What dark alley his mind has found and walked down—but this feeling, this dreadful feeling—Nelly knows it's real. Gone or not gone, Frank is her husband. He belongs to her. So she drives, and she hopes the Shadow survives the night, hopes her husband survives the night.

When she finds Terrell's house she leaves the car sputtering curbside. Nelly knocks on the door and waits. The woman who answers wears hospital scrubs and a hair scarf. She doesn't smile or invite Nelly in. Just looks at her like, "What?"

"My name is Nelly Page. I'm Frank's wife." Nelly peeks into the house. Two handsome children sit at a table doing homework. There's no sign of brokenness in this woman, this home. The house is clean, immaculate really, no clutter and the comfort of vanilla scented candles. "I just . . ."

"I haven't seen him," says the woman. She doesn't introduce herself. Doesn't change her serious expression. She looks at Nelly like she's waiting for Nelly to leave. Then her expression softens a little. "Listen, Honey," she says. "Let me give you some advice. Worry about your son. You're raising that boy into a man. It's not your job to baby his father. I used to be you. Running around looking for Terrell, driving through the southeast side crying, my boys in the backseat asking me what's wrong. I get it. I do. But don't come knocking on my door again. You understand me? You're gonna scare my kids."

Francis Street is quiet for a Friday night. Empty porches. No one creeping up and down the sidewalk. Not even the usual noise: the not-so-distant sirens, domestic situations, the chirp chirp of patrol cars harassing every black face that's outside after dark. It's serene, almost. A strange vibe in the air. Like tonight, just tonight, everyone in the vicinity is taking a break from polluting the air with their problems.

The only thing killing the quiet is Isaac. Relentless with questions. Asking about the past, about the glory days, on constantly about Joey's rise up from out of the driveway and into some packed arena. The last couple of weeks the boy has crawled out of his shell. Tonight Joey wishes Isaac would crawl back into it.

"Joey," Isaac says. "You're only twenty-six, dude. It's not too late. You could go to college, or try out for the Pistons."

Joey pulls on a Camel and exhales smoke out of his nose. His mind on Lorenzo: the epitome of southeast-side shit. The felon. The drug-dealer. Forty years old and living with his mother, walking up and down the sidewalk with his pants hanging past his ass, bullying teens, holding a bottle of malt liquor in a brown paper bag, looking like a movie extra in his own life. What could Tara possibly see in that man?

"I've been smoking for eight years," Joey tells Isaac. He pulls on the Camel again. "It's over, little man. My lungs are done. Knees are gone, ankles too."

Tonight though, Lorenzo is scarce; Joey saw him pop his head out the house around eight, when he first joined Isaac in the driveway, Lorenzo looking up and down the street, seeing Joey and smirking, shaking his head, and then going back inside.

"Quit smoking," says Isaac. He dribbles twice and shoots. Flick. Snap.

Joey ignores him. "Your shot looks good," he says. "Now you have to work on those handles." Joey looks down the street toward Lorenzo's house.

"Joey. All you have to do is quit smoking."

"How about this: how about you make it for both of us? On my word, Isaac: you ever have a game, I'll be there. Every one."

"Daddy?" Lyric stands in front of Joey and Isaac, wearing pajamas, wiping sleep from her eyes. She's only a couple years younger than Isaac, but Isaac seems so much older; the things he's seen, been through. Lyric's in this shit too, this neighborhood, but besides being caught in the crossfire of the occasional Joey/Tara argument, Lyric is oblivious to this block, confined to this driveway and the safety of this house.

"Mommy's not home," Lyric says.

Adorable. Coily curls. Her mother's light brown eyes. Joey's girlish mouth. Joey wishes she could stay like this forever. "Baby?" Joey says. He lifts his daughter and kisses her cheek. Isaac stops dribbling and holds the ball. The Olds is still parked curbside. Tara must have crept away on foot, must have snuck out the backdoor unnoticed, then slipped along the other side of the house. Joey carries Lyric inside. "Tara!" he says. "Tara?" He walks up the stairs and into the bathroom. There's steam on the mirror. Makeup cases scattered across the sink. Flatiron left plugged in.

"What's wrong, Daddy?"

"Nothing. Nothing, baby."

Joey carries Lyric down the stairs and back outside. Isaac is waiting for him on the porch, still holding the basketball.

"I need you to sit with Lyric for a minute. Can you do that?" asks Joey.

"Yeah," says Isaac. "What's wrong?"

Joey looks down the street, cracks his knuckles, his neck, and loosens his shoulders.

"Joey?" says Isaac.

"I'll only be a minute." Joey turns toward Lorenzo's. His Nike sandals slap the concrete as he walks. A cool breeze against his damp beater. He's buzzed off adrenaline. His hands trembling. Everything he could have been is behind him. Everything he has become breathes within the walls of the house on Francis Street. And now it's come to this: walking down the sidewalk with his mind on violence. He's walking into chaos, no chance of winning, not caring; no reason to fight, but ready to; not knowing what exactly he's fighting for.

Joey beats on Lorenzo's door. He rings the bell three times, then holds it down with his left hand, and continues beating on the door with his right.

The door cracks open and Joey pushes against it. It's held shut by a chain. "You looking to die tonight, muh fucka?" Lorenzo is shirtless. More built than he looks with his clothes on. Aging tattoos on muscled shoulders and arms.

"I know she's in there," says Joey.

"Thunderbooty?" Lorenzo smiles.

"Shit ain't funny, Lorenzo. Where is she? Tara!" he yells.

"Look, white boy. You need to stop with all this goddamn noise. You about to make me lose my cool."

"Fuck you."

"Fuck me?"

"Fuck you. I know she's in there, Lorenzo."

Lorenzo laughs. "Yeah, I got your bitch, nigga. She's upstairs waiting on me."

Joey lowers his shoulder into the door. It doesn't budge.

Lorenzo unbolts the chain. He grabs Joey by the throat. Punches him on the ear. Joey staggers, but gets a hold on Lorenzo's arm, pulls him onto the porch. Joey sees the silhouette of a woman standing in the house at the top of a stairway.

Lorenzo smashes Joey's head against the porch's concrete pillar. He twists Joey onto his back. Joey lays still. Lorenzo slaps him across his skull. "Look what you made me do, white boy." Lorenzo stands and looks up and down the street. He lights a cigarette and takes a drag. "Come beating on my door? *My* goddamn door. Like you're gonna do something." Lorenzo kneels next to Joey, barely conscious now and bleeding from the mouth. He puts the cigarette out on his forehead. "Look at you now, white boy. Mr. Superstar. White Michael Jordan. Ain't shit now, are you? No different than the rest of us niggas."

"Tara," whispers Joey.

"You's a dumb muh fucka, you know that?" Lorenzo stands and turns to walk into the house.

Joey is coming to his senses, seeing Tara standing at the top of Lorenzo's stairs. His head throbs. He licks blood from the corner of his mouth. The night is noiseless.

Joey tackles Lorenzo in the doorway and they fall against a shoe rack, knocking it to the floor. They wrestle for a moment before Lorenzo gets Joey onto his back. Joey looks to the top of the stairs and sees a large Hispanic woman wrapped in a green blanket. Lorenzo lowers a forearm into Joey's throat and puts his weight behind it. "Breaking and entering." Lorenzo pulls a pistol out of his waistband.

"Lorenzo, no!" cries the woman from the top of the stairs.

Joey looks into Lorenzo's face and knows he's going to die. Steel slides across steel when Lorenzo cocks the pistol. The sound is loud and its echo eats the empty night. Joey stares into the barrel of the pistol. He's swallowed by blackness and emptied into a dim-lit bar. Tara is there with two girlfriends. She twirls a straw in a fruity-looking drink, bored, listening to her friends talk but her eyes are fixated on the pink cocktail. Tara checks her cell phone. Scrolls through her contacts. Finds ♥♥♥Joey♥♥♥ and keys in *I love you*. She readies herself to hit send and then changes her mind. The scene dissolves, becomes black and fluid and Joey is spinning, backward, fast, until the barrel spits him out and he's staring into Lorenzo's cold, brown, remorseless eyes.

Joey hears sirens in the distance.
He tries to imagine a different life.
But can't.

Mourn
Summer 2007

THE SHADOW STALLS ON MADISON AVENUE, CLOSE enough to Garfield Park for Nelly to coast into the lot. After trying three times to bring the car back to life she gives up. She locks the doors and sets out on foot. The moon looks sick. It's pale. She thinks of a line Jack Nicholson said once in a movie. You ever dance with the devil in the pale moonlight? Dancing with the devil. That could be Frank, not the devil, but the devil's dance partner. Seduced beneath the pale moon, so deceived into pleasure that he can never turn back.

Nelly turns down Francis Street. It's dark and she's alone and she isn't afraid. She should be, but she isn't. All it would take is a crackhead with his eye on her purse, or a pervert with a beastly desire to take what he can't have, or a stray bullet, or a drunk driver hopping a curb and plowing through her. All of this could happen, yet Nelly feels no fear. This place is home. She walks down the empty sidewalk past empty porches. Through a bizarre silence that seems to last much longer than it should. And then she finds out why. The night's chaos has collected in front of Lorenzo's. An ambulance. Four police cars. So many lights.

Nelly pushes through the traffic of onlookers, people with their beers, their cigarettes—people are gathered in front of Lorenzo's house, surrounding the yellow tape. Tara pounds on a police officer's chest. Then she is restrained. She's face down in the grass, the officer's knee pressing into her back, he's asking her to please calm down, please. Joey

Cane is on a stretcher. His face, his body is covered, but Nelly knows it's Joey. Isaac and Lyric sit in the back of a police car.

The look Isaac gives her is harsh. Like her being gone caused this. Like Joey being carted away, it's all her fault. She cannot fully process the scene. Her racing heart is out of sync with the world. The way it's all slowing down. The voices blending together to make one warped and pulsing noise. Lips are moving but whose words are whose Nelly cannot tell. The dim ugly moon watching it all. Tonight is not real. Joey Cane is not dead. Isaac, her sweet boy, he's not seeing all this, he's not growing up too soon, not losing his friend, the last thing Isaac has, the only thing he has left in the life she brought him into.

"Miss! Wait, Miss!"

"He's my son," she tells the officer. Then Isaac and Lyric are out of the police car and into Nelly's arms.

Tara's head pounds. Tears and vodka and an empty bed. A Joeyless bed. There are phone calls to make, arrangements to be made, decisions, so many decisions: headstone inscriptions, burial or cremation—she and Joey never talked about death, they never had a plan. The worst of it will be his mother. Her need to control, her need to impose her whiteness on every situation. For him to die like this, the way he did, in *this* neighborhood, the bitch is not capable of restraint or tact, hell no! She'll most certainly be bringing a Rich White I Told You So, and it'll be all Tara's fault, because she never should have gotten pregnant, never should have kept the child, and never should have allowed Joey to turn down that scholarship.

Whatever!

Tara finds a clean facecloth and washes up in the bathroom. Her eyes are swollen and her throat is dry. Her neck hurts. It's amazing how much her neck hurts. Amazing how the mind tries not to cry and the body imposes its will. Amazing how much better you feel when you finally give in, let it all pour out of you.

Tara walks down the stairs and steps outside. She's offended by the shining sun. She feels like, shit, she feels like Joey just died last night, even the sun should mourn. She's filled with gloom and the sun is mocking her, mocking her loss, mocking her mourning, giving everyone else in this city a reason to smile. The yellow tape still surrounds Lorenzo's porch. A witness heard Joey down there screaming Tara's name last night, before Lorenzo killed him, before Lorenzo ran, before Lorenzo got shot sixteen times by the police and died facedown and shirtless in the middle of the street. Why was Joey even down there? Why was he screaming her name? What was said or implied about her and Lorenzo that had Joey acting all crazy.

God, she loved that man. She believes he loved her too. She has to believe it. Deep down in that complicated Joey way he had to love her. Maybe she had been too greedy? Asked him for too much. Maybe a man should be allowed to keep something to himself, those deepest darkest thoughts that she would try to pry away from him, that Joey always withheld from her? Maybe she was just in her own way? In the way of love. Plucking at the wrong strings, or pushing the wrong buttons. Yeah, maybe that's it. The love was real, but the communication was broken.

Tara sees Joey's basketball lying in the grass. She picks it up and walks next door. Nelly's been crying too. She was nice enough to keep Lyric over night, but nothing is forgiven. Tara knows what Nelly was after. She doesn't think Joey would actually cheat, especially with this skinny bitch, but still . . . Lyric's sleeping on the couch and Isaac's sleeping on the floor. Coffee brews in the kitchen. Nelly asks her if she wants some. Asks her if she wants to sit and talk. Tara does. She wishes she doesn't but she does. She wants to accuse Nelly of having an affair with her man. She wants to take all this pain she's feeling and shove it in her face. But she doesn't. Doesn't have the energy to fight, to yell. Doesn't have the energy to feel.

"How are the kids?"

"Not good," says Nelly. "Isaac spent the night crying and Lyric's pretending like nothing happened."

To be a child that young and lose someone who loves you. Someone you need. Your whole life is altered. What side of a tragedy do you land on? The side that remembers that love, that relationship and moves on, or the side that becomes crippled, unable to let go, unable to live. And is Tara thinking about the kids now, or is she thinking about herself? She hands Nelly the basketball. "I want Isaac to have this. This ball meant a lot to Joey. Isaac meant a lot to him." Tara sips her coffee. "He reminds me of Joey, you know," Tara says. "Not just the basketball, but the seriousness—Joey was always in his mind, off someplace else. Isaac seems the same."

"He is," says Nelly. "Before he met Joey . . ." she starts. "I don't know what Isaac's gonna do now?"

"That boy is strong. He'll deal. He will deal and move on."

"What about you?"

Joey had no life insurance. There will be funeral costs. They have no savings. They'll have to get an apartment they can afford. She'll have to get a job. Doing what? All she's ever been is Lyric's mom. This new world is heavy. Tara can feel the weight of it upon her. In her bones, her spirit. Something inside of her is cracking and hardening, making her both strong and cold. There is no room for fear in this new world. In this Joeyless world she has to go it alone. "I don't know," Tara says. "I just know I gotta get away from Francis Street. I just know I gotta get the fuck out of that house."

The house on Jefferson is a beacon on the gray street: painted pink and purple with a baby blue door. Boarded windows. It's as silent as a morgue. This place is not your traditional crack house, not that Frank has anything to compare it to, but really it's more like a crack-themed brothel. Cesar keeps the traffic manageable with a ticket system. His street dealers keep the tickets and give them out at their discretion, and the dealer's discretion, for the most part, involves women, women who still look decent and are at that point, that crack point where there's nothing they won't do. They come here with their tickets and they wait downstairs to be summoned, and when they're called they ascend those steps and they do as they're told, they are given their drugs, and then they leave. Getting high in the house is not allowed.

The overseer of this place is DeMarco, a six-foot-six mountain of mean, and Cesar's right-hand man. DeMarco is Philistine huge, huge like the pistol he carries is redundant, like he could take a baseball bat to the head and smile at you, like Mike Tyson would piss his pants. So needless to say, this place has order. Frank's only been here once before. And when his name was called, and he gave DeMarco his ticket, and he ascended the steps, Frank was led to a room with no furniture but a single mattress and a small table. On the table was an ashtray built out of plastic skulls. The room smelled like piss and shit and pussy. A balding white man waited for Frank there. He wore blue jeans and a button-down shirt. He was clean, normal, other than his scared-shitless demeanor.

"Knock twice when you're finished," DeMarco said. He locked the door from the outside.

"What's your name?" asked the man.

"No names," Frank said.

"Okay." For a moment the man said nothing. He waited like he thought Frank knew the score, like Frank was the one running the show. "I already paid," he said. "The man said you'd do it. He said I'd be able to watch."

Frank smiled. The terror he had felt since entering the room and seeing this man was gone. He knew what the ticket meant, knew he was coming for sex, but had imagined some lonely deformed woman, or someone terminally sick looking for one last thrill before she met her maker—the thought of squeezing The Cock into this Average Joe's poop shoot, or the thought of having one shoved up his, Jesus. A self-service hand job was a cakewalk. So Frank unzipped his pants. He loosed The Cock and tugged on it a few times to get it started.

"Fuck," the man said, and he reached into his back pocket for his wallet. Frank feared the worst. Because he knew he had a price. For the right amount of money there was nothing Frank wouldn't do. The thought came to him to knock the man out, take his wallet, and bust down the door, to run past DeMarco, down the stairs, out of the house, and brave the consequences of Cesar Bolden's wrath. But then the man peeled out a $50 and set it on the table. "Please," he said. "Just let me put it in my mouth."

Today, though, Frank has no ticket. Neither does Terrell. They both stand in DeMarco's "office." Chairless besides the one behind a large Steelcase desk where he keeps the dope locked in a drawer. DeMarco sits spinning his stainless steel pistol on the naked desktop with a long thick finger. Worried. Scared maybe. Looking much less menacing while he's slumped in his chair. What was it he used to be: a ballplayer, a boxer? Frank checks DeMarco's tattooed arms for clues, but can't decipher the ink against his dark brown skin. He gives up trying, thinking, everyone's a former something. "Cesar says don't move." DeMarco stands and paces. Leaves his pistol on the desk. He has a thick scar across his jawline that looks like someone slashed him with a broken beer bottle.

"Wait here?" asks Terrell.

"That's right." DeMarco opens the sex room door. "Fuck!" DeMarco checks his mobile phone. Frank looks at Terrell and Terrell looks at DeMarco pacing. He called Cesar a half an hour before, whispering into his cell phone. Frank could hear Cesar yelling on the other end. DeMarco hasn't said much since. If Cesar is coming, it's trouble. The man rarely shows his face around here. Frank wonders what's in that room that has DeMarco so scared. Did he kill someone? Frank heard from that mixed-chick Erica that DeMarco likes to sample the goods. The pretty ones that come here with their ticket, Erica told Frank, don't leave pretty. She said this with a black eye. She said this with claw marks on her shoulders. She said this then said, "I'm never going back there, Frankie. Never."

When Cesar steps into the house he has his pistol drawn. Frank watches from the upstairs doorway. Through opaque Ray Bans Cesar scans the room. "Everybody out!" He doesn't wait to see if they listen. He stalks up the stairs, past Frank, and grabs DeMarco by the shirt. He shoves him against the wall.

Frank and Terrell turn to leave.

"Not you," Cesar says. "You two stay put." He presses his pistol against DeMarco's temple. "Give me a reason not to kill you, nigga," he says through clenched teeth.

"Cesar, I—"

"You what? You just had to fuck her, right? A skin and bones raggedy bitch and you had to slide your dirty dick in her. Even after I told you she's off limits." Cesar slaps DeMarco with his pistol and draws blood on his cheekbone. "Even though you didn't shoot the shit in her veins you're the one that gave it to her. For that you get no forgiveness. For that, nigga, you owe."

DeMarco glances at his pistol, still sitting on his desk. A few quick steps away from being in his hand.

Cesar smiles. He grabs DeMarco's ear like you might grab a child's. "You want that pistol, D? Huh? Go on, then. Go grab it. See what happens if you do." Cesar lets go of DeMarco's ear. "Go ahead. What? I don't see you moving. I didn't think so." Cesar turns to Frank and Terrell. "Big Frank," says Cesar. "And you, dirtball nigga," he says to Terrell. "I want to show you something." Cesar wipes the blood off DeMarco's cheek with his finger. He wipes his finger on DeMarco's shirt. "You can take your bitch ass downstairs and make sure none of them junkies are on the lawn."

Frank closes his eyes as if when he opens them he'll be a stronger, better man. But who the fuck is he kidding? He's here because he's been summoned. He's here because he needs to get high.

"On the other side of this door we have ourselves what you might call an ironic situation." Cesar opens the door and steps into the room. Frank and Terrell don't move. "Y'all need to stop dragging ass."

They follow Cesar into the room.

Joy Green lies dead on the mattress. One hundred pounds and naked. Needle still in her veins. Her brown eyes made black by death. "Look familiar?" he asks.

Frank and Terrell nod.

"I need you to dump her in the river," says Cesar. "No need to weigh her down. Just let the bitch float. They bag DeMarco, so be it. They bag you two clowns, so be it. The way I see it, you got two options: A. Put her in the back of Frankie's truck, drive down to the river and dump her in it. B. DeMarco comes back up these stairs and puts a slug in both of you."

•

Frank feels like an interloper. He's driving down Francis Street at five miles per hour with his headlights off, easing his truck into the driveway like a thief. He doesn't know what he'll do or say. He has no plan. No plan but to convince Nelly and Isaac to leave with him. Get out of this city and start over. He doesn't know where and he doesn't know how. There is no money and his truck barely has any gas.

He leaves the truck running. Nelly has changed the locks. Frank beats on the door and waits for the sirens. Maybe he's paranoid. Joy Green is dead. She was wrapped in a brown tarp when Frank threw her in the river. Two bungee cords kept the tarp around her. Still her arm shook loose and dangled when she hit the water. When he ran the current hadn't yet taken her under. He wore black gloves, O.J. style, stolen from Meijer, and he burned them when the deed was done. How long until the body is found? How can a junkie, someone already gone be perceived as missing?

Terrell is on his own. He bailed out when they got to the river. Running, the coward, running and leaving Frank to do it by himself. When Cesar finds Terrell he's as good as dead. But when Joy Green's body is found—did Frank touch her before he put the gloves on? When they were lifting her onto the tarp, shit, he touched her, under the thigh and the armpit, Frank on one side and Terrell on the other. They'll find the prints. They always find the prints. Then what will Frank say? His demeanor screaming CRACK and the movie, shit, the porn flick. They'll think he was friends with Joy Green. They'll think they were lovers. Pin the whole thing on him.

Frank beats on the door. Nelly opens it, but hides behind the door chain. Isaac stands behind her. Emotionless. Hard. "Don't let him in," Isaac says.

"Isaac," says Nelly.

"Baby," says Frank. "I'm home, baby, I'm really home."

"Don't, Mom."

"Isaac, he's your father."

She shuts the door and Frank hears her loosen the chain. He doesn't wait for her to let him in. Frank's in the house and he's stalking around. This place is foreign. The furniture moved. There are plants. There are flowers. It smells like cinnamon. They watch him pace. He doesn't know where to begin, what to pack. Money. They need money. But that's what they're waiting for. They're waiting for him to say the words, because the last time . . . the last time he asked for money, the last time . . . "We need to get gas," Frank says. "We need to pack our things. The truck needs gas." No one moves. His voice carries no weight in this house, not anymore.

"Frank," says Nelly. "You're acting crazy."

"We have to go," he says. "We have to get out."

"Frankie. What have you done?"

She knows. The police have been here already. This is a setup. The body was found and examined. They found the drugs in Joy's system, found Frank's prints, asked around—"Yes officer, known associates." "Yes, Officer, both junkies." "Yes, Officer, they were in a porn flick together." That'll be enough to book him. Who will speak up against Cesar Bolden? How much time will the police spend investigating the death of a junkie? "What did they say to you, Nelly?"

"Who?"

"I didn't do what they said I did. Do you believe me? Damn it! Answer me, Nelly do you believe me?"

"We're not going with you," says Isaac. "You need to leave."

"You little shit. You don't know what I've been through. What I've seen. What I've done."

"I don't care."

Frank looks past Isaac to Nelly. "Is that what you want? You want me to leave?"

Nelly nods.

"Okay," says Frank. "I'll leave. But I need some money."

"Frank, let me get you some help . . ."

"I don't need help. I need money. Don't you understand? I need money. Just give me the money."

"Leave!" says Isaac. "Get the fuck out!"

Isaac holds a basketball. GH written on it in black marker. He looks pale, changed. Different. "Go to bed, Isaac," says Frank.

"Fuck you!"

Frank grabs Isaac by the arm and throws him against the couch. The basketball falls out of his hands and rolls across the floor. Isaac stays where he lands, his eyes on Frank, his face saying Hate. He's not Frank's son. Not anymore. This is not his house, his family. He is an interloper. "Nelly, give me the money." He says it calm, watching Nelly take a step back, he's feeling the change coming, the heat, the red, his hand grabbing the back of a wooden chair, Nelly shaking her head, telling him No, we're not giving you money, and then the chair is soaring across the room, and Nelly's falling, and her eyes are blank, and there is so much blood, a river of blood, a Nile, pouring from her head and soaking the carpet, and Frank's saying, Oh God, no, Please God, no, but Nelly's gone, she's gone and Isaac's a stone statue, and Frank's finding her purse and he's pulling out money.

He's leaving.

This house. This city.

Frank Page is leaving.

Iggy's Place
1995–1996

Joy Green steps out of Iggy's Place and into a surreal summer night in downtown Grand Rapids. A white moon hovers over the city like a curious eye. Puddles of light spill onto the Grand River. Music rides the wind. Nights like tonight you could almost be mesmerized by the moon and the music and the pillars of buildings on the other side of the river. But Joy sees a peeled and browning city teetering on the threshold of rot.

It's like the river is cutting the beauty in half and leaving this side for dead. Across the water the J.W. Marriott reaches toward the sky. The building is dark besides six squares of light that look like jack-o-lantern teeth against the cylinder-shaped mass. She imagines floating across the river and spying through those windows like some Peter Pan. Imagines who is in those rooms, insomniacs or workaholics, people drinking wine or scotch, working on a Saturday night, occasionally looking out of their window, seeing the loud lit sign: a massive black top hat traced in white light. "Iggy's Place" in blinking bubble letters next to the hat. Obscene in the night. A beacon to anyone on the business side of the river restless and alone.

She'd be lying if she said it didn't sting a little being back in Grand Rapids. The city rolling its eyes, laughing at her, at the way she turned up her nose when she left and never looked back. And now being here at Iggy's Place, she might feel a little shame, a little embarrassment. An hour before she stood in front of a glass stripper cage that looked like a large vase skewered by a chrome pole. The pole cast a wicked gleam. The sweatprints of whatever tits and ass that last wrapped around it were Windexed away. When she stepped into the glass enclosure something inside her tried to cry. She was a bird that soared away back with broken wings. But Joy refused to cry. Fuck that. This city will not get the satisfaction of seeing her tears. So she ran her hand across the glass thinking I'll be this right now, I'll be a bitch in a fish tank. Then she heard her name: "Innocence" and the cage ascended into the den of men. It was dark at first. But then she was bathing in the spotlight, naked besides a red silk robe. Every eye in the room was hers. A synchronized deep breath. Hundreds of men waiting to exhale.

The front door to Iggy's Place opens and a man in a tight T-shirt, a mixed kid with hulkish arms and a superhero chin walks out, lights a Newport. He cuts Joy a fatherly glance and says, "Never thought I'd see *you* up in there." He sucks in smoke and blows it out of his nose. "Didn't believe Iggy when he said you were coming down here."

"Do I know you?"

"Long time ago you did," he says, "before Uncle Iggy and your father fell out."

"Little Jackie?" Joy smiles, then realizes he'd probably seen her in there, robe hitting the floor, feigning an orgasm while she flicked her clit with her fingers.

"I stopped being both Little and Jackie a long time ago."

He's about six feet one and two hundred twenty pounds, Joy guesses, imagining what a motor his heart must be, pumping all of that blood into all of that bulk. "Jackson Carter," she says, "well I'll be *got* damn. You sure grew up."

"That's right," says Jackson, "grew up real fast."

Has she really been gone that long? Joy takes a few steps forward and grips a railing. To her right a sidewalk leads to an old trestle bridge that no trains have crossed in years. It's now used as a walkway to this side of the river. Over here there are titty bars, dives, and a hip hop club called Spider's that keeps getting shot up, keeps getting shut down. It's like the big bright buildings across the water have dominion over the bleak structures surrounding Iggy's Place. And the way US 131 runs through the back end of this armpit, it pins Iggy's Place and everything else against the water, creating a concrete island.

"Why are you down here?" Jackson asks.

Joy shrugs. Considers reaching into her cleavage and pulling out the roll of sweaty cash she earned tonight. But this boy used to worship her. And though she knows she's fallen face-first from her high horse, Jackie Carter might be the last person on the planet who still sees her for who she was. "I'm sorry about your dad," says Joy.

Jackson pulls on his cigarette. Exhales through his nose. "Don't know why you would be."

"He was a good man—" Joy stops herself. No point in trying to bullshit someone who knows better. Jerome Carter had a cheap vodka habit and a fetish for teenage girls. His fat fingers finding their way inside her panties on more than one occasion. Jackie sleeping on the couch, Joy holding the TV remote, flipping through channels, Jerome staggering into the house and wedging himself between them.

"Well," says Jackson, "at least he left me the house."

The memories Joy had in that house on Griggs Street. Babysitting the lovesick-boy-version of Jackson Carter. Fending off his drunk and horny father, offering a hand job to keep Jerome from putting the thing inside of her young body. Too many of those nights. Taking long hot showers to kill the smell of Jerome's cigar-stained hands, the haunt of vodka on his steamy breath. "I heard about your knee, Jackie," says Joy. "I wanted to call, but you know—. Listen, it's been a long time, baby. How are you? What's your life like?"

"I work campus security at Grand Valley. Pick up some shifts bouncing for Uncle Iggy when I can. Occasionally work the Van Andel. I work." His voice hides his regrets well but he wears them in his eyes. "What really happened with Motown?" he asks.

"They didn't like the album," Joy says matter-of-factly, the pain gone, the tears cried, the disappointment already dealt with. The whole truth something she won't ever reveal. Not to Jackie or anyone else. "They had me on standby for a few years before they finally dropped me."

"So then *this*?" Jackson slants his head toward his uncle's club, taking another hit on the Newport.

"Boy, stop talking to me like you're my daddy. I knew you when you were a baby, when you were just a kid, wiping your snotty nose with the back of your hand, walking around with that dirt streak across the side of your face." Joy mimics the way Jackson used to run his hand across his face as a child during those carefree Grand Rapids summers, a then-runty Jackie Carter running the streets with a ragged leather football, looking like he had a dinosaur egg tucked in his arm.

"You ain't that grown," says Jackson.

"Twenty-seven," says Joy. "Three, four more years, these titties will start sagging—I gotta get this money now, Jackie. While I still can."

"That's sad."

"That's life."

"Don't have to be."

"You tell me then, smartass. You tell me what I should do, Mr. Grown. Mr. Working Man."

"Don't know," says Jackson. "I'm just saying I think you're worth more than a pair of tits."

"You don't even know me."

"I know who you were. I know who you were to me."

"You don't know shit."

Jackson pulls on the Newport again. Blows smoke out of his nose. Turns to Joy. "Be humble," he says. "Go to George and Ivy."

"Ain't no way I'm going back to my parents' house. My mom's too busy taking care of my daddy to deal with me and my shit. Plus, I'm not really trying to hear their I Told You So's."

"Then what?"

"I'm only thinking about today, Jackie."

Iggy Carter stands in front of a two-way mirror feeding fire to a half-dead cigar. On the floor below, R-Kelly's "Sex Me" blares through the speakers. Big booty Cori is in the glass cage, slow dancing with the pole, her naked right thigh pressed against her chest, arms wrapped loosely around her elevated knee, grinding against the stainless steel rod to the rhythm of the beat.

She was up here earlier asking for a raise, on and on about her baby needing diapers and whatnot. Iggy has heard it all. Every sob story, every angle. Iggy told Cori like he tells each and every one of these hoes: You earn what you earn. I get twenty percent. No exceptions. Then she smiled, this twenty-two-year-old girl, and touched Iggy's cheek. I'm sure there's something we can work out, she said, as if Iggy hadn't been a character in that scene a million times.

Now Cori has her forehead pressed against the pole, her hands raised and gripping it, legs wrapped around it, still working her hips. A couple years ago Iggy would have broken her off. He would have face-down-ass-upped her on the bed, thrown on his hardhat, and put in some serious work. He used to hit them all. When they'd confront Iggy on the edge of their plummet. Sob story rehearsed. All these girls come to Iggy's Place believing it's temporary. And it is. Only it's never temporary on their terms.

The nightlife down here used to be jazz music and fedoras. Dance floors dense with the funk of fully clothed working men and women, loosened ties, untucked shirts, sweating their week away. Before it devolved into pussy and the music became sex. When Iggy Carter and George Green were in business together. Two young, ambitious black men in a town full of Dutch furniture money.

But like a fool Iggy went and fell dumb-in-love with his best friend's wife. Old oblivious cocksure George never saw the betrayal coming. Not from Iggy or Ivy, who had the kind of cool in her veins that could have taken their secret to the grave. Iggy's done his best to keep those days stashed away in the cellar of his mind. But when George and Ivy's daughter Joy showed up last week asking for a job she wiped the cobwebs off of a complicated past.

Downstairs, Iggy's nephew, Jackson, enters the club, limping. He's wearing Dickies boots and it's mid-summer. He's dragging on a Newport short, smoke swirling in his wake as he prods along. Jackson's been bouncing here for a few weeks and Iggy's liked having him around. But the boy is a gloom cloud. Drunk off disappointment. Dealing with his own kind of plummet. Working three jobs. No Plan B on the horizon.

Jackson Carter is a genuine tragedy if you ask Iggy. It was run-nigger-run in high school. Every major college in the country came to Grand Rapids selling their football program. Of the whole Carter family, Jackson was the only one who amounted to shit. Only one who had a chance at something different in life. To get out of this place. To see the world.

The city loved Jackson. Iggy would be at those games watching his nephew bowling- balling down the field, bodies bouncing off him, scoring those touchdowns. The unruly crowd at Houseman Field thick into the thousands. Folks tailgating like it was some kind of college game. They loved Jackson Carter. But when Jackson blew out his knee it didn't take long for the love to fade. It wasn't long before Jackson was nothing more than another beige face in the sewer side of the city.

Below, R-Kelly's song is coming to an end. Cori is motionless against the pole. Iggy watches Jackson. His arms crossed, shaking his head, staring up at Iggy like he can see him through the glass. The boy shouldn't have been here tonight. He should have never told Jackson that Joy Green was coming.

Earlier, when Joy's stage name, "Innocence," was called Iggy had watched Jackson slink into a dark corner of the room. Iggy had felt a pang of guilt as Joy twisted through the floor. He shrugged it off, kept his Grinch heart intact, telling himself business is business, knowing his profits would probably increase by a third with a former Motown star working the cage.

The cigar has died so Iggy relights it. He walks over to his mini-bar and pours himself a glass of Hennessey. He sits and sips and stares into a cloud of exhaled smoke. He's never told a soul about Ivy Green. What they had done, they did in darkness: against bathroom walls at crowded parties, in backseats of parked cars, once at a park playground; they climbed a ladder to a castle structure and they made love under the moon, Iggy looking down on her that night, a cool breeze drying the sweat off their bodies, loving this woman and feeling so low at the same time. His best friend was managing the club that night, and Iggy was sneaking around behind his back, and Iggy knew it wouldn't last with Ivy, but still he couldn't end it, because he loved her. He knew he was a sucker for it, but he loved her.

He and Ivy talked the way Iggy believed human beings are supposed to talk. About the lives they wished they were living. About the past. About the uncertainty of the future. They questioned everything, scrutinized their life choices, each wearing a white glove, dragging it across each other, across humanity, Ivy whispering into the phone while George was asleep, Iggy sipping something brown and eighty proof, detailing the elaborate life they could have together if they didn't both love George.

Iggy takes another drag on his cigar. Three knocks on the door. Jackson. Iggy makes his way across the room and unbolts the lock. "Come in," Iggy says to his nephew. "Bolt the door behind you."

"What you drinking?" Iggy asks.

"Yac."

"Have a seat, Jackie," Iggy says. "Standing there pissed off won't do you no good."

Jackson sits down and Iggy pours him a drink. Refills his own glass. He stands behind the bar like he works there, waiting for Jackson to speak.

"How can you let her dance here?" Jackson eyes his drink for a moment before taking half of it down in one pull. "I mean, if Mr. Green—"

"I don't give a shit about what George Green thinks," Iggy says. "George Green is in the same coffin as the rest of the people from my past. He might be a living, breathing, God-fearing cripple, but to me that motherfucker's buried, dig?"

Iggy takes a drag on his cigar, then offers a hit to Jackson.

Jackson declines. "I don't understand that, Uncle Iggy. I mean—your best friend's daughter?"

"You wouldn't," says Iggy. "Cause you just the same lovesick boy you always were. And let me tell you something: loving Joy Green won't get you nothing but hurt. Won't bring you nothing but trouble. That woman ain't the girl you knew."

"So," says Jackson. He finishes his drink. "That's it then? You're just gonna throw her to the wolves?"

"Jackie," says Iggy, "Joy Green is a stripper. It's what she is. She couldn't make it doing music, but she's gonna be a cash cow in that cage. If she wasn't making me money she'd be making it for someone else."

When Joy Green showed up at Iggy's Place, Cesar Bolden saw the future. He recognized her immediately: The high cheekbones, the Cosmopolitan mole flanking her pouty pucker of a mouth. She stood in the stripper cage wearing the same seductive expression captured on the cover photograph of her single, released years before, and never followed up on. Cesar almost jumped when the base dropped, when Joy's hip snapped twice in sync with the loud drum. Cesar watched her reach above her head with both hands and press the glass, lean into it, and the silky red robe seemed to melt away. That's when the whooping and hollering began. She was Pam Grier on a pole. She was tall and black and busty and beautiful. She was sex. She was money. These simple minded fools emptying their wallets just to see some skin.

Cesar watches her now, out by the river, and tries to imagine where her mind is at. Going from a world stage to a glass cage (he kind of likes the sound of that). To be reduced down to flesh. Her psyche right now, Cesar decides, is fragile at best. There's something tragic about the way the moonlight hits her. It's like tonight is hers. The black sky looking down and shaking its head. Another one lost to this wicked world. One more of millions heading down the road to gone. What she needs is redirection. Some studio time and an investor. Someone to book shows, put out an album, take a percentage. What Joy Green needs is a fresh start.

Cesar goes to step out of Iggy's Place and approach her, but then Jackson Carter brushes past him. So he eases shut the glass door and watches from inside the club. A few years back Jackson Carter had the city buzzing too, calling him the next Jim Brown or something. Jackson blew out his knee his senior year of high school and the rest is economics. Instead of being some college boy, Jackson Carter is a working-class nobody, by Cesar's assessment, holding a grudge against a world that doesn't give two shits about his ass.

Jackson and Joy appear to be old friends. Jackson looks like he has some kind of juvenile crush on her. Joy looks at him like he is just a boy. Jackson's demeanor says love, infatuation, but Joy's says something else: family? Jackson Carter doesn't appear to be a threat. But love not returned ages sour. The threat could come in the form of jealousy. Not a problem. Cesar keeps the pistol stashed in his waistband for such occasions.

Cesar backs away from the door when Jackson finally comes inside. He watches Joy, looking out at the buildings across the river, probably wishing she was in the Marriot tonight, missing that lifestyle and all that comes with it. Cesar steps out of Iggy's Place and stands under the top hat sign, the blinking bubble letters throbbing light behind him. He adjusts his hat. Slides his hands under his suspenders and smoothes down his shirt. "Babygirl," he says.

"Shit, Man." Joy turns as Cesar approaches. "Don't be walking up on me like that."

Cesar sees she likes the way he looks, her eyes doing a once over, her own smile doing a sly flirty thing he has seen a million times. Her aggressive tone nothing but a front.

"Relax," Cesar says. "I just wanted to meet you."

"Okay?"

"You mind if I ask you something?" Cesar doesn't wait for her to answer. "Fuck you doing down here at Iggy's Place?"

"Question of the night," says Joy.

"I'm saying, down here you get those big booty girls, two and three different baby daddy's names tattooed on their bodies like scars. The kind of bitches that be drunk at noon and drop their bastards off with their mothers. You don't belong down here."

"Yeah? And where do I belong . . . uh, did you give me your name?"

"Cesar. Cesar Bolden." He extends his hand and she shakes it. Lets the attitude muscles in her face relax a little. She doesn't introduce herself. Joy Green knows she doesn't have to. "In a studio," says Cesar. "On a stage. On tour."

"What? You supposed to be a manager or something."

"No. I'm just a man. Just a man looking to invest."

Joy feigns a look of boredom. She pretends like she isn't interested in what he's saying, but Cesar saw her eyes light up when he mentioned music, when he mentioned money. "Look, Cesar, right? You got a card or something? I've had a long night."

"No, I don't have a card," says Cesar. "But I have a number. You have a pen? Something to write it on?"

"I have a pen," says Joy. "And I have a hand."

A Sunday morning sun slow cooks the concrete beneath Joy Green's yellow thong sandals. She and Cesar Bolden stand on the old trestle bridge, looking down at the brown-tinted river. The big buildings to the right gleam. To her left, Iggy's Place is dead, the top hat sign a thing of gaud without the night as a backdrop, a scab on an aging building. Joy imagines the building being smashed to the ground. Replaced by a high-class restaurant, a patio with outdoor dining, a boardwalk perimeter where lovers can take nighttime strolls. There could be a college down here. Something shiny and proud. A positive presence in what is otherwise gloom. Something stacked with floors and glass walls, the river reflecting in its windows.

"So tell me," says Cesar. "What's your mother like?" A middle-aged white couple pedal past on their mountain bikes. Cesar nods hello, but they pedal hard, eyes forward.

Ivy Green and her tough love. Her, "Life don't owe you a damn thing." Her, "Cover up those titties, you look like a hooker." Ivy's beauty, hidden beneath her stony expression, an emotionless gaze, like she's staring into the next life, one where she doesn't work fifty hours a week to take care of a rheumatoid afflicted man and a redbone diva with her head in the clouds.

"What's she like?" Cesar asks again.

"Old school," says Joy. "And hard. She's the type of mother who would stand in my bedroom doorway," says Joy. "She'd whisper into the room that she loved me only when she thought I was sleeping."

"Stingy with love, huh?"

"Yeah, but my daddy is worse. You know he used to be in business with Iggy?"

"Yeah?"

"That's right." Joy's mind drifts to the mid-eighties. Lawn parties. Alger Heights. Music blaring from porch speakers, loud, and back in those days the neighbors never cared. Back then Iggy was Uncle Iggy and he had the kind of laugh that when you heard it you couldn't help but laugh too. But that was before everything changed. That was before Iggy Carter and her father severed ties and went their separate ways. "But then Daddy found Jesus." Joy doesn't look at Cesar. Her eyes stay on the river, watching the water, seeing Iggy's old Buick parked on the curb in front of her parent's house, the heaviness of her house key when she placed it in the lock, the thick silence of the house besides the noise in the bedroom upstairs. "Then arthritis found Daddy. He got old so fast. It was like he aged fifty years. He changed. Daddy buried himself in the church and became a bitter old man. He disowned me when I signed with Motown. Said I was doing the Devil's work. If he found out Iggy's letting me dance, he'd probably be down here with a shotgun."

"Yet Iggy lets you dance."

"He understands. If I wasn't dancing at Iggy's I'd be dancing somewhere else. Down here he feels like he can look after me. Plus, I'm good for business. Iggy ain't stupid. I got a face people recognize."

"Do you miss it?" asks Cesar. "Singing."

"Of course I miss it," says Joy. "Motown though, was a bitch slap right across the jawbone." And it was. Twenty-three years old with advance money. Cameras flashing. Grand Rapids, Michigan nothing but a distant past, another life, everything about it and everything in it nothing more than a vivid dream she once had and woke up from. But when the single dropped she had nothing to follow up with. No other songs recorded. The song hit quickly and fizzled just as fast. After months in the studio, everything coming out flat, Motown set her aside, and focused on this juvenile rap duo from Detroit, who hit just as fast as she did and had an entire album recorded and ready to release.

"Coming home," Cesar asks, "fresh start, or last resort?"

"A fresh start," says Joy, "I hope."

"Fuck hope," says Cesar. "All you need is a plan. What if you got involved in the local music scene? Did a few shows, recorded some songs? It's been a few years since your single hit the charts. You need to create a buzz. You need to build some momentum. Coming home doesn't make you a failure. Get involved in the music scene the city will embrace you, maybe even love you."

"Music scene?" says Joy. "That's some funny shit, Man. What? You want me down at Spider's performing on a piss-stained stage. Dodging bullets? Singing hooks on some no-talent thug's rap song?"

"I'm not talking about Spider's. I'm talking about bigger things. I'm talking about a movement. Bringing some big names in. Getting some big venues: places like the Orbit Room, Delta Plex, the Van Andel. Having some local talent open for them. This city might not have much of a music scene right now, but the city is waiting for one," says Cesar. "All it takes is one nigga with vision and enough dough to make it happen."

"And you're that nigga?"

"Could be I am."

"Hmm."

They watch the river in silence. Cesar Bolden is an obvious hustler. Dirty money all over him. So dirty she can almost smell it. But dapper. Not in that obnoxious, hustler way—Cesar Bolden could pass for a banker on his day off. Brown slacks and beige sandals. Light-brown Ray Bans propped atop his head even though the sun's blaring down. And Joy's thanking God they are; it'd be a damn shame to filter the magic thriving in those sexy gray eyes.

Maybe she could fuck with this man. See what ride he might take her on. He'd look handsome enough holding her hand. And he has money—that much is clear, this man has money. And Cesar Bolden has the demeanor of a king. He has this cool way of capturing each moment, like the space he occupies, he owns. This authority gives her confidence, has her thinking maybe he can help her get back the spotlight. And maybe, just maybe, she and Cesar Bolden can have a little fun along the way.

Iggy steps out of the club just as Joy Green and Cesar Bolden part ways. Joy's hips swaying as she walks. Cesar cutting her one last glance as she goes, then shouting something Iggy can't decipher. Iggy watches Joy stop and turn back to Cesar. Direct Cesar toward her with an index finger. He watches Cesar comply. Watches him hug her. Kiss her cheek then let her go. Iggy watches Cesar stand with folded arms watching Joy cross the bridge and disappear into the city. Iggy lights his cigar. He pulls deep and holds the smoke long enough to cough. Knowing. Just fucking knowing. Trouble's coming.

Cesar Bolden isn't the Devil, but he might be the Devil's son. He's the wrong guy to owe anything and Iggy owes 275. And we ain't talking hundred. It wasn't a sweet deal, either. It was the only deal. Iggy's landlord was selling—some white man with money was trying to clean up the riverfront, trying to buy up buildings so he could knock them down and build something new. Iggy and George had been renting from their landlord for years and the landlord was a cool enough guy. He told Iggy if he matched the white man's initial offer that Iggy could have the building. So it was buy or get out and Iggy didn't have the money, didn't have the credit, and just when he was coming to terms with that fact, that's when he met Cesar Bolden.

There was no official contract involved in the deal. The terms were written in a small black planner that Cesar pulled out of his back pocket. The deal was made with a pistol lying on the table. Cesar Bolden's reputation was his lawyer. Iggy had only heard whispers, but the truth isn't something bellowed—the truth is found in the wind, in the cracks of the concrete, in the eyes of people not saying a word, not trying to plead their case. The truth is silent and loud. And the truth about Cesar Bolden is if you cross him you come up missing, no evidence, no leads, you end up gone like you were never there at all.

Iggy looked Cesar in the eyes that day and shook hands with the Devil's son. He accepted a $200,000 loan and agreed to pay Cesar $75,000 interest. He bought the building from the landlord and since then he's flourished. Iggy's halfway paid off on his loan. He's halfway there. And now as Iggy watches Cesar Bolden approaching, sliding his sunglasses down from the top of his head and concealing his eyes, stepping across the bridge, down the walkway to Iggy's Place, Iggy's thinking half-way there is a long way to go.

"Joy Green in a glass cage," says Cesar. He phonies a smile. "You're something else, Old Man. I gotta give it to you, you're something else."

Cesar's been through them all. He catches them while they're fresh, before the drinking gets out of hand, before the drinking becomes drugs. Tapping each and every one of them. But never, not once, has Iggy seen him with a stripper out in public. And on a Sunday morning to boot. Iggy manufactures his own smile. "They'll get sick of her. They get sick of them all."

"How'd we do last night?"

We. The worst part of the deal. Cesar always hovering over the edge of things. Never all the way in; always tip-toeing the perimeter, asking questions. Lots of questions. None of it's his business. Not really. The deal was $10,000 a month and Iggy's never been late on a payment. The money's due the last Sunday of the month, but every Sunday morning Cesar's here, even when it's not time to collect, just to assess the situation. "The door did just over ten. Bar did around fourteen."

"Okay. Okay, Old Man. We're doing okay." Cesar goes to walk away.

"Joy Green," says Iggy. "What you want with her?"

"What? You suddenly got a conscience?"

"Curiosity."

"Curiosity? You know what they say about curiosity, don't you?"

"Something about cats." Iggy pulls on the cigar and blows smoke in Cesar's direction.

Cesar laughs an unnerving laugh. Something low-toned and forced and showing no teeth. "That's right, funny nigga. Something about cats." Cesar puts his hand on Iggy's shoulder. Iggy feigns cool and stares into the brown lenses of Cesar's sunglasses, trying to find his eyes. Cesar lightly slaps Iggy across the face, playful, a slick disrespect that says he owns him. He turns to walk away then stops. "You'll be doing yourself a favor, Iggy." Cesar says.

"By staying out my motherfucking business."

From the outside Cesar's apartment looks condemned. Peeling paint. Bars on the windows. Discrete. Cesar told Joy he likes it that way. She watches him pull out a set of rattling keys and unlock three separate locks on a reinforced steel door. Solid. Too solid. Overkill, thinks Joy. If a tornado came through the southeast side of Grand Rapids, Cesar's front door would be the last thing standing.

On the inside of the apartment the stained-wood floors have a Pine Sol shine. The living room is made cozy with a large Egyptian area rug and a few framed reprint paintings of melting clocks and creatures on stilts. No photographs of people. No framed Scarface posters, or dogs playing poker, or nude African artwork. None of the usual wall décor Joy has discovered in the dens of black male bachelors.

"Make yourself at ease, babe." Cesar walks into a small kitchen that is attached to the living room, the wood becoming brown tile, an island countertop the same shade of brown as the floors, all surfaces clean. Joy sinks into a plush beige leather couch and stares at the ceiling. A yellow watermark with a small crack runs across the ceiling, the only blemish she's found in the apartment. It's like a scar on a beautiful face.

Cesar returns with an uncorked bottle of Bordeaux and two wine glasses. He sits beside her on the couch and pours them both a drink. "I've been listening to your single. Been thinking about your video."

"Yeah?" Joy sips from her glass. "And what have you been thinking?"

"I think I know why things didn't work out with Motown."

"Shit, Man," says Joy. "If we're going to have this conversation, you're gonna have to give me something stronger than wine." She laughs.

Cesar says, "Seriously. It's not a matter of talent. You got the pipes. There's no denying that. It's just something about the music was false. It's like they were trying to sell Disney World or something. They had you on some teeny shit. And baby, seeing you at Iggy's Place, to put it mildly, you ooze sexuality. You'd be more natural doing grown-woman music. Think Toni Braxton or Sade. Something sexy and smooth."

Joy watches Cesar. His excitement turns her on. She's got a small bag of cocaine in the purse still strapped to her shoulder. She wants it loud. It feels as heavy as a brick. Joy's wine glass is empty and Cesar hasn't touched his, hasn't even glanced at it. She doesn't want any more wine. "Seriously," says Joy. "You got anything stronger than wine? It's a Friday night."

"Yeah," says Cesar, with a curious expression, like he's seeing something in her, but cannot quite make out what it is. "You want something dark or something clear?"

"Dark," says Joy, watching Cesar take her empty glass into the kitchen and leave his untouched glass where it lay. He returns with a tumbler containing something reddish brown and sets it on the coaster where Joy's wine glass was. "Okay, baby," says Joy. "You were saying."

"Image change," Cesar says. "What you need is an image change."

The man is beautiful. Genuinely beautiful. He is bronze. He is artwork. All night she could swim in his eyes, darker now than they are in the sunlight, more silver than gray, they are steel, they are mercury. "Okay, I'm listening."

"I'm talking about a whole new sound. A whole new style. Motown signed a Joy Green who was a tease. Someone teenage boys crushed on. I'm talking about bringing a Joy Green who seduces men. A Joy Green grown women can vibe to, can emulate."

"Okay," says Joy. "I like it. But we'll need writers. We'll need producers."

"You don't write your own music?"

Another slap in the face. Another reason Motown had her singing that bubble gum shit. She could sing anything under the sun, but couldn't write a word of music. Because if she could she could write about pain. She could write about loss. She could write about what it means for your family to fall apart. She could summon those memories. She could stand outside her parent's bedroom door and listen to Ivy and Iggy fucking, listen to them stabbing her Daddy in the back, and she could hate her mother all over again. She could relive it. She could cry for her Daddy. She could call on that hurt and write something beautiful. If only she had the words to match the memories. She could do it. Because the worst hurt in the world is losing your father's love. The worst hurt in the world is watching his eyes change when he looks at you. When the marriage trudges forward but the family gets divorced. And your mother can't stand you for telling on her. And your father resents you for being the one who found out. And they both, in their own ways, move on without you.

But she can't do it. Memories are memories and words are words. She is no more than a voice and that voice has never been her own. "Is that a problem? It's never been a problem before," Joy says. She watches Cesar process what she's saying. He has an expression like she's thrown a wrench in his plans. "Hey, which way to your bathroom?" Joy asks.

"Through the hallway," Cesar says. He looks at her suspiciously this time. Like he can see through her. Like he can see her need. Like she carries a glass purse and the bag of cocaine is on display. "On the right. If you make it to the bedroom you went too far."

When Joy finds the bathroom she locks the door. She spills coke on the sink counter and kneels on the floor. She lines up two hits with a credit card. One for each nostril. When she's finished she stands. She turns on the faucet and stares at her reflection in the mirror. "You are Joy Motherfucking Green," she says. She kisses her reflection and leaves a lipstick smear on the glass. She is so much more than this. So much more than Motown. So much more than a bitch in a fish tank. "You are Joy Motherfucking Green," she says again. "And you are a star."

Cesar admires his handiwork. Joy sleeps atop mangled sheets soaked in sweat and sex. He lay pressed against her, leaning on the pillows, his fingers feathering the crevice between her hip and high thigh. He drags an index finger over the bushy center of her thighs, across her flat stomach, between her breasts, circling and dotting a nipple. BET is on television, the volume on low. Cesar's watching *Midnight Love*. Kind of. He's seeing this woman lying beside him and it's blowing his mind a little that she's lying in his bed. It's funny the way someone might be on TV and seem so unreal, so unattainable, but then you find out they're nothing but flesh and blood like the next one, moaning, coming, curled up next to you. We're all just people. Television twists that. It sells you a dream. But what is it like to be a part of that dream? What is it like to be Joy Green, unreal, unattainable. And who do you become once you're obtained.

Joy cannot write music. That complicates things a bit. Because it doesn't matter how well you sing when the song's no good. And though Cesar doesn't mind paying, he imagines music industry writers, no matter how much money you're willing to pay, are selective about who they sell their songs to, because that's their art and their vision and ultimately their royalties, which fluctuate depending on the commercial success of a song. So if you're a one-hit-wonder like Joy Green, you are a risk, and finding legit writers to sell you songs, Cesar imagines, is a difficult task.

So what then is the best approach? On the television Brownstone's "If You Love Me" video is playing. All three singers are dressed in white. They stand behind glass with water pouring down it. It's like they're singing in front of a window on a rainy day. They are attractive but not beautiful. Sexy but not sexual. Cesar's heard of the group, but doesn't know their music well. They're not En Vogue, or SWV, or TLC. They're kind of in that second tier, that Jade, Changing Faces, Xscape tier. A group, Cesar's thinking, he could book for $10,000 or less. And more, for the right price, maybe he could even get Joy a cameo, some kind of one-night collaboration. He could bring Brownstone to Grand Rapids, plug Joy into the headline, and have some local cats open up for them to ensure the house is packed.

He could see Joy Green headlining a group. Maybe that's the way to go. Provide the context for her to shine, rub shoulders with a semi-major act—all Cesar Bolden ever needed was an in—he can learn this business just like he learned the drug business—experience and adaptation and innovative thinking. Tomorrow he'll make some phone calls, assess the temperature, and then he'll move quickly, because Joy Green has this volatile essence about her that Cesar cannot quite put his finger on. But it has him feeling urgent. Has him feeling like he needs to act without delay. Before this opportunity passes.

A trail of round vague lights are nestled in the ceiling. An ambient path of white that makes Joy feel angelic in the darkness. She's in the room the other girls fear. That thousand-dollar room where almost everything goes. The room has a panic button, small and red and right by the door, and when you press it a bouncer comes storming into the room with a free pass for violence.

Joy loves this room. She loves the tension she creates in it. The control she has over her patron, a large black pleasant man who wears a wedding ring and a sloppy-fitting suit. Who politely makes his requests with a gentle voice that is too small for his size. She loves that Jackie Carter stands outside the door ready to burst inside and kill this man if Joy presses that button, if her patron sets one toe out of line.

"Can I take it out?" the man asks. Shy almost.

"Maybe," Joy says. But first I want you to tell me about your wife.

The man looks at his shoes, which Joy notices are a bit aged, with frayed laces, yet they are polished to a flawless shine.

"I'll tell you what," Joy says. "If you tell me about your wife I'll take it out for you."

The man loosens his tie. He unbuttons the top button on his shirt. "What do you want to know?"

"Is she pretty?"

"She's beautiful."

"Is she prettier than me?'

"No."

"You're lying," says Joy. "You looked up and to the right before you answered. That means you're lying."

"I'm not lying," says the man. "Don't call me a liar." His voice has an edge to it.

Joy smiles. She walks over to the red button and lets her index finger dangle over it. "My body guard wouldn't like you talking to me like that."

"I'm sorry," the man says. "I just don't feel comfortable talking about my wife."

"Okay," says Joy. "Does that mean I'm putting my clothes back on? Does that mean we're done here?"

The man pulls out his wallet. He peels out five one hundred dollar bills and sets them on the coffee table that flanks the couch he's sitting on. "No more personal questions," he says. He isn't asking.

Joy nods. She takes her finger away from the button. The man hasn't put the wallet away which means an offer's coming. Her mind drifts back to a Ramada suite in suburban Detroit. The air swirling with smoke. Weed, cigar, and cigarettes. So much cocaine. Line after line. That night she called herself an Escort. She and a Thai girl named Millie, a girl Joy met in the limousine, got paid $5,000 a piece to party—that's what the man called it, a Party—he was old and rich and had enough powder that night for Joy and Millie to gallop through the night on that white horse, right up to the Ramada suite and do all sorts of nasty things to each other while this old man watched and waited for his Viagra to kick in. And when it did this old gray man got his money's worth. Four hours and a half-a-dozen condoms later, Millie passed out on the floor, Joy lying beneath his sweaty, hairy body, he finally fell asleep, half-erect, still inside her, and Joy slipped away, promising herself she'd never be an escort again.

"How much?" the man asks.

"How much for what?"

"I think you know for what."

"I wanna hear you say it."

"How much to fuck?" he asks.

"How much to fuck Joy Green?" says Joy.

"Yeah."

"Ask me."

This is her temple. In this room she is this man's God. Right now he's thinking about his mortgage, his car note. He's crunching numbers, figuring out a way. He's staring at Joy Green's naked body and deciding she's worth it. Worth risking the white-collar life he built on blue-collar effort and student loan debt. His boring beautiful wife, his job—this shit here, it's better than cocaine—if you could bottle this power Joy's feeling and sell it, if you could roll it and smoke it, if you could chop it, line it up, and suck it in your brain through your nose.

"How much?" the man asks. "How much to fuck Joy Green?"

"You don't have enough." She believes it. Imagines her price, her for real, strip-tease-over, roll-on-the-condom, and slide-down-on-his-dick price, and it seems so large until this man starts peeling hundreds from his wallet. Like this was his plan all along. Like he went to the bank on the way here and had it in his mind to offer Joy something she couldn't refuse. And the man must have seen the change in her demeanor because he's closed his wallet. He's put the pile of hundreds in a neat stack next to the five he'd already placed on the coffee table. This is his show now. He knows it and Joy knows it. She watches him unbuckle his belt, unzip his slacks, and pull out a long thin cock with an awkward curve.

I'm Joy Motherfucking Green, she tells herself, watching the man slide on a condom, Jackie Carter feeling so close now on the other side of this door. So close she can hear his boots slapping against the floor while he paces. So jealous, so in love, just waiting to come busting through this door when the hour is over, panic button or not, and beat Joy's patron to an irrational pulp.

Jackie reminds her of back in the day. Before she grew tits and drew attention from men. Back when she was no more than a girl that loved singing, that loved being on a stage, when life had this magic to it, a magic she was a part of, a princess who was loved and could do no wrong. Jackie makes her feel ashamed. She's gone down a few dark roads in her day, but she's always had a moral out, a rational way to call what she's doing something else. Even that Ramada night, in Joy's mind that night was not like this—that night she was paid to party, what happened when she got high wasn't scripted, but just another part of a wild night, another experience.

But this. Joy cannot find a rational way to call this anything but what it is. And something about Jackie being on the other side of that door. Something about the prospect of him walking in, seeing her doing it. It's too much money to turn down, she tells herself. She lost count at $2,500 and that's two weeks' salary, a nice cushion before Cesar gets this music thing popping again. Before she's back on the scene. Back doing what she was born to do. This is just another dark road she has to go down to get where she's going.

•

All it took was one phone call to set up Joy Green's comeback event. Brownstone was fresh off tour, a tour, their manager told Cesar, that didn't go as well as he'd hoped. A tour where one of the girls, Mimi Doby, got some kind of respiratory infection, and was going to have to take some time off. Name dropping Joy Green was all it took to book Brownstone for a dirt cheap $8,000. And Cesar knows why too. He knows Mimi Doby isn't really sick, knows if you put three women on stage together four nights a week for six months at a time then something is bound to go wrong. He knows that this is a tryout for Joy. What Brownstone's manager doesn't know though, is Joy Green is not for sale.

Cesar has his own vision. This show, as bright and loud as he hopes it will be, is nothing more than a what if? The show is context. Imagine Joy Green on a stage with two beautiful background singers. Imagine a group. Not Brownstone, but a group featuring Joy Green. Sometimes you have to show it before you sell it. It's simple business. No different than weed or coke or crack. You give these motherfuckers a sample of the goods and if your product is right your product is going to sell. Calling writers and producers and suggesting Joy Green headline an RnB group is one thing, sending them a recording of her on stage with Brownstone is another. All Joy has to do is kill it. If she kills it the rest will be easy. Cesar can find two more girls. Two girls with decent voices and the right look to compliment Joy. He can do business with the writers and the producers. Then he can get this thing started independently.

But it all hinges on this show. Brownstone is late and the southeast side is present. The Orbit Room has never been so black. Cesar isn't one to control the masses. You put him in a room with one man, sure, Cesar knows how to impose his will, but large groups are not his forte and the big burly bouncers he hired to keep order are too busy hollering at hood rats to keep the impatient crowd from getting too drunk and acting too stupid. The first opening act is a rap duo that calls themselves Natural Disasters. A skinny white boy and a fat mixed kid. Their lyrics are nice, but the beat, though hard hitting, is basically a loop, an amateurish lion roar sample coming around every eight seconds or so. They

bones. And it's just getting started with her. The only way out is to slay it and Joy's not the slaying type. Now Cesar's calculating his losses and he's livid, with himself, blinded by his own ambition, too stupid to see that thing in her, knowing that beast is going to eat and thinking . . .

Why not be the hand that feeds it?

Jackson Carter is beating on Joy's dressing room door and she feels like a caught child. Cocaine is spilled on the bench beside her clothes. She sweeps it off with her hand and then drops to her knees and blows off what remains. Jackie's been stomping around Iggy's Place pissed off since that day he stood guard outside the door while Joy lost the last strand of her dignity. He never did bust down that door, but when the patron walked out Jackie grabbed him by the shirt and shoved him to the ground—the patron probably weighed over 300 pounds and Jackie tossed him like he was nothing, for no other reason than jealous rage. Then Jackie looked at Joy and said nothing. Just shook his head and walked away.

Joy knows he loves her. She knows Jackie sees the best parts of her, those buried parts hiding someplace inside her, protected from the world, from all the hurt, from all she's been through. Jackie sees those parts because that's what he remembers. He's clinging to that Joy like that Joy's still in there. Jackie knows no better. He knows nothing of those dark roads she's travelled, those dark deeds she's done, the doors she's locked her innocence in. That Joy Green is gone. Those keys are lost. Jackie loves a memory, that's all, and what good did love ever do anybody anyway.

"Joy," Jackson yells. "Open the damn door!"

"What? Jackie, shit! What the hell do you want?" She finds her robe and wraps herself in it. Opens the door. "Jesus, Jackie. What is it?"

She should jump into Jackie's arms. She should cry into his chest. Let him run his fingers through her hair and tell her everything will be okay. But when was okay ever good enough for Joy Green? And Jackie is just a boy disappointed with his life and desperate to be loved. What could this boy ever do for her? Nothing. Nothing besides kiss her ass. "It's cute seeing you all concerned, Jackie," says Joy. "But I'm a grown-ass woman."

"I heard about the Brownstone show, Joy."

Not her finest moment. The alcohol. The drugs. That feeling in the air. Brownstone coming to town, Joy's mind on stealing Mimi Doby's job, on making Brownstone her own. She'd memorized the songs, she'd put in the work, she was ready—Lord, she was ready—then backstage the bottles started being passed around and she was feeling herself, really feeling herself, feeling like a star again, she was buzzing and she wanted to buzz some more, and by the time she realized she had a too much to drink the room was twitching like it was thinking about spinning, and she needed clarity and focus, so she pulled out that powder, and the last thing she remembered was the trimmed bush of that cute little blonde.

She woke to Cesar watching her. The show over and the Orbit Room emptied. Her head pounding. Her left breast exposed. "What happened," she asked Cesar.

"Brownstone bailed," he said. "You fucked up. You lost me over twenty grand." He delivered his words like he'd been watching her for hours, like his anger had subsided considerably during that time. "We'll be blacklisted. Brownstone will talk. No one will take us seriously."

"I'm sorry."

"You're sorry? You think I give a fuck about I'm sorry? You backed us against a wall, Joy. You hear me? I thought you were serious about doing this thing."

"I am, Cesar," she said. Then she let that man see her cry. She couldn't stop the tears from coming. That show felt a whole lot like a last chance. Cesar was right, she did fuck up. It would have been easy. One good show and the rest would have fallen into place. Now it would be hard. The sacrifice. The grind. The small and epic moral battles you lose along the way. "So what's the plan?" Joy said. "Tell me what I need to do."

Jackson's expression has softened some. His heavy hand rests on Joy's shoulder. "Listen," says Jackson. "You need to leave this place. You need to leave Cesar Bolden alone. There's an extra room at the house. You can stay rent-free for as long as you like. Figure out your next move."

"Jackie," says Joy. "I'm a singer. I don't need your free rent. I don't need your time. All I need is to sing. And that's what I'm going to do."

"Is it true what they're saying about you?" Jackson asks.

"What, Jackie? What the fuck are they saying about me?"

"That motherfucker's got you doing porn?"

The word *porn* did it. Got her reaching into her purse for the coke. Turning into the dressing room and spilling some of it on the bench. Chopping at it with her driver's license. She doesn't look at Jackson, but she feels the fire of his gaze. She lines up the coke, breasts swaying casually beneath the robe as she leans into her work. She's breaking his heart; she knows it; wants to stop, but can't. It's time. It's time to set Jackie Carter free. "It's gonna be a one-time thing, Jackie. One time," she says. Not believing a word of it. "I'm getting back in the studio and then—"

"Bullshit," says Jackson, "you really believe that bullshit? You're getting turned out, Joy. And you're too stupid to know it. Or worse, too stupid to care."

Joy finally looks up at Jackson. "I got me, Jackie. All I got is me." She kneels next to the bench and snorts a line.

"Maybe Iggy's right," says Jackson. "Maybe you're nothing but a hoe."

"Yeah, Jackie," she says. "Maybe that's all I am."

Cesar Bolden stands here in Iggy's apartment-slash-office-slash-bedroom and it kills Iggy to offer Cesar a drink. But he does. And Cesar accepts, but doesn't drink it. He places his glass on the mini-bar then sets his white Kangol hat next to it. He walks over to the two-way mirror and looks downstairs. "The white girl got an ass on her," says Cesar.

Iggy steps from behind the bar and joins Cesar at the mirror. Two cubes of ice float in four shots of cognac. He sips. Downstairs, Bel Biv Devoe sing "Do Me." The white girl, Lacy, or Lucy, or something is managing to stay on beat. A long braid as thick as a climbing rope swings across her tattooed back.

"Where you find her?" says Cesar.

"She found me," Iggy says. He sips. "They all find me."

"What's her story?"

"College student. I'll give her two weeks. Soon as she gets trapped into a dark corner she'll go running back to her work study job."

"Shit, Uncle Iggy," says Cesar. "With your nephew running around here scowling at everybody, puffing his chest out—I don't think any of these hoes got a thing to worry about."

Another thing Iggy hates about Cesar: Never straight to the point. He lets you simmer in the possibilities of what he wants from you, what he's going to take from you, like he ain't got a care in the world until you cross him. Then his eyes take on another shade and his face goes stone. It's like Cesar Bolden is two men: The one on the inside evil incarnate. The one on the outside nothing more than a walking, talking skin costume carrying all that wicked around. But tonight Iggy's not in the mood to be pawed at. "What is it you want from me, Cesar?"

Cesar smiles his arrogant smile that always makes Iggy cringe. "Old Uncle Iggy," he says. "I don't want nothing from you but what you owe. As long as you keep making good on our arrangement, me and you won't have no quarrel."

"Then what is it?"

"Why's it gotta be something? Why can't two old friends just be shooting the shit? Enjoying some scenery?"

"This is about Joy."

Cesar's smile is gone but he doesn't take his eyes off the white stripper. "Just thought I'd extend you a courtesy," Cesar says. "Joy Green is done here, Old Man. She's moving on to bigger and better things."

"Bigger and better things?" says Iggy. "Is that what you call fucking on film?" Iggy's thinking about Ivy. About his own part in this. About how if ever he stumbled across Joy's mother again how he could look her in the eye.

"Iggy," Cesar says. "You know exactly who that girl is. You know exactly what she has inside her. You can keep your hypocritical guilt trip to yourself. I'm going to make a polite suggestion to you. Because I like you."

"Yeah. What's that?" Iggy finishes his drink and watches Jackson downstairs pacing, Newport wedged behind his ear, unshaven, looking even meaner than he usually does. He won't take it well. Joy Green stripping is one thing. Cesar Bolden is going to walk her right off the ledge of a building. And Iggy's thinking: Jackie might just be stupid enough to try and stop him.

And like Cesar is reading his mind, he turns toward Iggy. "Keep that nephew of yours on a leash. Cause if he comes barking my way I'm gonna put him down."

Joy sips Jack Daniels straight from the bottle. A whiskey buzz hums in her head, but buzzing isn't enough. She has to get gone. Cesar watches her. The place is lit dim and one lonely bed centers the room. The rank air is cold enough to make her nipples stand. Low budget, but lower, an abandoned warehouse. She was with Cesar when he kicked in the door and set up shop. Was with him when he interviewed locals, not for a chance to be in a film, but for the pleasure of getting paid to fuck Joy Green.

She was excited at first. When she set aside the shame. When she let go of the reality of what it was she was doing. There was something hot about the idea of being watched, being filmed. There was something powerful about the idea of people paying to see her. That's what she told herself when Cesar broke down his plan. "We cannot undo the Brownstone show, baby. But we can build off it. Controversy, notoriety sells. Look at Lil Kim and Foxy Brown. Shit, look at Madonna."

Joy hits the bottle hard. She sits on a steel foldout chair in a cubical Cesar's calling a dressing room. She wears that same red robe she wore at Iggy's Place. Like it's a uniform. Silk and so thin the cold chair is leaving goose pimples on her ass. "You couldn't rent a space? Or get a cheap motel? Or get something with some heat?" Joy asks Cesar. She hits the Jack again.

"It ain't about money. It's about aesthetic." He's talking with a forced calm. Both of his hands balled into fists. Joy's never seen Cesar lose his temper, but today could be the day.

"Ass Thetic?" says Joy. "Nigga, you don't even know what that means."

In the same forced calm Cesar says, "The actors are already paid. You need to get your shit together."

"Actors my ass, Cesar. Actors rehearse lines, Man. Actors don't pop pills and pull on their dicks."

"You want to pull the plug?" Cesar asks. "You want to go back to Iggy's Place and wrap yourself around that pole? Tell me," Cesar says. "You tell me how long that Iggy's Place money's going to last you? Tell me how long that body is going to last you? How long before the world sees you as Joy Green the stripper and not Joy Green the singer?"

"I ain't no hoe, Cesar."

"I know that."

"Do you? Cause last I checked you had three niggas lined up waiting to fuck me."

Cesar pulls a balled-up bag of coke from his pants pocket. He spills coke onto a table and pulls out the card. "You did this to yourself. The Brownstone show would have made things easy. Now we have to go a different route. If you're serious, if you want this thing, now you'll have to walk through fire to get it. I'll pull the plug if that's what you want. I'll take another financial loss. We can shake hands and go our separate ways. You can go it alone. You can chase your dream to exhaustion by whatever means you see fit."

She knew he was right. Knew the porn flick would sell. She knew sex was money and what fame she had left would make this thing a big deal. But there would be no coming back from this. There would be no dark room to lock this shame in. All the shame would be on display, the wind taking the stink of it far beyond the borders of Grand Rapids. This would make some noise. And if she did this one thing. If she made the sacrifice, took this moral loss—if she did it, just got it over with, and then really got focused—leave the partying in her past, then maybe she could find herself on a stage again. Maybe. "No," says Joy. "I don't want you to pull the plug. I can do this. I'm just a little nervous."

"Then do a line," Cesar says. "Give yourself ten minutes to get your shit together. Find your courage. And when you're ready to start chasing that dream, then you can get your ass in the bed."

C esar knows it before she says it. The failed concealment of morning sickness singing its throes over faucet water and ceiling fan chatter. The subtle recoil when he touches her breasts. The scared shitless daze she had wandered into the past couple weeks. She's pregnant and Cesar knows it's his. He's been watching the signs and trying to find ways to deny that fact, but all attempts have been fruitless because he feels it, stupid as that might sound if he said it out loud, it's true, he knows Joy is pregnant and knows he's the one who made her that way. He stands outside the bathroom with his hand cupped to the door, his ear in his hand. He knocks twice. Joy doesn't speak but the water stops running. Again he knocks.

"Open the door, babe," Cesar says.

Joy fumbles with the lock, but the door remains closed. Cesar twists the handle. Pushes it open. Joy is sitting on the floor in front of the sink, leaning against the cupboard. A wreck. A bottle of wine beside her and her makeup smeared from crying. Cesar's feeling like the dumbest man on the planet because he never used protection. And the words of his father now echo in Cesar's head. *Never come inside a bitch unless you don't mind her having your baby.* The words are cold and true and taunting Cesar now. "You're pregnant?"

"Yes."

"How?"

"How the fuck do you think, Cesar?"

"You're on the pill." But Cesar knows better. How many times did he have to remind her to take it, her trying to double up the day after missing, Joy freaking out like the sky was falling, then doing the same damn thing two days later.

"Cesar," says Joy. "You know I forget sometimes."

He could strangle her. He could. This bitch is becoming his bane. Maybe he needs to cut ties entirely, let her chaos loose, free that beast in her and let her be devoured. He feels the need to punish her. To hurt her. "Are you saying I'm the father?" He lets his voice do the smiling for him. Takes pleasure in her anger, the homicide in her eyes.

"Really? You're really saying that to me right now?"

"Yeah," Cesar says. "I'm really saying it."

"Because I'm two months pregnant, Motherfucker! And there was nobody else."

"You think I don't know what goes on in those private rooms at Iggy's Place?"

"You don't know shit!" Joy stands and slaps him. He almost lets it slide. He takes a deep breath and then touches his face where it stings. He watches Joy back away. Watches the homicide in her eyes peel into fear. Cesar backhands Joy so hard she sails across the bathroom, tearing down the shower curtain when she tries to catch her balance.

She's pathetic. Already she's getting that running look. Anytime life gets hard Joy Green's going to put on her track shoes and be gone. She's going to run. She's got no heart, no fight—Joy Green is weak— she needs comfort, she needs easy, she needs to pretend everything is okay. She's heading for the first exit door that gets her out of the fire.

"You need to kill it," says Cesar. "Kill it before you love it. Cause a bitch like you . . ." Cesar says. "You have no business being a mother."

"Who you calling a bitch, nigga?" Joy says. "You don't know me. You don't know who I am or what I can be." He doesn't, Joy's thinking. All she ever was to this man is an opportunity to make some money. They both were playing the game, playing each other. And maybe emotions got involved a little. Maybe she feels something. And maybe her feelings are hurt right now because Cesar's being so cold. But to feel your body begin to change, to carry life—this man can't understand what that does to you, that initial fear, the acceptance, that budding confidence in her spirit that she can be better, that YES, finally Joy Green has something real in her life to live for.

And this nigga has the nerve to say, *Kill it*. She can't be around him right now. She needs space. Joy imagines a fetus in handcuffs. Policemen on either side of it, leading it to its death, strapping it into a toaster-sized chair. Skin smoking. It stares at her with betrayed gray eyes. Guilty of nothing but being shot out of Cesar Bolden's dumb dick. Being the fastest, strongest swimmer. Breaking through the egg and creating itself. She runs a hand across her stomach. She imagines a gray-eyed black boy wearing crisp jeans and rocking finger waves and a fade. "You don't know shit," Joy says. She stands and walks past him. Drags her suitcase out of his closet and begins filling it with clothes.

"Where you gonna go, Joy? Huh? Where you gonna run off to?"

She ignores him. There's only one place to go. Griggs Street is only a few blocks from here and Jackie Carter will open his door. Jackie loves her. What's wrong with letting him? And who knows: maybe if Cesar doesn't get his shit together, Joy's thinking, maybe she'll give Jackie a chance.

"I've seen a thousand of you," Cesar says, just before Joy walks out the door. "And each and every one of you meet the same end."

Joy takes a final look at Cesar's apartment, his expensive things, the shining surfaces, and then the watermark on the ceiling. "I'm having your baby, Cesar," Joy tells him. "Whether you like it or not. Maybe you should start thinking about what it means to be a father."

A Miles Davis Song
1996–1998

WINDOWS ROLLED DOWN. ON US 131 heading south toward
nowhere. The dark hours of the morning. The sky starless with
gray plumes of cloud half concealing the moon. Cesar's pulling on a
thick-bodied Swisher, letting weed smoke drift out the Caddy when it
wants to. Chopin on low, a cello creeping behind a piano while the car
floats down the road. He likes to leave the city to think. He likes to get
out of the gloom and breathe new air. A long drive alone always works
out the kinks when a situation twists inside his mind.

The concrete's been talking. In that slick whispered tone it's hinting Cesar Bolden might be slipping. His first inclination was to drive
straight over to Griggs Street and make Jackson Carter give head to the
pistol. To drag Joy Green out the house by her weave. Beat the baby
right out of her. But after an hour on the road and the mellow of the
buzz: Cesar chose to let it marinate. Let her get a dose of the broke life.
She can hide in the house all day getting swole, face breaking out in
bumps, flicking a TV remote, while Good Man Jackson Carter works
himself weary just to pay the bills. She'll be back. When reality settles
in, when that broke life starts biting at her, she'll come crawling back.

It's black on both sides of the road. It's like Cesar's driving through
an abyss. His car reminds him of a miner's helmet, providing only
enough light to see ten feet in front of him. He cruises through the thick
night, his high amplified by the silence outside, and for the first time he
imagines what it would be like to have a child. Someone to inherit his
empire. The thought makes him smile.

But then he thinks of his own broken past. His mother ninety pounds and jobless, belt wrapped around her bicep, slapping at her forearm, a teardrop from the tip of the needle. He thinks of his father, before his mother got on that shit, when she'd let him in the house, when they'd do it in the bedroom with the door open, and when he was finished with her he'd leave, and she'd cry, and she'd open a bottle of vodka, and she'd drink it straight, and Cesar would get out of bed and go lay on her lap while she watched reruns of *I Love Lucy*.

Cesar was ten when she killed herself. When he found his mother naked in the bathtub, one arm hanging out of the tub, the other laying across her body. Cesar shook her, his clothes soaking wet, the bathroom floor covered with blood and water, the razor blade cradled in her bent fingers. She'd been dead for hours and Cesar kept shaking her, crying, asking God to bring his mother back to life.

Then he went to live with his father. His father and that pea-green Monte Carlo. Its seats pocked with cigar burns. Its interior stained with the smell of smoke. Cesar felt like a prince in the front seat of that car. They'd go in and out of the apartments of women. Dozens of them. Sometimes his father would leave the car running, a few dollars would be exchanged, and then they'd leave. Other times they'd stay awhile, Cesar put in front of a television, while his father disappeared into a bedroom for an hour or two.

Cesar felt grown and his father seemed huge, a star. A Black N Mild cigar behind his ear and one in his mouth. His collection of hats. His shoes always shined. The women, they loved him, and they loved Cesar. They called Cesar Pretty Boy. They called him Handsome Little Man. They called him Young Adonis. And Mia Tate, a skinny dark-skinned women with large breasts, when Cesar's father was napping on her couch one Saturday afternoon, she took Cesar into her bedroom and taught him how to please a woman with his tongue—he was thirteen and she was thirty—and when Cesar turned and saw his father standing in Mia's doorway, his father was smiling. "My nigga," his father said. Proud. "You got five minutes. We gotta ride."

The man was not fit to raise a child. But how different is Cesar? And what kind of mother would Joy Green be? The beast might free her for a season, but it will never let her go. It's got her on a long chain. Just enough slack to get to the edge of a yard. After the baby is born, after Joy tastes a bit of what it means to be free, she will be snapped back to where the beast wants her kept. It'll call to her and she'll answer the voice.

What happens to the child then? Abandoned to the state. Another bastard, another motherless, fatherless southeast side child. What are the odds though that Joy finds strength in motherhood? Maybe her baby is a good enough reason to be better? Maybe she could find the courage to change. Joy said she's having the baby, so already she's made a choice. But what does that mean for Cesar? When his child is born—could he let the child be a bastard, is Cesar's heart that dark?

He tosses the half-smoked blunt out the window and brakes. It's been at least ten minutes since he's seen another car. Regardless he will pull the trigger. He will send a bullet screaming into the future. Joy Green cost him over $25,000 when she ruined the Brownstone show. He'll get back that loss. Ten thousand copies of *Innocence Gone Wrong* will be pressed at seventy-five cents apiece. He'll sell them at eight bucks a pop. He won't edit the tape, just let it ride in its raw form, so minus the two grand he paid each of the dick throwers, and the two hundred he paid the cameraman, he'll make a cool $66,000. The thing will sell itself. They paid a twenty-dollar cover at Iggy's Place just to see Joy Green wrapped around a pole. Cesar nods his head and smiles. He veers right and pulls off an exit to a small town, every resident asleep, and drives past an abandoned gas station, before hopping back on US 131 heading north.

•

It's like Jackie never sleeps. Late at night Joy keeps her back turned to him, her eyes closed but awake, listening to him breathe. His bear arm around her like she's his cub. His large paw stroking her shoulder. In this house there's just not enough oxygen to go around. And when he's gone, all she can do is stare at the walls. Jerome Carter still haunts this place. The yellow whites of his eyes floating in the dark. The front door closing. His quiet footsteps toward the couch where she and Jackie used to sleep as kids, the TV still on—sometimes when she's sleeping she feels Jerome's fingers crawling across her skin as plain as if it's real.

Joy's breasts are tender and heavy and she's beginning to show. She sprawls across the bed, alone, the only time of day she feels okay, a Jackson-sized imprint lying beside her, and no longer the need to pretend. She rises from the bed, steps out of the room, and down the hallway to the bathroom. She leans over the toilet and vomits twice, flushes, walks to the sink and runs the faucet. She washes her face and brushes her teeth. Lifts her breasts and lets them fall. She has to tell Jackson today.

She walks downstairs to the kitchen and brews coffee. She hears Jackson in the basement busy on the heavy bag. The loud thud of his fists against the canvas echo across the concrete walls. She tiptoes down the steps to watch him, glazed with sweat, broad shoulders, back muscles like a prizefighter. When he hits the duct-taped bag the rafters creak. It sways on a rusted chain. Little Jackie Carter all grown up. The man has a body like a Spartan soldier. A big old heart. Any woman with a teaspoon of sense would want him. Any woman but Joy Green.

"Jackie." It's hard to look at him. He's eleven all over again, mean-faced with the eyes of a grown man. The scowl he wears now just an infant then, but present—a boy destined to go through life pissed off. He's fifteen and teary eyed as she's leaving town, and she's blowing him a kiss from the backseat of a limousine like she's Marilyn Monroe.

Jackson turns. He wipes his forehead with a tattered black boxing glove. "Good morning."

The lie rocks back and forth in her throat. It's so hard to look at him. He's eighteen with a busted dream and a blown out knee. And she's pacing a hotel room in downtown Detroit with a glass of red wine. She knows she should call him, but won't. She doesn't care. Because her dream is already ending. And it feels good for Jackie's dream to be ending too.

The guilt tears start coming, so she looks away. She knows Jackie's a sucker for love. And it kills her that she's the bitch he's a sucker for. And the guilt hurts, so she lets the tears fall. "Baby," she says, then stops herself.

Jackson walks over to Joy and puts a hand on her shoulder. "What's wrong?"

"I'm pregnant." She waits to be accused, but isn't. Jackson just looks at her cautiously, like he's being careful with his next words. He didn't ask a lot of questions when she showed up at his door. He just asked about Cesar. Were they finished. Was Cesar going to come looking for her. And Joy told him they were through and Cesar wouldn't come looking. And she meant it at the time, but after a couple weeks she and Jackie started fooling around, and her clothes gradually moved from the spare bedroom to Jackie's closet, and she woke up one day realizing that she was playing house, she panicked, she packed up her things when Jackie was at work, and she almost hit the road, she almost went back to Cesar. But something stopped her at the front door.

The problem wasn't love. She loved Jackie in her own kind of way. And there is lust too, the man is fine, but it's almost like being intimate with a friend, and sometimes late at night, when Jackie's finally snoring, Joy sleepless and watching his chest move, it just feels weird, like she cannot get over the fact that he's the same snotty-nosed little boy she used to babysit, that this is the same house where she lost it, that thing a girl can never get back, Jackie sleeping on the couch downstairs on a dark cold December night, when Jerome Carter asked her nicely if she'd go up to his bedroom with him, and she was scared and didn't want to say yes but she followed him up the stairs anyway and she didn't say no.

"How far along are we?" Jackson asks.

But on those long sleepless nights it's Cesar Bolden she's thinking about, imagining him cruising through the southeast side in his Caddy, some new bitch riding shotgun, Joy and her baby forgotten. It wasn't love with Cesar. It was excitement. Being with that man was to buzz just by breathing his air, being around him, the cool way he owned a room, the way when he fucked her he could make her toes curl without even trying. Being with him was easy without a baby involved. And now with this child growing inside her she misses that feeling—she misses being with Cesar—but Joy cannot imagine a domesticated life with Cesar Bolden. She can't imagine any version of House that Cesar would play along with.

She could imagine raising a child on Griggs Street though. She could imagine Jackie Carter pushing a lawnmower. She could imagine her child drawing on the sidewalk with chalk. Having sweet tea in a large jar, sitting on the porch, baking in the sun the way her mother used to do it. Joy thinks of her father before everything went down with Iggy. Smoking his pipe and laughing his belly-born laugh. Miles Davis or Charlie Parker or Sam Cooke bouncing off the walls of their house in Alger Heights. Entertaining small groups on nights and weekends, records always spinning even after the rest of the world sold out and started playing cassettes.

Miles Davis Green, Joy's thinking, imagining the baby is a boy. I'm doing this for Miles, she tells herself. What other choice does she have? Raise this baby alone? And Jackie would be a wonderful father. He would. "About six weeks, Jackie," she says.

Jackson kisses her forehead. "Everything's gonna be okay," he tells her.

Jackson drags on a Newport. Shirtless. Black Champion sweatpants. His white Reebok Classics stained green. Lawnmower stalled because it choked on trapped grass. He stands in the yard. Focused on the taupe Cadillac parked curbside three houses down. It's the third time he's seen Cesar Bolden this week. Sniffing around. Trolling by yesterday morning on Jackson's way to work; parked at the old condemned church two nights ago when Jackson was out for a jog.

Jackson finishes the Newport and lights the other. He stalks down the sidewalk. Cesar's engine revs. The Caddy peels out and speeds past,

Cesar's profile barely visible through the window tint. Jackson leaves the lawn half-mowed and steps into the house. Joy is sleeping on the couch. Her bottom lip droops. Slobber trails down her right cheek. Pringles Cheezums are spilled on the coffee table, the container fallen over and lidless. Dean's French Onion dip is left open, the top lying face down, stuck to a pad of notebook paper.

Jackson kicks off his shoes. He walks over to Joy and wipes the drool from her face. Peels a throw from the back of the couch and covers her with it. Shakes his head, disgusted. She barely gets off her ass. Never leaves home. It's like she's living in a jail cell. Lately Jackson's feeling like the warden. He wonders if Cesar's been creeping in the house when he's not around. Jackson wonders how long it will be before Joy loses the energy to keep up the façade.

Jackson walks into the kitchen. Dishes piled in the sink. The last bit of coffee burned to the bottom of the pot. He unplugs the machine. Lifts a stack of porcelain plates and smashes them on the floor. He grabs hold of the refrigerator door and tries to tear it from the hinges. A carton of milk shakes loose and breaks on impact. A white river crawls out to the edge of the living room.

Jackson follows the stream.

"Jackie, what's going on?" Joy stands now, holding the Pringles carton.

"You been letting that man in my house?" A deep breath. "Has Cesar Bolden been coming in my house?"

"Shit, Jackie." Joy sets the Pringles down. Walks over to him. "Baby," she says. "It's me and you now. It's just me and you."

She hasn't done a thing to her hair in days. Sleep crust in the corners of her eyes. Dried spit on her lips. Wearing the same clothes she's been wearing all week: pajama pants and one of Jackson's white T-shirts, stained now with coffee and food. "Baby, what's the matter?" She wets her lips. She touches Jackson's chest. "Baby?"

Jackson remembers a family barbeque, Joy singing Jackson Five songs on a rented stage, her hair greased back in a thick ponytail, wearing a green headband and a baggy T-shirt with a dark green peace symbol airbrushed on it. Jackson remembers sitting on her lap while she read him books, playing Candyland, Chutes N Ladders, UNO. He remembers when he was ten and Joy was sixteen. She was babysitting and had to drive to the bar to pick up his dad, the bartender taking his keys, calling Joy to drive him home. Jackson remembers his dad staggering, slurring, Joy brushing his hand away when he placed it on her thigh.

"Jackie, say something."

He remembers Joy growing breasts and painting her face with makeup. He remembers her attracting grown men, but dating teenage boys with thin wisps of hair on their upper lips. Jackson remembers shaving his bald upper lip at age eleven, hoping his own thin wisp would grow. He remembers at age twelve she let him touch her breasts through a Michigan State sweatshirt. Teaching him how to tongue kiss on a vanity couch pillow.

Jackson remembers her gone, off recording demos, trying to get signed. Age seventeen buying a copy of her single, "Boys," and running his finger over the vast gap of the cleavage, the curve of her lips. Playing the song and holding the CD case insert with his left hand and masturbating with his right.

"Jackie?"

Then he sees her riding shotgun in Cesar Bolden's Caddy. Wearing big black sunglasses that looked like a fly's eyes. Weave blowing behind her. Her face forward and defiant, like she was being forced where she was going. At Iggy's Place now they talk about her and laugh. Legs spread in an old warehouse on Franklin Street. Cameras rolling. Folks already yapping about the porn flick dropping. Her rep plagued in a way she won't ever recover from. And Jackson knows he's no more than her fool. A fool seeing something in her that isn't there, maybe never was. It's only a matter of time before Cesar Bolden comes knocking. Only a matter of time before he comes back to claim what's his.

Jackson swats her hand away. The milk trail is soaking into his socks. "You think I'm stupid, don't you?"

"What?"

"You think I don't know whose baby that is? Huh! You think I'm that stupid? Tell you what . . . you need to get the fuck out of my house. Go back to your baby's daddy, Joy. I know that's what you want."

"It's not."

"You use the people who love you, Joy. The least you can do is come clean. The least you can do is tell me the truth."

"Jackie, I'm so sorry," Joy says. "I mean it, baby. I'm sorry."

"I'm not your baby."

"I'm sorry."

"You're ugly," Jackson says. "You know that? You're an ugly human being."

C esar hasn't slept. It's been a night of pacing and waiting. A night of calls to the doctor's office. A night of timing contractions. They're ten minutes apart now and the pain is getting worse. He has Joy in a warm bubble bath and he's rubbing her shoulders. Her eyes are closed and she's breathing short choppy breaths. "Miles is coming," Joy says. "Cesar, your son is coming."

"Now?" Cesar asks.

"No." Joy smiles. She touches his hand. "Not now, baby. But it's time to go."

Joy didn't come back crawling, like Cesar predicted she would, she came back different. She apologized for leaving and Cesar let her, not telling her about the porn money piling in, and he listened to Joy talk about their baby, a possibility for a life together, and how she wanted to make things work between them.

Off coke Joy is calm. She is cool. She is filled with the light of God. The pregnancy has changed her, or maybe gotten her back to her roots, before the spotlight, brought back that special something about her that made her a star. Now she sings while she's doing the dishes. And she talks long into the night, Cesar listening, letting her hold his hand.

The sound of her voice is soothing in the darkness. She knows she won't ever be a star again, she knows—she doesn't admit it, doesn't say the words, but she knows. She talks around it, saying motherhood is her focus now; motherhood is what she's going to do. It's a distraction, an excuse maybe, but Cesar doesn't hold it against her. He lets her talk and he listens.

When the morning sickness stopped and the corner of his bedroom became space for the baby, a crib, a dresser, some toys, he got used to the idea of a child being around. Some nights he'd watch Joy sleep, cradling her stomach, and he'd allow himself to believe this was more than a moment. He'd think back to a time when his own parents were together, to a vague Christmas with a neglected tree drowning in lights, its brittle needles all over the carpet, all over the presents. He'd think back to when things weren't bad—they were never good, but at some point in Cesar's memory they weren't bad. His father never lived with them, but his father was around. Then he simply wasn't and Cesar never knew why.

"Okay," says Cesar. "Shit, okay, baby. Okay."

Joy smiles. "Relax," she says. "We got this."

•

The delivery room is cold and it has a view of the city. A view of smokestacks and snow-kissed rooftops. An industrial grid of squares that seem to go on for miles. And the snowflakes have wings. Big white butterflies suspended in air. The kind kids like to catch on their tongues. The nurse is obese and monotone and self-important. She has seventeen years of experience, she's told them, and six children of her own. She said this after missing Joy's vein twice while trying to hook up her I.V., after Cesar asked for her supervisor, when Joy's pain went from a six to a ten, when Joy said, "Bitch, just shut up and give me my goddamn epidural!"

Now they're fully dilated and Cesar's watching the monitor. An artwork of peaks and valleys being sketched on a scroll. The paper folding down into an open drawer, documenting Joy's labor, a history of contractions, Miles' journey into this world. The doctor enters the room donning light blue scrubs and a demeanor that puts Cesar at ease, a been-there-done-that confidence that begins with a handshake, a smile, and a Please-Call-Me-Dave. "You're doing great, Joy," Dave says, snapping on light blue gloves. "Does it feel like you need to push?"

For half an hour Joy labors. Cesar doesn't coach her, but he holds her hand—he kisses her from time to time to let her know he's with her, that they're in this together. Cesar notices the clock says 6:35 am when Dave asks for a delivery nurse and a table, when Joy's feet are propped into stirrups, when Dave screams NOW! and the obese nurse hesitates for a moment and Dave catches Miles, screaming, pale purple, when he enters the world. Dave sets the baby on Joy's chest. Two more nurses rush into the room. No one seems to notice Cesar's tears. No one but Joy. "He's beautiful," Cesar tells her. "Your baby is beautiful."

The doctor asks if Cesar wants to cut the cord. Cesar declines. He sits on a cold brown couch and watches the nurses work. The weight of his responsibility is real. This living breathing thing. His own. Something right in a lifetime of wrong. Cesar remembers a late-summer morning, his father drinking coffee from a thermos, the Monte Carlo idling in front of the Wealthy Street Train Bridge. The bridge trestles painted with rust and graffiti, the wooden ties slick with dew. Cesar followed his father, one cautious step at a time, watching the Grand River flow beneath him, through the cracks along his path, until they came to a scaffold. A rope ladder hung from the train tracks. They climbed down. The landing spot was muck. A small Coleman cooler floated in a pool of dead water. A wooden pallet leaned against a concrete column. On the column *Punk Island* was tagged in blue spray paint. A large red pitch fork skewered the words. The island was shaped like an egg, the tip of it jutting out under the bridge.

The place was hidden beneath a canopy of trees. Five gutted Chunky soup cans were scattered next to a row of tents. A couple Five O'Clock Vodka bottles, one with a missing cap, the other with the label half torn sat on a picnic table. An icy breeze coming off the river. The music of birds. Clouds hanging. The city's reflection painted on the water. Cesar heard traffic on the streets above. Engines and mufflers. Tires on wet pavement.

Cesar's father set his thermos on the picnic table and pulled out his pistol. "Johnny Redd!" he hollered at the row of tents. No one answered. Cesar's father fired two shots in the air. A baby cried. "Johnny Redd," said Cesar's father. "I want my money." Again, no one answered, but the baby was screaming. Cesar's father fired one more shot. "That's your last warning, nigga."

"Okay, okay, Moody, shit!"

A tall freckled black men zipped open the tent. He crawled out and stood, holding the crying baby. He gave Cesar's father his wallet, held his baby against his chest. Cesar has never forgotten the fear in that man's eyes and truly didn't understand it until now, his own child crying in Joy's arms, feeling for the first time in his life that he had something other than himself to live for. The man asked Cesar's father, "Please, Moody. Take what you want and leave us be." Cesar's father folded open the wallet and counted out forty-three dollars. "You're seven short," he said. "I want my money, Johnny. When I see you on the block you better have my money. Don't make me come back down here."

"Baby," says Joy. "Do you want to hold him?" Miles lies naked on Joy's chest. Cesar's surprised at how pale he is—his little white boy baby, a birthmark on his butt cheek that looks like a strip of bacon. He's so small, fragile. His eyes are closed and he breathes loud, his lips puckered like he's trying to suck air.

"He's beautiful," Cesar says. "The most beautiful thing I've ever seen."

"You want to hold him?"

"No," says Cesar. "Not yet."

Joy's full of milk but she can't get Miles to latch on. He pecks at her like a baby bird, his mouth open, screaming, Joy's uterus contracting. Miles is frustrated and hungry and she is failing him. And to pump is a pain in the ass. The machine yelping like a bullfrog, the baby crying,

Cesar swooping in to save the day with a bottle of Similac and his cool, calming voice. But her breasts hurt so bad and she's supernaturally tired. And her body aches. Her body aches like she can't believe. And Cesar is so present. In her wildest daydream, Cesar Bolden was never a great father, and now, now the moment he takes Miles into his arms the boy stops crying.

"Shit!" Joy hands Miles to Cesar, who is shirtless and sitting on the bed.

"You'll get it, babe," Cesar tells her. "Hey, Handsome," he says to Miles, rubbing his back. Miles heaves a couple more quiet cries and then he's calmed, relieved, it seems, to be out of Joy's arms.

"He hates me."

"He's hungry," says Cesar. "That's all."

The asshole didn't even sign the birth certificate. He wouldn't even give Miles his name, saying the name Bolden dies with him, that his father gets no legacy, that he wants Miles to make his own name. Bullshit. Cesar Bolden bullshit. The truth is the man doesn't want a paper trail. If the relationship goes south that'll be his out. Another nigga dodging the Friend of the Court. Joy knows it but hasn't called him on it, because shit, at least now he's involved. Besides, every dollar the man makes if off the books. As far as Uncle Sam is concerned Cesar Bolden earns nothing. What good is half of nothing going to do her?

She feels her hormones shifting. Crazy has come knocking and it wants to get in. Her emotional range changes within the span of a minute, within a moment. Like now, watching Miles, wearing nothing but a diaper, lying against Cesar's naked chest, it's beautiful and she loves this man and she's jealous and she hates him and she loves him again and she cannot be a mother, she can't, it's just too much pressure and she's going to be the best mother in the world and if Cesar asks her, she'll be his wife and give him ten more babies and she's not having any more babies, especially not with this monster who won't even sign his son's birth certificate, who likes to feed her cocaine and knock her up and make her do porn. The bastard.

She knows how she feels is not rational. How can she be mad at a man for being better than he was? For surprising her. For being willing to change to accommodate a child. What it is is jealousy. What she can't stand, if she's being honest, is that she's supposed to be the mother, it's supposed to come natural to her, and this cool, calm motherfucker . . . he's just floating through this thing effortlessly, and she's sinking, she's failing, which is hard enough to stomach, but to fail and watch Cesar flourish, that's the part that really stings.

"Cesar," says Joy. "I don't know if I can do this." She's getting that familiar urge to run but cannot think of a single place to go. Every bridge has been burned, every relationship ruined, nothing to her name but a few hundred dollars. And this is Cesar's city. He'll find her and beat her and drag her ass home. God, what is she thinking? It's just a baby, her baby, who needs comfort and love, who needs patience. She just needs the edge off. A drink, a line, shit, a few puffs of weed, something to calm her nerves, get her head together. The nurses told her the first couple months would be rough, that breastfeeding would take some time, that depression would be desperate to gain foothold. Fight, Joy Green, you can fight. You have to fight, fight for your son, for your life.

Cesar kisses Miles. He cradles him and puts a bottle in his mouth. Then he looks at Joy. She cannot see Cesar's face in the dark room. But it's like his presence has changed. That love has left this place. He's swallowed the last few drips of light and the temperature has dropped. Miles' father is gone and Cesar Bolden has returned. He waits a moment before he speaks and when he does his tone holds no emotion. "You don't know if you can do this?" he asks. Cesar takes a long pause before speaking again. "Bitch, you don't have a choice."

The apartment smells like piss and shit. A diaper bag is spilled on the living room floor. A box of wipes is open and dried out. The breast pump is plugged in next to the left-on television, the Lion King DVD on the menu screen, theme music playing on a loop. Miles lies in his bouncer. He's been crying for so long his voice is hoarse. His white onesie is soiled, stained yellow, his diaper soaked, and shit climbing up his back. "Joy!" yells Cesar. He finds a washcloth and wets it. Begins taking off Miles' clothes, cleaning him up. "Joy!"

"Hey, hey," Cesar whispers. He nuzzles Miles' neck. Finds a diaper on the floor and puts it on him. He finds a sleeper in the diaper bag. "Joy!" When Miles is dressed Cesar carries him into the bedroom. Joy isn't there. Miles' chest is still heaving but he's given up trying to cry. Cesar should have known better. A bitch like Joy Green. He should have known. Now he hurts in the worst way—the way he loves this boy. Miles is beginning to calm down now, but God knows how long he was crying, God knows how long he was left alone. And this is it. There is no redemption for Joy, no forgiveness, no second chance. She's lucky he doesn't put a slug in her head. Real lucky. Because if something were to happen to this boy . . .

The past week she'd had the running look in her eyes. That beast was back, whispering its will to her. Cesar should have known better. She wasn't ever going to be free of it. It wouldn't be hard to find her. A couple phone calls. A drive through the southeast side. But the stakes are different now. His lifestyle is not conducive to raising a child alone. Miles will not grow up like Cesar did, in drug houses and bars, on runs, living like a grown man and having to grow up too fast, or in the system, in group homes being hounded by CPS, no suitable family to take him in, unwanted by everyone but his father, who was not interested in fathering, but grooming a disciple, a young Moody Bolden with a pistol and a pocket full of cash.

Cesar makes Miles a bottle. He sits on the couch and feeds him. He'll have to pack everything. Leave no trace of Miles in this apartment. No trace of Joy Green. There will be no parenting time agreement, no court-appointed visits. He'll send money. Plenty of money. George and Ivy Green live in Alger Heights so Miles will be close, close enough to keep an eye on.

"I love you, Son," Cesar says. "You understand me? I'm always gonna love you." He could kill her. He could. He hates himself right now. Hates himself for hoping she could change, that the change he saw in her was real—that someone weak as Joy Green could ever be the mother of his child. Miles is barely a month old and she's already failed. And to leave a baby alone. To abandon him and just run.

Cesar knew better. He did. And love. Love just makes a man weak. A woman, a child—doesn't matter what face the love has, love makes you stupid, it takes you out of your character, twists you, folds you, it drags you out into deep waters and drowns you. Love has you thinking about all the things you buried. All the things you left behind. It has you thinking about your mother, who was a nurse once, wearing scrubs and coming home late, before all the fighting, before the vodka, before the heroin, before Cesar found her in the bathtub sleeping in her own blood.

Love has you crying on the couch while you're feeding your baby. Not even a month old and you're leaving him. Not because you want to, but because of love. Because you love him and you know he's better off with somebody else. Because it's the right thing to do. But righteousness doesn't take the edge of the sting. Because it hurts. Because he's looking up at you. His eyes wide in awe like you're God herself. Your son cannot understand a word that you're saying.

He doesn't understand that you're saying goodbye.

Letting Go
2000-2003

MAE MCCOY HAD IT ALL FIGURED OUT. SHE took her 4.0 high school GPA three hours away from the Detroit suburbs and majored in English at Grand Valley State University in rural Michigan. No distractions. Get that degree, land a teaching job, and get on with her life. For four years she'd kept her head down and now she's a senior. One last semester then she's certified to teach. Job already secured working for Grand Rapids Public Schools.

She's a pretty girl; tall and slim with light brown skin. But she gives the boys no play, rolling her eyes when they spit their game, telling them no when they ask for her number. The white girls call her prissy. The black girls call her bougie. Mae calls herself focused, and that's exactly who she was, that is, until she met Jeff.

For weeks she watched him from across the classroom in American Literature. This white boy with skater bangs and eyes the color of pale olives. He has a passion for Updike and Roth, and a distaste for Vonnegut. She adores the way his cheeks redden when he disagrees with another student's opinion. The way he gently pounds the table when he's driving home a point.

Jeff gave no indication he even knew Mae existed. And why would he? Curves hidden beneath a baggy sweatsuit. Hair always pulled back in a ponytail. Barely saying a word in class, drifting off, daydreaming, watching him twirl those gorgeous white boy bangs.

So she straightened her hair and showed some cleavage (a tank top beneath an unbuttoned shirt). And she raised her hand during an Updike discussion, defending him against racist allegations by a critic who thought Updike stereotyped the African American male in *Rabbit Redux*—Mae cited realism and authenticity, and even sold out a little (by her own code of ethics) by pointing out she was the only black face in the entire class and *she* wasn't offended.

Jeff's eyes met her eyes. Then Jeff's eyes met her breasts. And for the past two weeks she noticed him glancing at her from across the room. So now as he approaches Mae, sitting in the food court alone, she isn't terribly surprised.

"Hey," he says. "Mae from Tuinstra's class, right?"

"Yeah." She wants to pretend she doesn't know him, to play it cool, but the words have already left her mouth. "Hi, Jeff."

"So you like Updike, huh?"

"Updike? Not especially. The Rabbit series, I love though."

"The sentence-level writing, the realness of his world . . . Updike is my favorite."

"I know," says Mae. "You've told Tuinstra about a million times." She smiles.

"Listen," Jeff says. "Here's my address." He hands her a folded sheet of paper. "I'm organizing a study group for Monday's test. You'd be a great addition. If you're interested swing by Friday around eight."

•

The night is that brittle kind of cold that feels like you're breathing broken glass. The snow has a thin glaze of ice over it that cuts into Mae's ankles as she steps up Jeff's unshovelled walkway. And Mae feels—what does she feel? Giddy or girlish, a fist-sized lump of nerves collected in her chest, working its way down to her stomach.

Jeff answers the door wearing athletic shorts and a tank top. He is long and thin and hairy. He is holding a twenty-four-ounce Pabst Blue Ribbon beer can. "Babygirl," he says, sarcastic almost. "C'mon in."

Mae hugs her backpack. She can't tell if Jeff is drunk or just buzzing. She's never been much of a drinker.

"C'mon," he says. "I won't bite."

Mae steps into the house and Jeff shuts and locks the door behind her. "Where's everyone else?" asks Mae.

"You know, running late—Friday night and all. Let me·take your coat."

Mae sets her backpack on the floor and unbuttons her coat.

"The Beatles?" asks Jeff, pointing at Mae's T-shirt. "Cool. I'm more of a Stones man myself, though." Mae hands him her coat and Jeff drapes it over the couch. "Do you want to get started now, or should we wait for the others?" he asks.

"We can wait."

"Have a seat," says Jeff. "Can I get you a beer? Maybe some wine?"

"Wine," says Mae.

Jeff returns with a bottle and one glass. He pours. Hands the glass to Mae. "I'll be right back." He returns moments later with an unopened Pabst. He cracks it open and lifts it in the air. "Cheers," he says. He sips.

Mae downs the glass of wine in one pull and then pours herself another. Maybe they're right? Maybe she is prissy, or bougie. Four years, all this hard work; maybe she should have had some fun? Maybe she could have been a little more reckless. One semester away and what memories has she made? She takes a few sips of wine and succumbs to the warm, gentle buzz that's easing its way through her skin. She doesn't flinch when Jeff places a hand high on her thigh.

"You know I'm crushing on you, right?" he says.

"Is that right?"

"It is." His hand creeps a bit higher.

She'd only ever done it once, the day *before* prom (Mae McCoy does *not* do clichés) on a Friday afternoon while her parents were at work, in her own bed, with Brandon Arrington, a preacher's son, and it didn't hurt, but didn't feel good either, and the look on Brandon's face was so dumb when they finished, and Mae was thinking two things in that moment:

1. How could such a handsome boy look so silly. 2. Why'd she even bother spending hours the night before making a lose-my-virginity mixtape, when the whole thing would be over before the first song (Al Green's "Let's Stay Together"), had even finished playing.

Mae finishes her second glass of wine. Pours herself another. Downs it. This boy is so cute—what's the word they used to use in those old TV shows, those white girls wearing sweaters with skirts? Dreamy. This boy is so dreamy. Smiling at her, wanting her. She takes Jeff's hand and places it on her breast, the wine deading the nerves, making her brave. She's surprised by how easily he undoes her bra clamp. How quickly he has her out of her clothes.

Jeff takes off his shirt. The Star of David is tattooed around his left nipple. His shorts hit the floor. Mae lies naked on the couch, covering her breasts. "Protection?" she asks. She can barely get the word out of her mouth.

Annoyed, Jeff leaves the room, but when he returns he's smiling. "You're so fucking beautiful," he says. He pushes a pink condom over his short, fat penis. It hurts when he puts it in. She closes her eyes and waits. Waits for it to feel good. Jeff sucks a nipple. Hard. Too hard. He bites her. His beer breath hot against her chest. She opens her eyes. Jeff is no longer Jeff. His eyes are mean, greedy. He's biting down on his bottom lip. He has her knees pinned to her shoulders. His forehead sweating, beading. His face red. *Stop.* Did she say it out loud? She doesn't know.

"Stop."

"What?"

"Jeff, I said stop."

"I'm about to come."

He pumps three more times before pulling away. The same dumb look as Brandon Arrington. He wipes the sweat from his forehead with the back of his hand. The pink condom dangles from his penis. Jeff walks into the bathroom. Water runs. A toilet flushes. Mae finds her clothes. It's like she's floating down the stairs, a passenger in someone else's skin. The winter air stings and she realizes she's left her coat in the apartment. She doesn't care.

"Mae, what the hell?"

Jeff is beside her. Pulling a sweatshirt over his head. Shoes untied. "Mae, wait. What the hell, Mae?"

"You know what the hell," says Mae. She stops walking and faces him.

Jeff crosses his arms. "No," Jeff says. "I don't."

"You don't?"

"I don't."

"Okay." Mae walks away

"Wait, Mae. I'm sorry, okay? I'm sorry."

Mae keeps walking.

Then Jeff grabs her. "Just talk to me. You owe me that."

"I owe you?"

A black boy approaches on foot wearing tattered brown Dickies boots. He carries a flashlight and wears a campus security uniform, a wool cap, an unzipped brown leather bomber jacket. "Miss?" Mae hears him say, then "Miss, are you okay?" He looks at Mae and then he looks at Jeff. Jeff backs away. "You're freezing," he says. He takes off his jacket and wraps her in it. "Is this guy bothering you?"

"She's my girlfriend," says Jeff.

"Yeah?" says the campus security guard.

Mae shakes her head.

"Look, bro," says Jeff. "I just want to talk to my girlfriend. We had an argument, that's all."

"Bro?" The security guy crosses his arms. "I suggest you go inside, Little Fella. Before your mouth signs a check your ass can't cash."

"Just give me five minutes, aight?" says Jeff. "*Aight?*"

"Miss," says the security guy. "You want to talk to this clown?"

"No," says Mae.

"Kick rocks," the security guy says.

Jeff turns to walk away. "Fucking niggers," he says.

Mae watches the security guy's face change from amused, to calm, to something like a cool quiet rage. "No!" she yells.

•

"The sirens are getting closer," says Mae. "You should get out of here."

"For what? So they can get my address from the school and pick me up tomorrow?"

"Jeff's not moving."

"He'll be out for a minute," says the security guard. "I caught him dead on the chin."

"Are they going to take you to jail?"

"Yup."

"And you're fine with that?"

Before the security guy can answer the police arrive, patrol cars throwing lights across the snow, sirens screaming. They exit their cars with guns drawn. The security guy puts his hands in the air. Three policemen shove him face first into the concrete. Another helps Jeff to his feet.

They put the security guy in handcuffs. They take him away.

Mae McCoy sits on the curb, in the snow, wrapped in his coat.

The holding cell smells like freshly mopped floor and unshowered men. Like ammonia and funk. Like failure. Or hard luck. Jackson paces the small space he shares with four degenerates: drunk drivers, or child support dodgers, and he decides *fucked over* would best describe his own scent. He had a white mother but was born beige. The average hick-town cop, when giving him the eye test, sees nothing more than nigger. Whatever whiteness Jackson had was buried with his mom.

He called Iggy first, but Iggy didn't pick up—probably knee deep in one of those big booty things he stocks his club with. Then he tried his supervisor and got the man's voicemail, left him a message explaining the situation. Out of people to call, he'd been led to the holding cell to wait. Jackson figures his worst case scenario is a small fine and misdemeanor assault charges. Unless he broke the white boy's jaw. Then he'd have to do some time. It would be worth it though. Motherfucker will think twice before he drops another n-bomb.

Two armed guards approach and a couple of the degenerates perk up, hoping they got bailed, or that they're being transferred to a cell.

The other two are sleeping: one next to a stainless steel toilet, the other balled up on a bench using a roll of tissue for a pillow. The two hopefuls grunt when it's Jackson whose name is called, who's led out of the glass cage and into the lobby.

He scans the room for Iggy, but Iggy's not there. Standing by the doorway is the girl from Grand Valley. She wears a vanilla pea coat and a tan scarf. She is holding Jackson's coat. She isn't smiling, but isn't in pieces either. "Mr. Carter," she says.

"Jackson."

"Mae McCoy."

"Pleasure," says Jackson as Mae hands him his coat. He puts it on. Opens the door for her.

"My car is down there." She slants her head toward the metered street parking a half a block away. "Can I give you a ride somewhere? Or maybe we can get some coffee or something?"

"What about a drink?"

"It's not even noon."

"Extenuating circumstances."

"I don't feel like drinking," says Mae. "But I'll sit with you."

The man has an edge to him, an anger, a hardness. But beneath the surface intensity, Mae sees something more. Passion. Honor. Something much louder than anger in Jackson Carter. A thing he doesn't seem willing to let the world get a glimpse of. She wants to ask him what he's hiding from, how the world hurt him, but decides against it, twirling the lemon in her ice water with a straw, watching him swallow a third shot of cognac and take a fifth swig of a tall beer. "Jeff isn't going to press charges," says Mae.

"Is that right?"

"Yeah."

"Just like that? Knock a white boy out and he's just going to let it slide?"

"It's more complicated than that," says Mae.

"Complicated?"

"Yeah." An image of Jeff flashes through Mae's mind. Scrawny and shirtless and much stronger than he appears. She looks at Jackson Carter, sipping his beer and staring her down. There is something about the strength of this man. He makes her feel safe. Almost like nothing even happened last night. Almost like today is a new beginning. Almost. "Are you going to lose your job?"

"I don't know," says Jackson. "Probably."

"I'm sorry."

"Don't be. I have two other jobs." Jackson finishes his cognac without a cringe. He downs what's left of his beer. He's reckless but he's lit with passion. He's like a man ready to fight only he doesn't know who or what he's fighting—just believes in never backing down. "So, what was last night about? This Jeff guy; is he your boyfriend?"

"No."

"Was he?"

"No."

"So what then? Why all the drama."

"Just leave it alone, okay?"

"Right," says Jackson. "Complicated." He nods over to the bartender and holds up two fingers. Then he looks back at Mae. "So when do you graduate?"

"April."

"Then what?"

"I'm taking a job at a middle school in Grand Rapids."

"You from here?"

"Detroit."

The bartender arrives with a double shot of Hennessey. Jackson takes it to the head. He chases it with another swallow of beer. "I had plans for college," he says, "but life had other plans for me."

Mae watches Jackson Carter set his large hands on the table. His knotted knuckles are thick with scar tissue. His brown fists are covered in blonde hair. Mae wonders how many unjust men have had to face the wrath of Jackson Carter. He reminds her of a flawed superhero or a vigilante. A pissed off man seeking vengeance against anything and everyone he doesn't deem right. He flinches when she touches him. When she smoothes the palms of her hands over the hairy fists of his. It sends a shiver through her, feeling his skin beneath hers. She watches him turn to the bartender and nod for another drink. "Mr. Carter—"

"Jackson."

"Jackson," says Mae. "Don't you think you've had enough to drink?"

He smiles. Takes her right hand in his and brings it to his mouth. Kisses it. "Yeah, I think I have." Then he places her hand back on the table, and holds two fingers up to the bartender.

George and Ivy Green had a closed-casket funeral. They had been blindsided by a cement truck. Dead on impact. The Grand Rapids Press said they never felt a thing. Maybe a moment's fear before the lights went out forever. By chance Joy's young son, Miles wasn't in the car with his grandparents. He'd been on a visit with his mother, who Jackson heard from Iggy, was clean for the moment, and had been going through the process of getting custody of the boy, who'd been living at George and Ivy's since just after he was born.

Jackson played the back wall at the service waiting for Iggy, but Iggy never showed. Joy sat in the front row. Crying but not carrying on. No Lawd Jesus. No Why God Why. Just the occasional sniffle; Joy holding Miles against her chest. Jackson crept out the back before she saw him. He was too bitter for condolences. Too afraid of the feelings Joy was stirring up in him. The way when he saw her, or thought about her, he always went back to being a boy. A boy beneath her thumb. Plus, his mind was on Iggy. So Jackson slipped out unseen and made his way to the riverfront. Now he stands in the wreckage of Iggy's apartment. A record player spins, but no sound comes from it but the scratch of the needle. The two-way glass is cracked and looks like a large spider web. A

Hennessy bottle shattered on the floor in front of it. Another Hen bottle half-empty on top of the bar. Iggy lay face down on the bed, wearing a black suit, dead besides his snoring.

Jackson walks over and touches his uncle on the shoulder. Iggy lies in vomit. He hugs a bouquet of white roses, mumbling incoherently as Jackson tries to shake him awake. "The past," says Jackson. He walks over to the bar and pours himself a double. "Grief times two." He swallows his drink and begins cleaning the apartment.

When Jackson blew out his knee Iggy never left his side. There never was a backup plan. Just run. Run and knock over anything that got in the way. It was a cheap shot that ended his dreams. Helmet first. This bitchass safety from Union named Robert McIntosh going low to avoid being punished by Jackson's shoulder, going too low, a direct shot to the knee, Houseman Field silent but Jackson's screams echoing in the night.

Jackson finds a broom in Iggy's cleaning closet and sweeps up the glass. Cleans the vomit with a wet paper towel, sprays some Lysol on it, then finishes the job with a hand rag. Iggy finally stirs, inhaling the chemicals, his head twitching before he turns away from the stench.

"Unc," says Jackson. Then he says it louder.

Iggy opens his eyes.

"You missed the funeral." Jackson feels stupid as soon as the words leave his mouth.

"No shit." Iggy rubs his eyes. "Fix me a drink."

"You had enough."

"Boy," says Iggy. "Fix me a drink. Then fix yourself one."

Jackson walks behind the bar and watches Iggy sit up on the bed. Eyes swollen like he'd been crying. Tie loosened. Shirt untucked. Top two buttons missing. Iggy stands, walks over to the bar, and sits on a stool. "They send 'em off right, Jackie?"

"Closed casket," says Jackson and watches Iggy nod. "Peaceful," Jackson says. "No dumb shit."

Iggy glances at the two-way mirror. "Shit," he says. "That's gonna cost a couple grand to replace."

They both sip their drinks. "I had my share of ass," says Iggy. Hundreds of girls. Black, white, Asian. Hispanic. None of them were touching Ivy Green. You think Joy has curves? Her momma had tits *and* ass, pussy so good, Jackie, it was like it was singing to you."

Jackson takes in Iggy's words but doesn't speak. Vague memories of the Carters and the Greens getting pried apart. No explanation but an unspoken something. No more barbeques. No more Saturday nights. Only Joy and Jackson on the couch on Griggs Street. Then she was gone too.

"I loved her," says Iggy. "Still love her."

"Mrs. Green?"

"We were having an affair. Joy found us out and told it all. Rebellious, see? Pissed off at her momma. Tired of all the rules and regulations. Ivy kept Joy's fast ass on a tight leash. So Joy told George and the shit hit the fan. After all that sneaking around, all those what ifs, Ivy still chose George."

Jackson wants to question him about Joy, about letting her strip, about spite. He decides to save that attack for another day. And something about seeing his uncle slumped on the stool, broken by a wrong love, fills him with rage. The ghost of his love for Joy Green still lingers. Sleepless nights imagining her out there running the streets. Stung by those few weeks he thought she loved him back. After all that hurt, all these years, there is still that quiet old love that no amount of disappointment can seem to dissolve. How can he love Mae McCoy with Joy haunting around?

"My whole life, Jackie. I only loved one woman. And look at me— just some sad old fuck. All these goddamn years—same gaping hole in my chest."

"I'm sorry." It's all Jackson can muster.

"Don't be," says Iggy. "I should have known better. It's common knowledge: human beings crave worst for what they can't have."

•

Outside sirens whine in the night, but Mae feels safe beneath Jackson's arm. He is naked under the covers, sleeping. Mae lies on her back staring at the ceiling. A cool breeze sweeps in through the cracked-open window, and Mae needs it, the cool. She's still hot, something like the simmering coals that remain after a fierce fire. Glowing from the soul side out. It's like the sun rose somewhere in her stomach and sent heat through her from the waist down, her skin feeling the way a foot feels when it falls asleep.

They were kissing and whose hands wandered first she isn't sure, but then their clothes were off, and he was inside her body, and she liked how he felt, but then she closed her eyes and saw a white boy with eyes morphed into mean, then her pleasure morphed into pain, and she was sitting on the curb wrapped in Jackson's coat all over again, and Jackson must have read her mind because he stopped, and she opened her eyes, and Jackson said, "Baby, are you okay?" and Mae nodded, but the tears started coming, and Jackson kissed her forehead and said, "You're not ready" and he smiled and said, "We can wait as long as you need to," and there in that moment she knew she was falling in love.

But it was time to take control. That night at Grand Valley, Jeff, the little bastard, did not deserve the space he was occupying in her mind. Mae would not be ruled by fear. So as Jackson stared at her, his brown eyes lit by the moon, caressing her lips with his index finger, Mae said, "I'm ready, baby" and Jeff wasn't gone, but he was so quiet she could hardly tell he was there. Mae was healed the same way a wound heals, sealed with a scar, no longer feeling the pain, but left with a permanent reminder of where she'd been and what she'd endured.

Now her mind spins with new possibilities. Her plans never included a man. In her daydreams she was always alone, independent, in vague classrooms filled with featureless kids, who occupied seats but had no discernible faces. In fact, in her daydreams no one had faces. She'd see herself spending summers on exotic beaches, nose in a book, renting a small cottage—she always had neighbors, but they never had names—kids were always playing around her, but they were never her kids, there was

never a husband, or even a boyfriend. Sometimes she'd see herself traveling Europe. She'd be riding on a train from city to city, reading a map, people always near, but never with her. Now when she closes her eyes all she
sees is Jackson Carter. It's everything else that is vague.

And what would Daddy say? "You can do better." That's exactly
what Daddy would say if he saw Jackson with his working class clothes
and his working-class boots and his working-class house in this low-
er-class neighborhood. But Daddy would be wrong. He'd stand there in
his dark lawyer suit and tell Mae, "An educated black woman needs an
educated black man." The same philosophical rhetoric he'd been spewing for years, since Mae started high school and the stakes became real,
even after the divorce, when he left his beautiful-educated-black wife
for his average-looking-white secretary, the rhetoric hasn't changed.
He'd roll his eyes and do that deep, heavy-breath thing he does when
he's disappointed, if Mae told him the truth: That she was sleepwalk-
ing before she met Jackson Carter. That Jackson Carter woke her up
and made her feel alive. He'd say she is behaving like a child, and maybe
he'd be right, because Mae feels like a giddy little girl, laying here next
to this man.

Sleep is not claiming her any time soon. She slides from under
Jackson's arm and out of the bed. She kisses him on the cheek and
dresses. Steps into the hallway and down the stairs. Into the kitchen.
She runs dishwater and wets a rag. She wipes down counters, the stove
top, the inside of a refrigerator, which is empty besides a carton of milk,
some lunchmeat, and a few slices of Swiss cheese.

The cupboard beneath the sink is flooded with Schlitz cans. Spilled
beer aged into the wood; a reek so ripe Mae has to cover her nose. She
bags the empties and finds six spent Hennessy bottles hidden behind
the mountain of cans. She throws the bottles in the trash. A red flag goes
off in her mind, but her loud heart has committed to this feeling of love.
She imagines Jackson on nights they aren't together sipping from those
bottles. Drunk. Alone. Numbing his mind. But to what?

When the dishes are done she goes upstairs. She climbs into the bed with her clothes still on. Jackson reaches for her and wraps her in his arms. A hint of alcohol on his breath—a nip snuck from a stashed bottle when she wasn't looking, maybe. Or a few shots to the head before she arrived. We all have our demons, Mae rationalizes, with a slight swallow of fear. She's falling for this man. But what? What exactly is she falling for?

A crisp November breeze blows off the Grand River. Fallen leaves from nearby trees have been grabbed by the wind and are captured in dead weeds, tangled in the unkempt landscaping rocks in front of Iggy's Place. Iggy stands under the top hat sign, tugging on a cigar, smiling as Jackson approaches. Jackson hugs his uncle and kisses him on the cheek. He holds him for a moment before letting go.

"She why you been scarce, Jackie?" Iggy nods his head toward Mae McCoy, who's standing on the trestle bridge, her flat-ironed hair falling out of a wool hat, leaning over the railing like she's reading the graffiti on a concrete pillar.

"Been scarce because I'm switching careers. I start truck-driving school next week."

"No shit?"

"That's right. Fifty stacks a year driving an east coast route."

"That's all right, Jackie. All right." Iggy smiles. "So," he says. "Who's the girl?"

You don't see a girl like Mae McCoy coming. Not a loud thing about her but her soul. She's sexy but she doesn't know it. Strong willed and big brained. And humble. She baffles Jackson with her ability to hide all that body in her clothes.

"Her name's Mae, Unc. She's a good one. College graduate. Now she's teaching English over at Burton Middle School."

"Hmm."

"Hmm?"

"Yeah, hmm. You talk about the girl like you're reading me her resume." Iggy pulls on the cigar, skeptical eyes squinting, his head slanted at Jackson. "You know Joy Green came down here the other day."

"That right?" Jackson lights a cigarette and takes a deep drag. He blows smoke out his nose then glances over toward Mae to see if she's watching. She hates it when he smokes.

"Down here for what?"

"For her job back. Some sad shit, really. Looking rough. Real rough. When's the last time you seen her, Jackie?"

"Haven't seen her since the funeral." Jackson watches Iggy out the corner of his eye. "How you holding up, by-the-way?"

"Shit, I can't call it, Neph. What can you do? I'm breathing. Blood's coursing through my veins. At least George and Ivy went together. At least they didn't feel no pain."

"Let me ask you a question, Unc." Mae McCoy is everything that Joy Green isn't. Jackson can't imagine a scenario where Mae would be down here stripping at Iggy's Place. He can't imagine her falling for a con like Cesar Bolden. The drugs and porn and who-knows-what-else. Mae McCoy doesn't need rescuing. "Can a man love a woman when he is still thinking about someone else?"

Iggy puts his hand on Jackson's shoulder and looks out at the river. "Jackie," he says, "I spent my whole life thinking about Ivy Green. What good did that get me? A whole lotta ass and a whole lotta empty."

Jackson's uncle waves from across the river and Mae waves back. Jackson's only living family. She wants to meet him, but doesn't, Jackson offering, Mae declining, saying she'll meet him another time, that she didn't think it appropriate for the occasion: Jackson telling Iggy he was leaving his job at the club. But in truth she isn't ready. She hates to pass judgment, but judgment is pulling at her, making her wonder what type of man Iggy Carter is. Wonder what type of man runs the kind of club he runs. If a meat shop owner can even be a "type."

Mae watches Jackson hug his uncle goodbye and walk toward the bridge. Limping from an old football injury in a permanent way, like the past is part of him, something he wears as he moves through life. He smiles plenty, but Mae knows a lot of it is feigned. A front. She loves him and she thinks he loves her. Though Jackson's love is vague, elusive. The moment she begins believing in it his mind goes someplace else. She feels it when they kiss but there is so much he is not saying. So much Mae is scared to know.

Jackson stands beside her on the bridge. He reaches for her hand but doesn't look at her, just stares across the river to Iggy's Place, watching his uncle walk inside, thinking about who-knows-what or who-knows-who.

"What's over there you can't let go of?" Mae asks.

Jackson forces a smile, but can't stop his eyes from telling on him. He kisses Mae's hand. He cracks his neck. Left, then right. He takes a long breath and then stares at the sky. "I think I might love you."

"Yeah?" Mae says. "But what's stopping you?"

"Who says I'm being stopped?"

"The tone of your voice says."

"The past is one complicated motherfucker."

"True," says Mae. "But the present is simple." She kisses Jackson's cheek. "Simple as letting go."

"If I didn't know better, Mae McCoy—I'd say you were falling for me."

"And if I were falling? What would you say?"

"I'd say take me with you."

Jackson stands behind Mae with his hands on her naked hips. His chin is nestled between her neck and shoulder. Her bare ass feels cool against his thighs. The city below reminds him of Gotham. Darkness descends upon lit buildings, parked cars, the headlights of traffic. A swollen moon casts a pallid shadow across the river. From the twenty-seventh floor window of the Amway Grand Plaza Hotel it all seems so small.

Jackson felt like an orphan at the wedding. Most of the guests were Mae's sophisticated suburban Detroit family, no one there for Jackson besides a handful of Iggy's people, Iggy standing as his Best Man, smiling, drink in hand, cigar in mouth at the reception, charming the ladies, not bothering to notice he was way out of his league.

Jackson had spent the whole day nervous, sweating in his tux, waiting for a cracked-out Joy Green to come busting into the church and start flipping over pews. Hank McCoy's dark eyes following Jackson's every move, aggressively shaking Jackson's hand, his face softening when he submitted to the force of Jackson's grip.

Jackson kisses Mae's neck. His eyes still on the city below. "Your father can't stand me," he says.

"Daddy doesn't like anybody, baby," says Mae. "Besides, it isn't my daddy you married." She reaches around him and grabs his ass. Leans against the large window.

Jackson holds her tighter. Kisses her again. It's past midnight on a Saturday. Somewhere down there, away from the riverfront, out in the southeast side, Joy Green is on the prowl for her fix. His mind drifts to those weeks they spent together and he feels ashamed. His arms around his new bride, their honeymoon night, and still, after all these years he's thinking about Joy Green.

"Baby," says Mae. "Let's go back to bed."

Being with Mae was so much different than being with Joy. Joy was all body and no mind, no soul. Physically there, but her thoughts someplace else. But Mae, Mae is on another plateau. Her body, as ample as it is, a secondary thing, a vessel. Sex is a place they crawl into together and find something more.

They lie on top of the covers. Mae pulls Jackson close and presses her forehead against his. "I want to have a family with you," she says.

"Baby, we've been through this."

"I know, it's just—"

Jackson thinks of the injustice of it. A world that allows Joy Green to get pregnant taking that chance from Mae. Something about an ovarian cyst, some kind of cancer or something, a surgery. Mae gave him the biological breakdown, but she may as well have been speaking Spanish. The medical jargon, Jackson grasping only some of it, but the gist of it easy: Mae cannot get pregnant. In truth though, he is relieved she's barren. Kids were never part of his plan.

"A girlfriend I went to Grand Valley with is a social worker," says Mae. "She could get us some information about adopting, or foster care."

"That's really something you're interested in?" Jackson strokes her face. He kisses her forehead. He thinks of his father Jerome, missing one of his front teeth, smelling like vodka and Certs. He was a laugher before Jackson's mother died, before the cancer chewed her away. But when Annie Carter left this world she took Jerome's joy with her. There was no more laughter in the house on Griggs. The only smiles left were the smiles of a cynic, a bully, a sadistic prick with wandering hands and a quick temper, and no longer interested in being a dad.

"Two people don't make a family, Jackson."

Jackson thinks of the Hennessy. Those bitter nights. His childhood dream thieved by bitchass Robert McIntosh on a Friday night in November. The way the anger has its mitts on him. The way the beer is no longer enough to edge him down. He tries to imagine himself being a dad, but can't. He only sees Mae. Him and Mae in the haunted house on Griggs Street.

Is it Mae's imagination or is this woman being smug? With her tight, perfect, sandy-blonde ponytail. With her ten-dollar pen wedged behind her ear. With her condescending smile—that's what it is—that PhD grin she keeps flashing after every sentence, no teeth, just lips, scrunching her forehead a little and nodding, hoping to convey she's much more than a doctor, that she's someone who cares.

"Ms. Carter . . ."

"Mrs."

"Mrs. Carter," she tells Mae. "I'm sorry, there's just nothing we can do. Your uterine cavity is completely scarred. You're not getting enough blood supply to your endometrial lining. It is not possible for an embryo to implant."

"I've heard all of this," Mae says. "But you're supposed to be an expert. Is there no procedure? Is there nothing you can do?"

"I'm sorry."

Mae nods.

"Maybe," the doctor tells her. "It just wasn't meant to be."

A bronze cross hangs next to the bookshelf behind the doctor's desk. A framed picture of the doctor's family is propped against a row of thick hardcover books. Her husband is a wavy-haired strong-jawed ox wearing a teal Polo shirt. Their three handsome children pose with cross legs and folded hands.

"Have you considered a surrogate?" The doctor asks Mae.

"My husband would never go for that," Mae tells her. "Thank you very much for you time."

The doctor hands her a stack of pamphlets. "In case your husband changes his mind," she says. Another PhD grin.

Mae drops the pamphlets in the waste basket on her way out the door. She knows she should call in, but doesn't. She only ordered a half-day sub, is what she's telling herself, but it's probably not that big of a deal—a sub usually wouldn't mind staying another couple hours, or an interventionist or parapro could cover for her. The truth is that Jackson is on the road and she doesn't want to be alone. Not today. Not now.

Her classroom is empty when she arrives. Lunch will be over soon. This moment of silence will be swallowed by the noise of laughter and gossip and the awkward tone of pre-pubescent voices. All of these children. Jesus, what was she thinking? Making that appointment. Investing hope into a hopeless situation. And Jackson, as supportive as he's been, as convincing he's been when he tells her that she's all he needs, that kids don't matter to him, he couldn't possibly understand what this makes a woman feel like. How it makes Mae feel. Like a failure. Broken. Inadequate. Some kind of second-hand wife.

The sub has left a note. Kind of. *C.J.?!?!?!? Wow!!!* is all the note says, followed by a large drawing of a frownie face. The sub's talking about C.J. Grady, a bright boy, a truly bright boy, who always tests high, but never hands in his homework. He has a disinterested father and an overworked mother who has no time for conferences, no time to answer phone calls, or emails, or notes home—no time for any correspondence at all.

Mae should have taken the rest of the day off. She will. Right now before the kids come in asking where she was and she has some kind of psychotic breakdown in front of them. Because she feels it coming: the anger, the hopelessness. The pain and no place to put it. Mae grabs her purse just as the bell rings and beats the hallway traffic. She steps into the office and finds Maggie the admin and just as she's about to speak she sees C.J. Grady sitting outside the principal's office, wearing a picked-on expression, folding a piece of paper into some kind of origami animal. The boy is dreaded and a head taller than most of the seventh graders in the school. He's no stranger to the office, though he rarely gives Mae any trouble.

"Hey, Mrs. Carter," he says.

"Hi, C.J." Mae says. "Why are you down here?"

"Your sub's racist," he says.

"Racist?"

"Yeah. Racist. I told her when I grow up I'm gonna be the first black president. Bitch laughed at me. Told me I better cut my hair."

"So you called her the 'B' word? That's why you're down here?"

"Whatever," says C.J. "She is a 'B' word."

Mae starts to laugh, but she manages to keep her composure. Outside the office door stands a women wearing a hair scarf and a scowl like hell's coming. She buzzes the intercom and taps on the glass window of the wooden door with her bony fist. "Get your ass over here, C.J." She says when she's finally let in. She bites down on her bottom lip then says, "now" without taking her teeth off of the lip.

"Miss Grady," says Maggie the admin. "If you want to have a seat, Mr. Powers will see you in a minute."

"I don't wanna see no goddamn Mr. Powers. I had to punch out to come down here. You hear me C.J.? I had to punch out to come down here. The third time the last two weeks. You're gonna get me fired! Then what? You gonna go live with that deadbeat nigga you call your daddy? Can't shut your goddamn mouth and be respectful—I'm gonna lose my job, C.J. You hear me? I'm gonna lose my job!"

First Miss Grady is crying and then something changes in her. The scowl is back. Hell is back, leaking out of her eyes, aching to fill this room. Maggie the admin is already reaching for the phone. Then Miss Grady is choking her son, his head, his dreads bouncing against the wall, and Mae watches Mr. Powers and some other suited man rush out and pause for a moment, and in the space of that pause, Mae's anger finally boils over, her hopelessness comes to a head, and she's livid, and before she realizes what she's doing, she has Miss Grady by her scarf, and she's yanking back her head, and screaming, "Leave that boy alone!" Then the woman's eyes change back into the eyes of a mother. *A mother*, thinks Mae, disgusted, bitter, watching C.J.'s mom, who now has love and guilt all over her, and Mae's thinking this bitch doesn't even deserve to be one, before she lets go, shoves the woman aside and stands between her and C.J. "You should be ashamed of yourself," says Mae. "This boy is precious. And you don't even know what a gift you have."

J ackson shouldn't be down here. That's what his conscience is saying. Watching Joy walk up and down Division in busted heels, one with a chipped kickstand, the other with a broken strap dangling across the front. He watches her step up to a parked car, braless, her breasts hanging as her frail arms lean against the passenger side window. Her son sits on a curb digging into a sidewalk crack with a twig, toying with ants, nonchalant, like his mother out here tricking isn't new digs.

Jackson sits in his black Ford F150, curbside, about ten feet away from the boy, about thirty feet from Joy, his hands gripping the steering wheel, the truck idling, its engine humming. He considers snatching her up. He thinks about tossing Joy and her son into his truck, dropping her off at rehab. But where would the boy go with George and Ivy dead? With Cesar Bolden? Into the system?

"Fuck you then!" yells Joy. Jackson watches the car peel away. Joy adjusts her hair. She looks left and then right. She brushes off her shirt like she trying to put herself back together, gather her confidence. Then she notices Jackson. She picks up her son and starts toward him. Jackson shifts the truck into drive, and pauses before pulling off. "Jackie, wait!" Joy screams when Jackson lets off the brake and drives off, feeling small, watching them in his rearview mirror.

M ae answers the doorbell and finds a heavy chested black woman and a small gray-eyed black boy standing on the porch. The woman's on something, or needing something. She's obscenely thin, her nipples showing through a pink Puma T-shirt with a grease stain around the collar. Her eye sockets are like caves. Her eyes like she's only half-alive. The boy is wearing high-waters and his hair isn't brushed. He looks around five or six, smells like he hasn't bathed in a week. His facial expression screams *save me.*

"Where's Jackie?" asks the woman.

"Who are you?" says Mae.

"Bitch, who are you?"

"I'm Mae Carter," says Mae, "Jackson's wife."

At this the woman smiles. Adjusts her hair. Wets her ashy lips with her pale pink tongue. "Aw shit," she says. "Jackie finally found somebody."

"Okay," says Mae, "and who are you exactly?"

"I'm who you ain't," she says. "You just a replacement bitch. I'm the one he couldn't have. I'm the one who chose another nigga."

"What's your name?"

"I think you know my name," she says, scratching her arms. The boy looks at his shoes.

"I'm sorry," says Mae. "I don't."

"Joy," she says. "Joy Motherfucking Green."

"Jackson never mentioned you," Mae says. But she wonders why. The woman looks familiar, but from where, Mae can't say. Whoever she is, or was, she is no more. Clearly on drugs and maybe in trouble, glancing down the block, the boy now staring up at Mae like he's begging to be let in the house. "Why are you here, Joy?"

"My son, I—"

"What does this boy have to do with Jackson?" Mae wonders if the boy is Jackson's. Wonders if Jackson could keep something like that from her.

"I just—"

"Leave him," says Mae. She didn't see the words coming, but they came, soaring from her chest, out of her mouth, and smacking this Joy Green right across the grill.

"With you?"

"What? You'd rather bring him where you're going?"

"Bitch, you—" she starts, but then she picks up the boy. "Miles, baby," she says. Joy Green kisses her son on the cheek. The boy frowns and turns away. He wipes the kiss off of his face. "Baby, Mommy will be back, okay?"

All week Jackson had been on the road. Ohio. Pennsylvania. New York. Brooding behind the wheel of his big rig, searching for the root of Mae's strange tone of voice the last time they had spoken on the phone. His suspicion was a miracle pregnancy. Something hiding in her words: happy or excited, something too big to tell him until he got home.

The truth comes the moment he walks through the front door. A lump under a blanket on the couch. Jackson walks over and peels back the cover. A young boy is sleeping, smelling like Dove soap and lavender shampoo. Jackson knows who he is. Why he is here, Jackson imagines, is Joy Green has finally met a rock bottom she couldn't bring him to. Jackson feels a tinge of guilt, remembering the day a few weeks ago when he saw the boy on Division.

Jackson limps up the stairs and finds Mae awake in the bedroom, nose in a book, the bedspread folded over her waist, reading lamp beaming across her serious brow.

"Is he yours, Jackson?" Mae asks, not looking up from her book.

"No."

"Who is Joy Green?"

"A sad story," says Jackson. He walks across the room and kisses Mae on the cheek.

"That's not good enough, Jackson."

"Joy Green's nothing but a ghost, babe."

"Who is she, Jackson?" Mae finally looks up from her book. No tears but they're coming. Her bottom lip quivering. "Do you love her?"

Jackson tells her everything. The same story of his past only this time Joy Green is in it. He's not alone on that couch when his father's off drinking, when his mother's dead. This time he tells Mae how it broke his heart when Joy Green left for Motown. About the anger he felt when she was stripping Iggy's Place. About Cesar Bolden. About the weeks Joy Green was living in this very house.

Mae takes it all in with no expression. She doesn't cry. "Come here, baby," she says. She folds her book and sets it on the nightstand.

Jackson sits on the edge of the bed.

"Tell me it's me and only me. If that's the truth, Jackson, tell me. Tell me that and I'll believe you."

Jackson takes her hand. "It's only you, Mae. Since I met you, it's only been you."

There's a silent moment between them before Mae finally lets the tears fall. She smiles and wipes her eyes. "Okay, baby. Okay."

Jackson leans over and kisses her. Rubs her shoulder and then stands. He takes off his shirt, his jeans, until he's down to his boxer shorts, opening dresser drawers, finding clean clothes. "How long has the boy been here?" Jackson asks without turning around.

"A couple days."

"What's he like?" Jackson wonders how involved Cesar Bolden has been in the boy's life. What kind of crack houses the kid has been in and out of? What kind of shit he's seen his mother do, or get done to her?

"Funny," says Mae. "And never stops talking. Listen, Jackson, I don't think his mother is coming back for him."

"No?" Jackson turns. Fresh boxers in hand. Some clean shorts to sleep in.

"No. She had this look in her eyes when she left. Like she was saying good-bye for good. Don't be mad, baby, but I talked to my friend Doreen, the social worker. She's going to find out what we have to do to keep him."

"After all I just told you?"

"The boy deserves a chance."

"The boy has a father," Jackson says, and knows how stupid the words sound coming out of his mouth.

"Five minutes ago his father was the devil himself. Listen, Jackson, I want to do this. I know it seems strange, this woman, the past—it just," Mae says. "It just feels like the right thing to do."

The Wreckage
Summer 2008

IT'S ELEVEN ON A SUNDAY MORNING. THE sun hides behind the clouds. Lyric's hand hurts in her mother's firm grip. She's being dragged along, her mother wearing what she calls her business face, showing no teeth, her eyes lost in dark sunglasses. Two men sit huddled on a concrete slab under one side of an old blue railroad bridge. They share a twenty-four-ounce Steel Reserve Beer. A beer Lyric's mother drinks nightly, Just One, her mother likes to say, but the empties are piled beneath the sink in their two-bedroom apartment, enough beer spilled and soaked into the floor of the wooden cupboard to make the kitchen smell stale.

Lyric waves as her mother leads her across the bridge. One of the men waves back, his hand partially hidden beneath a fingerless black glove. The other takes his turn with the beer and gazes out at the river like there is something there besides the brown water.

Joey used to bring her down here sometimes. They'd walk a cement path to the Fishladder where men would be flicking bamboo poles, occasionally pulling out large ugly fish with gaping eyes. They would watch them for a while and then cross back over the bridge to a grassy area. Her father would thread a night crawler onto a hook, cast out their one line, and hand the pole to Lyric. They would wait for the bobber to move, but it rarely did.

"Mom, why are we walking so fast?"

"I have to see about a job, baby."

"You have a job."

"A better job."

"Why can't I go to Grammy's?"

"Me and Grammy ain't talking right now, baby."

They reach the end of the bridge and step up a walkway toward a small building with a large black Abraham-Lincoln-hat-looking light cocked sideways on the roof, *Iggy's Place* in bubble letters next to it. They approach a man with black hair streaked with silver. He's smoking a cigar. He lifts his brown-tinted sunglasses and lets them settle on top of his head of tight curls. "Tara?" he asks.

"That's right." Lyric's mother folds her arms.

"Iggy Carter." The man looks down at Lyric and smiles. "And what's your name, Little Momma?"

"Lyric."

"That's a pretty name." Iggy reaches into his pants pocket and hands her three sour apple Jolly Ranchers'.

"Thank you," Lyric says.

"You're welcome."

Iggy leads them into the building and Lyric notices a glass cage connected by ceiling and floor. It reminds her of those capsules you put money in at a bank drive-through. She imagines climbing in, hitting a button, and being transported to another world.

"What's this, Mr. Iggy?" she asks him.

Iggy ignores her. He looks at Tara the way Lyric's Grammy does sometimes. "This ain't no place for children," Iggy says. "You got babysitter issues? Cause if you bring her to work with you, you'll be sent home."

"No issues," says Tara. "baby," she says to Lyric, "why don't you go over there and play on that stage. So me and Mr. Carter can have some grown-up talk."

•

Isaac Page rides shotgun in a Chevy Cavalier. Backpack between his feet. The Grand River behind him. The tall business buildings flanking its banks disappearing in the car's rearview mirror. Isaac's hooded head rests against the window. He watches his breath appear and then fade into the glass. Almost twelve years old now, Francis Street behind him, Isaac thumbs the tattered skin of the late Joey Cane's basketball.

"We can get you a new ball." The driver is a social worker named Doreen, a square-bodied black woman with shiny pink lip-gloss and micro braids. "One without the rubber showing through the leather."

"No, thank you." Isaac looks past Doreen and gazes out at the city. To his left is Veterans Memorial Park. A place where the homeless like to gather. They lean against pillars. They sit on the edge of a fountain. One man lies in the grass with his head propped on an Army duffel, sipping from a pint of Five O'Clock vodka. Beyond the park is the public museum and beyond that is Grand Rapids Community college, the place where Isaac's parents met, when Frank Page was a janitor and Nelly Terpstra was a Calvin College exile. But Isaac doesn't know that story.

"You'll like it at the Carters," says Doreen.

Isaac has already been briefed. The dad: a former high school football star turned truck driver. The mom: a schoolteacher. The foster brother: another hard-luck kid like he is.

"I mean it," Doreen says. "I've known Mae Carter for years, Isaac. It won't be like the group home, I promise."

The group home: Fight back or get beat down daily. Fight back or they take everything that matters to you. Break a bully's nose and they leave you alone.

Doreen makes a right onto Jefferson Street and guides the Cavalier into the bowels of the southeast side. They pass aging brick buildings with concrete lawns. They travel over potholed roads. Past the Kent County Human Services building, a three-story tomb of brick and glass, its sidewalk perimeter stained with cigarette smokers, curb squatters, people walking back and forth talking to their hands.

Houses are pinched together with only feet between them, paint peeling like sunburnt skin. Porches lean. Sidewalks are cracked and raised by roots. Chain-link fences sag and bend. Brittle brown grass is dying on unmowed lawns. The Cavalier hooks a left onto Griggs and brakes in front of a powder blue house with a concrete porch. Doreen doesn't look at Isaac when she says, "We're here."

•

Jackson Carter sets Isaac's suitcase on the living room floor. His beige head is shaved bald and casts a baby oil gleam. Two days' stubble surrounds a snarly black goatee. He looks like a giant to Isaac, like a power forward, or an out-of-costume Batman. Jackson's smiling but his eyes are cold. Like his face is fixed in a permanent state of *Motherfucker, please.* Isaac knows this look, knows the numbness. A look like Jackson has seen life's worst and has emerged scathed and changed. A look that Joey Cane had.

Mae Carter is tall and slim and light-skinned. Soft spoken. Her breath smells like orange Tic Tacs. Isaac notices a small scar on her left cheekbone and wonders how she earned it; imagines her in a slapping match with another girl, or falling off of a banana-seat bicycle and going face-first into the sidewalk.

The foster brother, Miles is a handsome long-limbed kid with light brown skin, a sly smile. He hovers on the edge of the room, a smirk lurking in his silver eyes. Isaac wonders how Miles landed at the Carters. Wonders his history, what he'd been through—why, after whatever he'd been through, he's standing here now smiling, like the past never happened.

The Carters' place is strange and friendly. Isaac feels as if he's slipped into a dream, or another world. It scares him, what seems like a functional family—he's so used to hiding in Joey Cane's driveway, or his books, or his journals, unseen. He notices a massive stained-oak bookshelf that takes up most of a wall. There are hundreds, possibly a thousand titles organized by author. Isaac stands in front of it, running his index finger over bindings, checking them for dust, finding none.

Mae, watching Isaac, says, "Doreen told me you like to read, Isaac. If you want, you can have the far right corner for your own books."

Isaac flinches when Mae touches his shoulder and she steps away. Isaac cradles Joey Cane's basketball in his arm. The backpack strapped to him contains his own modest collection of books (*The Adventures of Tom Sawyer, The Adventures of Huckleberry Finn, The Hobbit, The Lord of the Rings Trilogy*), and four spiral notebooks. Isaac tells her thanks, but no thanks without taking his eyes off of the shelves.

He is worried they will ask about his parents, but they don't. They don't ask about the group home he had lived in the five months before arriving here. They don't ask him anything. Just watch him like he is standing in an invisible cage.

"Miles," tries Mae, "has been with us since he was five."

Isaac pretends not to hear her. He thumbs through Mae's books, books he's never heard of, authors he's never heard of, still hiding under his hood, rolling the basketball against his ribs. The Carters study his silence. They urge Miles over to him with head nods and hand signals. Jackson Carter clears his throat.

"Sup, bro," says Miles, extending a fist.

Isaac taps it with his own. "Hey." Isaac sees Jackson put a bulky arm around his wife, sees Mae Carter smile.

"Miles," says Mae, "why don't you help Isaac bring his things up to the room?"

Isaac follows Miles up the stairs and into their shared bedroom. The walls on Miles's side are plastered with magazine cut-outs of rappers and athletes and half-naked women. Miles sets Isaac's suitcase on one of two beds and shows Isaac which dresser and closet is his. Isaac places Joey Cane's basketball next to the suitcase and begins unpacking his clothes. He puts socks and boxer shorts into drawers, hangs shirts and pants in his closet, which is empty besides a couple dozen thick plastic hangers.

"You don't talk much, huh?" says Miles.

Isaac ignores him.

"Silent type," Miles says. "That's cool. I'm telling you now, though, you better keep that hood off in the house or Jackson's gonna kick your ass."

Isaac peels back the hood and picks up the basketball, flips it in his hands.

"You hoop, yo?"

"A little," says Isaac.

"What does G.H. mean?" asks Miles.

"George Hessler."

"Who's that?"

"Some asshole." The same response Joey Cane had given him. Two words. Two nails in a coffin. Case closed.

"Fuck you got some asshole's initials on your ball for?"

"It was my friend's ball. He wrote the initials on there."

Miles thoughts go from brain to mouth, no filter, harmless but annoying—like his words are a finger tapping against Isaac's mind.

"Where you from?"

"From here," Isaac says. "I used to live on Francis."

"Why don't I know you?"

Isaac shrugs.

"This your first foster family?"

"Yeah."

"What about your parents?"

They didn't ask a lot of questions at the group home. They just assumed you were the same kind of unlucky as they were: orphaned or abused or neglected. Handed to the State of Michigan with an invisible *Treat With Care* sticker stuck to your forehead and herded into the system.

But Isaac's surprised Miles hadn't heard what happened—the news coverage—Frank Page gone missing, Isaac's mother lying dead in the living room.

"My mom had a deal with Motown but she got shelved," says Miles. "You know what shelved means?"

Isaac shakes his head. Those loud knocks. All that blood. The light in his mother's eyes gone.

"They didn't put her album out," says Miles. "They sat on it for a couple years and then dropped her. Then she started stripping and got all messed up on drugs. That's how I ended up here."

Isaac shuts off his mind and focuses on Miles. He doesn't know how to respond. Miles doesn't seem too bent about his ordeal. He speaks like he's reciting facts from a book, like he's summarizing someone else's life story.

"Last year they found her floating in the river. Just another dead junkie. The Carters didn't tell me that," says Miles. "My daddy did. And Jackson don't like him. One time he came down here and Jackson snatched him out of his Cadillac and beat the shit out of him. My daddy threatened to come back and kill Jackson, but he let it slide. He still comes around from time to time—catches me out at Garfield Park, gives me a few dollars. But like I said, Jackson don't like him, so you gotta keep that secret, okay?"

Isaac wonders why Miles isn't living with his dad if his dad is around. Wonders where Frank is. Wonders if he's still alive. First Joey then Nelly. Too much death.

Isaac agrees to keep Miles' secret with a nod.

"The Carters are cool, bro," Miles keeps on. "Jackson don't play, though. Disrespect that man and he'll put you on your ass. Mae's like Claire Huxtable—but this ain't *The Cosby Show*. She can be as sweet as she wanna be, but when Jackson hits that bottle the walls start shaking around here. Trust me—you see Jackson drinking Hennessey and Coke, keep your distance."

"Okay," says Isaac.

"Hey, bro, you feel like going up to Garfield? You wanna hoop?"

"Sure." Isaac stuffs the last of his clothes into the dresser and picks up the ball. He stands there looking at Miles like he needs permission to leave the room. Miles leads him down the stairs.

"Hey," Mae says, "you guys are leaving?" She's aproned and oven-mitted. Smiling and motherly. Miles was right: Mae Carter is a sitcom mom. Not like Isaac's mother was, with her forced smile and worried eyes, waiting until she thought Isaac was asleep and then slithering out of the house and into the night, past Joey Cane's and down the street to who-knows-where.

"Park," says Miles.

"Dinner's at six." Mae's smile is real and it's weird feeling wanted. Like they bought him from a store. From Goodwill. Like the Carters walked through the aisles of the second-hand mart and saw something with potential. Like Isaac was a thing they could bring home and polish, tinker with, see what they could come up with.

When they step outside Miles scans the street. "Look, Man," he says, "just be cool. Let the block get used to you. Ain't too many white boys around here."

"I'm not scared," says Isaac.

"You don't have to be scared to get your ass kicked, yo."

Isaac tucks Joey Cane's basketball in his arm. Pulls his hood over his head.

"It's summertime, Man. Fuck you wearing a hoodie for?"

Isaac shrugs and steps down onto the walkway. He dribbles through his legs, alternating hands with each step. "You coming?" Isaac asks.

Garfield Park has two basketball courts leaning back to back. A concrete runway of faded paint surrounded by a multitude of empty benches. Half-chewed nets hang from thick rims. They sway to and fro in a crisp lifting breeze. Isaac dribbles a few times, grips the ball with both hands, raises it to eyelevel, and shoots. The ball spins on its arc. The net snaps. "Change," he says and Miles passes him the ball.

"You gotta step back, bro," Miles says, "NBA range for change."

Isaac dribbles through his legs as he takes a few steps backward behind the three-point line. Flick. Snap.

"For real, Man, how you learn to ball like this?"

"I made friends with the concrete." The words of Joey Cane. He runs his fingers across the G.H. on Joey's old ball. Francis Street is only a few blocks from here, but it seems so much further. A different state. Another realm.

"Shit, Man. You might do okay around here. Me, I hoop a little, but my shit is music. You got flow?"

"Huh?"

"Can you spit? Rap, man, can you rap?"

Isaac had grown up around hip hop music on Francis Street. Bass lines and f-bombs spewing from the open windows of rusted cars with large wheels, gleaming rims, and squealing tires. He heard the music, but like background noise, or backdrop noise, a mural of noise-graffiti floating somewhere in the traffic of his mind. It was the music of the southeast side that Isaac wrote to. Filing Mead notebooks to the sounds of dogs barking, sirens, women shouting at their men. The drunken laughter of smokers on porches. He wrote to no audience but himself. But as the months droned on and the journals filled with words, when Joey Cane went from being in Isaac's life to being gone, what he was doing on the page began to evolve. What was once a rant was becoming something more; Isaac knew it, but didn't have a name for it. He needed it, the release. Where the concrete kept his pain at bay, the page gave the pain a place to go.

Flick. Snap. "No," says Isaac. "I can't rap. I never tried."

A couple black kids walk up, one gangly, rocking a mid-high fade, wearing baggie And 1 shorts and a matching top. The other not quite as tall, but stocky, wearing a Jordan brand jersey and a red Nike hat that's cocked sideways.

"Sup, Geno. Sup K.D.," says Miles.

"Who's the white boy?"

"This is Isaac," he says to the gangly one, "Isaac, this is Geno." He looks at the stocky one. "That's K.D."

"Hey," Isaac says.

"Sup," Geno and K.D. say in unison. "Y'all wanna run twos?" says Geno.

"Run it," Miles says. "Zick, shoot for rock."

Flick. Snap.

"I got the white boy," says Geno to K.D. "You d-up Miles."

"Check." Isaac flips the ball to Geno. Geno tosses it back. "Ones and twos make-it-take-it?" says Isaac. "Game 11 win by 2?"

"Bet," says Geno.

Flick. Snap. "Two nothing," says Isaac. "Check." He learned at the group home no one gives you respect. You have to earn it. There was one rim on one small slab of cement, a freethrow line and a three-point arc spray-painted on the court haphazardly, the trail of black paint kissing a wall of weeds just after it began to curve.

Flick. Snap. "Four," says Isaac. "Check." Isaac wasn't the smallest kid at the group home, but he was the only one who was white. To stay on the court, you had to win. There were no fouls called, no rules, few openings to shoot. When you got the chance to get off a shot you couldn't miss. In Joey's driveway it was fundamentals. It was theory. At the group home they shoved you into the grass when you tried to shoot it. Took out your legs when you left the ground.

"Bet you don't make another one," says Geno.

Flick. Snap. "Six," says Isaac.

"Play d, bro!" says K.D.

Isaac pump fakes and gets Geno off his feet. He dribbles past him and K.D. comes over to help. Isaac drops a dime to a slashing Miles and Miles lays up the ball. It rattles around the rim before falling through the net.

"Fuck!" Geno slams the ball against the concrete and it soars into the air.

Isaac catches the ball off the second bounce. He watches Geno's hands, clenched in fists; Geno pacing back and forth.

"Seven," says Isaac. "Check." He tosses Geno the ball.

Geno holds the ball for a moment and cocks his head. He chews the inside of his cheek. A devilish smile crawls across his face. He turns to Miles. "This muh fucka an orphan, Miles?" He glances at Isaac, then back at Miles. "He a Carter Kid, like you is?" Geno is six inches taller than either Miles or Isaac, at least a couple years older. Big hands. Bony knuckles. A small hole in the right toe of some black Nike throwback Dopemans. "Aw shit! Muh fucka's an orphan, K.D."

K.D. laughs. "Little Orphan Annie."

"Where'd y'all find him, Miles? Was he digging in the Carters' trash, yo? He looks scurvy," says Geno, laughing hard now.

"Check up," says Isaac.

"Did the stork take a shit on your porch, yo?" says K.D.

"Aw, Miles, look at your white boy. Muh fucka's pissed. Look at those eyes, yo! He looks like a wolf." Geno feigns throwing the ball at Isaac's head and Isaac flinches. "Now I gotta hit you, white boy. Two for flinching, right?" Geno taps Isaac on his shoulder with his fist once, then blasts him on it the second time.

Isaac looks to Miles for help and Miles looks away. It was the same at the group home. Catch a kid one-on-one and he acts like your best friend in the world. Soon as the bullying starts your best friend no longer knows you.

"Where'd you get him, Miles? You find him in the wilderness. Little Tarzan muh fucka with a basketball? Little vending machine kid: pop in a quarter, out jumps a scurvy little white boy. Aw shit, this muh fucka's gonna cry, yo!"

"Check up," says Isaac.

Geno tosses the ball to Isaac. "Here, white pussy. My Uncle Rosco would be all over your ass. Nigga's crazy about white pussy. Bet you don't score again though, white pussy."

Isaac pumps but Geno's feet stay planted this time. Isaac dribbles left, hesitates, and then crosses right. He accelerates toward the basket, goes to layup the ball, and Geno shoves him into the pole. Isaac falls to the concrete. Geno stands over him. "Said you wouldn't score."

•

A heavy rain slaps the concrete. Puddles form in low cracked portions of the court. A dark ceiling of clouds makes the evening look like night. Miles ran home when the lightning sprawled across the sky. Others retreated when the first drops of rain fell. But Isaac embraces the weather, the sound of it, the feel of it pelting against his head—it puts him at ease. He is alone and freed. The eyes of the block are gone. There is no need to crawl into his mind and hide.

Griggs is only a few streets away from Francis and it's the same shade of gray. Men with forty ounce beers sitting on porches. Talking shit to anybody walking down the sidewalk, hollering at young girls, thirteen-year-olds with tits and ass and aching with stupidity. Stopping when they're asked to stop. Smiling when they're told they're their cute. Pregnant before they're out of middle school.

Joey Cane told Isaac to never smile when he comes outside. Watch the block without the block knowing you're watching. Keep your mind on what you're doing and they'll leave you alone. Isaac dribbles his basketball and keeps his eyes on everything and nothing. They see him and he sees them and no one says a word. But Joey won't leave this place. He's a southeast side ghost. Isaac still hears his voice. Still sees him puffing on a cigarette. Cracking his knuckles. Walking down the street toward his death.

The gunshots became louder after Joey died. Isaac's been hearing them on the southeast side for years, but before Joey was murdered they were nothing more than loud snaps in the night. Now they are real. Bullets that hit something. A car door. A window. A ball. A child playing with her Lincoln Logs in the living room. But most times they hit nothing. Nothing according to the news. All these guns and all these bullets—only occasionally someone shot or killed. Imagine this place if the shooters had aim.

Isaac watches Jackson Carter's Ford F150 pull into the parking lot, windshield wipers chasing the rain, horn honking.

Dribble. Dribble. Flick. Snap. The ball dies in a puddle beneath the hoop. Isaac retrieves it. Dribbles out to the three-point arc.

The horn honks again.

Flick. Snap. Again, the ball dies.

Jackson cuts off the engine. He's soaked by the time he reaches the court. Isaac retrieves the ball as Jackson approaches. Jackson's expression teeters between angry and impressed.

"Boy, what the hell are you doing out here?" Jackson says.

"It's just rain," says Isaac. He shoots. The ball rotates on its arc and rolls off the rim.

Jackson catches the rebound.

"You're late for dinner," says Jackson. "You got Mae worried. Day One, Isaac, and you got Mae worried."

"I'm sorry, Mr. Carter."

"Jackson, Isaac. Just call me Jackson."

Jackson watches Isaac weave the basketball through his legs, each step a dribble, the ball as much a part of his body as his hands. The sun pulses in a cloudless sky. A hot, sticky Sunday, Michigan-humid and just past noon. Isaac has been at the Carters' house for the past six weeks and by Jackson's assessment is adjusting well. The kid puts it all into ball. Not unlike Jackson as a child, up before the sun like a black Rocky, doing push-ups, pull-ups, jogging to Houseman field and jumping the fence, running the bleachers until his legs burned.

"The kid has skills," says Miles.

Jackson nods. He pulls off his sweaty white T-shirt and stuffs it in the back pocket of his jean shorts. A woman unloading groceries from her car breaks her neck to check him out, smiling from across the street.

"Show off," says Miles. He smirks.

"When you got it," says Jackson, "you got it." Miles is the spitting image of his punk-ass father. Often Jackson has to fight the urge to backhand the smirk off of his face. Jackson can't help seeing the Cesar Bolden in him. Jackson's believes nurture can overcome genetics, but the boy has something slick about him. Hopefully it's an innocent slick. A sly or crafty slick, not a Cesar slick, the kind of slick that knows how to finger fuck the world.

"Well," says Miles, "you might be diesel, Jackson. But you sure as hell can't hoop. Yo, Zick," he says. Again, that smirk. "This man shoots bricks so hard you can hear it from down the street."

They approach the court and Isaac dribbles ahead and lays up the ball. Jackson walks behind him. A small circle of boys off to the side of the court are doing that rap battle thing they do. Jackson's eyes are on Miles, standing at the edge of the court, weighing which way to go. Jackson remembers Miles' mother, the Joy Green of his youth, standing in his living room, holding a television remote like a microphone, Jackson and his rubber Hulk Hogan, Iron Sheik, and Junkyard Dog wrestlers propped up on the couch like an audience.

"You know you're too pretty to be a rapper, right?" Jackson steps onto the court. He shakes his head and smiles when Miles goes the other way.

"I don't run much anymore," says Jackson to Isaac, "but I can catch rebounds for you."

"Thanks." Isaac stands ready to shoot from the top of the arc. Flick. Snap.

"Couple more years you'll be in high school," Jackson says. "You keep practicing and the college recruiters will be beating down the door." The kid isn't impressed. He dribbles a few steps back and shoots. Misses. Jackson palms the rebound and casually hooks it through the hoop. "You ain't thinking about college ball?"

"Don't know."

"No hoop dreams? NBA fame. Millions?"

Isaac shrugs. Jackson tosses him the ball. "Then why five in the morning, Son? Why in the rain. Shit, winter time you'll probably be out here in the snow, freezing your little nuts off, shooting this beat-down ball through a frozen net."

Flick. Snap. "I don't know," says Isaac. "It's just what I do."

Jackson twirls Isaac's battered basketball in his hands. He remembers the old football he used to run around with, a present from his late grandfather, the source of his white roots and his large frame. A former quarterback at the University of Iowa, a heart attack taking him at age fifty-two, and after his death, the entire family beginning its spiral downward.

"This was your friend's ball?"

"Yeah."

"He's the one who taught you how to play?"

"Yeah."

Jackson admires the boy's strength. How he's managed to keep his shit together is beyond Jackson. With his friend getting murdered. Being there when his mother died. Doreen said Isaac's father was on drugs. Said the police found Isaac's mother lying on the living room carpet. Head split open by a thrown chair. Frank Page went missing, vanished. Jackson suspects he's dead. O.D'd or murdered. Owing money to someone he shouldn't have owed. Isaac gives his grief to the concrete. It makes sense. But Jackson can't help but wonder: what happens when the concrete is gone? What happens when the grief digs itself out of the darkness?

"Everything good, Isaac? I mean, they treating you okay out here?"

"Yeah, Jackson. I'm fine."

"Okay. But if you need anything..."

"Alright." Isaac shoots and the ball bounces off the rim. Jackson turns to catch it and sees a taupe Cadillac pulling into the parking lot. Washed. Waxed. Shimmering in the sun. The ball rolls off the court into a small patch of grass next to the sidewalk leading to the parking lot. Miles hasn't noticed the car. He has his back to the lot, head bobbing, hand cupped and making a motion like it's pushing down air.

Jackson scoops the ball and tosses it to Isaac. He shields the sun with his hand and stares down the walkway at Cesar Bolden's ride. Tires screech when the Caddy peels away. Jackson watches Miles' eyes follow the car out of the parking lot, watching it pimp-turn onto Madison Avenue.

•

Jackson opens the freezer door and pulls out a pint of Hennessey and a tray of ice cubes. He twists off the cognac's cap, sips, and then sets it on the counter. Jackson opens a cupboard door and takes out a large glass. He bends the ice cube tray and loosens the cubes. He drops two into the bottom of the glass. Pours in half the pint of Hennessey. Takes another sip before twisting the cap back on and placing the bottle and tray back into the freezer.

Jackson steps into the living room and sits in his recliner. He goes for the television remote but then changes his mind. He needs silence. He needs to calm himself down and wait for the hum-of-the buzz-of-the Hen to quiet his mind. That man. Jackson knows Cesar Bolden's been creeping around, seeing Miles on the sly, and who knows what lies he's putting in that boy's head. So Jackson sips, and waits, and drinks a couple tall boy Schlitz, and then pours the rest of the Hennessy in his glass, and sips some more.

By the time Mae walks through the front door Jackson is buzzed and brooding. And Mae takes one look at him and knows. "It's the middle of the afternoon, Jackson," she says.

"That's right."

"And you're already drunk?"

He lets her words hang for a moment. He's sees that taupe Caddy. Imagines the smirk of Cesar Bolden as he peeled out of the parking lot earlier. "I think Cesar Bolden's been coming around seeing Miles," Jackson finally says.

"And?"

"What you mean, *and*? You aren't worried about Miles?"

"Are we talking about Miles or are we talking about you, Jackson?"

"What's that supposed to mean?"

"Nevermind. Where are the boys?"

"They're still at the park."

"Okay." Mae sits in her recliner. She doesn't look at Jackson when she says, "You know, I'm real tired of you glooming this house with your regrets."

"What regrets?" Jackson takes a large swig from his glass.

Mae shakes her head. "That's your answer for everything." She waves her hand in the direction of the Hennessy. "Numb it away."

"Regrets? What regrets? I'm trying to protect this family."

"Whatever."

They sit in silence. Jackson knows he's drinking too much. Too often. Knows she's right. Mae's changing. Or sick of Jackson choosing not to. Isaac was her idea and Jackson didn't like it: bringing a white kid into a black home—after all the boy had already been through. Jackson conceded though, to buy some time. Something had to be done about himself, he knew it. He just wasn't quite ready to have it done or have the strength to do the doing. "Isaac," says Jackson. "He seems to be doing okay."

"He'll adjust. These things take time."

"Yeah," says Jackson, "but he seems like he's doing okay here, right?"

"Isaac talks, but he doesn't really say anything. Straight answers. Yes or no. He's either in his room or at the park. He doesn't trust us yet."

"He's been through a lot." Jackson sneaks a sip of the Hennessey, remembering what it was like to be a boy alone: his own mother dead, his dad a fun-loving drunk, becoming a mean drunk. When Jackson was a child a red-faced Jerome Carter would pay him a penny-a-push-up and Jackson would rattle off a hundred of them with ease, entertaining his father's friends at those small Saturday night get-togethers. By the time Jackson was twelve that same red face took on a shade of angry and Jackson grew used to being backhanded by his father for no reason besides being in the same room.

"Isaac will come around," says Mae. "It's you I'm worried about, Jackson. Your drinking's getting out of hand."

"I know."

"Then stop."

"I will." Jackson takes another sip. Glances over at Mae, who gets tipsy off a glass of wine, who can't possibly understand what the liquor does to the darkness. How it holds his hand through it, the regrets, how it helps him deal. "When I'm ready to."

Lyric stands sandal-footed in wood chips. Her Grammy sits on a bench, giving herself a headache over a crossword puzzle. Deep-set wrinkles on dark brown skin. A face that scares Lyric sometimes. Grammy's always so serious, always complaining about something or someone, mostly about Lyric's mother, Grammy's only child, who she's constantly criticizing, about not going to college, about stripping, or about getting knocked up by a white boy. But once you get past the noise of her, what you find is that Miss Netta James will do anything for the people she loves. Lyric's Grammy loves hard.

"Girl, why you hiding over there in the shade?" Grammy asks. "You need to get out and get some sun. Get some color in your skin."

Lyric moves enough to satisfy Grammy. She slides over by the swings and kicks around in the wood chips. She watches Isaac Page shoot a basketball with his trademark flick of the wrist, taught to him by her father, polished and perfected in the year since Joey Cane died. A shirtless, bald, muscle-bound black man rebounds for him, occasionally catching one of Isaac's missed shots and lobbing it through the rim. Isaac looks different. A few inches taller and hoodless. And happy. No, happy isn't quite the word. Okay. Isaac looks okay. Not like when she'd last seen him, dead-faced and broken, shooting his basketball in her driveway, Lyric watching him from her mother's bedroom window.

She'd walked down Francis Street earlier this summer and stood in front of his house, hoping to see him out in the driveway shooting on her father's rim. But the Pages' house was as ghostly as hers was, worse really, with boarded windows and gang art graffitied on the porch. The neighborhood unchanged, just a little more aged, a little more decayed. The Pages were gone, Lyric's family was gone, life moving on as if they were never there.

Seeing Isaac Page here at Garfield Park makes Lyric feel some kind of way. It's like she feels played, or betrayed, only she doesn't know by who. This life she landed in. Her mother leaving her home alone when she's out stripping. Grammy refusing to babysit on nights Tara is working at Iggy's Place. Some nights her mother brings home men. They come in loud and drunk in the early-morning hours. Some mornings Lyric finds her mom naked and alone. She'll wrap her in the bed covers and fix herself breakfast. Other mornings Tara is crying in the bedroom. Lyric will stand in the doorway watching. Tara's makeup smeared, she will tell Lyric to come in. Then she'll hold Lyric in her arms, against her naked breasts, and she'll tell her she's sorry. Tell Lyric she loves her.

And Lyric never stops thinking of Isaac. That night on the porch. The sirens. The gunshot. She and Isaac were supposed to be kindred mourners. That hooded white boy with the sad face and the pretty blue eyes. Seeing Isaac here uncloaked and not frowning. It's like he's moved on and left her behind. That's what it is. It's like she hasn't moved on from that night and Isaac has. It's like he has forgotten. It gives Lyric an overwhelming urge to run. Not toward Isaac, but away. She does. Grammy screaming after her. She loses one sandal in the woodchips. She loses the other in the parking lot. She doesn't care. Lyric runs across the concrete barefoot, ignoring the traffic, the horns honking, people yelling from their cars. She runs back to Francis Street. She sits on her father's porch and hugs her knees.

It's the simple things she misses. The way she felt so small in his arms, like a baby, when he'd scoop her up and hold her, kiss her cheek and tell her he loved her. She misses the smell of cigarettes. She misses his coffee breath. They had this game they played, Joey would say, Baby I love you. Lyric would say, I love you too. Then Joey would say, No, NO, NOO, I love you so much more. Then Lyric would say No way, Daddy, I love you more! Then Joey would come up with this huge number, a number Lyric couldn't even comprehend. He'd say something like, I love you six gazillion, four hundred billion, six hundred sixty-six million, twenty two thousand, four hundred ninety nine, point nine nine nine nine nine. That was her favorite part of the game: the nine nine nine. He would keep saying it until she laughed. Until she admitted that he loved her more than she loved him.

Her dad always looked so angry. He didn't like to smile. But he'd do it for Lyric, and that made her feel special, feel like the most important person in his world. Because his smile was beautiful and it was hers, hers alone. The little smile was for the rest of the world. The fake one. But the smile he gave Lyric was huge—it started in his eyes and stretched across his face—he meant that smile. He loved her. Lyric knew it. That smile is what she misses the most. And when she pictures it, it makes her sad. She's sitting on her father's porch with her eyes closed now, thinking about that smile. She's sad, and she's hugging her knees pretending her arms are her Daddy's arms, but she isn't crying.

She's not going to cry.

It is summer's end. Leaves are morphing, falling from trees, bringing shades of orange and red to the neighborhood's gray. Even the southeast side of Grand Rapids must bow to the beauty of a Michigan fall. A late-August morning brings a hint of what's to come, a chill in the air, the whisper of a slow-approaching winter. It's cold enough to keep most kids away from Garfield Park until the sun begins beating down. Isaac had the court to himself until about an hour ago.

For the most part the block has left Isaac alone. Today, like every day, he lets the city exist around him. He inhabits his concrete planet, listening to teenage boys rap battle, Miles among them, not rapping but beat-boxing and adlibbing. Isaac stands at the free throw line, holding Joey Cane's worn-down-to-rubber ball, the fuzz dribbled off, now more nectarine than peach. Expiration date looming.

Dribble. Dribble. Flick. Snap.

The memory of Joey Cane is quieting down. Now more lucid than real. More memory than ghost. And his parents: buried so deep inside him—Isaac wouldn't even know they were there if he wasn't the one who did the digging. The Carters have been good to him, but still, there's this feeling like the bottom could fall out—like they could change their mind. On some whim Mae and Jackson could ship him back into the system. And that loud possibility is a roadblock for letting go of the past and submitting to love.

A taupe Cadillac, bloated with base, rolls into Garfield Park. Gold rims and window tint. Hood ornament folding light like a prism. A black man exits the vehicle. He looks like money: dapper, fingerwaves doing somersaults across his dome, a gold rope chain with a cross dangling from his neck. He walks up limping, not like he's injured, but like he's too cool for the sidewalk. Isaac notices the man's gray eyes, his arrogant smile, the proud way he's looking at Miles—after listening to Miles rave about the man all summer, Isaac cringing, dreading the day he'd have to meet him—for the first time, Isaac knows he is laying eyes on Cesar Bolden.

Dribble. Dribble. Glance.

Flick. Snap.

Isaac watches Cesar approach Miles, stop at the edge of the rap battle, arms crossed, head bobbing to the beat. Miles nods his father's way, but doesn't quit beat boxing, spit flying, the noise of music bouncing off his lips.

Dribble. Dribble. Flick. Snap.

Glance.

Isaac watches Cesar reach into his pants pocket for a bankroll, flipping through hundreds. Cesar stands there like a false God letting the teenage boys worship him. He extends fist pounds and daps. Gives away a few dollars. Miles sips from the limelight. Isaac thinks of Miles' dead mother. He tries to imagine what she looked like and summons that lead singer from En Vogue, then tries to imagine her on drugs, then sees a flash of Frank Page, bone-faced with nasty teeth.

Dribble. Dribble. Flick. Snap.

Miles leaves the battle circle and embraces his father. There appears to be real love between them, but Isaac can't help but think Miles foolish, a sellout—According to Miles, Cesar tried to save his mother, tried to help her get clean, but she was too far gone. Something about that story doesn't feel right to Isaac. Something about Miles living with the Carters while his father cruises through the southeast side in that Cadillac, coming and going as he pleases, seems off. Isaac watches Cesar slide Miles a few bills and then look Isaac's way.

Dribble. Dribble. Flick. Snap.

Glance.

Miles leads Cesar onto the court. Off to the side, the rap battle continues.

Flick. Snap.

"You got a nice shot for a white boy," says Cesar.

For a white boy? thinks Isaac. "Thanks," he says.

"Cesar Bolden." Cesar extends his hand for a dap.

Isaac accepts it. "Nice to meet you, Sir."

Cesar wets his lips then smiles. "I ain't no tight-assed Jackson Carter," he says. "You can lose the 'sir,' white boy."

Isaac thinks, *You can lose the white boy, SIR,* says, "Alright, Cesar."

"Listen." Cesar flips through his wad of cash. "You a friend of my son, you family, dig? You need to hold something?"

"Huh?"

"He's asking if you want some money." Miles shakes his head.

"No, thank you," says Isaac.

Cesar raises a suspicious eyebrow and cocks his head to the right. He looks at Miles like he can't believe what he just heard. "Jackson been talking to you about me, white boy?"

"No, Sir," says Isaac.

"Boy, I told you about that 'sir.'"

"Sorry, Cesar."

"It ain't no thing," says Cesar. "Say, these neighborhood niglets still giving you problems?"

Isaac looks at Miles. Miles shrugs.

Cesar doesn't wait for an answer. "They better not be," says Cesar. "They do, you let me know."

"Okay, Cesar."

"Look, Boy, you keep shooting that rock. I respect your hustle. You remind me of myself when I was your age. Hard work will get you places. Will get you this." Cesar pulls out his wad of cash. Peels through layers of hundreds that become fifties, become twenties. "Hold twenty, white boy," he says, "don't hurt my feelings."

Buried

Summer 2011

IT'S EARLY JULY AND THE LAKE MICHIGAN WIND hasn't yet conceded its bite. At the Grand Haven Beach before noon it's hot enough to swim, but not hot enough to sweat. Isaac walks the pier with Mae and Miles. He dribbles his basketball, two-years-worn, a gift from Mae, brought home in the last days of the ball Isaac inherited from Joey Cane. When it was all rubber and only a small island of fuzz, a sad patch still tattooed with a markered G.H. With the new ball Mae came home with a bronze trophy cup that Joey's ball now rests in like a shrine on Isaac's dresser.

There is no G.H. on the new ball. Joey's last name is Sharpied in thick letters on the faded orange skin, between the black rubber seams, beneath the word "Spalding." Isaac navigates the hazardous cement walkway, watching boats sail by, an occasional awkward bounce off the cracked and jagged pier not affecting his lordship over the ball.

Today Mae is smiling for what seems like the first time in weeks. She wears big oval sunglasses and an almost-comical straw hat. Her flower-print sundress flaps in the breeze. Large kites hang over the vast beach. The three of them step off of the pier and onto the hot sand. A group of boys toss a football and when they catch it they dive into the waves, pretending it's an end zone. Men fish off the side of the pier. Small children cart buckets of water into the moat of a large sand fortress supported by beach drift, dead hunks of wood, and straw unearthed by the wind.

Miles, shirtless and wearing opaque sunglasses, chases a couple of teenage girls down the beach, catches up with them, and attempts conversation while the girls laugh but keep walking. Mae and Isaac return to their spread. A large pink sheet held down by a cooler, a beach bag, and two separate stacks of towels.

"Aren't you going to swim, Isaac?" asks Mae. She sips Evian water.

"Not yet," Isaac says, "I'm not hot enough."

Mae kicks off her sandals. "I am." She turns away from Isaac and slides down the right strap of the dress. She has a dark brown mole on her upper back. She slips off the left strap. The sundress gathers at her feet and she steps out of it. She Frisbees the hat onto the sheet but keeps her sunglasses on.

Isaac watches her toe her way into the water one slow step at a time. He watches men and boys ogle her, turning their heads for a second look, awed by the sleek figure in the white bikini. After three years living in her house, Isaac realizes he has been deceived. Mae Carter is a woman. Her stern way, her librarian glasses, her all-business pinned-back hair, her fashion-police-red-flag-Miss Prissy sweaters and slacks: it is a disguise, a lie. Underneath it all Mae Carter has curves that could snap a man's neck, could crash cars.

Mae steps out of the cold lake, bikini top clinging to her, nipples hard and pushing through the fabric. Isaac looks away. He rolls onto his stomach.

"The water feels great," says Mae. "Cold, of course, but great."

Isaac looks up and watches her dry her arms with the towel. Her legs. He watches her lay the towel next to him on the sheet. Isaac is thinking, *Please put the dress on, please DON'T put the dress on.*

Her cool arm brushes against his ribs when she lies on her back beside him. "Do you have sun block on?" she asks.

"Yeah," Isaac lies, knowing it is in the beach bag in the opposite corner of where he is laying. Knowing his erection won't die anytime soon.

"I'd put some more on, baby," says Mae, and this time the "baby" lands differently in his mind. Almost like a tickled whisper in his ear working its way through his body. *Oh, baby. Oh, baby.*

"I'm good," says Isaac. "Really."

Mae rolls onto her stomach and reaches for the beach bag. Isaac glimpses her golden brown ass, peppered with sand, bikini bottom creeping into her crack.

"Here," she says, tossing Isaac the bottle.

Isaac rubs it on his arms and forehead.

"Hand me the bottle, baby," says Mae, "so I can get your back." She sits cross-legged and squeezes lotion onto Isaac's back. She rubs it in casually and with obviously innocent intentions, but for Isaac it is the stoking of a lust that is sure to have no good outcome.

Cesar stands on the old trestle bridge looking down at the Grand River. The rising sun a pallid orange in a purple soup of hues. The city yawns and stretches. A lazy Sunday morning opens its eyes. Cesar's always loved it down here. The water flowing beneath him. The city surrounding the ancient river. A bright green canopy of trees far off in the distance. Cesar's always appreciated the beauty. He's always thought it was a perfect juxtaposition of urban and God.

To his left is Iggy's Place. Now a relic on the riverfront. No longer the loud lit attraction it once was, but still turning a profit, still the premier flesh club in the city. Iggy Carter has long-since made good on his loan. He's had Cesar paid off for years. But Cesar was so used to coming down here on Sunday mornings that when he received his last payment from Iggy he just kept coming.

Joy Green's body had washed up in front of the Marriot. Almost directly across from Iggy's Place. And since Joy's death Cesar's been dealing with something that feels like guilt. He comes down here and he treads in the past, and he searches for the right apology, the right words to set his conscience free. If he had the words he'd speak them into the breeze. He'd let the wind take his apology where ever it wanted and maybe it would find Joy, maybe then his mind would be at ease.

Some things are just too difficult to let go of. And Cesar's grudges have a fierce grip that only time can loosen. So after George and Ivy Green died and word got back to Cesar that Joy was back on the block, feeding the beast, her custody of Miles fucked up and forfeited, his son living with Jackson Carter, who'd finally let go, finally accepted Joy Green for who she was—Cesar welcomed his cracked-out baby's mother back into his life with a video camera and middle finger. He got his revenge. One scene, one movie at a time, his heart hard and his mind on business, he told her story.

But seeing her that day with the needle in her veins. There may have been a moment, if only a sliver, a glimpse, Joy pregnant and happy and clean, Miles on his way to being in this world—Cesar might have loved her, maybe. Because he hurt when he saw her lifeless body. Though he knew Joy's path had one direction, one conclusion, with or without Cesar opening the door and leading her down it, he knew he was responsible. Joy being the mother of his child should have been enough to stay his hand.

This place is a graveyard. Behind Cesar, two bridges back, is Punk Island. Frank Page and Terrell Lewis are buried there. Sometimes Cesar can hear their decaying hearts beating in his head. Their voices coming out of the dirt and calling into the breeze. Sometimes he sees Joy Green's ghost floating across the water and he remembers when they first met at Iggy's Place, Joy beautiful and full of life, only one foot then on the road to gone. One Sunday morning maybe he'll have the words for an apology. But today is not that day. Just like last Sunday and the Sunday before that.

Cesar exits the bridge on Iggy's side. He finds his Caddy and makes his way toward Griggs Street, toward the Carters, where karma has him lurking in the shadow of his own son. Watching the house and hoping he goes unnoticed. Jackson can't stand Cesar. Cesar knows it, knows Jackson has his reasons, knows Jackson's love for Joy Green twisted his mind into seeing things one way, seeing Cesar one way. A man like Jackson Carter cannot be reasoned with when he has his mind set on a thing. So Cesar plays the monster. He allows himself to be the villain that ruined Joy Green. He lives on the edge of Miles' life, loves his son from a distance, and keeps his deep gratitude for Jackson Carter to himself.

Cesar's knows he's done some unequivocally evil shit. That's not something he can deny. And when a man changes, or in Cesar's case, something changes a man, the change isn't always seen by the world. Our flaws are announced with a chorus of trumpets and a blinding spotlight. Always on display for anyone with eyes. But from day one Cesar's done right by Miles. No one with eyes can deny that. Though that one thing may not redeem a lifetime of bad shit, Cesar clings to that one thing, eyes or no eyes, it's something he owns.

Cesar parks the Caddy a few houses down from the Carter's house. He checks his watch. It's almost 8:30. They sleep in on Sundays. Everyone but Isaac Page. That boy is probably already up and around, probably already at Garfield Park dribbling his fingers raw. You talk about a trip. You talk about a wild coincidence. The son of Frank Page and the son of Joy Green living in the same house, oblivious to their dark intersecting histories, crack and porn and death. One day maybe. Maybe one day Cesar will tell Miles, but that's not a truth Cesar's ready to reveal, not yet, not when Miles is too young to truly understand.

The chaos that followed Joy's body turning up in the river. The news footage. DeMarco in handcuffs being dragged out of the house on Jefferson Street. Channel 8 doing a special on crack, calling it a plague that is claiming the city, shots of the southeast side, people from the neighborhood being interviewed. DeMarco won't talk. He'll do his five years in silence, just like Cesar would have had he been the one in the house when the door was kicked in. But it's only a matter of time before Frank and Terrell's bodies are found. Will DeMarco adhere to street code when facing a life bid?

Cesar had been in the drug game his entire life, before he was even out of his teens, and he's never caught a case. He has no criminal record. Not so much as a parking ticket. How long would that luck last? How long would intelligence be enough to beat this game? It was time for a change. It was time to go legit. Start a business, pay taxes. It was time to get out before it all came crashing down.

The obvious choice was porn. He'd already made a killing off the Joy Green movies. But that was in the nineties, when internet porn was still in its infancy, before it became the flea market it is now. The evolution of the internet complicated things a little. There were too many sites where you could view porn for free. These sites were neatly categorized in a way that allowed any pervert with a computer free access to virtually anything he desired. Busty. Asian. Latina. You click on the category and can scroll through thousands of scenes until you find what you want to jerk off to. It was bootlegging at its best. Anyone could upload a movie or a scene onto one of these sites. And if you owned the rights to these movies, like Cesar owned the rights to the Joy Green movies, there was no way to police the bootlegging. Go to any of these sites and type Joy Green in the search engine: every scene Cesar ever shot, every movie he ever sold, is available for free viewing.

The days of making a real profit selling physical copies were dead. So Cesar adapted. He chose the six baddest strippers at Iggy's Place and interviewed each of them. Got them talking on camera about their lives, their likes, dislikes. About their fetishes, their favorite sexual positions, their dirtiest secrets. Each interview ended with the same question: How much money would it take for you to fuck on film? Each girl had her price. The answers varied but they were all offered the same deal. $2,000 for three hours of footage.

Then he created something like a mixtape for each girl, a highlight reel of sex clips to grab the viewer's attention, and then after showing the sex, the music faded and the interview began. Each girl had a story. The hook was to make it personal. He leaked the mixtapes into all the major free sites and linked the mixtapes to his own website, a pay site, where you could view the mixtapes for free, but if you wanted access to hours of actual footage you had to provide your credit card information.

What Cesar hoped was that the exclusivity and intimacy of the process would trick the porn viewer into thinking he had ownership. He paid his money, it's his girl, his alone—he's special and he wouldn't want to share. Wouldn't want any asshole with an internet connection and a mouse to get a free view of what he paid for. Cesar found this to be true, for the most part. There was the occasional leak. He'd police the free sites once a month, or if he noticed a particular girl took a dip in action on his site. If she was leaked she was replaced with a new girl and the process would continue. It worked. The money was good. But lately Cesar's thinking a man needs more than money. A man needs to leave his mark on this world before he dies. Because when God finds you and holds you accountable for your life, what do you say? Do you make excuses? Do you give reasons? Do you make a lawyeresque argument to justify a lifetime of greed and manipulation? What would Cesar say to God? What mark has he left? The only good thing Cesar's really accomplished is Miles.

There is movement in Jackson Carter's house. Jackson's wife has drawn the curtains, is letting in the sun. Isaac Page is late for the day. He notices Cesar's car when he steps out the house, basketball weaving through his legs while he walks down the sidewalk. So much history. So many secrets. Only Cesar knows it all. He eases the Caddy into Drive. He nods at Isaac Page when he cruises by and Isaac looks away, ball still weaving through his legs, getting smaller in Cesar's rearview.

Mae sits in her recliner, enjoying the cool quiet inside. The boys are gone off to the park. Jackson's outside pushing the mower, the sound of the blades chopping at grass soothing her mood. It always has. She used to love watching Jackson push that ancient thing around the yard, his shirt stuck to his back, his muscles stretching its seams—those days, though, are just another thing left behind.

She stands and walks over to the window. She should bring him a glass of ice water, but doesn't. Just watches him work. It's almost one hundred degrees and humid. Grass sticks to his arms and legs, his clothes. She turns away from the window and walks back to her chair. She's not going to love this man today.

The lawnmower cuts off and Jackson comes inside. Mae watches him take off his shirt and wipe his brow. In spite of the drinking he's still got a build. Broad shoulders. Broad chest. Only a thin layer of fat across his mid-section. Jackson notices her watching and smiles. She doesn't smile back, but she doesn't look away either.

"Sure feels good in here," he says.

He's sober. Mae can tell by the way his voice sounds. Testing her, throwing out a line. He's innocent at the moment and assessing whether today is a good day to stay that way. Knowing the boys won't be home until dinner. Assessing whether Mae is in the mood to fool around.

"Sure does," Mae says.

"Been a hot summer."

"It has."

"Be a good day to walk down by the river if you want to?"

"Too hot." She doesn't mean it. The breeze coming off the water on a day like today—it's worth slapping at those big river mosquitoes—it used to be their favorite thing to do, holding hands, walking through the city. They'd share an ice cream and talk, not casually, but really talk, that sun and that breeze and all that love between them.

"Too hot?" Jackson frowns. He nods his head like he's working something out in his mind. Assessing.

"Yes." Mae serves it to him cold. Watches Jackson come to terms with it, close his eyes, and then nod his head again. He kicks off his shoes. Touches Mae's shoulder when he walks past her and into the kitchen. Mae waits to hear the freezer open, the ice cubes breaking in the tray, the Hennessey pouring into the glass. Assessing. When the freezer opens and the ice cubes break free Mae walks over to the bookshelf and grabs John Updike's *Couples*. She walks upstairs into her bedroom and closes the door.

•

Mae is almost asleep when Jackson staggers into the bedroom. Her eyes open with her back to him, she listens to her husband slap at the light switch a few times before giving up and closing the door. She hears his clothes hit the floor before he joins her in bed. She doesn't want to feel him next to her, but it's too late to pull the covers tight—he'll know she's awake. When he gets this drunk he's emotional; when he's emotional he wants to talk. Mae isn't in the mood. Doesn't have the patience for his half-assed vows of sobriety. So she stomachs his arm wrapped around her. Breathes through her mouth to avoid the rot of his breath. Suffers through his heavy hand on her breasts. Waits for the snoring.

When he's finally asleep, Mae rolls out of bed. She stands watching him for a moment. Jackson's mouth is open, eyes half-closed and rolled up into his head, mostly whites showing, only the lower curve of his brown irises visible. She's too tired to be pissed off tonight. She hides Jackson's naked body beneath the covers and grabs her portable CD player.

Mae tiptoes down the hallway to the bathroom. Plugs the CD player into the wall, sets it on the sink counter, and presses play. Mary J. Blige. Sweet Mary. Take me away, Mary, thinks Mae, take me away. She lights a cocoa scented candle. Runs bathwater. Slips out of her nightshirt and panties. Fills the tub with Epsom salt and bubbles. Slides into the hot water and feels the day's stress begin to leave her bones.

Mae draws water until the bubbles spill over the side. Turns off the faucet. She closes her eyes and lets Mary take her someplace else. She thinks about her cousin's offer to move to Mississippi. Free room and board until she gets state certified, lands a teaching job, gets established, and is able to afford a place of her own. But it's just not doable now. A drunk can't raise boys into men. Isaac and Miles are starting high school in a couple months. And Isaac, Isaac has come so far—hardly a shell of the boy he was when he first moved in. If she left it would break him, Mae knows that. "Four more years." She finds comfort in hearing the words spoken out loud. At least she has a plan.

She should have listened to her daddy. What did he say about her and Jackson? Unequally yoked. Daddy probably didn't know he was quoting bible scripture, but now, his words sing true. He's right. He's been right the whole time. An educated woman has no business with an uneducated man. A good heart doesn't make you a good person. It's the way you live your life that matters. Daddy looked at Jackson all those years ago and saw something flawed. Mae saw it too—but Mae, Mae thought she could mend the broken parts of him. She thought love would heal him. Mae now knows you can't mend the past.

She lets the thought go and listens to Mary. Lets the pain in Mary's voice and the bath water calm her. It's like Mary knows her and feeling known makes Mae strong. The bathroom door creaks and she opens her eyes. Isaac is frozen where he stands. She wants to scream at him, but doesn't; he's as shocked as she is—the two of them snared in this moment. She slides deeper into the water.

Isaac turns and runs away. Mae is submerged to the neck, taking her time, processing this thing. He's a fourteen-year-old boy. Puberty full-blown. Six foot something, long arms, size thirteen feet. The equipment of a man. But he's still a boy. Her son. Seeing her in a way he never should have seen her. And they can never take this moment back.

N as's "One Love" instrumental is on repeat in Isaac's iPod. He loves that New York sound. The slow heavy drums. The simple piano melody. The vocal sample chants: *One love. One love. One love. One love. One love. One love.* Isaac leans against the arm of the couch, sharpened pencil wedged behind his ear, pencil shavings spilled on the end table, another pencil in his hand, scratching words in a spiral notebook.

Quiet nights make the mind more loud.
A concrete beat, the echo of the ball on the street
No peace, can't quiet the gunshot in my mind.

He lips the words as he writes them. Tries to twist them into the rhythm of the instrumental, but cannot make them fit to the beat. It's a puzzle, one Miles could help him solve if Isaac asked him to, but he won't. This is Isaac's struggle. His constant struggle. Finding the space in the confines of the beat. Making his words fit in it. But there are too many restrictions. There is not enough space to free his words.

Mae walks into the living room and Isaac closes the notebook. He plucks out his ear buds and switches off the iPod. Mae holds a coffee mug that says *Number 1 Teacher.* She's wearing a Grand Valley State sweatshirt and a smile. "Good morning," she says.

Isaac looks intently in her eyes, scared to glimpse anywhere else. "Morning."

"What are you up to today?" Mae places the mug on the table propped between her and Jackson's recliners, walks over to the bookshelf, and grabs a title decisively.

"The usual," Isaac says.

Isaac watches Mae settle into her chair and sip from the mug.

"You?" asks Isaac.

Mae lifts a book, something Isaac hasn't heard of, the name DeLillo printed in big letters across its binding. "The usual." She sets the book on her armrest. "So how are things, Isaac?"

She has this inquisitive posture she gets sometimes. Gazing over her glasses, intense, psychoanalytic, never actually asking the questions she wants answers to. Instead Mae probes and hopes and makes herself available—that's what she likes to say when she doesn't get what she's looking for—she's available if he ever wants to talk. This started about a year ago, after Isaac switched counselors for the third time, Mae asking Isaac, Is it a trust thing, baby? And Isaac told her the truth. He said he feels fine. That he knows he's been through a lot but he has his own way of dealing with it. But that wasn't good enough for Mae. He overheard her talking to someone on the phone shortly after that conversation and she said Isaac was repressing, but he wasn't. Not really. He thought about the past all the time. He wrote about it in his journals. Just because he doesn't like to talk about it, doesn't mean he's repressing.

These past three years Mae's been so good to him though. His memories of his own mother are vague, fluid and loose, she might ruffle his hair or sit with him on the couch and watch cartoons, or smile, sometimes he can see her smiling in his mind, he can almost remember her happy, she'd be up in the morning cooking him breakfast, drinking her coffee, sometimes Isaac would wake up with a gift under his arm —she liked to do that, bring home small gifts from her job at Meijer—a notebook, a pack of pens, a movie; she'd tuck them in his arm and Isaac would wake up with them, "Hey, Isaac," she'd always say, "Good morning. I love you." But the most vivid memories are the bad ones—those are the ones he sees clearest: his father throwing her around, hitting her, her head split open, all that blood, and that gravestone, plain with only her name, the year she was born and the year that she died, no epitaph citing accomplishments, or providing hints to what she meant to the people she left behind. He wishes he would have written something. He wishes he would have honored her in some way.

"How are things with you and Jackson?" asks Isaac. Always the perfect way to deflect her.

And on cue Mae smiles. She opens her book. "Well," says Mae. "On that note . . ." Within moments she's totally immersed, neglecting her steaming coffee. Isaac tries in vain to find the imprint of her nipples beneath the thick layers of bra and sweatshirt. If Isaac could draw, he could sketch the artwork of her curves, the birthmark: a dark brown splotch on her left breast, the plump brown nipples like two islands on a light brown ocean of skin, the thin twisted trail of hair that runs from the edge of what was hidden by bubbles up to her navel.

Isaac adjusts himself so his erection presses against the waistband of his shorts. He holds the notebook in front of him, and leaves the pencil shavings on the table, when he walks past her and up the stairs to his bedroom. Miles snores under his covers, mouth open. Isaac opens the top drawer of his dresser and pulls out a Mary J. Blige CD, stolen from Mae's collection weeks before.

He walks into the bathroom and turns on the ceiling fan. He fills the bath with bubbles. Lights a candle. Plays the Mary J. CD on low. He recreates the scene, imagining Mae lying there, only this time her hand churns beneath the surface, asking him to join her. Isaac thrashes in the water, drowning the candle, soaking the floor mat. He lets the water drain down and does it again. And then the guilt of love and lust returns. It feels wrong, these thoughts, seeing what he saw, but his body keeps asking for more, in spite of the guilt, in spite of the wrongness.

Lyric stands on a black marble path. Enormous trees made of bone stretch through another world, skeletal branches twisted together like gripping fingers, making this bizarre forest a singular thing. Glass leaves fall and shatter into dust that floats over the path, becomes intense grains of light that drift past the glowing bone trees and into the darkness. The voice of a man whispers from somewhere beyond the trees.

"Shorty, come here. Let me talk to you for a minute." The voice repeats it. Then repeats it again.

Lyric walks. The voice follows. "Shorty, come here. Let me talk to you for a minute."

She wants to run but everything is slow here. She wants to run but something else is controlling her pace.

Another voice, "Babygirl, let me holler at you."

The first voice, "Shorty, come here. Let me talk to you for a minute."

Then the trees are gone and there is only darkness.

"Babygirl, let me holler at you."

"Shorty, come here. Let me talk to you for a minute."

Something touches her. Something with a thousand fingers. Enough fingers to cover every inch of her skin.

"Babygirl, let me holler at you."

"Shorty, come here. Let me talk to you for a minute."

The voices stop. The path ends in a circle of light. Her dead father is standing in it alone. She wants to hug him, but he shakes his head. He is crying.

"Babygirl, let me holler at you."

"Shorty, come here. Let me talk to you for a minute."

"Babygirl, let me holler at you."

"Shorty, come here. Let me talk to you for a minute.

The voices are louder. Closer. The light at the end of the path begins to fade. Her father is no longer her father. He is a giant eagle. Still crying. The eagle turns and flies away.

Mae wakes to Jackson's hand in her nightshirt. Hennessy breath on her neck. His erection pressing against her. He's breaking her rule and he knows it. He waited until she was good and asleep and started working his fingers. The drunk. But tonight she's too tired for principles. And she's already too aroused to call him on the drinking. She allows him to enter her from behind while she lies on her side. Then she maneuvers herself on top and arches her back. Jackson can't last two minutes when he's this drunk. It's like he's not even here. He's like a crash test dummy with a penis. Jackson's on autopilot, the only proof he's alive is his erection.

At this late hour, the house asleep, the passion in this marriage gone—the sound of sex is a lonely sound indeed. She's angry and her anger turns her on. When he's sober Jackson is a selfless lover. He discovers what Mae needs and takes pleasure in giving it to her. The orgasms come in abundance, each one a gift she receives from Jackson. Tonight she feels like a thief, claiming that pleasure for herself, racing toward climax, as fast as she can ride this thing, because if he goes first it's over, and she's close, God she's close, but then he softens and slips out, and she turns and finds this jackass snoring. Unbelievable.

Mae punches him in the chest and the thud echoes. Jackson mumbles something and scratches his head but doesn't wake. Mae lies in bed for a while staring at the ceiling. Her arousal has waned, but now she's awake. Restless and awake and pissed. And fixated on the fact that he broke the rule. No sex while drinking, Jackson. Period. She made her position clear. Don't come up here smelling like liquor or beer and put your hands on me. Too many of those nights. Drunk sex. Not making love, but fucking, fucking like a couple of stray dogs, no foreplay, no connection, just two bodies pawing and pounding each other. Oh, she's pissed! She's pissed at Jackson and she's pissed at herself. Where's your self-control, Mae Carter? Huh?

She'll deal with Jackson in the morning. In the morning she'll give him a piece of her mind. For now though, she'll find something to do with this anger. Maybe she'll go clean the hell out of the kitchen. Maybe that will settle her down. And some tea. Some chamomile tea. Mae puts on her robe and goes downstairs. She stands in the kitchen ready to start the teakettle then hears a noise in the basement. Someone is up and moving around. She opens the door and finds the light on. It's late for laundry. She walks down the steps.

She finds Isaac on his knees. Naked from the waist down. He's holding her photograph, the one that should be hanging in the living room, her extremely dorky senior picture that Jackson won't let her take off the wall. Her panties dangle from the end of Isaac's penis. It's long and pale and shouldn't belong to a fourteen-year-old boy. Mae's speechless at first, but then the anger comes back, a few drips at a time, Jackson upstairs snoring after breaking her rule, and Isaac the little shit, how dare he, with her picture and her panties, oh, she's livid, the anger pouring through her now. "Isaac!" she yells. "What in the name of God are you doing?"

Isaac looks like a caught puppy. He drops the picture and glass shatters, which makes Mae even more upset. "How dare you!" she screams. She slaps him. Then she clenches a fist and punches him on the back. "How dare you, Isaac!" She picks up the framed photograph and hurls it across the room.

Isaac covers his face with his arms. "I'm sorry," he says. "Mae, I'm sorry.

•

Lyric opens her eyes and sits on the edge of her bed. The TV is loud in the living room, studio laughter from some sit-com, otherwise the apartment is still. She opens her bedroom door and walks down the hallway, into the wreckage. Empty Budweiser bottles litter a glass coffee table. A few soggy cigarette butts float in the bottom of a half-finished beer with the label torn off. A used condom sits next to an uneaten slice of pizza on a greasy paper plate.

Lyric's mother sleeps on the couch, naked besides a bra. She's got Thunderbooty tattooed across her ass like she's proud of it, like it's the only thing she has going for her. A large black man sleeps beside her, leaned back against the couch, wearing nothing but a gold watch and socks, one hand on her mother's ass, the other on his own thigh. His weird-shaped penis rests on his big balls, the tip of it bigger than the rest of it, reminding Lyric of a toadstool.

Lyric finds a blanket and covers them with it. She steals a Marlboro Light from her mother's open pack. She smokes it right there in the living room, hovering over the couch, standing beneath a framed picture of her dead father. How did this become her life? She shakes her head. Disgusted. She blows smoke toward her mother and this man. She ashes on the carpet. Drops the cigarette in a Budweiser bottle. Goes back to bed.

Jackson is already gone when Mae wakes up. No sign of him ever being in the bed. Not even bothering to wake her up to say good-bye. No matter how bad things have gotten between them, these kinds of slights still hurt her feelings. She's amazed at the man's capacity to recover from a night of drinking. Up at 4:30 every morning like clockwork, a quick work out, a shower, and then his day begins. They never talk anymore about anything that matters. Nothing that matters besides the boys. They have their good days. If Jackson's not drinking and she's not chastising him—they might go see a movie, or out for dinner. But it's like the pulse of their marriage is gone, it's flat lined, and a "good day" is nothing more than a jolt back to life until it flat lines again.

Mae wraps herself in her robe and goes downstairs. Jackson was nice enough to brew the coffee before he hit the road—his apology for last night—these days the words "I'm sorry" never pass between them. She still smiles at his thoughtfulness though, and pours herself a cup, no sugar no cream, and puts her mind on Isaac. He'll be up soon, basketball in hand, off to the park. She has to catch him right away and nail this thing down. Clear the air between them.

The thoughts that must be running through that boy's head. The way he used to flinch when she hugged him. Those awkward moments when she kissed him on his cheek. And God forbid Mae actually said those words. Actually told the boy she loves him. And now this. She tries to put herself in his shoes. That night in the bathtub, walking in like that, seeing her, seeing everything. Jackson used to say her body was a well-kept secret. All those curves, baby. All those goddamn curves. How the hell are you hiding all those curves? But Mae's never seen herself as sexy, or sexual—it was her mind, her character, that mattered; at least to her. So why mislead the world? Whatever she had going on beneath her clothes belonged to Jackson, so why make men think she's advertising something when she's not? Why send their dirty minds spinning toward a thing they can never have. Still, Isaac's just a boy. A boy seeing a naked woman. Of course he's going to get confused. Of course he's going to be affected. But her panties, her photograph, Isaac went too far.

Mae sits at the kitchen table and waits, sipping from her mug, listening to the stairs crack beneath his weight, the basketball bouncing off the living room floor. Isaac emerges moments later, stopping at the edge of the room when he sees her. Mae just smiles. "Good morning, baby," she says.

"Morning." Isaac looks at his feet.

"Boy, lift your head up."

It's like he doesn't know where to place his gaze. Mae watches him struggle to maintain eye contact, the front of her robe tugging his eyes downward, Isaac fighting the urge to steal a glance. "Come have a seat," says Mae.

"You're not going to tell Jackson, are you?" Isaac says, sitting at the table and then looking at his hands. "Please don't tell him."

"I won't tell him, Isaac. But we need to clear the air. We need to get an understanding."

Isaac relaxes a bit but still won't look her in the eyes. "This is awkward," he says.

"I know, Isaac. But if we don't talk about it, things are going to get weird between us."

"Okay."

"First off, I'm sorry for slapping you. I'm sorry for punching you. I was a bit shocked and I . . ."

"It's okay."

"Well, I've had some time to think about everything. We never talked about that night you walked in on me. I mean, I know it was late. I know you didn't do it on purpose. I understand. You're young and your hormones are going crazy . . . how you saw me is unnatural. I know I'm not your mother. But for all intents and purposes, Isaac, I *am* your mother. Seeing me like that, I imagine, was very confusing for you. And you're at that age where you're experiencing with your body, and . . ."

"Mae, please. This is really awkward."

"It needs to be said." The boy is looking at the table, humiliated. Is she making the situation worse? "Listen, Isaac. I'm sorry. I'm just saying that there are better ways to . . ."

"Mae, please."

The problem is you cannot unsee. You cannot forget. The bathtub scene is another image added to the movie roll in Isaac's mind. It's imbedded, she's imbedded, and he's fourteen with nothing but his imagination to compare her to. What can she do? Buy him dirty magazines? Buy him porn? Plant more lustful images in his brain and hope they out trump her own image. There is no solution to this problem but time. And she'll have to be really careful with Isaac from this point on—dress the right way, always be aware when interacting with him, so nothing can be misconstrued. And most importantly, just keep loving him. Understanding and love. That is the only way to handle this. "Okay," says Mae. "So, to the point?"

"Yes. Please."

"You're a teenage boy, Isaac. What you do in private is your business. We're going to pretend none of this happened, the bathtub, the basement, but I have one condition . . ."

"Okay."

"Leave my personal items alone."

L ast night's wreckage is gone. The man is gone. Tara's hair tied in a ponytail, running a vacuum over the carpet, dancing while she does it. She has dishes soaking in bleach water. Incense trying to overpower the Marlboro stink from the night before. Lyric stands in the living room but her mother doesn't see her. Tara dances around like life is just gravy.

Tara is startled when she turns and sees Lyric watching her. She cuts off the vacuum. "Hey, baby," Tara says, smiling. "You startled me."

Lyric wishes she were big enough to whoop her mother's ass. Because she would. She feels the birth of the word coming in all of its ugliness. From her chest, to her throat. But it stops at the tip of her tongue. Maybe it's her late-father's blood coursing through her veins, telling her it's wrong. Telling her there is too much history behind the word, too much hate. She wants to vomit it out. Has to. "Where'd," she says. "Yo." She waits on the edge of it. "*Nigga* go?" It feels good when she says it. Empowering. The word's not allowed in Tara's home. A shot to her mother's gut that leaves her momentarily speechless.

"What?" Tara's smile is gone. It's like it was never there. "What did you say?"

"That mushroom dick nigga you had laid up on the couch last night." This feeling. These words. It's all coming from someplace else.

And it feels good, seeing her mother cower beneath her, eyes wandering around in their sockets, mouth moving to speak but unable to say a word.

Lyric is so lost in the feeling she doesn't see the fist coming. Doesn't feel a thing when it lands. When Lyric comes to her senses, Tara is dragging her across the carpet by her hair. Lifting her and tossing her onto the couch. Tara grabs her by the hair again. "You ever speak to me like that again—" She says it through her teeth. Her lips barely even move. "I swear to God, Lyric. It'll be the last thing you ever say on this Earth."

She won't cry. Her defiant eyes are fixed on her mother. She is tired of keeping her mouth shut. Tired of those nights and all these men. With their wandering eyes and their wandering hands. Tara seeing it all. Saying nothing. Lyric is tired of playing pretend. "This is not my life," Lyric says.

Tara loosens her grip on Lyric's hair.

"If my daddy—" Lyric starts.

"Your daddy is dead, baby. It's me and it's you."

"This is not my life."

"It's not mine either," Tara says. Reaching for her pack of Marlboros. She lights one. Inhales deep and exhales from her nose. She looks up at Lyric's daddy's picture. "But we still have to live it."

When Isaac sees the black sedan parked curbside he's hurled into the past. Back on Francis Street, sitting in that police car with Lyric Cane. Joey's body being carted away, Joey's girlfriend beating the earth with her fists, face down in Lorenzo's yard, her screams clawing the night, a cop with his knee pressed against her back.

A black sedan had pulled into Joey's driveway the next morning. Isaac held Joey's ball, rubbing the GH, and watched a dark-suited clean-cut man step out of the car and knock on Joey's door. He and Lyric were outside playing, and she didn't seem sad at all, and Isaac didn't understand, because every time he thought of Joey he hurt, and he couldn't stop the tears from coming, but this girl, this girl who loved her daddy so much, just played, singing with such a pretty voice, like Joey wasn't even dead.

Isaac steps inside the house to find Jackson and Mae sitting in their recliners. A dark-suited clean-cut man sits on the couch, coffee mug steaming in front of him, unsipped and lonesome on the table. He has a slightly crooked jaw and a pineapple-shaped head. The man's smile is irksome, one of rehearsed concern, showing no teeth and no patience, like he just wants to say what he's obligated to say and leave. Jackson and Mae exchange a glance.

"Miles?" asks Isaac. This man means death and Miles is the only one missing.

"He's upstairs, baby," says Mae. "Please, Isaac. Have a seat. This is Detective Mahoney. He has news about your father."

Isaac sits and listens to Detective Mahoney, who tells Isaac his father's body was found buried on a small island on the Grand River, by the Wealthy Street train bridge. That his father was discovered by a fisherman and his young son, illegally camping, digging a hole to make a fire. Mahoney mentions a funeral service, but Isaac shakes his head. Out of words, Mahoney finally sips the coffee, like it's the only thing left to do.

Isaac turns to Jackson. "They're not going to make me leave are they?" he asks.

"Oh, baby," says Mae. She walks over and hugs him. Squeezes in between Isaac and Mahoney. "This is your home, baby. This doesn't change a thing."

"Is that it then, Detective?" Jackson asks. He stands.

The detective reaches into his suit pocket and hands Jackson a card. He sips his coffee again, sets it on the table and rises from the couch. "In case you have any questions," he says.

Jackson lets Mahoney out of the house.

"I'm not going to any funeral," says Isaac. Those first few weeks, Isaac wishing it was his father dead, not Joey Cane, finding refuge in the concrete. Shooting that goddamn ball until his hands were raw, his fingertips smooth. Joey's daughter watching him from the window. Then she was gone too. A moving truck. Isaac's mother and the Joey's girl-friend hauling boxes, Isaac and Lyric playing in the driveway.

"It's your choice, baby," says Mae. "But don't you think you need some closure?"

"He killed my mom," Isaac says. "He's dead. That's all the closure I need."

C esar stands outside of Miss Netta's house The place has a brick body and a wooden white hat. Her small green square of yard is fenced in and littered with gnomes. The house next door is missing a window. Plastic is stapled around its frame. Four bullet holes are in the passenger side door of the blue Impala parked in the neighbor's drive-way. A long skinny black man leans shirtless on the trunk of the car smoking a blunt. A pistol handle peeks out from his waistband. Cesar knocks twice on Miss Netta's door.

"Uncle Cesar!" A young girl hugs Cesar's leg when she opens the door. The girl's probably five or six years old and Cesar can't remember her name or who she belongs to. This house is a circus of bodies. A revolving door of family and close friends—Miss Netta's the matriarch of the madness, a Franklin Street Saint, if you ask Cesar, placing hope where it isn't deserved and giving refuge to any and all who ask.

Three boys sit on a beat down couch playing a video game, some first person shooter that has the television screen cut into thirds, each boy with his own view, each boy hunting the others down. There's laughter coming from the kitchen and the smell of fried food. Miss Netta sits in the far corner of the room smoking a cigarette. She rocks in a wooden chair beneath a bronze cross. She doesn't smile when Cesar enters her home. The carpet is ragged, flat, and caked with dust, still Cesar kicks off his shoes.

He walks over to Miss Netta and kisses her on the cheek. Cheap perfume and Salem smoke. The combination is enough to make him gag. Miss Netta carries herself hard, but Cesar knows better. This woman has about the softest heart of anyone he's ever known. "How's

D.J. holding up?" Cesar asks her. There's no place close to her he can sit so he stands.

"Like any thirteen-year-old boy," says Miss Netta. "Missing his Daddy and trying to act tough. DeMarco wasn't always the best father," she says. "But he was around. That's more than a lot of these men out here."

"Yeah," says Cesar. He tries to remember the last time he saw DeMarco's son, but can't place it. Just a few flashes of a boy in diapers, always into something, hardheaded, always getting his ass whooped for being told twice. "Is he here?" Cesar asks.

"Yeah," says Miss Netta. "He's here. Nitty, run and grab your brother," she says to the little girl who answered the door, now pushing a plastic shopping cart through the living room and humming the theme song to some cartoon that sounds familiar to Cesar.

Moments later D.J. stands in front of Cesar staring him down. Hate all over him. In his posture, in his eyes, in his clenched fists. "What you want, nigga?"

"Boy, you watch that tongue in my house!" Miss Netta slants her gaze at him and readies herself to stand.

"My bad, Auntie," says D.J. He smiles and then his demeanor changes immediately. "Hey, Unc," he says. Sneaky. Smooth. He daps Cesar and half-hugs him. Glances at Miss Netta to see if she's satisfied. She is. Lighting another cigarette and looking in another direction, as if she's giving D.J. and Cesar some privacy, as if there's any privacy at all in this house.

"Hey, Nephew," says Cesar. Punk Island was all over the news. It didn't take long to trace Frank and Terrell's bodies back to DeMarco. Didn't take long to book him, to add two life sentences to his five-year bid. DeMarco is never coming home. The problem is Cesar paid him to do it. If the feds start asking questions, if the feds come to DeMarco with a deal, Cesar's getting hit with conspiracy charges. And if they do ask questions, if they find the right streets, the right corners to walk down—if one or two crackheads start running their mouths—if Cesar's name starts getting tossed around . . .

"Good to see you free," says D.J. "My Daddy ain't so lucky."

"I'm sorry," Cesar says.

"Sorry? That was my Daddy's crackhouse they raided, right? It was my Daddy who killed those men, right? Justice served, Unc. Ain't no reason to be sorry. Be happy you free. Be happy you still alive. That's what I'd be doing if I were you. I'd be enjoying my life for as long as I'm living."

"D.J."

"It's Dee."

"Dee," Cesar says. You ever need anything you call me."

"Put some money in my Daddy's commissary, Unc. That's all I need from you."

When D.J. walks away Miss Netta apologizes to Cesar. "The boy has all this anger, Cesar," she says. "And he don't know what to do with it."

"Anything you need for DeMarco's kids, Miss Netta. You let me know, okay?"

"Okay."

"Listen," says Cesar. "Can we go somewhere and talk in private?"

"Only private place in this whole house is my bedroom and no man has been there in years." Miss Netta smiles. Her teeth are straight and her gums are healthy. She'd have a beautiful smile if her teeth weren't stained gray by the Salem's.

"I'll be on my best behavior, Miss Netta. I promise."

Cesar follows Miss Netta down a hallway into her bedroom. Her bed is sunk in like she's been sleeping in it for years, the same spot, her body at the same angle. It smells like mildew and old smoke in here. It smells lived in. Like a lifetime was lived in this room. But it's clean. The floor vacuumed and no clothes lying around. Framed photographs on the wall. An associate's degree from Grand Rapids Community College. "Culinary Arts," says Miss Netta when she notices Cesar looking at it. "I used to want my own restaurant. I just love to cook. I never could figure out how to turn that into a business though."

"This is you?" Cesar asks. He points to a picture on Miss Netta's dresser. A tall slim woman in a red evening gown. A large dapper black man holding her arm.

"It is," she says. "Now *that* woman . . . your 'best behavior' act would be out the door."

They both laugh. Miss Netta settles into a small recliner that sits next to her bed. "I'd offer you a place to sit down, but . . ."

"It's okay," says Cesar. "This will only take a minute." He takes a large roll of hundred dollar bills out of his pocket and sets it on her dresser. Miss Netta's smile is gone.

"What's that supposed to be? Some kind of bribe?"

"Bribe?"

"We can smile and flirt and play nice, Cesar Bolden. But don't think for a minute that I don't know who you are and what you do. Don't think for a moment that I believe all this was my nephew's doing. That your hands aren't just as dirty as his."

"Miss Netta," says Cesar. "This money is for D.J. and the little girl . . . for Nitty. When you talk to DeMarco," says Cesar. "Will you just tell him I came by. Tell him his kids are taken care of."

"Why don't you tell him yourself?" says Miss Netta, lighting another cigarette. "You know where to find him."

"You know I can't go there," Cesar says.

"Yeah," says Miss Netta. "That I know."

The Season
Winter 2013

THE FURNITURE IN THE LIVING ROOM is rearranged to accommodate a Goliath of a Christmas tree. A tree so large the tip of it bends against the ceiling. A tree so large it makes the house smell like pine. The tree was paid for and chopped down by Jackson the day after Thanksgiving. And decorated as a family, with blinking lights and garland, an assortment of homemade and store-bought ornaments, and about a hundred candy canes, which will be plucked off and eaten before Christmas day arrives.

Christmastime at the Carters feels a lot like Christmas on Francis Street. Isaac remembers his father humming Christmas tunes, pink-cheeked and smiling. He remembers eggnog. He remembers watching Frosty the Snowman, The Grinch, and that movie with the boy who wanted a bb gun, the "You'll shoot your eye out" movie that Frank and Nelly always watched together, sitting on the couch under a blanket.

During Christmas season the Page house took on a different hue. Maybe it was the tree and the lights. But the mood was different too. There was this vibe—that's what Isaac remembers most—there was this vibe in the house that felt like no matter what happened, everything was going to be okay. That was before everything changed.

Isaac peeks out the blinds, checking the driveway for Mae's Camry. He makes sure the door is locked and then twists the deadbolt. No one ever locks both when they leave the house. Should someone come home unexpected, having to use the key twice will give Isaac more time. Isaac walks back upstairs and then locks his bedroom door. He has a laptop and lotion and tissue.

This always ends the same way. When he does the deed it's always while watching the same kind of girl. That makes Isaac curious and confused and in those guilty minutes after he's finished, when he lies back in his bed with his fingers interlocked behind his head, he looks for meaning in this, understanding the source of his desire, but wondering if it ever will change, evolve, become something else. Or is the incident with Mae imbedded in his brain forever. Will his desire always coincide with what he saw? Will he compare every potential sexual partner to her? Or seek out only those that resemble her.

So on nights like tonight when he finds himself alone, he likes to challenge that curiosity. He avoids what he *knows* he desires for as long as he can. He begins with teenage blondes. Their skin pale or tanned. Their nipples pink. He scrolls through a dozen thumbnails and tries watching a few clips. It's enough to get him hard, but not enough to make him want to do anything about it. He types *Big Booty* in the search bar. These girls are mostly black and Hispanic, the occasional white one. Isaac loses interest after watching a few clips. He types in *Busty Ebony*. He takes off his shorts and unbuttons the front flap of his boxers. He's looking for a light-skinned woman with big breasts. He wants her lying on her back. He wants the camera zoomed in close enough to see her face.

He's looking for Mae. In the end he's always looking for Mae. The closest thing he can find is a girl with a panther tattoo on her shoulder. Her nipples a little lighter, a little smaller than Mae's are. But she's pretty. Like she would be pretty if she wasn't in porn. And when it's over, and the tissue is thrown away, and he's dressed, and his hands are washed, and the laptop is back on his dresser, Isaac lies on his bed considering Oedipus. He's trying to extinguish the flames of guilt by rationalizing that Mae isn't his biological mother. And he feels cheated, really, that's how he feels. One moment. One half-asleep-stumbling-into-the-bathroom moment and he's fucked for life. Feeling all kinds of unnatural feelings. Loving this woman and having that love corrupted in the most primitive way.

Mae stands on the threshold of Miles and Isaac's bedroom holding a basket of laundry. Even when the boys are gone she's always leery to step inside. Teenage boys are nasty creatures indeed, with their hormones, their oily skin, their odors. They burp. They fart. They masturbate into condoms and tissue, leaving the waste paper basket filled with the evidence. But Mae braves the room. She empties the boy's clothes on their respective beds for them to put away later, or in Miles' case, to throw on the floor of his closet. When she turns to walk out of the room she notices one of Isaac's notebooks left open on the dresser. She sees her name sketched in the margins of a half-finished poem, or rap song, or something. It's titled "Kidnapped by Oedipus."

Keep walking, Mae Carter, look away and keep walking. But she cannot. She only makes it to the doorway before she turns back toward the dresser. "Shit," she says aloud. Then she's sitting on Isaac's bed, her hands sweating, reading his journal. *If I could draw, I'd sketch the artwork of her curves, that birthmark: that dark brown splotch on her left breast, the plump brown nipples like two islands on a light brown ocean of skin, the thin twisted trail of hair that runs from the edge of what was hidden by bubbles up to her navel.* Mae glances at the doorway then back at the unfinished writing. There are notes jotted below the first paragraph: *Love? Lust? Cheated?*

She glances back at the door, then flips to the beginning of the journal. The first page is titled "Those Crackhead Eyes." *When I think of my father's eyes I'm reminded of blood. I'm reminded of hate. I'm reminded of death. How in a moment, the time it takes for an old wooden chair to soar across the room, the time it takes for a bullet to leave a gun, it can all be over. But the memory, the sound of a gunshot, or those Cheshire eyes of my father, glowing on their way out the door, those memories will echo in my mind forever.*

"Jesus," Mae says. All of these years. All of these deadends. All of these therapists. Mae turns the page. This one's titled "Bullets." *Gunshots used to be nothing. No more than loud snaps in the night. Now they are real. Sometimes I imagine a bullet's journey from the gun barrel into the air, into a car door, a window, a ball. Into a child playing with her Lincoln Logs in the living room. But most times they hit nothing. Nothing according to the news. All these guns and all these bullets—only occasionally someone shot or killed. Imagine this place if the shooters had aim.*

"Mae Evelyn Carter." Jackson's standing in the doorway. "You should be ashamed of yourself." He shakes his head and frowns but he's smiling with his eyes. Mae starts to defend herself, but she knows Jackson's right. She sets the notebook on the dresser and follows him down the stairs.

"Jackson, wait," she says, filling with excitement. "Jackson," she says. "This is it."

"What are you talking about?" Jackson sits in his chair.

"All of these counselors, Jackson. All these years. This whole time Isaac's been counseling himself. His journals. You have to see what he can do."

"I'm not looking in that boy's journals, Mae. That's an invasion of privacy. How would you feel if someone was going through your personal things?"

"Okay. Okay," Mae says. "You're right." She's annoyed with Jackson taking the moral high ground, but he's right.

Jackson picks up the television remote and changes the channel to Sportscenter. He finds his glass of Hennessey and sips.

"Jackson, will you please turn the TV off and talk to me. This is huge. You don't understand it, but this is huge."

Jackson turns off the TV and looks at her with disinterested eyes.

"Jackson, Isaac can write. I mean, he can really, *really* write. He's raw, but for a fifteen-year-old boy . . . we need to encourage him."

"Isaac's always writing in those journals, Mae. Seems like he doesn't really need it. Encouragement, I mean. Isaac's a self-starter."

"He needs to read, Jackson. We need to encourage Isaac to read. He has a gift. For that gift to fully develop he needs to read."

"Do you really think we should push him? Seems like if he wanted to read he would read."

"Not if he didn't know how important it was. You'd have to see the journals, Jackson. Isaac is searching for answers in his writing. More, he's editing, improving. His writing suggests he wants to do something with it, with writing. It's a tried-and-true fact. All great writers are passionate readers."

"What makes you think Isaac wants to be *a great writer?*"

"Jesus, Jackson. Why are you being so difficult?"

"I'm just not sure we should be pushing him."

"You're such a damn hypocrite. Who's been shoving college basketball down his throat? Who's been signing him up for all those camps, A.A.U.?"

"That's different."

"How?"

"Isaac's already playing basketball. I'm encouraging something he's doing on his own. We don't know why he's writing. We don't know how important it is. If Isaac wanted to pick up a damn book he'd pick up a damn book."

"I know how important it is," Mae says. "*I know.*"

Jackson turns the television back on and sips his drink. He reclines in his chair.

"Asshole," says Mae.

L yric wakes to the clanging of dishes and the deep-throated humming of some man. She pops her head into Tara's bedroom. Tara is sleeping, an empty Courvoisier bottle on the nightstand. The faint scent of marijuana lingers. Her mother's digital alarm clock tells Lyric it's 4:06 in the morning. A gray fedora rests on the cap of a lampshade, a subtle glow in its belly like the fedora is part of the lamp's design.

There's an anemic white Christmas tree in the living room. Blinking red, white, and blue lights hang from its fragile plastic branches. Four presents lean against the tree's white plastic stand. On Christmas day Lyric will open them alone. Her mother will stay in her bedroom. They won't visit Grammy. There will be no feast. There will be no festivities at all. Because neither of them want festivities. There is no yuletide joy to be had in December. Not in this apartment. Christmas died when Joey died. The first couple years they pretended—they went through the motions of Christmas—in the end though they decided it was easier, that it felt better, to just let the season be what it was: Depressing.

In the kitchen the man making the noise is an older white guy with a hairy back and matted-down black hair. He stands in his boxers and socks, rinsing and stacking dishes. Lyric clears her throat to speak and the man jumps.

"Jesus," he whispers, "you scared me." Then he smiles. Straight white teeth. The teeth of a man with money. "You must be Lyric," he says. "I'm Clyde."

"Hi." Lyric takes him in, guessing he is in his late-forties or early-fifties. A lawyer, maybe a banker. She's had her share of these conversations the past couple years, but none of them ever occurred while a man was doing dishes.

"I didn't wake you, did I, Hon?"

Hon. This one is married. He probably told his wife he was away on business. Probably has his own kids at home. Abercrombie kids with electronic gadgets who wear bike helmets when they pedal through their safe neighborhood. A Brent and an Amy. Both with flowing blonde hair and clear braces. All smiles, these two, and daddy's just the biggest hero on the planet.

Lyric wonders how much Clyde paid to ride the Thunderbooty. Wonders how much her mother would charge a man like this: old, fat, hairy. One hundred, two hundred, five hundred? He is handsome though, in a used-to-be-handsome kind of way, the captain of something in high school maybe, his looks faded but still somewhat sexy, his money doing now what the looks used to do for him.

"You don't have to do that," says Lyric, "the dishes, I mean. I do them in the morning."

"Well," says Clyde, "I guess tomorrow morning you get a day off." Clyde winks.

Never trust a winker. "So, uh, Clyde," says Lyric. So far removed from giving a fuck. She loves these moments. She loves fucking with these men. "How much did you pay her?"

"Excuse me?"

"For sex."

"I'm sorry?"

"You're not sorry," Lyric says. "You're doing the damn dishes."

Clyde adjusts his hair. His straight white teeth shine bright beneath the dim light of the kitchen. His dark eyes crawl across her and she can feel them like fingers. She crosses her arms over her breasts, nervous but fronting, and musters a raised left eyebrow and a slanted head, says, "*What*, motherfucker?"

"Nothing." Clyde touches her shoulder as he walks past her, out of the kitchen, and into her mother's bedroom.

Jackson wipes steam from the bathroom mirror. He watches Mae's silhouette through the glass shower door. Her movements are smooth and seductive and she doesn't even know it, she's never known it—that's Jackson's favorite thing about his wife—she's oblivious to how beautiful she really is. Jackson spits in the sink and puts his toothbrush away. He gargles Listerine and takes off his towel. He grips the shower door handle and hesitates for a moment—Mae might hate him today, if it's a hate day, then he's going to get shut down. He decides he'll risk it.

"Hey!" says Mae when he steps into the shower. She smiles. She tries to cover herself. All these years and she's still shy about her body. "What are you doing?" she asks.

"I want to make love to my wife," says Jackson. He grips her wrists and pulls her against him. The water comes down against her hair. Shampoo washes down her cheeks. "So you do love me today," Jackson says.

"I love you every day, baby. Our problem has never been love."

•

Jackson watches Mae stopper the tub and run water, pour in bath salts and body wash, and then settle between his legs, lean back against his chest. Jackson plays with her ear. Her cheek. Her lips. He watches her stop the faucet with her toes when the bath is full. "What are your plans for the day?" he asks her.

"Christmas shopping," she says.

"Where?"

"The mall."

Jackson hates Christmas shopping. Hates the mall. In the beginning he used to let Mae drag him all over the place, comparing prices, looking for deals, spending hours popping in each store and then doubling back. Just to save a few bucks. When the marriage turned that last bend and emptied into what it is now, Jackson started saying no to shopping and eventually Mae stopped asking. "Can I go with you?" Jackson asks her.

"Jackson Carter," says Mae. "What are you up to? Why are you kissing my ass?"

"We've been doing a lot of fighting lately," Jackson says.

"I know."

"I've been thinking," he says. "I'm willing to see a counselor. I hate having all of this animosity between us. I know when you brought it up before I scoffed at it. I'm just saying . . . I'm willing now." Jackson's fingers slide down Mae's ribs, to her hips, to her thighs. He grips a handful of bubbles and watches them dissolve.

"Honestly, Jackson," Mae says. "I don't think we need counseling."

"You don't? What changed your mind?"

"Time," says Mae. "A ton of time and a ton of reflecting. You're a wonderful husband. A loving husband. A wonderful father. You invest everything into our family. You do. We don't have a marriage problem. A marriage counselor cannot help us."

"Then what can?" Jackson asks. But he already knows what Mae is going to say.

"Only one thing, baby. Just one thing. And you know what that is."

"Yeah."

"You just have to choose. The marriage or the bottle. It's as simple as that. I love you, baby . . . and I'm happy we're having this conversation now, when we're not upset . . . but it's important that you know. Love isn't enough for me to spend the rest of my life living like this. You need to know that. If you love me, if you value our life together, you're going to have to stop."

"Okay."

"Okay, like you're agreeing? Or okay, like you heard me, but you're going to keep doing what you're doing."

"I'm agreeing, Mae. Okay? I'm agreeing."

The floor creaks when Clyde takes his first sock-footed step into Lyric's bedroom. His fat shadow stretches across the moon-kissed wall. Through her cracked-open window, she hears the noise of cars driving by, the exhale of the night, wind tossing through the parking lot, slapping around an empty beer can. She sleeps on top of her covers, as she always does, under a cool, thin blanket that was hand crafted by her father's mother, a grandmother she used to see in another life, a phantom woman with a face like a black hole.

The blanket only covers the top half of her body. She wears panties and a T-shirt, nothing sexy, something cotton and Hanesie. At fourteen, she's already a bra size bigger than her mother and lugging around an ass that seems to grow thicker with each meal. She remains still as Clyde approaches her and stands over the bed.

Lyric grips the small blanket, closes her eyes, and waits for the pain. She knows other girls who have done it with men. They all say it hurts until it starts to feel good. This act. This fucking. Lyric knew her first time wasn't going to be special. That happens to girls in movies, girls without dead fathers, girls without stripper-turned-hooker moms, girls who don't cut class to get high, girls who live in houses with manicured lawns, those green-grass bitches, those picket-fence bitches, not concrete-dwelling hoodrat bitches like Lyric, who has to play at adult, tuck in her drunk mother, and fend for herself in a world of wicked men.

She wants to tell Clyde, just do it. Get it over with. Why she isn't screaming rape, she doesn't know. Why she isn't calling for her mother, she isn't sure. Does she want this? She can't want this, can she? But Clyde doesn't put it inside her. His trembling hand touches her ass and Lyric opens her eyes. She watches Clyde's shadow while he strokes himself, breathing fast, and trying not to make noise. Then it's over. A hot, sticky mess on the small of her back, Clyde wiping it off with his fat palm, wiping his hand on her bed sheets before leaving her lying there.

His shadow climbs up the wall and across the ceiling when he exits the room.

Isaac is hood cloaked. He leans against a wall at a house party in Kentwood. A party for the cousin of some girl Miles is messing around with. Adults sip cocktails in the kitchen. Teenagers get high outside on the dark side of the house. The patio is misted with fog, steam mixing with the cold December air, the hot tub uncovered but empty. Isaac saw it all when he followed Miles through the party, through the streamers taped to the basement doorway, until Miles went off to mingle and Isaac found his wall.

Now Miles argues with whoever is controlling the sounds. The bass line thumps. The walls rattle. A voice repeats: *Ass and titties. Ass and titties. Ass. Ass. Titties. Titties. Ass and titties.* Isaac ignores the words and creates his own.

The past is a cold ghost that won't leave you alone.
You can hear its whispers in your bones blood and soul.
Time ticks like bullets penetrating your skull.

My path is my own. My path is alone.

He'll scribble them into a notebook later. Twist them around. Try to make them make sense. That's the hard part. Feeling the words is easy. What is it about the confines of a song, the structure that makes it so hard? Miles has lost the argument with the DJ. He stalks toward Isaac, feigning pissed off.

"Bro," Miles says, leaning next to Isaac on the wall. "There's a lot of honeys here tonight, feel me?"

Isaac nods. His flow is broken. The Ass and Titties song switches to something Isaac has never heard. "Do me a favor, Miles," says Isaac. "Don't do what you do, alright? Not tonight. I'm not in the mood." Miles: self-proclaimed hound dog for the wet spot. Lost his virginity early into their freshman year and has spent the last year and a half trying to lose Isaac's for him. Sneaking girls into the house before Mae gets home from work. Taking one up to the bedroom and leaving her friend with Isaac on the couch, awkward conversations, Isaac not the type to make a move, the girls feeling put off because he didn't.

"Shit, Man. Stop being so goddamn sensitive. Tell you what: I'll do me. You do you."

"Whatever, Miles. You asked me to come; I came."

"Okay, Gloom Cloud." Miles scans the room. His eyes find the girl who invited him. "Well, I'ma go get on some of these honeys. Don't let that wall fall down, a'ight?"

Miles walks across the room. He hugs the girl who invited him: a brunette wearing too much makeup. An Ottawa girl Isaac has seen in the hallways, but hasn't actually met. She says something to Miles and Miles shrugs. Begins a conversation with the girl's friend. Isaac pulls his hood lower and looks for an escape route. To make it to the stairs he'll have to walk past them.

The girl with the makeup signals for Isaac to join them. When he doesn't move she walks toward him, switching her hips for Miles' benefit. "Are you shy or are you just an asshole?" she asks, standing in Isaac's space, looking up at him, chewing gum vigorously with the left side of her mouth.

"Are those my only two choices?"

"Huh?"

"Nothing," Isaac says. "Asshole," he says. "I'm an asshole."

"Whatever." The girl laughs and grabs Isaac's hand.

She leads him over to her friends. "I didn't do anything," says Miles. "I swear, Zick. She went over there on her own."

He's introduced to the girl's cousin, Nikki, the girl who the party is for, a white girl wearing an army fatigue shirt unbuttoned, probably an older brother's, the name Mack stitched across an open breast pocket, the flap resting on the propped-open pack of Marlboro Reds. Beneath that she is braless in a green wife beater. Isaac glances at the imprint of her pierced nipples then up at her curious green eyes. Nikki wears no makeup. Doesn't need to. She has a shy smile like she's self-conscious about something not obvious.

Nikki shakes his hand while her cousin throws questions at him like rocks. Isaac answers quick and concise, looking for a way out of the conversation, the party.

"Yes, me and Miles are brothers."

"Yes, foster brothers."

"Yes, I hoop . . . Look, I'm sorry, where's the bathroom? Be back in a minute."

He ascends the steps into another kind of noise. Loud, drunken talk. Laughter. No music but the conversation. Seven adults stand in a kitchen over a liquor buffet, an island of opened and unopened bottles, sipped-on and finished cocktails.

Isaac flips down his hood. He stands with his hands in his pockets, waiting to be seen.

A bald forty-something man with a graying goatee and John Lennon glasses seems to be the host. He's red-faced and loud, refilling drinks. Standing next to him is a thin tanning-bed-tan woman with a blatant boob job. She laughs at everything the host says. A couple. Funny, to Isaac they look related, like the woman is a female version of her husband. Like he shaved, lost weight, put on a wig, and stuffed a bra with silicon bags. Vanity, Isaac thinks: the man is so in love with himself he married his reflection.

It's the woman who notices Isaac first. She walks toward him, drink in hand, and starts asking him questions: who are you? Where are you from? Who did you come with? She's real touchy feely. Touching Isaac's shoulder. Feeling his chest. Grabbing him by the arm when she leads him to Liquor Island. The laughing and the loudness stops. The adults have gone back to being adults. Asking questions. Making eye contact.

The host says, "Wait, wait, wait . . ." He walks into the living room and returns with the sports section of the Grand Rapids Press. "This is you," he says. "Isn't it?" The headline says, *Ottawa Hills Sophomore, Page, Nets 37 against Rival Creston.* The picture beneath it shows Isaac pulling up for a jump shot. His tongue peeks out of his mouth, touching his top lip. His eyes are focused on the target, shooting elbow emerging from four defensive hands.

"Yes, sir. That's me."

"No, I don't know your daughter. I just met her tonight."

The host walks to the top of the stairs. "Nikki! Nikki!"

"The bathroom?"

"Yes, I was looking for the bathroom."

Isaac washes his hands and stares at his reflection in the bathroom mirror. He presses his forehead to the glass. He inhales, holds it for a moment, and then exhales slow. Isaac steps back into the kitchen and waits on the edge of the conversation. It's Nikki being interviewed now.

"Yes, art school."

"Yes, Chicago."

"Black and white photography."

"No, I don't plan to teach. I plan to travel. Freelance. Maybe photo journalism."

"Isaac," says her father. "There you are. Nikki, I believe you've met Mr. Page, here?"

Isaac's eyes meet Nikki's and they take each other in. Recognition. They've been in this situation before; they just haven't been in it together.

"I was just telling Nikki, Isaac—"

"Mom, stop." Nikki's tone is cold and her eyes are rolled. "Look, Isaac. *Isaac,* right? You wanna go for a walk or something?"

Isaac follows Nikki outside. The crisp air bites his cheeks. He hears the low hum of laughter and conversation from the weed smokers gathered in the darkness. The driveway is filled with cars. A basketball hoop with a rusted pole presides over one side. No net hangs from a bent rim. A chunk of backboard is missing like it was smashed by a thrown rock.

"My Uncle Mike and Aunt Myra." Nikki waves her hand toward a couple arguing in front of a parked car. "Every time someone looks at her boobs he gets jealous. Every time she drinks she flirts." Nikki lights a cigarette when they walk past them. "You're welcome, by the way."

"Huh?"

"I could tell you wanted to leave. Shit, I was ready to leave. I didn't even want a party. My parents wouldn't take no for an answer."

"Birthday?"

"A Nikki-got-accepted-to-art-school-in-Chicago party."

"That's cool. Congratulations."

"Yeah, thanks. But all they're really doing is congratulating themselves on their parenting. Can't wait to get the fuck out of here."

She offers Isaac a cigarette and Isaac says no. "Ah, yeah, forgot. You're some kind of basketball god, right? Some Mr. Everything. That's why my parents called me upstairs. So we can meet and talk and fall in love. Maybe share a romantic moment under the stars? That would complete my success as a daughter: a strapping young man on my arm."

Nikki's not like other teenage girls Isaac has met, traveling in packs, shallow, and desperate to blend in. No, Nikki is clearly "Nikki." A middle-class suburban white girl who resents it. Pierces her nipples and goes braless just so her parents' friends will look, just so they will smile their fake smiles, and the minute she turns her back, talk about what a problem child she is.

"Sorry to burst your bubble though, Isaac," says Nikki, just as Isaac is considering the possibility, "but you're not my type."

"Okay. But thank you, anyway. I *was* ready to leave."

"Anti-social?"

"I just like to be alone."

"We have that in common." Nikki finishes her cigarette and flicks it into someone's yard. "So this superstar thing—it doesn't really fit your whole hide-under-a hoodie way of existing, does it?"

Isaac lets her words land and disappear. Instead he says, "The fatigue shirt. Your brother's?"

"Yeah. My brother James. He's in the Marines. He's stationed in Afghanistan."

"I'm sorry," Isaac says. "Must be hard. The worrying, I mean."

"Worried?" Nikki coughs out a laugh. "Worst thing that happens to James over there: he breaks a nail. My big brother sits at a desk all day. Enlisted for the GI Bill. He gets out next year. Plans to come home and go to music recording school or something. Your brother met him when he was home on leave a few weeks ago. Apparently they have big plans for the future."

Nikki leads Isaac down a cement pathway that leads into a park. They step off the path and cut through the grass, down a snow-covered hill, across a soccer field and into a playground. "You mind if I get high?" she asks him.

"Not at all," Isaac says. He sits beside her on a wooden structure that looks like a small boat, only there are monkey bars above it, and a small slide on the backend. He watches Nikki pull out a long joint and light it, lean back and smoke it, staring at the sky. Isaac leans back beside her.

"Too bad you're a goody goody," Nikki says. "It's a nice night to get high and look at the stars."

"You assume too much," Isaac says. Not really wanting to try weed, but wanting to prove he isn't afraid to. They all have him in this box. This Basketball Is His Life box, like he breathes for it, like that's who he is. It's always Isaac Page: That ballplayer. Or Isaac Page: That white boy who plays for Ottawa. He takes the joint from Nikki and hits it. Coughs. An ash lands on his cheek and it burns. He brushes it off. He hits it two more times before passing it back to her, feeling nothing at first, but then the stars appear to have a pulse that's in sync with his heart, now beating loud in his mind like a tribal drum—and the stars, the stars swell with each beat, and the thin pale clouds in the black sky seem to collapse upon him.

"How do you feel?" Nikki asks him.

"High," says Isaac. His voice sounds like someone else's. Or rather, it's his voice, but he's someone else, listening to the real Isaac Page speaking from another room.

Nikki laughs. "Do you want to play a game?"

"What kind of game?"

"A game of confessions."

"Okay."

"You first."

"I don't know what to confess."

"I don't know," Nikki says. "Something you're embarrassed about. Something I'd be surprised to hear."

"Okay," says Isaac. "I'm a virgin."

Nikki laughs. "Isaac," she says. "You have *virgin* written all over you. Something better. Something good. I mean *really* good."

"You first," says Isaac.

"Okay," Nikki says. "Hmm. Alright. I have one. Are you ready?"

"Yeah."

"I used to steal cars."

"Bullshit."

"I did, I swear. The first time I did it on a dare. We were playing a game a lot like this one and that's the dare I got. So my friends drove me around until we found a car left running—you know, someone thinking they're going in and out of the store. I was scared shitless, but I did it. I only drove a few blocks and then I parked the car and took off running. But that rush . . . I wanted to do it again. So on nights I was bored, or lonely, or sad, that's what I'd do. I'd do it right now if you dared me to."

"That's the truth?"

"It is. I'm hardcore, right?"

"Why'd you stop?"

"A felony wouldn't look good on my college application."

"Ah," says Isaac.

"Okay, Isaac Page. Your turn. And it better be good. I just confessed to multiple felonies. You know my name. You know where I live. Give me something good. I want you to shock me."

His skin is numb. His lips are numb. His brain is numb. It wouldn't be hard to shock Nikki; the shit he's seen. The shit he's been through. But the one loud thought in his addled brain is Mae. She's his confession, he can feel it like he's going to throw it up, like he needs to speak it into the air, like he needs someone to know. "I'm obsessed with my foster mom."

"What?" Nikki's voice is curious, but not judgmental.

"A few years ago," says Isaac. "I walked in on her in the bathtub. I saw everything. It fucked me up. I started fantasizing about her. Jerking off thinking about her. One time," says Isaac. "Shit, this is embarrassing . . . one time she caught me doing it. I took her picture off the wall and wrapped her panties around my dick. She caught me."

"Damn," Nikki says.

"Yeah, *damn*. The worst part is it changed me."

"What do you mean?"

"I'm only turned on by black women. Black women with big breasts."

"So your foster mom is black?"

"Yeah."

"That's deep," Nikki says. "Hey, there's a little bit of this joint left, you want it?"

"No," says Isaac. "I'm too high. My mind . . . shit's starting to get too real."

"So let me ask you something . . ."

"Okay."

"You're white."

"Obviously."

"But you aren't attracted to white girls?"

"I don't think so."

"So if I kissed you . . . *nothing*? Or if I reached into your pants?"

"I don't know."

"Hmm. Too bad I'm into girls," says Nikki. "That would be a fun experiment."

"Is that your next confession?" Isaac asks. "That you're into girls?" Now his voice seems to come from a mile down the road, or from another planet, or from deep in the dungeon of his own mind."

"No," says Nikki. "Everyone knows I'm a lesbian."

Isaac's mother is dead. Isaac's father is dead. Joey Cane is dead. They're buried in the earth. Their bodies are rotting. He can see their bodies rotting. He can see them racing to rot. First Joey died. Then his mother. Then his father. But there is size to account for, body weight. All things considered his mother would rot the fastest.

"Isaac," Nikki says. "Are you okay? You don't look so hot."

Isaac is going to die. He'll be buried. Covered with dirt. What if he isn't really dead and they bury him alive. What if they cremate him? What if he wakes up while it's happening?

"Isaac?"

Everyone's dead. Everyone's going to die. Jackson, Mae, Miles. Nikki, she's going to die too. Everyone he knows. Everyone he loves. Everyone. Maybe it's him? Maybe he's some kind of plague—a curse— you know Isaac Page and you're pregnant with death.

"Isaac . . ."

Joey Cane looked like a wax sculpture in a velvet lined box. His skull reconstructed by morgue art, swollen, but no evidence that a bullet ever destroyed through it. Isaac glanced at Joey and walked away fast, his head down. Tears soaking a suit that was too tight around the collar. Bumping into a pew. Looking up and seeing Lyric. Sitting with her Grandmother. Looking bored. Like she was sitting at church. And Isaac didn't understand. Not yet. Not until it was him. Not until a few weeks later when it was his mother's turn to sleep in a coffin. Not until it was Isaac's turn to pretend that his life as he knew it wasn't coming to an end.

"I can't breathe," Isaac says.

"Isaac, chill out."

He's a pervert. Nikki knows it now. She's judging him. She can't wait to tell everyone that Isaac Page wants to fuck his foster mother. He'll be called a foster mother fucker. Jackson will find out. Isaac will be sent away. Everyone will know. "Fuck," Isaac says. "Nikki, how do you get this to stop? I'm too high."

Nikki laughs. She's laughing at him. Everyone's going to know. Fuck. No more weed. Never again. "*No. More. Weed.*"

"Isaac, calm down," says Nikki. "Breathe, Isaac. All you have to do is breathe."

Lyric sprays her mother's perfume on her wrists and neck. She slips into a black thong she'd stolen from Macy's earlier that day. She feels the Ecstasy begin to kick in, the pill popped a half hour ago, stolen from her mother's nightstand drawer.

Lyric's legs tingle, like butterflies in her stomach, but just her legs. Then the feeling rises inside her, expands, fluttering heart, surreal vision, bedside lamp throbbing.

She picks up her baby blanket, hugs it, holds it against her hot skin. It's cool, other side of the pillow cool, loose threads like tiny cloth worms crawling across her chest. She's aware of all of its parts, her scratchy embroidered name, the ribbon-y red border.

She slips out of her bra and she touches her nipples. A warm rush between her thighs. Footsteps in the hallway. When Clyde opens the door Lyric is lying on her stomach, her own thunderbooty swaying as she rocks back and forth on her hips. Clyde stands in the doorway, a black figure wearing a cape of light. Tara's probably passed out drunk in the other room, leaving Lyric to deal while she walks through life with the cold gaze of someone refusing to mourn. But Lyric knows better. She can see it. Her mother wears it in her eyes: the grief, the regrets, the guilt. She has the body of a twenty-year-old. Eyes like she's fifty. Dark purple circles. Wrinkle wings along the edges. This woman who used to fill her mind with princess stories, castles and dragons and magic rings that transported Lyric to other worlds. But there are no castles on the southeast side. And the only princesses in Grand Rapids are white and Dutch and oblivious to this life.

Lyric feels the full effect of the Ecstasy now, wanting to be touched, wanting to hurt her mother, wanting to be hurt.

What will this prove?

Clyde steps into her bedroom and closes the door.

Christmas day has arrived. Isaac wakes to Bing Crosby's rendition of "Do You See What I See." He knows it's Bing Crosby because for the past three years Mae's told him it's her favorite Christmas song. Isaac knows Jackson and Mae are downstairs in their pajamas. He knows they're both drinking coffee. He knows they had sex last night and woke up giddy this morning. He knows it's early. Six, seven in the morning. Miles is sleeping with his headphones on. His hand stashed in his sweatpants. Better Isaac wake him up than Mae. Because Mae has this shrill morning voice she uses sometimes—tone deaf and persistent—better to be shaken out of sleep than annoyed out of it. Isaac walks over to Miles and shakes him. Miles takes his hand out of his pants and wipes his face with it.

"Wake your nasty ass up," says Isaac. "It's Christmas."

"Give me an hour," Miles says. He takes off his headphones. Rolls over on his side.

Isaac licks his index finger and sticks it in Miles' ear. Jumps out of the way when Miles swats at him. "You better get up, Miles," says Isaac. "Or Mae's gonna be up here. You know she will."

The boys walk downstairs together. "Merry Christmas!" say

Jackson and Mae. Practically in unison. Jackson has a Santa hat on and they both wear red and green pajamas. They are genuinely corny. But it's nice to see them happy. Jackson sober and Mae with that glow like she loves him—Mae and Jackson on one of their good days, now that's a thing to behold—so much love between them, Mae calling him *Baby* like she's hugging him with the word and Jackson never too far from his wife, always finding an excuse to put his an arm around her.

Presents surround the tree and spill out across the living room. They always go overboard. They'll open gifts, one at a time, and then Jackson and Mae will cook together while Isaac and Miles sort through their things, the scent of bacon, sausage, and eggs filling the house. The scent of homemade cinnamon rolls. Isaac sits on the couch and Miles sits beside him.

This year Isaac receives book after book after book. After book. After book. Thirty of them in all, written by authors he's never heard of, guys named Colum McCann, Michael Chabon, and Junot Diaz, women named Zadie Smith, Connie May Fowler, and Ellen Lesser. And the grand finale, for Isaac, is a massive bookshelf that he will probably have to assemble himself, Mae over there smiling, Jackson cutting her a glance that seems to convey *What the fuck?*

"Isaac," Mae tells him. She's still smiling. "I know there are a ton of books. I know you haven't been reading much the last few years. But I always see you writing. It seems like something you're passionate about. If you write, that makes you a writer. And well, reading is a writer's weight room."

"Thanks, Mae. Thanks, Jackson," says Isaac. He watches Miles with his electronic gadgets, his new clothes, and feels a little played, then a little guilty for feeling ungrateful. So he opens the gigantic box his bookshelf is in and begins the daunting task of putting it together.

•

Jackson has gone missing. Breakfast is almost finished. The living room is covered with boards and screws. Isaac needs help. He needs Jackson's help. But Mae is in the kitchen alone. Isaac tries upstairs first. He's not there. He checks the driveway for Jackson's truck. It's still parked behind Mae's Camry. Downstairs, maybe? Isaac walks down the steps and finds Jackson sitting on the washing machine. A bottle of Hennessey pressed against his lips. The past couple weeks he's been sober. Supposedly. The arguing has been on hiatus. Jackson's been sleeping in his bed. The slow jams have been playing late into the night.

"Shit, Isaac." Jackson goes to hide the bottle at first, but it's too late. He knows Isaac's seen it. He shrugs, cocks his head to the left a little, and then downs as much as he can in one pull. "Please," says Jackson. "Don't say anything to Mae."

"I won't," says Isaac. "But I need your help."

"With what?"

"My bookshelf. It's a pain in the ass to put together."

Jackson laughs. "Man, I told her . . ."

"Told her what?"

Jackson gets this weird expression. A caught expression he gets sometimes when Mae busts him drinking. "Nothing. Nothing. No problem. Give me a few minutes and I'll knock it out for you."

•

Mae knows. Isaac can tell because she's glaring at Jackson from across the table. The only reason she hasn't called him on it is because it's Christmas. And Jackson knows she knows because he's kissing ass. Volunteering to do the dishes. Clean up the living room. "Relax, baby. Just relax. I got you." Even Isaac recognizes the slur in his speech. The change in his eyes. The smell. That's the biggest giveaway. Jackson's a sweater. The alcohol always comes out of his pores. Isaac glances at Miles and shakes his head. Miles knows too. Everyone knows. And Mae doesn't have it in her to hold her tongue.

"It's ten in the morning, Jackson," Mae says.

"Yeah?"

"It's Christmas."

"Uh huh."

"Okay. I'm glad we're on the same page." She waits. Isaac knows she's trying to not to do this. He also knows she can't help herself. A big hot steaming pile of shit is about to hit the fan. The problem is the praise she had been giving him. Isaac heard her, at least a dozen times the last few weeks—she told him how proud she was, how happy she was that he was sober. "So where is it, Jackson?"

"Where's what?" He looks at Isaac. Isaac shrugs.

"You know goddamn well what."

"Mae, it's Christmas."

"Exactly. It's Christmas. It's Christmas and it's ten o'clock in the goddamn morning." She throws her plate at him and Jackson blocks it with his arm. A piece of scrambled egg sticks to his beard. Everyone notices but him. "Where is it? Huh? Where's the bottle?"

Isaac flashes back to Francis Street. He sits at a table with his father doing a puzzle. A large beer sits on a coaster. Frank doesn't look up from the table when Nelly walks through the door.

"What do you want me to say, Mae? It's Christmas. Can't we deal with this tomorrow? For the boy's sake, Mae. Bitch at me tomorrow."

"Bitch at you? It's ten o'clock in the morning on Christmas and you're drunk. Drunk. At ten in the morning. On Christmas. Does that register with you? Does that compute as a problem?"

"I'm sorry."

"So you admit it?"

"Is that what ends this? You need me to admit it? Fine. I've been drinking."

I'm sick, Isaac's father said that night. *I just need money. Where's the money, Nelly?* Those eyes, remembers Isaac. Those crackhead eyes. *When I think of my father's eyes I'm reminded of blood. I'm reminded of hate. I'm reminded of death.* The table flipped over, the beer rolling across the floor, the puzzle lying face down on the carpet. The way his father's voice changed when he said it again. So calm. *I just need money.*

Mae stands. The veins in her neck are prominent. Her eyes spew flames. Her small bony hand is clenched in a fist. It only takes her two quick steps to get around the table. It takes only one right cross to break Jackson's nose. Blood lands on Isaac's plate. On the table. On the floor. Jackson pinches his nose and stands. He holds Mae back with the hand not pinching the nose. She flails.

"Stop!" yells Isaac. "Jesus Christ. Just stop!"

"Are you calm?" Jackson asks Mae. "If you're calm I'll let you go."

"I'm calm." Mae looks at Isaac. His expression softens. Jackson lets her go.

"All these years, Mae." Jackson says. "All these years and you never asked me why?

"Why what, Jackson?"

"You ain't ever asked me what's so hard." He's let go of his nose and more blood pours out of it. He wipes his hand across his mouth and then his hand on his shirt. "I was supposed to be somebody, Mae. Don't you understand that?" Jackson's crying. Isaac's never seen him cry. "I was supposed to be somebody," he says. "Don't you understand?"

"You are somebody, Jackson," Mae tells him. "That's what you don't understand."

Exodus
2014–2015

THE DIM LIGHT FROM A READING LAMP yawns across the bed.
Thunderbooty's passed out, looking like a three-star narrative in a
two-star movie, another southeast side story with a predictable end.
She has a ten-gallon ass and a need to numb her life with liquor.
Another Iggy's Place girl, stripping because hard times swallowed her.
Calling excuses reasons and trucking forward, believing like a million
other girls believed, she's taking control of her life, fighting to leave
this game with her soul intact, thinking she's one of the few who will
defeat the odds.

Cesar leans against the headboard licking a Cigarillo, stuffing it
with weed, then rolling it thin and tight. This life is getting old. Cesar's
getting old. He's almost forty-five now and still sleeping around, still
immersed in the underbelly of life, feeling more and more as he ages, as
the sex game becomes more mundane, the need to settle down. To shut
down the website and try something else.

He stands and digs into his pants pocket for his cash. Puts a hundred on the nightstand. Thunderbooty didn't ask him for a dime. He's
here because sometimes he comes here. He's here because he isn't bored
with the booty yet. He's here because she isn't clingy, or talking crazy, or
hinting toward him being anything more than late-night company. But
you never can be too sure. So he pays her anyway. Better to pay than let
her get it twisted. Better to pay than have her crying at your doorstep.

Cesar wedges the blunt behind his ear. He steps out of the room, down the hallway, and into the living room. The apartment is covered with framed photographs of this lost family. All these smiles jailed in the past. A baby's daddy dead and gone, murdered, enshrined on these walls. These people haven't learned how to mourn. They haven't learned how to let go. The past is upon them. Within these walls, in the air they breathe—a constant reminder of what they lost.

Cesar opens a sliding glass door and walks out onto a balcony. He leans against the railing with his back to the moon. Cesar lights the blunt. He inhales deep and holds the smoke in his chest for a moment before exhaling out of his nose. Then Thunderbooty's daughter slips into the living room wearing nothing but a T-shirt and a thong. She's young and dumb and heading down the same path as her mother. She nods Cesar's way before walking into the kitchen, pouring herself a glass of orange juice, and drinking it in one pull. She's got her mother's ass. And she's fast; too fast. Only God knows what she's seen or done within these walls, out on this block, in the dark corners of the bleak southeast side streets.

"Little Thunderbooty," says Cesar, when she joins him on the balcony.

"Cesar Bolden," she says. She reaches for the blunt. "You thought about what I asked you?"

Cesar hits the blunt one more time then hands it to her. The girl isn't even as old as Miles and Cesar sees her whole life trajectory. The same trajectory as Joy Green. The same trajectory as her mother. He could tell her the truth. Stay away from the flesh game, Babygirl. Get that student financial aid. Go get yourself a degree. But for what? Why waste the words? The truth is too real, too hard. It's too much work. That sex money is easy, in the beginning, and people with easy on their mind can't see beyond the end of a day.

"I already told you. I don't fuck with fifteen year olds," Cesar says.

"I'm about to be sixteen."

Cesar shakes his head. "I can't help you, Little Thunderbooty."

"There's gotta be something," she says. She chokes when she says it. Laughs when she hands the blunt back to Cesar. "Let me clean your apartment," she says. "Or wash your car. I ain't afraid to work. Ain't afraid to get my hands dirty."

"You ain't ever gonna see the inside of my apartment. And washing my car is a crackhead's job."

"C'mon, Man. There's gotta be something."

"Holler at me when you're seventeen," says Cesar.

Tara wakes to find Cesar gone. No surprise. Another empty bed. Another empty morning. A fifth of Captain Morgan has four swallows still in it. The bottle sits on the nightstand next to the hundred-dollar bill Cesar left her. She's not one of those girls. Those girls that listen to the drunken whispers of men while they're giving lap dances, dry-humping cock and auctioning the booty to the highest bidder. Those girls walk through a door that locks from the outside. There's no coming back through that door. Iggy won't let you dance with a black eye. Iggy won't let you dance when you're knocked-up by some horny fool that pinned you to the bed and snapped off his condom.

Sometimes though, it's nice to lie next to a warm body. So if a man is a regular, and he has good manners, and he's smooth enough to take off his wedding ring before he shows up at Iggy's Place, and he wants to talk about Tara's life and not her ass—sometimes she'll call it a date— sometimes she'll pretend she's being wooed instead of used, pretend it's not two o'clock in the morning, pretend that Lyric's not sleeping in the room next to hers.

She never asks for money, but most of them leave it, and when she finds the cash she adds it to the stash she earned the night before. She clings to the fact that she didn't ask for it. That fact, she tells herself on these empty mornings, makes her a single woman on a date and not a stripper moonlighting as a whore.

No. Tara's not one of those girls. Those lazy, greedy little girls who are all body and no brains and low self-esteem. Or those foolish girls that Cesar plucks from the glass cage and puts on his website, a few clicks away from being seen by their family. Or those girls that show up for a few weeks and then disappear, not because they wanted to, just because they did, nothing in their wake but rumors, and tight-lipped Iggy Carter isn't one to answer questions. Nope. Not Tara James. Thunderbooty's the one shaking her ass. Tara James has a bank account. Tara James has no debt, no car note, and a 720 credit score. Tara James has $40,000 saved for a house, and when she gets $50,000 she's done, she's getting a job and establishing what Jason Burke, a loan officer at Fifth Third Bank, likes to call legitimate employment, and then, with a low mortgage and a substantial nest egg, Tara James will start thinking about her exodus from this life and into a better one.

Yes. Tara James is a woman with a plan. She rolls out of bed and peels the wet sheets from the mattress. The infamous Cesar Bolden. They call him cold-hearted and cruel, but Tara respects his game. She sees a man just using the tools God gave him. He's the rat in the bar-rel with the sharpest teeth, the biggest claws. Besides, she's not look-ing for love. All she needs in this life is a chance at a better life, and to get that she works, she sacrifices, she tells her morals to shut their damn mouth, or turn the other way when shame starts poking its nose around. Cesar's convenient. He's a late-night text. He's on call, a doc-tor, and the dick is nothing more than medicine. He doesn't ask for any-thing, doesn't need anything—there's no fear of stalking, there's no fear of him getting sex confused with love.

Tara tosses the bedding toward a dirty clothes hamper and misses. She picks up the bottle of Captain Morgan and goes to dump its remains in her bathroom sink, but then she changes her mind. She twists off the cap and takes the rum down in one pull. She's no alcoholic, it's just not in her to waste. Besides, the liquor is good for the hurt. That's what she tells herself. Some nights she feels alright. Those nights she's sober. Nights off from Iggy's, curled up on the couch with a blanket, watching a movie. But some nights are hard. Some nights the edge is too sharp and the memories too real. And those Iggy's Place nights—the glass cage is no place for sobriety.

Tara walks into the bathroom with the empty bottle and drops it in the trash. She washes her face. Brushes her teeth. Lyric is up and around. Dishes clanging in the kitchen. This girl. She's filled with fire and fury. Fifteen years old and her teenage years already gone. Stealing cigarettes and weed from Tara's stash—well, not even stealing, taking, helping herself and daring Tara to say something. It's like Lyric has been collecting moments, and one day, one day she'll unleash a whole life-time of bad parenting on Tara, she'll throw it right back in her face. And what could Tara say then, because Lyric wouldn't be wrong.

But she's still required to say something, isn't she? It's almost ten in the morning and the girl should be at school. Her words can go in through one of Lyric's ears and out of the other. They can float through the room ignored. But she has to say something. So why the fear? Confrontations have never been a problem for Tara. Why now? Is it shame? Thin walls keep no secrets. Lyric knows all. Tara suspects Lyric has her own loud and vicious words rumbling around in her head. Are those words what Tara fears? Being called out. Being stripped down to bare bone and exposed by the one person, the only person who matters to her.

Your life is fragile indeed when confronting your child is an act of brav-ery. But Tara is brave. You have to be in her line of work. You have to put on a business face and pretend you're unfazed. You have to pretend you don't hear them call you bitch, cunt, hoe—that you don't see them jerking off in the furthest corner of the room, the corner the servers bid out when it's their night for cleanup duty—and when the patrons break the rules and touch you, when you feel their hands on your hips you let it slide, because you feel their money against your skin, so you press their hands down and turn over your shoulder and scold them with a smile that says okay, okay, but don't go any further, but sometimes it doesn't do the trick, and even when their fin-gers creep a little lower you have to keep cool, because though the bounc-ers never let things get too out of hand, cash rules in Tara's line of work, and Tara knows her beating heart doesn't stop her from being a product, and in her line of work product comes second to the cash.

Tara steps out of her bedroom and finds Lyric in the kitchen. Lyric glances at her then returns to the dishes. Can she blame the girl for her lack of respect? Should wearing the title Mother grant you some sort of free pass with your child, or should you be held accountable for your failures, your continued failures, no matter how noble your intentions are, no matter how things look on the surface: the stripping, the . . . the date nights. Why should Tara, as Lyric's mother, have to break down her plan and give a teenage girl reasons, show her an account statement, a letter from Loan Officer Jason Burke of Fifth Third bank, should she, wearing the title Mother have to cross that line with her daughter and just keep it real? Tara doesn't think so.

"Good morning, baby," Tara says.

"Late night?" asks Lyric. She rinses a plate and wedges it in the strainer.

"I had to work."

"Cesar Bolden was here last night. Is he what you're calling *work*?"

"He's a friend."

"Whatever." Lyric pulls the stopper from the sink and lets the water drain.

"Why aren't you at school?"

Lyric shakes her head. Tara watches her dry the dishes with a towel and put them in the cupboard.

"Answer me," says Tara.

"You're ridiculous."

"I said answer me."

"Because it's Saturday, Mom." Lyric nearly bumps into Tara when she walks out of the kitchen and down the hallway.

Today the world is a pale shade of gray. It's going to rain. Cesar's always loved the rain. The steadiness of heavy drops against the roof or the road. Tapping against the Caddy. Life likes to slow down. Street corners are vacated. The sidewalks are emptied. Even the crackheads stay inside.

Cesar watches Miles plug his iPod into the stereo. His son riding shotgun in the Caddy reminds him of the past. A place Cesar no longer avoids. That hurt confronted and devoured. Moody Bolden forgiven though no forgiveness was ever asked for. Cesar's childhood a place he visits sometimes so he can reference point those loud moments in his life, those scariest scenes, when he was asked to act grown when he was only a boy—he likes to revisit those moments and measure himself against who he is now. Against who was and who he's become.

Miles presses a few buttons on the iPod and a chorus of strings, something both dark and somehow inspirational, bellows from the speakers. A teaser base drop. One loud thump and then another, introducing what's to come. Miles slants his head and glances at Cesar. That's when the Darth Vader theme music comes in, The Walk, and it loops on what Miles calls an eight-bar count, marrying the now-pounding baseline beautifully, and the strings bringing something that sounds like glory to the beat. The composition reminds Cesar of an army's march toward an epic battle.

Miles has his mother's talent and his father's brains. And though it pains Cesar to admit it, Miles has Jackson Carter's work ethic. Cesar's son will not fail. He's been honing his craft since he was young, dreaming of being a rapper, finding his niche instead as a beat maker, a producer, teaching himself on a keyboard Cesar bought him a few summers ago. He's only seventeen years old now and already stacking his dough. Already well on his way toward success.

"Dope," says Cesar. "Your style is evolving."

"Thanks," Miles says. He turns the stereo down to low.

"Do you need anything? Equipment? Anything at all?"

"I'm good, Cesar. I got everything I need for right now. Unless you got an Emcee. That's what I really need, someone real nice to do an album with."

"There has to be a thousand rappers in this city."

"I'm not looking for one in a thousand, Cesar. I'm looking for one in a million."

"When it's time," Cesar tells him. "When you get your ducks in a row. I want to invest. When it's time, Miles, just say the word." Yeah. Miles will not fail. Every move he makes is a calculated move. A gift Cesar bestowed upon his son. Talent and business savvy is a deadly combination. It feels good seeing himself in Miles. The best part of himself. What Cesar gave up, letting him be raised by another man, playing the lobby in Miles' life—seeing Miles becoming the best version of Miles—that makes it all worth it. "I just want to say . . ." It's always so hard in these moments. It's still hard to cross some lines, to allow himself to be vulnerable. "I'm proud of you, Miles."

"Thanks, Cesar," he says. "Listen, you mind dropping me at Garfield Park? I'm supposed to link up with Isaac."

"Yeah," Cesar says. "No problem." Thunder claps and the rain comes down hard. People run for their porches and cars. A few stragglers at a bus stop cover their heads with whatever is in their hands and continue waiting.

"Nevermind," Miles says. "Jackson's on the road. You can drop me at home."

"What about Isaac?" asks Cesar. "You want to scoop him on the way?"

Miles laughs. "Naw," he says. "Isaac goes home when he's ready to. Rain, lighting, don't matter—there could be a flash flood and Isaac would still be out there, finding a way to tread water and shoot jumpers."

"Damn." Cesar remembers Isaac's father. He wonders what Frank Page's life was life before it all went to shit. Before drugs and porn. Before he was running through the southeast side with that dirtball nigga Terrell. Before a slug with Frank's name on it came screaming out of DeMarco's pistol and into what was left of his cracked-out brain. Before he ended up buried under the Wealthy Street train bridge, on Punk Island, surrounded by the Grand River, a cool breeze swooping over his unmarked grave.

"Mark my words," Miles says. "Isaac Page is going to the NBA."

Isaac Page. Another fatherless child. Another owed apology.

Another living, breathing reminder of Cesar's sins. Another enemy, if Isaac ever knew the truth. A truth Isaac would certainly share with Miles. Some secrets are best left with God. "He's that good?" asks Cesar.

"He is," says Miles. "And he's that pissed off."

It's like he's underwater and the thousands in attendance are above the surface. That's how they sound, here, but not; the ball echoing off the hardwood floor is so much louder in his mind. They are elevator music. Incidental. This is his Matrix. Everything moves slowly: the defender reaching for the ball, the teammate slashing toward the basket, the backside help adjusting their position in case he passes the ball, a man spilling his popcorn in the first row of the bleachers, a child breaking free of his mother's grip and running courtside with a wild devilish smile.

Isaac guides the ball behind his back, away from the defender's reaching hand, and elevates.

Flick. Snap.

It's the first round of the Michigan Regional high school basketball tournament and it's being played at Grand Valley State University, Mae's alma mater. Isaac glances over at Jackson. A few rows up and focused on Isaac, his index finger twisting his goatee. Mae sitting next to him, clapping. Above the quiet noise Isaac hears her yell, "Good shot, baby!" He wonders what they feel when they watch him? A senior in high school now and a national hoops phenom. This hardluck kid all grown up and thriving. Pride? Is that what they feel? A sense of accomplishment?

He defends the man bringing up the ball. He could rip him if he wanted to, he could rip him at will, stride down the court, throw it down with two hands, beat his chest with his fist and point up to the Ottawa Hills student section. But he doesn't. He lays back. Only applies pressure when the kid's in shooting range. Smothers him. Makes him pass the ball to another player. It's too easy.

This isn't what he asked for. It's what they told him to do. *You have this gift. Don't waste your gift.* Joey Cane once said something about God and talent. Something about spiritual balance, about seeing God in the work of humans. He mentioned the Sistine Chapel and Mohammed Ali and these moments of human perfection being God incarnate. But Isaac's beauty was found in solace. His love for basketball born when it was just him and the concrete. The echo of the ball and the snap of the net. He never found God in those moments alone. And he loved being good at something, having something to invest in, but he never wanted to share his talent with the world.

This crowd, this team, these cameras, the interviews, the recruitment letters. This was Joey's dream. This was Jackson's dream. This was not his. It was never a gift; it was refuge. It was his hole. A coffin he crawled into. And now it's like the world wants to crawl in it with him. The same world he is trying to hide from.

There's not enough space.

Flick. Snap.

He wonders if this is what Joey missed, this spotlight, the greedy masses reaching out to touch him—this small-time fame, this stage— is this what Joey was looking for when he stared out at nothing, cigarette between his lips, another behind his ear, smoke rolling off into the night. What's Jackson thinking now? Quiet in the crowd. Is he living his dream through Isaac? Or is he stung by the past, lusting for it, lost in the nineties with his whole life ahead of him?

These lights are too bright for Isaac. The air is too thick to breathe. The world is too close. He dribbles past the half-court line and holds the ball. He looks up at Jackson and Jackson stands. Isaac calls a time out. He checks himself out of the game. He untucks his jersey and sits on the end of the bench. His coach doesn't question him. The game is well in hand. He's tired of the cameras. Tired of the questions. Of the looming decision. He closes his eyes. This used to be solitude. A calm other place. But the chaos has found him. It has become this place.

•

The boy is poetry. Fluid. Flawless. It's like he is playing against children, toying with them, a cat pawing at mice. But there is no soul in his motions. The passion, the anger Jackson admired in Isaac when he was younger is no longer there. He can't tell if Isaac has softened or hardened. If he has conformed to this life, or if he's simply burrowed deeper inside his own mind. Jackson used to wonder when this time would come. When the past the boy was suppressing would reemerge, impose itself upon him. When basketball would lose its healing power and Isaac would be left with flesh and bones and memory. When the boy would be forced, finally, to deal.

Jackson stands. He watches Isaac call a timeout and walk off the court. Mae, sweet Mae, oblivious and blind, cheering for the boy and not noticing his eyes ask for them in the stands. Jackson takes a step toward Isaac and Mae grabs his hand. She hasn't touched him that way in weeks. Her skin against his feels like a stranger's skin.

"What's wrong, Jackson?"

"Isaac. Something's wrong with Isaac."

Or maybe it's not the past, maybe it's the pressure? Constantly approached by people. The recruiters. The letters. The attention. The clock is winding down. Isaac is sitting at the end of the bench. The press lurking toward him. The Ottawa Hills students are out of their seats chanting down from ten. Cameras flash. The crowd rushes the court. The press is smothering Isaac. Asking questions. More flashing. "Back away!" Jackson yells. A few of them listen. Those that don't get shoved out of his way. Isaac stands and they face the press together. Jackson wraps an arm around Isaac's shoulder. "One question each, then you leave him alone." He sees Mae standing in the crowd of onlookers. She's smiling, looking at Jackson in a way she hasn't looked at him in years. Her eyes doing the smiling, her high cheekbones wet with tears. When the questions are answered she approaches Jackson and kisses him on the forehead. Jackson watches her hug Isaac and tell him good game.

Miles runs up and jumps on Isaac. "Bro," he says, "what'd you drop, like fifty on 'em?"

"Don't know."

It's moments like these Jackson wishes he could freeze. The four of them together. A family. The son of Joy Green, the son of Cesar Bolden raised right: Jackson's gift to the world. Mae paying attention to Jackson. Jackson. For once her eyes on him. Miles keeps talking but the lights are out in Isaac's eyes. He's someplace else. Looking through Miles like he isn't even hearing his words. Mae watching Jackson and smiling. Jackson glancing back and forth at Isaac and Miles imagining who they would be in different circumstances: Isaac left in the system, recycled in and out of homes. Miles being groomed by Cesar, schooled in the art of street, hustling, drug dealing.

Jackson watches Miles turn to Mae. "Can I get those Camry keys though, Momma Mae? I wanna take baby brother out to celebrate."

•

The engine in Jackson's Ford F150 growls. Led Zeppelin is in the CD player. He turns the volume on low because it's not Mae's thing. He steers through the campus of GVSU, the same place they met all those years ago that bitter winter, Mae a soon-to-be graduate, Jackson still trying to save the world one damsel at a time. Tonight Mae holds his hand. He's not thinking about the pint of Hennessy in the freezer. He hooks a right onto Lake Michigan Drive with one hand on the wheel, the other one wrapped in Mae's, his meaty thumb rubbing her smooth, unpolished fingernails.

"I don't understand," Mae says. "Isaac was so good tonight. What happened to him?"

"I don't know. I think it's the pressure. That boy likes to be alone. Those cameras in his face, the questions, all that attention . . ."

"I think it's more than that."

"I know it is. You don't survive what he survived without burying some of it. He's becoming a man. I imagine it's all coming back. His friend. His parents."

"I don't know, Jackson. I think it's always been there. He hasn't been hiding. He's been dealing. He's been doing it his own way, but he's dealing."

"You think I've been pushing him too hard about choosing a school?"

"Maybe. But it's not just you. I've been pushing Grand Valley real hard the last few weeks. Maybe we should lay off a little. Let him decide in his own time?"

"Yeah. I think you're right," Jackson says.

Mae squeezes his hand. "The way you went down to him, Jackson. The way you supported Isaac . . . today," Mae says, "Today I am so proud to be your wife."

Jackson lifts the back of her hand to his mouth and kisses it. He hasn't slept in his own bed in weeks. Sometimes he stands in the doorway and watches her sleep, curled up in her corner of the bed, the same way she used to curl against him. It's like she's sleeping with his memory, the invisible shape of who he was.

"What about tomorrow?" asks Jackson. The question is heavier than the words.

Mae loosens her grip a bit, but doesn't let go, stares out the window into empty pastures and cornfields, into the Allendale darkness. "I don't want to think about tomorrow, baby." Jackson's first "baby" in a long time. "I just want to be in this moment. This now. I want to feel like this about you forever."

They don't speak the rest of the ride home. Mae leans against his shoulder. Her free hand rests on his thigh. And he knows what she's thinking. She knows he's going to fail her. Even he knows he's going to fail her. But he hasn't failed her tonight. Not yet. He can't. He just cannot fail her tonight.

The walk to their front door feels like the first time. No words pass between them. Jackson's Dickies boots thud against the sidewalk. Mae is more graceful, her heels making no sound, like she's walking on paws. He opens the door and follows her inside. They stand in the living room for a moment, neither knowing where to go. Most game nights Jackson drives home alone, stopping at the package store for a pint, coming home finding Mae with a book, pretending he's not there, Jackson putting some ice in a glass and drinking it straight, in the open, just to spite her.

But tonight their routine has been broken. Mae stands in her teacher's attire: a sweater concealing her curves, a skirt that barely touches her knees. She hasn't aged a day, besides the sadness in her eyes. "Do you want to go upstairs?" she asks.

"No."

"No?"

"No." Jackson walks over to the entertainment center. Presses a few buttons on the disc changer.

"Al Green?" asks Mae.

"That's right," Jackson says. "Come here."

"What?"

"I want to dance with you."

Mae steps out of her heels and walks to him. Rests her head on his shoulder. Her breath against his neck makes his arm hairs stand. They lean into each other and barely move, just sway to the sound of the soulful crooner, a Grand Rapids native defected to Detroit. They listen to Al Green and listen to the house breathe, the hum of the refrigerator, the roar of the furnace, the sounds you notice when you're home alone.

Isaac runs a hand across the word *CANE* that is Sharpied on the basketball on his lap. He stares out the window of Mae's Camry, now parked against the curb, in front of Miles' friend James' uncle's house. Music thumps from windows. Smokers sit on the porch in lawn chairs. Isaac can see the lit parking lot at Garfield Park across the way and longs to be out of the car and onto the concrete, into the night alone, with no one around to muddy his thoughts. He's heard of people having a midlife crisis in their forties and fifties, death creeping closer, regretting their career choices, their marriages, feeling a sense of emptiness or depression, an irrational need to do something drastic with their life.

Isaac feels as if he's having some sort of crisis now. Basketball has become too loud, a circus, even the subtleties: the ball spinning on its arc, the sound it makes when the net snaps, the frustration of the man guarding him, always the best defender on every team, always so full of confidence when he takes the court, a quarter into the game he's confused, or angry because his confidence deceived him. To be good used to be some sort of redemption for Isaac. Some sort of *I told you so* to his childhood. He would not be broken. He would emerge. But now he's feeling like he *has* overcome. Like this chapter of his life is coming to a close. But Jackson and Mae, Miles, all these coaches and recruiters— they feel like Isaac is just beginning.

"I got something I want you to hear," Miles says. "This one's a game changer." Miles scrolls through his iPod and turns up the volume on the stereo. Listens as the intro to the beat comes in. A sample from an old Blaxploitation film, familiar, but Isaac can't name it—a man with a gravelly voice philosophizing about the art of pimping. Then a violin swims across the surface of a deep bluesy bass line. "Wait for it," says Miles, an open hand raised in the air. He drops his hand, scowls, and bobs his head when triumphant horns swoop in over the top of the beat.

Miles stopped wanting to be a rapper after Cesar Bolden bought him a Triton keyboard a few summers back. The keyboard, worth several thousand dollars, had to be hidden from Jackson until it could be explained off by Miles, who started borrowing the lawnmower and pretending like he was out working, saving money. He accepted praise from both Jackson and Mae with his trademark smirk and spent his summer nights wearing headphones, locked in the bedroom teaching himself how to make beats on the complicated machine. At the end of the summer he showed Jackson the Triton—Jackson knew nothing about keyboards and what they were worth—and managed to escape Jackson's wrath. In the process he created a few simple beats and discovered a talent and a passion that he never outgrew.

"I figure find one dope artist and put my money into his album," Miles says. "Get him some spins on the locals. Plug that shit into social media. Then build. I get plenty of dough selling beats. My name is out there. I just gotta start hitting them from different angles."

Isaac thinks of his stack of notebooks sitting on his dresser. Filled with lyrics he rehearses when no one is around. He imagines being on a dark stage, beneath a soft spotlight, hiding under a hood. A faceless crowd with upturned arms. They chant when he tells him to. He reaches them with his words. They love him for it. They're all looking for something to cling to. "How much you got stacked?" Isaac asks Miles.

"Five grand."

"Damn."

"It ain't work when you're doing what you love. Music is my sustenance. This shit is my food. Get Green Records is about to be a reality. My boy James is an engineer. He's in the recording program at Grand Rapids Community College. He's got that techy stuff down, Man. Mixing, mastering, you know? With me making beats and James running the mixing board, the quality of sound is going to be industry standard."

"That's what you keep telling me," says Isaac.

"What, Zick? What's with the tone? You got that face on, Man. You ain't about to fall into one of those zones are you? You got that look like you're in one of your moods."

"I'm just not feeling like being social tonight."

"Social? That's some funny shit. When does Isaac Page *ever* feel like being social? Let me ask you something . . . how come I ask you to come support me in my shit it's always a problem? This is James's party. He's going to help me get my label off the ground. I asked you to come cause it's important to me. You ain't right and you know it, Zick. You ever have to ask me to come to your games? Huh? Ever? Well, I'm asking for a little family support."

"Fine," says Isaac. He spins the basketball on his lap. "Is James' sister Nikki going to be here?" Isaac asks him.

"Doubt it," says Miles. "Last I knew she was backpacking across Europe. What? You into her or something?"

"No. She's just cool. Someone to talk to."

"Yeah. Good. Cause you know she digs chicks, right?"

"Yeah."

"Anyways," says Miles. "Let's go. And leave the damn ball in the car."

Isaac and Miles make their way up the sidewalk and Miles knocks on the door.

"Doctor Dre!" A bulldog-looking guy stands in the doorway. He's short, with broad shoulders on an otherwise small frame. His head is buzzed low to blend with a receding hairline. The man dap-hugs Miles. Looking at Isaac, he says, "And let me guess: you're the real Slim Shady."

Miles says, "This is Isaac Page. Isaac, this is Mike. He's James's uncle."

"I know that name," says Mike. "You're that hooper right? I was at the Creston game. My son Mikey—his youth squad was playing at half-time." Mike extends his hand. "Good to meet you. Mike Goslett."

"You, too." Isaac shakes Mike's hand. Firm grip. Blood-shot eyes. Sweating liquor. He leads them through a living room where a couple are cuddled together in quiet conversation, an agitated woman sitting on the other end of the couch playing with her cell phone, and into a kitchen where three men wait for Mike to rejoin their game of Spades.

"We got Doctor Dre and Slim Shady here, Boys," he says to the men at the table. The men are clearly annoyed, their collective demeanor like they've been tolerating Mike for hours. "You guys wanna do a shot of Jack?" Mike says to Isaac and Miles.

"Run it," says Miles.

Isaac says nothing. He lets Mike pour three shots and leaves his sitting on the counter when he and Miles toast to Mike's pending divorce. Mike mumbles something about bitches and takes Isaac's ignored shot of whiskey to the head. Then he goes on a ten-minute rant about his soon-to-be ex-wife, Myra, who is here tonight, according to Mike, just to spite him. Before he can finish his tirade Mike staggers into the table and gets steadied by a large black man wearing a gray thermal shirt and a white Nike beanie. "Whoa there, Mike. Maybe it's time you go lay down, Buddy. Sleep it off."

"No," says Mike. "This is my house. This is my nephew's party. Bitches," he says. "Fucking bitches."

"I know, I know, Buddy. Let's get you upstairs. Let's get you in bed." He stands and helps Mike through the living room, Mike mumbling the entire way.

Downstairs the walls shake. A strobe-lit dance floor is cleared center room and packed with drink-sippers, mingled together, singing along with the chorus of "Big Poppa." A white DJ in his early twenties sits in a booth, gesturing and lipping the words, a red hoodie half-covering his peroxide-blonde hair. The song ends and the DJ speaks into the microphone. "Oh, shit! Miles Davis Green is in the house. That cat that puts that fire on the track." Miles lifts triumphant arms in the air. Isaac finds a wall. Wu Tang Clan's "C.R.E.A.M." spews from the speakers. The DJ steps out of his booth and embraces Miles.

"Zick, James. James, Zick."

The two hooded white boys shake hands. Isaac a head taller and a little thicker through the shoulders. They step off the dance floor and away from the noise.

"Yo, I caught your game at Creston a few weeks ago. You got skills, bro."

"Thanks."

"For real. Miles said the recruiters been kicking in the door."

Isaac nods.

"I used to hoop a little," says James. "Wasn't good enough for college though. Went to the Marines after high school. Did my four years. Spent my last year in the desert dodging bullets."

Isaac looks intently at James and nods his head. The guy's scrawny and unaffected, not visibly anyway. Then Isaac almost laughs, remembering Nikki saying her brother had a desk job. Something about the worst thing that would happen to him is breaking a nail.

"No regrets, though," says James. "I served my country. Got that GI Bill. Now I'm about to do my thing, feel me? I'm schooling Miles on the subtleties of the craft, dig? Show this muh fucka how to get the best out of his sound. Your brother's got talent. No denying that. But the kid is raw. I'll straighten him out, though. Fine tune that rawness. Trust me on that—

"But, for real, Isaac," James continues. He's kind of jittery. Fast talking with busy hands. Coffee-buzzed or Ritalin-needing. "You decide you wanna wait for college—I mean, I know you're doing your thing on the court—I'm just saying, you feel uncertain about shit, you want to figure things out—no better place than the military. Free food. Free housing. Money for school. Plus, they pay your ass."

"Shut your ass up, white boy," Miles says. "You sound like a goddamn recruiter. Isaac Page in the Marines? You fucking kidding me? This muh fucka's going to the league. To the N," he says. "B." Another pause. "A."

"I'm just saying."

"Just saying what?" Miles asks. He laughs.

But Isaac isn't laughing. He slinks back against the wall and lets Miles and James continue the conversation without him. Imagines himself in fatigues. He remembers the beach scene in *Saving Private Ryan*, bullets piercing through helmets, bleeding men dying in the ocean, in the sand, the loud, quiet noise. He wonders what fighting for his life would mean. Fighting for something more than his own life. How welcome a bullet in the head might be. He thinks of that Vietnam movie from the nineties starring Lorenze Tate, Chris Tucker, and that bald guy, Bokeem something, who severed off a Vietcong head and carried it around in a bag. He imagines himself walking through some vague desert; weapon strapped over his shoulder, sipping from a canteen, no identity but Page, no history but the previous day.

Isaac watches James escape to the DJ booth. Watches Miles raise his hands over his head when Jay Z's voice bellows from the speakers.

H to the izz-o, V to the izz-a
Fo' shizzle my nizzle used to dribble down in VA

Isaac watches the dance floor. Miles now grinds on a weave-headed black chick wearing a silky black lie of hair. A white woman who looks old enough to be Miles' mother dances behind him, holding a wineglass with her left hand, Miles' belt buckle with her right. In the center of the dance floor a woman dances with her eyes closed holding a bottle of Jack Daniels, a small pink purse wrapped tight around her shoulder. She favors Paula Abdul—could have been her big-boned little sister. She has a cute speck of a mole flanking her upper lip and breasts that stretch the seams of a red Detroit Pistons T-shirt. The center of the floor is hers. She owns it. No one will go near her.

H to the izz-o, V to the izz-a

Isaac watches the woman dance. Her eyes are still closed. She's off-beat and tipsy and dancing on her own planet. When the woman opens her eyes she sees Isaac staring and smiles. She hits the Jack Daniels. She slow motions her index finger at Isaac and cycles it toward the dance floor, toward her. Isaac shakes his head, but feels a wisp of lust—this woman: entirely alone and all those curves.

The woman walks over. She's taller than she looked on the dance floor. And prettier. Her light brown eyes almost the same shade as her skin. "Hi, Sexy," she says. "I'm Myra."

"Mike's Myra?" James' Uncle Mike upstairs had called her a cheater, a whore, but a picture of their family still hung over the dining room table. Mike, Myra, two handsome boys, all dressed in corny sweaters, Mike a little less balding, Myra looking much plainer in the picture than she does right now.

"No one's Myra. Not anymore. You got a name?"

"Isaac."

"Why won't you dance with me, Isaac?"

"I don't dance." Isaac looks at her curiously, trying to figure out if she's Indian Indian or from India Indian.

"I'm half-black. Half-Mexican. Half-white," she says like she can read his face, like her looks cause ethnic confusion all the time.

"That's three halves," Isaac replies.

"That's right," she says, catching Isaac staring at her breasts. "I got a little extra, if you know what I mean." Myra offers Isaac a hit of Jack Daniels. He declines.

"Aw, so innocent." She leans against him, reaches up and around the back of his head. She pulls him closer. Whispers in his ear, "Maybe I should corrupt you." She steps into his space. Her breasts squish against his ribs. She runs her free hand across his upper thigh, between his legs. "Or maybe I already am?"

Isaac pulls away, leans against the wall. He glances out at the dance floor. Miles has a finger slitting his throat like a knife, shaking his head, lipping the word NO. But Myra is no teenage girl. She has Isaac feeling like his virginity is no longer a sacred thing. The way his balls tightened when she touched him—the loud shivers echoing through his bones—his body shutting down his mind, begging, just begging for Isaac to let go.

Myra takes another swig of the Jack. Steps back into his space. "C'mon, baby," she whispers. "I'm feeling reckless."

"Mike," says Isaac.

"Forget Mike." Myra takes Isaac's hand and this time he lets her. Somewhere there is an image of Mike Goslett in his mind, some defensive guilt, or a conscience that can give him the courage to tell her no. But Myra's already leading him out the sliding glass door and into the night. Into the cold, the quiet. The snow's starting to melt but there's no path to walk on. "Hold my arm, baby," Myra says. "I'm a little drunk."

Isaac hooks his arm in hers as they approach a slight incline on the side of the house. "Where are you taking me?" he asks.

"You'll see."

"My brother," says Isaac.

"You'll be back before the party's over," says Myra. "I promise."

At the top of the incline is a driveway with cars parked bumper to bumper. Myra's blood-red Dodge Durango is boxed in against a small garage, almost in darkness. A floodlight hangs from the side of the house, its pale glow stretching out into the driveway, kissing the passenger side of the truck. Myra lets go of Isaac's arm. "Hold this," she says, handing Isaac the bottle of Jack Daniels. She fishes her keys from her purse and chirps open the doors. "Get in," she says. Her demeanor has changed. Maybe the cold air has sobered her some? She looks at the house and shakes her head. Isaac looks at the Jack Daniels bottle, considers sipping from it, but then gets in the truck.

"Are you cold?" Myra asks, climbing in the driver side, starting the truck, and blasting the heat without waiting for an answer.

"No," says Isaac. "I'm fine."

"You want some music?"

"Sure."

Myra finds her iPhone in her purse and begins scrolling through it. "I'm old school," she says, adjusting the volume so it's just above a hum, and setting the iPhone on the dashboard. Raphael Saadiq sings about Southern California, his bizarre melodic voice claiming it never rains there, he's taking a plane, missing some girl.

"You got a girlfriend, Isaac?"

"No." But it's not like he didn't have options. Miles, always with some new chick who always has a friend, who always thinks Isaac is so cute, or so mysterious, always with their questions: Why don't you date? Why are you always carrying that basketball? Why are you so quiet? Are you shy or something? All these girls and they all want something. A cameo in an unwanted spotlight. To be the first girl to fuck Isaac Page. Like that is something. Like putting a round ball through a hoop is something. All these girls. If they saw the wreckage inside him they'd run. "You and Mike?" Isaac asks Myra.

"Over," says Myra. "So over." She remembers the Jack Daniels and takes it from Isaac. She twists off the cap, swallows hard, and cringes. She swallows again. "Motherfucker wants to run around here sleeping with every skank that bats an eyelash at him, but he can't handle the pay back."

Isaac wonders what the payback is, if he's the payback, but Myra's finished the bottle, and she's setting it down, and she's reaching over Isaac and reclining his seat, and he's hard before she even gets it out of his pants, and wraps her lips around the tip of it while Raphael Saadiq finishes singing about Southern California draught and begins singing about his anniversary.

Then Myra shimmies out of her jeans. She struggles to get the Detroit Pistons shirt past her breasts and over her head, and when she does she unclips her bra and she covers her stomach, and her breasts pour over her arms, and then she looks almost shy or insecure, and suddenly Isaac's nerves are gone and he's feeling like the bravest virgin alive.

"I don't have a condom," Isaac says.

"I'm on the pill, baby."

"Okay."

Myra now looks like she's on the edge of the building, no chute, reaching for Isaac's hand. She isn't asking to be saved, though. It seems she just wants Isaac to close his eyes and jump with her.

"I want to do this, baby, but you got to promise me one thing."

"What's that?"

"Promise me you won't fall in love."

It felt like a first and a last. An only. A one-night stand aflame in the drudgery of an ending marriage. Mae straddling Jackson like she used to, fingernails digging into his chest curls, her hips dipping into him like she wanted the moment to last, the night to last, knowing it wouldn't, knowing it was too late.

He's watching her sleep now. Naked with her back facing him, fetal-ed in the farthest corner of the bed, half-wrapped in a fitted but unhinged sheet. Is this what it feels like when It's Over has begun? He knows she won't leave until the boys finish school. But what's worse than being left when you're still living in the same house? The process dragging on. Sharing the same bed, the same memories. Both of them walking down a road called It's Ending. Neither one of them saying a word, or acknowledging aloud the unspoken bitterness.

He leans over Mae and kisses her lips. She turns away, burrowing deeper into the loose sheet. Even while she's sleeping she finds him repulsive. Can he blame her? He finds himself repulsive, weak. Downstairs the Hennessy calls him. The need is in his bones, his skin.

Its voice is in his head. Jackson slides out of bed and puts on his boxers. He walks down the stairs and into the kitchen. Opens the freezer door. Reaches for the Hennessey and changes his mind.

The bag, Jackson. Go downstairs and hit the bag.

He doesn't bother putting on his hand wraps. Doesn't bother with the gloves. He hits the bag until his knuckles bleed, the ancient thing swaying, thudding against his blows like it's losing its wind. He's weak and the whole house knows it. He stops swinging and stares at his bleeding hands. He looks up toward a God that he doesn't know. A God who doesn't know him. Like he could see through two floors and into the sky, beyond the stars to a place where a vague bearded giant looks down on him ashamed.

Then he's back in front of the refrigerator with his hand on the freezer door.

He stares at the Hennessy bottle a moment before he opens it.

He sips.

He shakes his head and sips again.

An hour later he's drunk and feeling guilty. Wanting to wake up Mae and apologize. To make another promise he won't keep. To curl up next to her warm naked body and pretend she still loves him back. But Mae will not tolerate his apology tonight. She'll feel played by it, like he only stayed sober for sex, like he got off, waited until she fell asleep, and then came down here to the bottle. Like that was his plan all along when it wasn't.

He considers taking a shower, gargling Listerine and brushing his teeth ten times to kill all evidence of drinking. But Mae will hear the water running and wake up. If he goes back to bed she'll wake up too, and she'll smell it on him. If he sleeps in the recliner, she'll catch him there too. Shit. He goes into the kitchen and opens a cupboard door. He moves some canned goods around and finds another pint of Hennessey. He walks into the living room, sits in his recliner, and sips.

He doesn't remember falling asleep but he wakes when the front door opens. The pint lay capless on the floor. Whether it spilled or he drank it, Jackson isn't sure. It's Isaac and Miles and one of them smells like pussy. He wants to call them on it but his voice isn't working, his words clank around in his head. "Pussy," he manages. "I smell it."

Miles laughs. Isaac tells him to shut up. "Sleep it off, Jackson," says Miles. "And tuck your dick back in your boxers. "Man-oh-man," Jackson hears Miles say on his way upstairs. "Mae is gonna kick that nigga's ass."

L yric wakes to her cousin Dee watching her. He stands smoking a cigarette, dressed in all black, a black beanie sits atop a picked mini-fro. He looks at her curiously but waits to speak. Noticing her garbage bag full of clothes lying next to the couch, he shakes his head and says, "Fuck you doing out here, Cuz?"

"Got into it with my mom," Lyric tells him.

"Okay," says Dee. "But why you sleeping in the fucking garage? Why didn't you come inside?"

"I don't want her to know where I am. Grammy would have called her."

"Auntie's sleep. She's been sleep."

Lyric sits up and looks around the room. She rubs her eyes. "What time is it?"

"Late," says Dee. "It's cold as fuck out here, Lyric. You need to come inside." He rubs his hands together. Reaches into the pocket of a hoodie. Pulls out a blunt and lights it. Hits it. Passes it to her. "You lucky I couldn't sleep," says Dee. "You might have froze to death out here." Dee sits down on the couch with her. They pass the blunt back and forth until it's down to ash. Until Lyric's heavy-headed high. Like her brain's growing inside of her skull. Like her thoughts have sound.

"Can you keep a secret?" Dee asks her. He's leaned back in the couch with his hands resting on his thighs.

"Yeah," says Lyric. "I can keep a secret."

"Cesar Bolden," Dee says. "I'm gonna kill that nigga."

Dee's been all fucked up since his father got sent to prison. Crazy. Like what he's saying could be just words or could be something more. Uncle DeMarco is Grammy's brother's son. Which makes him Tara's cousin, which makes him Lyric's second cousin, which makes Dee her third cousin. Lyric decides to keep her mouth shut about her mother and Cesar Bolden. And she definitely cannot tell him about her plan to make some money with Cesar. It'll only set Dee off.

"What's your beef with Cesar?" Lyric asks him.

"He's the reason my Daddy got sent away," says Dee. "He's the reason Nitty's growing up without a father."

"How do you know that?"

"I just do."

"And you're serious about killing him, Dee? You ain't just talking?"

He looks at Lyric. He's high, but the weed isn't enough to glaze the hate in Dee's eyes. Lyric remembers one summer back when they were kids. Uncle Slim was fucking with Dee. Like, going hard on him. They were playing dodge ball in the back yard: Lyric, Dee, and a few other neighborhood kids. Uncle Slim was out there too, barbequing, sipping something, watching the game. Then he set his drink in the driveway and joined in. Picked up the ball and threw it hard at Dee's feet. When Dee fell down Uncle Slim laughed, picked up the ball and hit Dee with it again. The third time he hit Dee, he made Dee cry. Called Dee a pussy ass nigga and walked back to the driveway and picked up his drink. He didn't see Dee pull a brick from the base of the house and follow him over to the driveway. Uncle Slim caught a beating that day. Dee was nine, maybe ten at the time, covered in his Uncle Slim's blood. It took Grammy's voice to get him to stop hitting him with that brick, Dee saying "Pussy ass nigga" when he finally did stop and drop the brick beside him. "Dee," says Lyric. "You're not serious, are you?"

Dee laughs. "I'm just playing, Cuz. Let's go inside. It's cold as fuck out here."

•

Jackson parks his Ford F150 in the GVSU parking lot. He empties a half-pint of Hennessey into a half-finished 32-ounce Pepsi fountain soda. Jackson steps into the ten-degree Michigan winter night. Ice cracks beneath his weight. He is clean-shaven besides his thick goatee. The frigid air stings the naked parts of his face and his aftershave bites his skin. Tonight he feels alright.

He finds Mae in the bleachers, there after a late day at work grading papers. She glances at Jackson's Pepsi and rolls her eyes. He kisses her on the cheek. She has threatened divorce when the boys leave for college.

Jackson sips his Pepsi.

It's the Regional Final. The game begins with Isaac hitting a three-point shot from four feet beyond the arc. Cameras flash. Isaac shoots. He scores. Only missing occasionally. Bored. His mind on something else. Jackson fingers his beard. "He's just going through the motions."

"What, Jackson?" Mae says, annoyed. She's that way now. Annoyed after everything he says. Annoyed just by his presence. Like when he's with her she's offended that they're breathing the same air.

"Isaac. Look at his eyes, Mae."

"You're drunk, Jackson," Mae says. "You're drunk and I'm not trying to hear you tonight."

Jackson scans the crowd. He finds Myra courtside, not watching the game, but playing with her cell phone. Heels. Skirt. Shirt showing a massive amount of cleavage, and Jackson has to admit: the chick is bad. Thick as hell. She reminds Jackson of his truck. An F150 of flesh. Ford tough, built to last. No wonder she's got Isaac's head in the clouds.

After the game Jackson limps down the bleachers. He watches Myra walk down to Isaac and kiss his cheek. Whisper something in his ear before walking toward the door. Jackson follows her. Her cell phone now at her ear. She's smiling at whoever is on the other end of her conversation.

"Hey!" he yells across the parking lot.

Myra turns. Long black coat now buttoned to the neck. All that body hidden in wool. Cell phone still at her ear. Expression like *Oh Shit* when Jackson approaches her, scowling and limping.

"You know who I am?" he asks.

"Let me call you back, okay?" she says into her phone. "No, everything's alright. Five minutes. Yeah. You too." She puts her cell phone in her coat pocket. "Yeah," she says to Jackson. "I know who you are."

"What do you want with my son?"

"Jesus, Man. You get to the point, huh?"

"Answer the question."

"Mr. Carter," says Myra, "no disrespect, but that's not your business."

"Isaac is my business," says Jackson. "Isaac's future is my business. And you make no sense. Or," says Jackson, "you make perfect sense." Jackson sips his phony Pepsi. "Explain to me why a twenty-seven-year-old-mother-of-two is interested in an eighteen-year-old boy? A boy who just happens to be getting recruited by every major college in the country."

"It's not like that."

"Yeah, what's it like then? Enlighten me."

"Look, Mr. Carter, I have to go."

"You're gonna ruin him," says Jackson. "You know that? You have any idea what that boy has been through? Any idea how far he's come?" The Pepsi is gone and so is Myra, pulling out of the parking lot, cell phone back at her ear.

"She's gonna ruin him," says Jackson.

Mae can't help but laugh at herself. Wine drunk. Crying like a teenage girl. Becoming the very thing she's been bitching about all these years. Doesn't matter that she's making the classier choice: wine over liquor. What matters is the hypocrisy, the guilt she's feeling. Hating Jackson for chasing the numb, then chasing the numb to quiet the hate.

She and Jackson share a dinner table, they share a living room, sometimes they share a bed. Together, separately, they support Isaac and Miles's endeavors. But nighttime gets lonely. The clock moves slow and the darkness drags on. And that night after Isaac's game at Grand Valley, when Jackson was sober, when they danced to Al Green and they made love like they did in the beginning, she wanted the moment to last, the night to last, knowing it was too late—but like a fool she woke up that next day and she allowed herself hope, real hope, and then found Jackson passed out in his recliner, his penis hanging out of his boxer shorts, an empty bottle of Hennessey on the floor.

There are two taps on the bedroom door. Her first thought is Jackson, but she reconsiders—that man is not moving tonight. "Come in." Mae watches the door crack open. Isaac pokes his head in the room, dangles the Camry keys before setting them on the dresser. He eyeballs the wine bottle she's holding, then the one on the nightstand. Raises an eyebrow. Mae sniffles and then she laughs. "I know what you're thinking," she says. "And I know I'm a hot mess. Come in, baby. Shut the door. Come talk to me."

Mae pats the bed with the hand not holding the bottle. Isaac sits. Mae sips. "This woman," says Mae. "I hope you're using protection—Boy, don't look at me like that. Coming home late at night, smelling like sex and perfume . . ."

"Jackson already gave me this speech."

"Well now I'm giving it to you." Mae sips. "You knock that woman up—well, you can kiss college good bye." The room spins a little. A few more sips and it will start spinning a lot. "I mean it, baby. I'm not going to try and tell you what to do. I just really hope you're being safe. Besides, we got semis to think about. Two more wins and we win state. You gotta stay focused." She hands the bottle to Isaac. "Set that on the nightstand, baby." She lies back against a pile of pillows. "Have you narrowed it down?" Mae asks.

"Michigan, Michigan State, and Syracuce . . . and Grand Valley, really Mae, I've been thinking about it. I have."

"I know they're Division II, Isaac. I know their basketball team isn't on the same level as those other schools. But the Writing Program would serve you well. It would."

"Don't those other schools have writing programs too?"

"Yes. I don't know? Probably," says Mae. "All I'm saying is that I've seen the GVSU Writing Program, experienced it, my English Major required some writing classes. It's a great program. That's all I'm saying. And it would be a great fit for you."

Isaac nods. "Really, Mae. I'm thinking about it. He stands there for a moment watching her. "You and Jackson," Isaac starts, but lets it hang over the bed.

"I don't want to talk about that," says Mae. "I'm tired of talking about that. Tired of thinking about it. Isaac leans in to hug her. She squeezes him tight. Too tight. Like she's scared to let him go.

"He still loves you," says Isaac.

"I know, baby," she says. "It's just become too complicated."

"What about me and Miles?" asks Isaac. "I mean, if you guys don't—"

"No matter what happens we'll all still be family. I love you, Isaac," says Mae. "Nothing is ever going to change that."

"I love you too." His words hurt her in the most beautiful way. Released unwillingly from his tightened throat and into a room that hasn't seen love in years. After all this time he's receiving love and giving love in return. And now she's leaving him. And she feels so low. Maybe she's never felt so low. She should be an adult and tell him right now. Face to face. But she can't. She just can't. Because if she does she'll never leave. Graduation is two months away and that's just too long. Another night in this house feels too long. Because it's no longer hers. This is not her home. It's time. Isaac would never understand, but it's time.

There's an energy in this place that Isaac feels apart from. There is one pulse, one beating heart, and then there is him. Alone in his skin, in opposition to the mood of the Breslin Center, where the Ottawa Hills student body run deep and the Saginaw Arthur Hill students run deeper still. Isaac is Achilles. He is the sword that will decide the war. But is Myra his heel? She's supposed to be here tonight, but Isaac can't find her in the crowd, among the students, among Jackson and Mae.

It's been a week since he's seen her and Isaac is lost in the void between then and now. She'd given him a place to go. Sex had given him a place to hide, to be lost, where the only thing that existed were his senses, her lips and skin, the otherworldliness of the act. No future had to be considered. No decision had to be made.

She's still living with Mike. Miles told Isaac that, told Isaac that he's just some young dick, Myra's side-piece to use when she's in the mood. Isaac doesn't want to tell Miles that he's right, that he knows he's getting played. That Myra only texts, she never calls—that she only texts at night, only texts for sex. Somewhere inside of Miles is a deep and thoughtful human being. The proof is the soul of his music, the emotion. A bass line may pump like a pulse, the snare drum might snap over the top of it, but the strings, the horns, are all pain, all reflection. But everything that comes out of Miles Davis Green's mouth is a player pump fake. Isaac knows this, but still, he doesn't like to be on the receiving end of some bullshit watered-down Cesar Bolden philosophy.

The buzzer sounds and Isaac finds the bench. He stands for the National Anthem, holding his hand over his heart, scanning the crowd for Myra, finding Jackson and Mae sitting both together and apart, finding Miles in the Ottawa section, but no Myra. Maybe she's up in the nosebleeds, too far up for Isaac to see her?

The Anthem is over and they are announcing the starters. Isaac shakes the hand of Saginaw's coach when his name is called. He checks the stands for Myra one last time. Isaac had made a couple incognito visits to a Marine Corps recruiting office. He talked to this eager red-headed Staff Sergeant named Hilliard, who rocked a god-awful high and tight, that government-issued hairdo. Hilliard was on about an All-Marines basketball team, seeing the world, all the pussy you get overseas. But Isaac's mind was on escape. Leaving the gray of the city; trading the Grand Rapids concrete for the Middle Eastern sand.

But would Myra wait for him? Is she even with him? Does Isaac mean a thing to her but dick, a late-night companion, a payback for her husband cheating on her? And how long does the payback last? When she feels satisfied in her revenge then does Isaac get kicked to the curb, is her marriage off pause and Isaac left wanting?

Ottawa wins the tip and Isaac scoops up the ball. He leans against the defender for a moment and stares down at him. There is no fear in the boy's eyes. There should be. Isaac has something building in him, an intense focus, a moment of clarity. He's made a decision, Isaac can't name this feeling he's feeling, he doesn't know it yet, but this will be his last game, the greatest game he'll ever play. No scholarship will be accepted. This chapter of his life will come to a close.

Isaac smiles. He drops his shoulder a little to gain some space. He takes two dribbles and pulls up just inside of half court, his eyes focused on the front of the rim, the Breslin Center silent, the defender below him, he flicks his wrist and doesn't watch the ball leave his hands, doesn't watch it spin across its arc, doesn't have to. Isaac leaves his follow through in the air, his wrist, his fingers on his shooting hand form a perfect goose neck, his left arm dangles now as he backs down the court, the defender turning to watch the ball travel across its arc, watch the net turn inside out and get tangled on the rim.

Flick. Snap.

•

The road home from Lansing is dark and rural. Jackson's playing classic rock with the volume on low. Miles rode home on the fan bus. Jackson and Mae drove separately. "Thanks for waiting for me," Isaac tells Jackson. "That bus home gets kind of crazy. I didn't feel like dealing with that today. I'm in the mood for quiet." Isaac checks his cell phone. He finds a text from Myra. *Sorry I missed the game baby. Sitter bailed* ☹

"You played a helluva game, Son," says Jackson. "55 points by my count. I never seen nothing like it. You looked like a man possessed."

"Thanks." Isaac texts Myra back. *NP*

"Boy, what the hell is wrong with you? You just won the State Championship. You're carrying yourself like you lost or something."

"I just got a lot on my mind, Jackson. That's all."

Jackson hits a button on the steering wheel and his window rolls down a little. He lights a Newport. "This about that busty chick?"

"Her name's Myra."

Can I make it up to you??? Myra has texted him back.

How?

"Listen, Son. I think it's real cool she's letting you sniff the pussy. I do. But you gotta ask yourself: what does a twenty-seven-year-old woman with two kids want with an eighteen-year-old boy? You think she wants something serious? You think she's looking for you to father her kids?"

I booked us a room. Myra texts.

I'm good. Tired from the game. Myra hasn't even asked how the game went. Hasn't even asked if he's won.

Really? U sure???

Isaac sets his phone on the dashboard.

"I just don't want you to fuck up your chances, Son," Jackson tells him. "My chance was taken from me. I'd give anything to get it back. It can all be over in a moment. All the sweat and blood. All the training. It don't matter when your fate finds you. My fate found me, Isaac. Each time you run over there to that Myra you're looking for yours."

Isaac lets Jackson's words linger for a moment. He's heard the speech before. A couple weeks ago on his way back from seeing Myra, Jackson drunk and mumbling about the decision, about married women, about marriage, about the past. "Okay, Jackson," Isaac finally says.

"Okay my ass, Isaac. I need you to hear me. You have a lot on the line. You have this great opportunity. You can go anywhere. You know how many people would kill to be in your position?"

Isaac checks his phone. He has three new texts from Myra. The first: *??????* The second: *U sure?!?!?* The third: a picture. She's topless and her face isn't showing. One arm holds her breasts together the other must be holding her cell phone.

Where should I meet you? Isaac texts back. *What time?*

Motel 6 on Alpine. Midnight.

"Jackson," Isaac says. "You mind if I borrow your truck tonight?"

"Boy, are you even listening to a word I'm saying to you?"

"I'm hearing you," says Isaac. "I've *been* hearing you . . . I'll be safe. I promise."

•

The room is painted pale green and smells like old clothes. Candlelight tickles the walls. Isaac's shadow folds into the ceiling. Myra wears pink lingerie and holds a bottle of wine. She leans against propped pillows. Isaac stands at the foot of the bed in his boxers.

"I'm so sorry I missed the championship, baby," says Myra.

"It's okay."

"Were you The Man?"

Isaac doesn't respond.

"I wish I could have been there," Myra says. "I really do."

"Really, it's okay."

"No, I want to make it up to you?" She smiles. "I'll tell you what . . . how 'bout you take off those boxers and come here."

"You don't want to talk for a while?"

"I only have a couple hours."

Isaac wants to ask her why, but doesn't. He wants to ask her why she's still living with Mike if they're supposed to be getting divorced. But Myra never wants to talk about that and if Isaac persists he knows her mood will tilt, she'll cop an attitude, and she'll start putting on her clothes—she'll call his bluff, she's done it before, and have Isaac apologizing, damn near begging her not to leave. Maybe he's just pussy whipped, like Miles called him.

Isaac's boxers hit the floor.

"Come here," says Myra. She sets the wine bottle on the nightstand. She slips out of the lingerie. Her heavy breasts sag. She has stretch marks on her stomach and hips. She's beautiful. Isaac crawls onto the bed. Myra smells like cocoa butter lotion and strawberry conditioner. He loves how when they start kissing, the blood rushes from his brain to his dick and it's like the world stops breathing. Her fingernails dig into his back. Soft moans, her hot breath tickling his ear.

She turns to all fours and looks over her shoulder. Isaac mounts her and strokes.

"Harder," she says. "Isaac, do it harder."

He's aware of the all the sounds in the room, a heater kicking on, a nagging beep from a smoke detector, its battery running low. He can hear the faucet drip from the bathroom. The headboard banging against the wall. Myra's ridiculous moaning, too loud, too exaggerated. It's like Isaac's just playing a role in her fantasy. He cannot get gone this time. There is no escape. Because now Myra could be anyone. She could be Mae in that bubble bath all those years ago. She could be any busty girl with light brown skin. This, Isaac is learning, is what it means to fuck. The difference between fucking and making love. This is what Myra wants, to be pounded, to get a few moments of pleasure and go home to her husband. When Isaac comes he's disgusted with himself. Understanding every ounce of fool he's become. Myra isn't offended at all when Isaac gets dressed, when he doesn't lay down with her after. She pulls the covers up to her neck and looks at him. "Damn, baby," she says. "You just rocked my world."

Isaac shakes his head while he dresses. He flips the hood of his sweatshirt over his head and stares her down.

"What, baby? What is it?"

"You're not leaving Mike, are you?" says Isaac.

"Baby, we've been through this."

"What are we, Myra?"

"What do you mean?"

"Am I your boyfriend? Am I your fuck buddy? Am I your side-piece? What are we?"

"Why do we need to define what we are? Why can't we just be?"

Isaac laughs. "You're still fucking him, huh?"

"Me and Mike have kids together," Myra says. "It's complicated. I can't just up and leave."

"So that's a yes then. You are still fucking him." Isaac heads toward the door.

"Isaac," says Myra.

Isaac doesn't turn around.

"I told you not to fall in love," she says.

The night is a cloudless. A black ocean pocked with stars. An ivory moon floating over the Grand River like an island in the sky. Mae leans against the railing of the Blue Bridge. A few men stand together off to the right talking, laughing, sharing a bottle. Music from Iggy's Place echoes across the water. It sounds like you could walk on it—like Mae could jump off the bridge and the music would break her fall, and she'd be carried off to wherever sound goes when it disappears.

Mae finds a pack of Camel Menthols in her coat pocket. She lights one, inhales too deep, and coughs. Recovers to a gentle high-headed buzz. Inhales again. The cold air and the menthol bite burns her lungs. She remembers standing in this very place with Jackson. All those years ago. Deciding to marry that man. A dumb giddy girl, too in-love to have her wits about her. And now starting over scares her. Terrifies her. Has her trying to rationalize her way out of the guilt that she's feeling. Because what kind of mother leaves? What kind of person? But what else is there to do, she asks herself, or tells herself— be miserable, being married to a man who's married to the bottle? Should she grow old waiting for the man she loves to stop treating her like his mistress.

Mae finishes the Camel and lights another. Watches Iggy's Place. Tries to imagine Jackson working there surrounded by all that flesh. Tries to remember him back then with all the apprehension, standing on this same bridge and looking over at Iggy's Place and asking Jackson what was over there he couldn't let go of, before she knew it was Joy Green he was holding on to. The thought of that woman pisses her off. So Mae lets the thought sizzle and burn. She inhales and coughs again.

A man leaves Iggy's Place and makes his way onto the bridge. He stops about ten feet from her. "Mae Carter?" he asks.

She glances over at him. It's too dark to see his face. But there's something familiar about him. His posture. The tone of his voice. "Who are you?" Mae asks him.

He takes a couple steps closer. "Cesar Bolden," he says. "It's late. You shouldn't be out here alone."

"Cesar Bolden," says Mae. Inhales. Exhales. "The Devil himself," she says. How many mornings has she seen that Caddy parked down the street? Cesar watching her house through tinted windows. How many times has she wanted to confront him, tap on that window and ask him, What? What the hell do you want? But there was enough drama at the Carter house already. No need for her to be starting some more. And Jackson, lord, if Jackson were to find out Cesar was out there, to have a repeat of Jackson's first altercation with Cesar Bolden—the violence—that's a side of her husband she hopes she never sees again.

"Let me walk you to your car," Cesar says.

"I'm not ready to leave yet."

"Then let me stand with you."

"Free country."

Cesar leans on the railing beside her. He's different than Mae imagined him. But how he's different she cannot quite name. There's nothing drug dealer about him. There's nothing porn, or sleazy, or corrupt. He's just a man. None of us are entirely villain, are we? And on the flipside none of us are entirely good. We all have our flaws. "Cigarette?" Mae asks him. She holds out her open pack.

"I don't smoke."

"Neither do I." She inhales, exhales, watches the sky.

"Me and Jackson," Cesar tells her. "We have our differences. But your husband is a good man. I could never say these words to Jackson, but they need to be said . . . I just want to thank you," Cesar says. "For taking such good care of my son."

Cesar's eyes look silver beneath the moon. And full of regret. So much history in his voice. The past has a way of doing that. If you're brave enough to remember and yet strong enough to move on. Cesar seems to Mae like he's that kind of man. Someone who decided to be better and had the courage to at least make an effort to change. "I don't know what to say," Mae tells him.

"You don't have to say anything," says Cesar. "I just wanted you to know I'm grateful."

Mae smiles and she nods her head and she closes her eyes. "Thank you for saying that," she tells him. "It means a lot."

"It's the truth," Cesar says. "Now, if you're done pretending to smoke cigarettes, I'd like to walk you to your car. It's late. You shouldn't be out here alone."

The Holiday Inn is strangely vacant for a Friday. It's almost as if Cesar had arranged it. Ghostly. So few cars. So few humans. The night holds its breath while the moon's gaze follows Lyric Cane, exiting the bus and heeling her way through the parking lot. Then she steps inside and moves through the lobby, up the elevator to the third floor where she waits in front of room 318.

On the other side of the door the noise of men. Laughter and raised voices. The scent of smoke: cigarettes and weed. It's not too late to walk away, but it's too late to walk away. Thunderbooty finally sending her packing, catching her red-handed in her bedroom, standing over her dresser, bag full of weed, fist full of twenties. Get this money, Babygirl. Get this money. "Get this money," Lyric says, and knocks on the door.

Inside big bright lights canopy an empty bed. Four men sit at a table sipping liquor and playing dominoes. One of them nods her way and the other three don't look up from the game. Cesar stands next to a man holding a video camera. Two other men sit by an open window sharing a blunt.

Lyric locks herself in the bathroom. She swallows two Ecstasy pills with a pull on a Courvoisier bottle. She sits on the edge of a bathtub and drinks. Waits for her body to go numb. Waits for her nerves, for the shakes in her hands to dumb down. Then she has this moment. This need for escape, and her mind races, she sees all these flashes, her whole life, the smell of coffee and cigarettes on her father's breath, Isaac Page in her driveway shooting a basketball, her mother when she used to smile sometimes, before Iggy's Place, before Clyde, before Cesar Bolden, and Lyric thinks for this one brief moment: What if? What other road could she go down? What else could she do? Could she be?

But then the moment dissolves. When she pictures her future she sees nothing. Nothing but the past. Dreams are created in childhood. Kids imagine themselves being policemen, teachers, fire fighters, ball players . . . Lyric's childhood ended before her dreams began. There's no career in being a princess. And in this life you need money. They say money cannot buy happiness. But shit. Money can get you the fuck out of the hood. Maybe the dreams will come later. But for now a bitch has to do what a bitch has to do.

"Little Thunderbooty." It's Cesar.

"Yeah?"

"It's time."

Lyric takes one last pull on the Courvoisier. She's beginning to feel the effects of the E. She hides her purse in the cupboard beneath the sink and covers it with towels. On the other side of this door is that money. Money she asked for. And she knows that if she bails out now she can never ask Cesar again. So she opens the door. Cesar has the bed boxed in with props. Tables have been moved. Five men are gathered around them. One man is missing. It's dark but the lights beating down on the bed.

Lyric slides past the men and finds Cesar.

"You ready?" he asks.

She nods. Get this money, Babygirl. Get this money.

•

M ae Carter has never been one to pull a punch. Never been one to stray from conflict in the name of what's right versus what's wrong. But there is only one way to do this thing and if that means being wrong, so be it. Because there are so many right reasons to stay. Isaac and Miles graduate in a couple months. Isaac still hasn't chosen a school. And Miles, straight A's and everything, hasn't popped off a word about college. There's still work to be done with those boys.

There will always be a reason to stay. But Mae hasn't done a thing for herself in years. And Jackson has made his choice. He's chosen the bottle over their marriage. Ultimatum aside, Mae knows she's in the right on that front. The man is a not-debatable drunk. A tried and true liquor hiding, liquor sneaking, sipping himself into a nightly stupor drunk. End of story. That is no marriage to be in no matter how much you love a man. If Jackson loved her back he'd stop. He hasn't. The end.

She's justified her exit strategy, the move to Mississippi, the fresh start, but apprehension is present now that the day has arrived. So what if she's sipping from a hypocritical bottle of wine. So what if she's playing ping pong with all these little white round thoughts, these reasons to stay. So what if it's ten p.m. and she still hasn't packed her bags and she's decided to run down the street and grab another bottle, to drink a little more in search of her courage. This is hard.

Letters. She'll write letters to Isaac and Miles. Offer an explanation, give them both some last minute motherly advice, apologize and plead for some time—give Mae a couple months, just a couple months to focus on Mae, away from Jackson, out of this house, let her establish herself, and then let's rebuild this family, complicated as it might be without her and Jackson together . . . let's rebuild it. After all, Mae's thinking, she'll always be Mom.

Miles' letter is easy. An explanation. An apology for missing graduation. Support for him choosing music over college, real support, because if she lets go of her own convictions, her belief in education, really lets go, she knows Miles will be just fine. So independent and so strong. So sure of himself and mature far beyond his age. He'll miss her, but he'll understand. Miles is even-headed like that. And he's ready for the world, which is what's most important. But Isaac, Isaac, baby, you have so much talent. I'm not talking about basketball. I've seen what you can do. I've read your journals. I'm sorry, but I have. You need to develop that talent. All you've been through doesn't make you weak, it makes you strong, it makes you special. Please go to Grand Valley. Go learn from people I know. People I trust...

God. Can she do this? She cannot do this. Shit. She wads up Isaac's letter and she tries again. Wads up that one and finishes the second bottle of wine. Now her ear is cupped to the door of Isaac and Miles' bedroom. No sounds but Miles tapping his fingers against the keys on his keyboard, headphones probably on, off in his own world. Mae sneaks down the stairs and finds Jackson in his chair, per usual, watching some game on TV, sipping his liquor. He nods when he sees her then looks back at the TV.

Maybe she's drunk now. Acting out of character. Irrational. Grabbing the remote from the arm of his chair. Turning off the TV. Reaching into Jackson's sweatpants and getting him hard. No. This isn't Mae. Leading him up the stairs and locking the bedroom door. Pushing play on the CD player. Stripping out of her clothes.

"Mae?"

"Shut up."

This isn't Mae's character. Face buried in the bed. Feet planted on the floor. Ass up in the air. Don't look at him. R-Kelly's voice. *One, we'll go to my room of fun... One, we'll go to my room of fun...* Something in her believing that this act could convince her to stay. Jackson, baby, convince me to stay. But his cold grunts could be a stranger's. He didn't even kiss her first. She didn't even ask him too. And for some reason she's thinking of Joy Green, that ancient spectral. Imagining Jackson with her, wondering what the bitch had that she didn't, and if Jackson still loved her, and if Joy Green was right, that Mae wasn't anything but her replacement.

One, we'll go to my room of fun, One, we'll go to my room of fun. One, we'll go to my room of fun... "Jackson, stop."

"*Stop?*"

"The CD's skipping."

She turns and sits on the bed. Watches Jackson walk across the room and kill the music. She lies back and closes her eyes. Tries to make Joy Green go away. Jackson pins her knees to her shoulders and penetrates her. She bites down on her lip, remembering the boys, careful not to leak a sound. She opens her eyes. Jackson looking down on her with not a hint of love.

"Stop, Jackson I said stop."

"What's wrong?"

"This isn't love, Jackson." She hears something new in her voice. It is flat and dead and final. All emotion sucked from it, dry, with unbiased clarity. This is no longer ending; this is the end. Jackson must hear it too. His face changes when she says it. Confusion to sadness to anger.

"This was your idea."

"I know, look, I'm sorry. I just—"

"You're sorry? Look at this." Jackson waves a frustrated hand at his erection. Looks down at it like he's disgusted with it. "You get yourself off, then just say it's over? Then you leave me standing here like this?"

"I need you to leave me alone right now, Jackson."

Jackson scowls and shakes his head. He strokes himself. Three, four, five times.

Ending: Hope long gone but the occasional glint—a sober day—an act of kindness that asks for nothing in return. A glimpse of what used to be, a moment, enough to keep that possibility tip toeing around in her mind. The end: coming now like an anvil from the heavens. Like God hurled it down himself.

Six, Seven. Thick curls of black hair cover his chest, his gut, his swollen balls. She returns his gaze of contempt. Eight, nine. Done. It shoots out of him and onto the bed, onto Mae's thigh. The dumb satisfied smirk on his face sets her off. She slaps him. He jerks back his head and wipes his hand on her shoulder. She watches Jackson get dressed while she puts on her robe. He opens the door. Isaac and Miles stand outside the room. Jackson glances at her one last time before walking away.

"One big happy motherfucking family, Mae," he says. "Just like you always wanted."

·

The living room is dark besides the blue hum of the left-on television. Jackson sleeps in his recliner. An empty bottle of Hennessey lies on the armrest. Two tall boy Schlitz cans sit on the coffee table. Mae sets her suitcase down, gets a blanket out of the linen closet, and covers Jackson with it. She throws the Hennessey bottle in the kitchen trash, puts the beer cans under the sink. She turns off the TV. "I'm leaving you, baby," she says.

She wants to peek in on the boys, but doesn't dare. She glances at her bookshelf. It's going to hurt leaving her books behind. Maybe Isaac will find some use for them. Maybe he'll take her advice. Maybe. Miles and Isaac's letters are sealed in envelopes. She sets them on the table between her and Jackson's recliners. Jackson has already been told. He doesn't know where she's going. He doesn't know she's leaving tonight. But Jackson's been told.

Mae kisses Jackson on the mouth. Her anger has subsided. She's beginning to sober. A couple hours removed from what happened. A cup of coffee drank and her large thermos filled. She looks at Jackson one last time before walking out the door.

"I loved you," she says. "I really did."

It Never Rains
Spring/Summer 2015

IT'S AN OVERCAST MORNING IN SAN DIEGO, California. The air is raw. Dense with the scent of looming rain. It's early June, and still, under the holstered sun, the California morning simmers like an August afternoon in Michigan.

Isaac's camouflage fatigues cling to his skin. The high-pitched cadence of a drill instructor drones. Soles of boots slap against the half-baked concrete. Recruit Isaac Page trudges forward with forty-nine others.

They haven't slept in two days. They were ushered off the bus when they arrived at the Marine Corps Depot, rushed to rows of yellow footprints with touching heels and reaching toes, and made to stand on the painted prints, at attention, arms flanking the hips, fists clenched, thumbs straight and stiff, facing forward along the pant crease. That's where Isaac got his first glimpse of recruit Snipes, wearing tight Wrangler jeans and a Texas belt buckle, shirt tucked in, bright orange Adidas on his feet. The drill instructor had made a comment about running in glow-in-the-dark shoes, getting seen by the enemy, getting everyone killed, calling him a clueless hick, and Snipes stood still and silent, stoic.

Isaac staggers as he marches, dragging, heavy with a sludginess he can feel in his bones. He marches in a daze, the world looking pinkish gray. A mirage of heat hovers above the concrete.

"Left. Right. Left. Right."

I was ten when I met him, eleven when he died.

"Left. Right. Left. Right."

I was eleven when I held his little girl and wiped her eyes.

"Left. Right. Left. Right."

The gunshot that took him, it still echoes in my mind.

"Left. Right. Left. Right."

That's when I crawled into the concrete and what's left of me survived.

"Platoon, halt!"

Isaac keeps marching. Crashing against the recruit in front of him.

"Jackass!" He hears a Texas drawl and finds himself on his hands and knees, pebbles pressing into his palms. A boot kicks against the small of his back and then he's lifted to his feet by someone who has hold of a fist full of shirt. He turns and finds Snipes, lesser in height, thicker in build, about six feet tall and doughy, his Marine Corps cammies crisp and perfect, every patch of stubble shorn off of his upper lip and jaw, a flawless military regulation shave. "Get your shit together, Recruit," says Snipes. "You're fucking up formation."

Isaac rubs pebbles out of his palms. He disregards Snipes. Returns to formation. The drill instructors are cluster fucking around the front of the chow hall, deciding which platoon will go in first. A hand grips Isaac's shoulder. "Hey, Asshole," Snipes says, a decibel above a whisper, a notch below conversational tone. "I mean it. Square yourself away. You're going to get us *all* in trouble."

Still facing front, Isaac reaches for Snipes' hand and flings it off of his shoulder. Then Snipes' fingers jab into his back. The drill instructors are inside now. Six platoons wait in obedient geometric herds. Isaac turns. He leans toward Snipes and says, "Put your hands on me again and—." He lets Snipes imagine the consequences. He lets him ignore his warning; believe in the romance of bravery. Honor. Courage. Commitment. Semper Fi. Hoorah, Devil Dog. Hoorah.

Isaac locks into formation. He waits, anticipating another shove. He leans against it, rotates his body, gains leverage with his right foot, and steps into the blow with his left. His right hand crashes against Snipes' temple and Snipes, as his consciousness fades, is in a limp-bodied free fall, his arms dangling at his sides, camouflage cap jarred crooked on his clipper-shaved head. Snipes lands on his back, his head bouncing twice on the concrete and his body twitches, mouth gaping, eyes rolled back into his head.

Snipes is a crumbled building—recruits clear out like they're backing away from asphalt and rebar. Isaac stands over Snipes, watching his body twitch. Then the drill instructors are on him, six of them, knees and elbows in his back, his neck, pressing him into the California concrete. "Are you calm?" one of them yells and Isaac says he is. He doesn't struggle, just absorbs the weight of the men.

They cuff him at the ankles and wrists, like he's a trapped beast or a runaway slave, restrained by a contraption you might see during medieval times, something dragged out of a dungeon and dusted off.

They haul Snipes away on a stretcher, stuff him into an ambulance that throws caution lights but sounds no siren. Two military policemen stand holding M16s, flanking either side of Isaac. A lieutenant and a few sergeants confer in a small circle just out of earshot, glancing and pointing and comparing stories, replaying the assault from various angles: did Snipes start the fight? How many times did his head bounce on the concrete when he got dropped? Was recruit Page really going to kick Snipes in the head even as he lay there having a seizure? These guys are supposed to be menacing, but Isaac finds them comical in their drill-instructor hats, the way the hats rest obnoxiously atop their heads, like their heads are too big or the hats are too small. These guys swell with Marine Corps killer pride, these former sixth-grade bullies, the kind of kids that used to set cats on fire, the ones that stopped growing at age thirteen, those that joined the Marines so they could kill something, bark commands, point weapons at the world.

There's a drizzle of rain and Isaac wishes it would beat down against him. He remembers the song by Tony Toni Tone: "It Never Rains in Southern California." Raphael Saadiq singing, Myra straddling him in that blood-red Dodge Durango. Her back arched. Her chewed-on nails digging into his hairless chest. "It never rains in Southern California," sang Raphael Saadiq. "Never." Bullshit, thinks Isaac. He closes his eyes, tilts his head toward the sky, and lets the drops fall on his face.

The rain falls harder. The cuffs around Isaac's ankles are loose but those holding his wrists cut into his skin. The lieutenant approaches while the sergeants linger, curious but stern. The lieutenant is short, muscled, and stiff as an erection. Rain pelts his military cap with an angry pang. It sounds like hail hitting a tarp. "They're gonna send you to the brig, Recruit," the lieutenant says. "You know what the brig is? That's prison."

•

Isaac sits in a small cold room. The walls are glossy brick painted pale canary, bare but a Michael Jordan poster, spread eagle, tongue out, MJ floating over the free throw key with the ball cocked next to his right ear. Isaac sits on one side of a desk, admiring the poster, a throwback— no one had the killer instinct like MJ—the talent, the work ethic, the refusal to fail.

"You hoop?" asks Senior Drill Instructor Staff Sergeant Lawrence. He'd been silent since Isaac sat down. The man's demeanor is cool compared to the rest of the DI's. Isaac has yet to see him yell. Bronze-skinned and handsome. Face like he's on the shore of smiling, but he has yet to show his teeth.

"This recruit used to, Sir!"

"Page, you can tone that shit down in here, Man."

Isaac slumps back into the chair. He cracks his neck. Senior's the fourth person he's spoken to since Snipes was hauled away. The first person who's offered him food: a Snickers bar, unopened in front of him on the desk. Isaac opens the Snickers and devours it. "I used to."

"Until when?"

"Until I came here."

They all told Isaac he was going back to training. That he'd get probation and a fine. That he was lucky he didn't break Snipes' jaw. But when Isaac said he wanted out they laughed. Said he signed his name on the line; the Marine Corps owns him. He enlisted for four years plus he was required to be a reserve two years after that, they told him. They told him there was no way out.

"You any good?"

"All-State."

"No shit? Any offers?"

"A few."

"Where?"

"Michigan. Michigan State. Syracuse."

"Why the fuck you join the Marines?"

At that Isaac couldn't help but laugh. Jackson looked like he wanted to kill him when Isaac told him and Miles the plan, regurgitating the recruiter's words, saying things like G.I. Bill, figuring out what I want to do with my life, seeing the world. Jackson couldn't say a word, just scowled and shook his head, while Miles paced the living room thoroughly breaking down the reasons why this was such a "bad fucking idea."

"This seemed like a smart way to figure things out."

"I played a semester at Alabama," says Senior. "Couldn't get the grades."

Isaac nods. Hearing something in Senior's voice that makes him sit up straight in his seat. Like Senior's deliberating something.

"Those scholarships still waiting for you, Page?"

"Probably."

Senior leans back in his chair. He interlocks his fingers behind his head. He smiles, finally showing his teeth, flawless white with gold fronts. "You messed up a great opportunity, Page. You get a second chance, you gonna mess it up again?"

"The base commander said I couldn't get out. Said I signed—"

"Boy, that ain't nothing but a scare tactic. You ain't even all the way *in* the Marines until you graduate boot camp."

"So what? They'll just let me out?"

"No," says Senior. "The probation and the fine was contingent upon you going back to training. You want out they're gonna send you to the brig. They'll charge you with assault and battery. Probably give you a couple months and a bad conduct discharge. You want out; that's the only way."

•

Isaac spends his days at the Camp Pendleton Base Brig filling sandbags: sit on a pile of three, shovel sand into another, tie it shut, then stack it on a pallet. He plays childish word games with men twice his age. Start with the letter A. Each man names an animal. Get stumped you're out. Last man surviving wins the round. Move on to letter B. Go through the alphabet (skipping X). Pick a new category. Start with the letter A.

It is hot and monotonous. The days are long. They eat dinner at five p.m. They are given one hour of recreation at six. Armed guards stand on the roof, betting on the four on four basketball games the prisoners play on a small square of cracked cement, with a rubber ball that is orange and bald and lopsided.

Isaac is mocked and called Woody, for the character Woody Harrelson plays in *White Men Can't Jump*. He gets thrown to the concrete. He gets up. He says, "Check." The pattern continues. They hate it when he kills them. From beyond the arc if they give it to him. Flick. Snap. If they don't, he's pump-faking and taking it to the rack. With two hands or one, he's throwing it down. Or he's tear dropping it in or slapping the backboard. A week ago he took an elbow to the face that purpled his eye. He has a month's worth of scabs on his elbows and knees. Stay down, Woody, this is a black man's game. But he gets up, checks the ball to a short black man with weight room muscle, a long-timer they say beat his commanding officer into a coma he never woke up from. His eyes look like a shark's eyes, like two big pupils, no irises. He talks to no one. No one talks to him. It's like he has no name. Isaac crosses him over and pulls up to shoot. Someone takes out his legs. The ball snaps the net. The concrete sizzles beneath Isaac's sweaty back. The man with no irises and no name stands over him. Reaches out his hand.

"Respect, white boy."

Isaac is scheduled to be released in a couple weeks. And then he will go home. He has no plans for the future but putting pencil to page. Just the spaces between the lines, the scratch of graphite. Mae said the Writing Program and Grand Valley will help him develop his talent, help him turn writing into a career. An author, a teacher, a copywriter— Isaac isn't sure of any of that—all he knows is he wants to write. Her letter stung twice. That she left was enough, Isaac understands her leaving Jackson, the marriage had been fragile for years—but to escape in the middle of the night, while everyone was asleep. To get an obliterating Dear John letter from someone you consider mother? That hurt hard. And in the letter she confessed to reading his journals. That may have even hurt harder. The betrayal. A person shares his thoughts at his discretion, or his art, that's what Mae called his writing. She called it art. To be robbed of that was a violation. One he isn't sure he can forgive her for.

Isaac sits on one end of a steel picnic table that is bolted to the floor. Four men play spades on the opposite end. This cocky Chicago native named Caleb talks fast as hell, talks mad shit, popping his card on the table when he knows he's won the book, scooping up the highest card played with his own concealed card and slapping it down when he trumps it with a spade.

The cell houses twenty Marines, some counting down the days to be discharged, others filing appeals to be allowed to stay in. Two rows of bunks on either side of a constantly mopped floor. Some men nap, other men shower, others write home to lovers who left them, lovers who are waiting for them, loved ones who are praying for them.

Two pay phones hang from the wall in the far corner of the room. Both are occupied. One by a suave looking black man talking low into the phone, the other by a stubby white man with red cheeks and auburn hair. The black man whispers. The white man yells, slams the phone down. Takes it off the receiver. Slams it down again.

Isaac glances at his notebook.

I was ten when I met him, was eleven when he died

I was eleven when I held his little girl and wiped her eyes.
The gunshot that took him, it still echoes in my mind.
That's when I crawled into the concrete and what's left of me survived.

He glances at the payphone. Finds the white man walking back to his bunk, back facing the rest of the inmates, trying to muffle his crying with his hands. Isaac closes his notebook and walks to the payphone. Dials Miles.

"Man, I don't ever get tired of these calls, bro," Miles says, then robots his voice, "Collect call from the Camp Pendleton Base Brig. Sounds like a space station. Like baby bro is calling me from Mars."

Isaac imagines him smirking on the other end. Probably rolling a blunt. He hears music in the background. A girl's voice. "Hold up," says Miles away from the phone. "I'm talking to my brother."

"How's things?" Isaac asks.

"We're getting there. Moved out to Kentwood a couple weeks ago. Built a studio in one of the bedrooms. We've been looking around for a space to rent, but haven't found anything we can afford. How are you feeling? Being locked up, has it given you any perspective? Has it got you thinking any clearer?"

"I think so."

"Fuck is your head at, really? This whole Marines thing. None of what you're doing lately is making sense."

To say he was trying to find himself would sound corny, though it would be true. To say he wanted to be as far away from the southeast side of Grand Rapids as possible would be true too, but those words would be wasted on Miles. He could say he wanted to throw himself into something blindly. Do something the world didn't expect him to do and maybe shake off the burden of expectations, misconceptions about who he is, where he came from, who he wants to become. He wanted to enslave himself in something so he could set himself free. But Miles wouldn't understand. Plus, Miles was right. Jackson too. The Marines was no escape. Just a day after arriving Isaac was ready to come home.

"I've been writing," says Isaac.

"You've been writing your whole goddamn life."

"Raps, Miles. I've been writing lyrics."

"Fuck you mean, bro? What? You gonna be a rapper now? Isaac, get your damn head out of the clouds. First you're a hooper, then you're a Marine, now you're writing raps? Turning down scholarships. Look, I know you're bent because Mae left. We all are. But shit, I mean, how many years did she wait for Jackson to stop drinking? It's not your fault. Wasn't you she left, it was him."

"I know," Isaac says, but he doesn't really mean it. He trusted Mae. Loved her. And he feels just as left as Jackson does.

"Fuck is going on with you, bro?" says Miles. "You spend your whole life doing one thing. You get to the point where you can make something of it, overcome everything that's ever happened to you, then you just up and quit. Zick, man, I can't even talk to you right now. You're pissing me off and I don't do pissed off."

A long pause. Isaac pictures Miles looking at the ceiling, eyes closed, covering the receiver while he takes a few deep breaths, collecting his cool.

"Look," says Miles. "Figure shit out and I got you. Just don't come back to G-Rap without a plan."

The Concrete
Summer 2015

DEE KEEPS THE CHROME ON HIS Ruger with a flawless shine. The weapon is small in his large hand. It's light. An extension of his fist. With one eye closed he stares down the sights, finds a Mohammed Ali poster on the wall, and focuses his aim on the icon's chest. He squeezes the trigger and waits to hear the click. "You're dead, nigga," Dee says, then he relaxes his hand. He has a snap cap in the chamber. It contains a spring-dampened false primer which absorbs the force of the firing pin, allows Dee to practice without wasting live rounds, allows Dee to dry fire without damaging the gun's components. He clears the chamber. The rubber bullet bounces twice on the bed. It's the color of blood.

Dee stands and places the Ruger on his dresser. He puts on a blue and black McDonalds polo over a white T-shirt. He slides into black slacks. Black socks. All black off-brand rubber-soled work shoes. He keeps his weed in the closet, stuffed into the deep pockets of an old Sunday suit he used to wear back when Auntie still had the energy to bully him into going to church. He counts out thirty dime bags and drops them on the bed. Finds his backpack lying on the floor.

Dee keeps the ammunition under his pillow. Gold Dot 90 grain. Silver bodied bullets with bronze heads. Hollow point. So when he hits his target the damage spreads. He picks up the Ruger and releases the magazine. He loads six in the clip and one in the chamber, flips over the safety, and drops the pistol in the backpack. Drops the weed in the backpack. Straps it over his shoulders and readies himself for the block.

"Bye, Auntie," he says when he steps into the living room. The uniform is half for her half for the police. Auntie knows all. Auntie sees all. Rocking in her rocker. Staring at Dee through a cloud of Salem smoke with her exhausted eyes. Auntie knows he quit his job at McDonalds, she has to—but Auntie's at that point in life where it takes less energy to play pretend. And the police see a young black boy out in the night he better have a damn good reason to be out there. Those white boy cops, looking for an excuse to slap those bracelets on you, they flash their lights and they see DeMarco Payne J.R. in his Mickey D's attire, they move on to the next nigger, the one with sagging pants and a throwback jersey three sizes too big.

"You be safe out there, D.J." Auntie says.

Dee doesn't look at her before he walks out the door.

Uncle Slim stands on the porch smoking a Black and Mild, chatting up this former-junkie named Kat. Kat has a huge gap in her smile, and a body like she used to have a body. She's Torey from down the street's side chick. Everyone on the block knows it but Torey's wife, who's either dumb as hell or doesn't want to know it. Kat bounces from house to house bumming cigarettes when Torey works his second shift job at the shelter. Where she and Torey go to do their business, Dee isn't sure, because it seems like Kat's always around but doesn't ever set foot in his house. And she has this way about her. Like she'd let you fuck her if you tried, like all you'd have to do was ask, almost like she's daring you to do it, but no one ever does out of respect for Torey. Why Torey has status like that, Dee isn't sure, other than Torey's a different kind of dude—same job for twenty years, coaching youth football and basketball, a community man, the kind of guy you might see on one of those food trucks wearing a Jesus Saves T-shirt handing out almost-spoiled yogurt to the homeless.

"Hey there, Nephew," Uncle Slim says when he sees Dee. Uncle Slim is Auntie's baby brother. He did his four years in the Navy and it's like he came home and decided those four years was all he ever had to do with his life. Uncle Slim's known for those all-day dinners. He'll start drinking and cooking around ten in the morning and the food won't ever be done before the sun goes down.

"Hey, Unc. What's the night like?"

"Quiet with a cool breeze," says Uncle Slim. His go-to response. Uncle Slim takes a pull on the bottle in his hand. Dee can't see the label.

"How you doing, Kat?" Dee asks her. The Ruger feels loose in his backpack. He wants more than anything to hold it again, to fire it, to feel what kind of power it has.

"I'm good, baby," says Kat. "You off to work?"

"Every night," says Dee.

"Cool. When you get back this way find me," she says. "I might have something for you." And that's her way right there. She could have said she might have some money for him, or some business, but Kat said she might have *something*. She said it with a sly look on her face too. Like she could mean pussy. Dee would hit it too. He would. Couldn't give less than a fuck about no *Jesus Saves* T-shirt wearing Torey from down the street. Because those forty-year-old bitches are where it's at. According to Dee's father anyway. He told Dee that a few years back, before they hauled him off to Jackson State Penitentiary. He said the young ones think they're God's gift to the earth. But you catch one in her forties, that's when she's thirsty for it. She won't fuck you like she's doing you a favor. She'll fuck you like she wants you to come back for seconds. A forty-year-old—they got that *good* good, you feel me, D.J.? Leave the young pussy alone and get you some of that *good* good. Trust me. Then you'll be a man.

"Alright, Kat," Dee says. "I'll come find you. I'll come see what you might have for me." He heads down Franklin Street on foot toward Miss Tracy's liquor store, a hot spot for crack and a place Dee hopes he can low-key his weed beneath the dope boy's noses. He's been hustling for a few months and the money's not coming quick enough. Miss Tracy's is a risk, but one he's willing to take, the Ruger in his backpack makes his dick feel just a little bit bigger, makes him feel just a little more grown, a little more brave.

Miss Tracy's is jumping tonight. A large yellow neon sign tricks eyes away from the aging brick walls. The dope boys stand nonchalant in front of a blue building with a rust-colored roof. They approach no one, don't need to, the crackheads know enough to linger at the bus stop on the corner and wait for eye contact, know enough to slide attention away from the store front, know enough to have their ten palmed and be ready to make the exchange and walk away with not so much as one spoken word. Dee walks past the blue building, and posts up on the sidewalk just past Miss Tracy's, hoping to blend in with the traffic of people on foot, walking from their houses or cars, or standing around talking. "I got that fire," Dee says. He says it quiet, almost a whisper. No one even acknowledges he's standing there. "I got that fire," he says again. Louder this time. A woman glances up from her conversation with two men standing in front of an Escalade. "Shut up, little nigga," the one holding the keys tells him. "You stupid or something?"

"Who you calling stupid, nigga?" asks Dee, but then the dope boys are on him. Three of them. They walk slow, circle him. "What up, cuz?" one of them asks, but it isn't really a question, he has a hand on Dee's shoulder saying, "C'mon, let me holler at you. Over here, little nigga, away from the noise." Dee takes the first punch like a man. He staggers a little, but he doesn't fall. The second one though, busts his lip and brings him to his knees. Then all three dope boys are stomping him out. Dee clutches the backpack straps and takes his beating. Until a voice brings the beating to an end. The voice could have been God's. The way this man said the word and the blows stopped coming.

"I know your face," says the man. He is short and fat and dark-skinned with dreads. He reaches out his hand, but Dee slaps it away, stands on his own accord. "You're DeMarco's son, huh? Y'all remember DeMarco. Used to run around with Cesar. Got sent to Jackson a couple years back. Your name's D.J., right? Why you out here being reckless, D.J.?"

"Dee." If the Ruger were out of the backpack and in his hand . . . Dee didn't feel safe stuffing it in his pants, the cold barrel against his skin, one accident away from shooting his dick off. But if he had been braver this moment would be his. He wouldn't be the one being told, he'd be the one doing the telling. And the Ruger feels so far away, loose and lying in a nest of dime bags. The Ruger won't ever be in that backpack again.

"Shut up, little nigga," the dreaded man says. "And don't let me see you out here again. Being Cesar Bolden's godson won't save you twice."

"Fuck Cesar Bolden," Dee says. His father is never coming home again and Cesar left the game squeaky clean. And Dee has this dream of taking that $50,000 bribe Cesar gave Auntie and dropping it at his feet. Putting the pistol in Cesar's mouth and making him get on his knees. Let the last thing Cesar Bolden ever sees is the son of DeMarco Payne.

"Fuck Cesar Bolden?" Dreads says in disbelief. He shakes his head at Dee and says, "Dumb little nigga, Cesar Bolden is the only reason you alive right now."

Dee slinks back between two houses and takes the backpack off his shoulders, drops it in the driveway and kneels. His lip stings. He can taste the iron in his blood. The dope boys have gone back to their post. Dreads has vanished. Dee unzips the backpack. Finds the Ruger. Flips back the safety. Miss Tracy's has slowed down some. The Escalade is gone. There are two cars in the parking lot. A few people at the bus stop. The dope boys lean against the blue building beneath the rusted roof. A bell chimes when a white woman walks out the store and checks her smart phone. It chimes again when her two black girlfriends join her outside. The three women linger by one of the two cars parked storefront. One lights a cigarette. Another, fidgeting with her purse, glances at the dope boys. The white woman scrolls through her phone.

Patrol lights decorate the street. Three quick chirps and a black Lincoln is pulled over. Two cruisers park behind it. Two white boy cops approach the Lincoln, one on each side of the car, each with his weapon drawn. The dope boys fade into the night. Two black men walk out of

Miss Tracy's. They join the lingering women and stand watching. It's
Pastor Moss they have pulled over. He gets out of the driver's seat with
his hands above his head. He's shoved face first onto the hood of his car.
Handcuffed. The older of the two officers presses his pistol to the back
of the pastor's skull. The white woman records the scene on her smart
phone.

"Pastor Moss," yells one of the two men watching. "Pastor Moss,
you okay?" The pastor doesn't respond. He doesn't move. Dee tries
to imagine what thoughts might be going through the pastor's head.
Wonders how much a man's faith changes when he's facing death. If the
pastor's calm now, praying to his God, just waiting for His will to be
done. Or if he's wetting the hood of his Lincoln with tears, wetting the
front of his pants with piss, faith faltering, begging God to let him live,
or questioning if his God even exists.

"You all go about your business," the younger cop says. He notices
the woman with the smart phone and takes it from her. Puts it in his
pocket. None of the onlookers leave. The younger cop returns to the
Lincoln and opens the passenger-side door. "Ma'am, please step out the
vehicle," he says. The pastor's wife doesn't move.

"Sarah," says the pastor. "Do as the man says."

Dee readies the Ruger to fire. He looks down the sights and finds
the back of the young officer's head. This is power. To take the most precious thing a man has. To have that choice, squeeze or don't squeeze,
this young cop, this racist, this bully, with the pastor's wife bent over the
car now, her legs spread, he's a little too thorough while he frisks her, a
little too friendly with his hands, does he go home to a wife and child,
does he go home feeling like he's doing the city a service? Would he feel
it when the bullet entered his skull? Would he have a second thought, a
moment of regret, before the world turned black?

"She's clean, Tommy," says the young officer. The older one unlocks
the pastor's cuffs. Both officers stand there watching Pastor Moss and
his wife climb back into the Lincoln. They holster their firearms when
the pastor drives away. Dee waits until they return to their vehicles.

Waits until the patrol cars are in motion until he straps on the back-pack, steps out of the shadows, and fires.

All seven slugs hit something. Metal, glass, flesh—Dee doesn't know. The five onlookers duck behind their cars. Dee runs before the tires screech. Before one officer crashes into a parked car and the other slams against the curb. He runs across the street and down the sidewalk. He heads left down Neland. The weed bouncing around in his back-pack. The Ruger in his hand. He runs beneath the cover of night and urban trees that stretch up into the power lines. The sirens are behind him. Someone holds down their car horn when he crosses Worden. Dee doesn't slow down. His legs burn. His chest burns. Dee keeps running. Across Prince, up to Watkins, past the Christian Reformed Church, then he veers slightly to the right and slows his pace to a jog, then a walk, when he sees Alexander Elementary school.

He leans against a chain-linked fence and tries to catch his breath. He vomits three times and almost collapses on the sidewalk. He used to ball when he was younger. He used to spend his summers at King Park running up and down the damn court and didn't ever get tired. Not like this, like he's got a railroad spike in the center of his chest and some-one's twisting it around. He has to get off the street before he's seen. There's no sign of the police but he can't have someone from the neigh-borhood notice him. Can't leave opportunity for a physical description. Right now he's "Young Black Male." So long as he stays that way he'll remain anonymous.

This school's too poor for security cameras, Dee's thinking, and then remembers they shut the school down last year. He looks for a place to lay low, his lungs finally filling with air. He stashes the Ruger in his pants and enters by a basketball court covered with cracks, thick grass growing from them. To the left he sees a wooden privacy fence attached to the school. He walks over and sits with his back against it, hidden from anyone who might be looking for him.

He pulls out the Ruger and strokes the barrel. He feels different now. Changed. Like he crossed some line that made him more man than boy. He thinks of Uncle Slim and Kat smoking on Auntie's porch. Kat with her flirtatious ass. Torey's probably off work now, so she's probably with him. They probably get a room. Yeah, that's probably what they do. Torey probably takes her to a hotel for a few hours and then he drops her off when he's done with her. Let's her sleep wherever it is she lives.

Dee thinks of his first time. His only time. Tiny from down the street. She wasn't pretty but she had an ass on her. Dee came too quick but Tiny didn't seem to notice, or didn't seem to care. He's tried a few times to hit it again, but Tiny wouldn't let him, saying, *Only if we're dating,* and when Dee said, *Let's date then,* Tiny told him no. Maybe one day he'll give Kat a try. Maybe he'll take his father's advice and go after that *good* good. Maybe he'll cut through all Kat's bullshit and straight up ask her can he fuck? Tell her he has the cash for a room and all the weed she feels like smoking. He pictures that scene. He imagines what kind of body Kat has hiding beneath her clothes, imagines what the titties look like—that trail of cleavage that goes on for a mile—the pink thong he glimpsed once when she dropped her phone on the porch and bent over to pick it up.

The sirens are gone. Dee sets the Ruger beside him and unzips his pants. His dick is hard and hot in his hand. His breathing has slowed. The breeze cool against his exposed skin. He closes his eyes and imagines Kat, her lips wrapped around his dick. He strokes a few times and then comes. He's only seventeen, but it's time to be a man, he's thinking, he's done with dime bags of weed, done with teenage girls. Revenge will be had. Even Cesar Bolden isn't smooth enough to dodge a bullet. Dee will take his time, be smart, wait until the opportune moment, until the sky opens up and God himself tells him it's time for that nigga to die. Dee puts the Ruger back in his hand and kisses the barrel. It's cold against his busted lip. It was his father's gun—toward the end, when he was getting more and more edgy, more and more paranoid, Dee watched his father downstairs pushing up a panel, watched him stash the Ruger in the ceiling and put the panel back in place. And that's when he saw Dee and told him, "Promise me you won't follow in my footsteps. Promise me you'll find your own road."

But this is the road Dee was left on.

What else can a nigga do but walk down it?

Lyric stands under the top hat sign at Iggy's Place. The P and the L are dead. ACE blinking in the night. When she was little she called it the Abraham Lincoln Hat sign. Back in those days when Thunderbooty first started working down here, dragging Lyric across that old blue railroad bridge because Grammy wouldn't babysit, not so long as Tara was stripping. She has this memory she can't shake, her mother dragging her across that damn bridge, two men sitting huddled together beneath it, facing the river, sharing a beer. And it was morning. That's what she remembers most, the sun hiding behind the clouds, it was morning and those men were sharing a beer.

Lyric opens the door to Iggy's and is stopped by the bouncer, this corn-fed white boy with a pervy smile. Some Zach or Steve, some Calvin College Christian, some rich boy who doesn't need the cash, who took the job so he could look at tits and ass all night for free.

"I.D." he says.

"Move over."

"I.D."

"I need to see Iggy."

"We've been through this."

"Call him. Tell him it's important."

Zach or Steve doesn't move. His arms remained crossed. Walkie talkie clipped to his hip. He's blocking the entrance.

"Shit, *please*, a'ight?" Lyric looks past him into the club. Iggy's glass stripper cage is empty at the moment. She glances up to the black glass window of Iggy's apartment. Zach or Steve finally grabs his walkie talkie and mumbles into it. A pause of static, then Iggy's voice. "Send her up."

"Move, Bitch," Lyric says. She brushes past him and ascends the staircase leading to Iggy. He's waiting for her with the door open. Not smiling like he usually is, looking sick and thin. "You got old," she says. She walks past him and stands in front of the two-way mirror, scanning the club for Thunderbooty.

"Your name's been on the wind, Little Momma," says Iggy. He steps next to her, suddenly looking larger than he was just moments before, overlooking his establishment like some Don. Lyric ignores him.

"You were a sweet girl, you know that? Even after losing your father you still had some light left in your eyes," Iggy says. "That light is gone now. I seen it happen a thousand times to a thousand girls."

She always liked Iggy. Some nights he'd let her sit up here and color, or watch cartoons. That was before Thunderbooty started leaving her at home, before she started doing more than just stripping, before she started bringing men home.

"You said my name's been on the wind. What's that mean?"

"They're saying Cesar Bolden got a hold of you."

"Shit, nigga—Cesar Bolden got a hold of Thunderbooty, not me."

"That's not what I'm hearing. And I know you know what I'm talking about. Pretty soon everybody's gonna know. Then what?"

Six men. No script. Twelve hundred dollars' cash. Two hundred dollars per dick. For two days straight she cried more than she didn't— bleeding from both the pussy and the asshole, going through six pads a day until the bleeding stopped, so sore she couldn't stand up in the shower and the bathwater stung like hell. And that was just the pain part of the recovery. The memories won't ever heal. They pulled out and came in her hair, her face, her eyes. One of them burned her ass cheek with a cigar. Another bit off a nipple ring.

Cesar sat there in a metal foldout chair and watched for awhile. And then there was this moment when Cesar looked at her like he was bored, or sorry, or like he was just tired. Like some kind of conscience was being born in him. And Lyric thought for a moment he would end it right there, but he didn't. Cesar just stood and walked away. He left her there and the cameras rolled on.

"Thunderbooty ain't stripping tonight?" Lyric asks.

"No," says Iggy. "Your mother don't work here no more."

"Tricks must be good."

"Ain't tricking no more either," Iggy says. "She asked me to give you this." He reaches into his back pocket and pulls out an envelope. Hands it to her."

"What's this?"

"Don't know," Iggy says. "She stopped by a few weeks ago and left it for you. Took a job at that plastics factory your daddy used to work at."

"Bullshit."

"That's what she told me. And let me tell you something, Little Momma—I seen a lot of women leave this place—they don't ever leave like that—the rest of them, they disappeared."

Lyric turns and walks toward the door, envelope in hand.

"Lyric," says Iggy.

Lyric keeps walking.

"She loves you," he says. "She always did."

Lyric closes the door and opens the envelope. She unfolds the sheet of paper inside of it. The note says, *Baby, come home.*

Jackson's head throbs. He leans back in his recliner listening to the noises of his parents' house, his house, the house he raised his own family in. Emptier now than it was in his youth. He had no idea how much space Mae filled in this house, in him. He picks up three empty Hennessey bottles and throws them in the trash. He vomits twice in the kitchen sink and a third time on his way upstairs. He'll clean up later.

Jackson walks into the bathroom and turns on the faucet. Wets his face. His head. He stares at his reflection, his bloodshot eyes, his pale, dehydrated skin. How many of these hung-over mornings? Waking up saying he was through. Isaac regarding him with those pitying eyes, Mae looking at him with shame, Miles looking up from his headphones and staring through him like he's not even there, not even a man. Walking around his own house feeling like he's overstayed his welcome, telling himself he's done drinking. By the end of the day back in the bottle, chasing the numb, saying *tonight* is the last time.

This is no quick fix. There is no Band-Aid big enough for his life. Jackson covers his face and head with a lather of shaving cream. He slices into the lather with a razor. He begins with his head and then works down his jaw line avoiding his goatee. His rinses his head and face and looks at himself in the mirror. He holds his belly with both hands and watches it bounce when he drops it. He twists his beard. Scowls at his reflection. "Fuck you," he says.

Then he hears a voice, not a voice, more like an awareness. It comes from someplace inside him. It's like a fist squeezing his heart, or like his bones fell asleep—he is full of this feeling, this conviction. The fist squeezes Jackson's spine and Jackson goes limp, drops to the floor, feeling like at any moment he'll be hurled across the room, tossed against the walls. Jackson's body is no longer his own. And this presence doesn't speak, it doesn't say words, but it tells Jackson it's time. Change or die, it tells him. You're better than this. You're better than who you've become. And then it lets go.

Jackson reaches up and grabs the edge of the sink. He pulls himself to his feet. Stares in the mirror. He's never been one to pray. He's never asked forgiveness for his sins. He's never asked for aid from some greater power. He's always held himself accountable. He's always been a man. But he'll do as he's told. That loss of control scared him. Maybe it's God? Maybe. Or maybe it's just the God inside of him, some consciousness that's fed up with the pathetic existence of Jackson Carter. Either way, it's time.

Jackson lathers his upper lip and chin. He shaves himself clean. He runs bathwater hot enough to make his skin turn pink when he dips himself into the tub. He lies back and closes his eyes. "Day one," he says. A day one that should have happened years ago.

•

Miles stands on his front porch wearing a Cheshire grin and holding a steaming mug of coffee. He rocks a charcoal gray Polo sweat suit and horn-rimmed Gucci glasses. Kentwood is green, surreal almost compared to the southeast side. Like each blade of grass was dipped in paint. Planet suburbia. Mini-vans and hybrids. A man two houses down washing his car in his driveway. A woman across the street pruning her garden. "Why didn't you call, bro?" Miles says, smiling. I could have scooped you from the bus station."

"I did," Isaac says. "Twice. But no worries. An hour trip across town wasn't gonna kill me; been on a bus for four days." Isaac steps onto the porch and hugs Miles.

"Shit, bro. You smell like a bus. Like the road."

"Kentwood, huh?" says Isaac, taking in the neighborhood, everything with a suburban polish, a store-bought shine. "Finally Jefferson'd your way up out of the 'hood."

"Needed someplace low-key, man. Someplace quiet. We're getting real close to making some serious money. Once the money starts coming in those southeast side eyes start taking on a different shade, feel me?"

They step into Miles's duplex. The living room has a brown leather sectional couch and a fifty-inch flat-screen. One wall has a framed poster of Bob Marley next to a same-sized framed poster of a dreaded depiction of Jesus. Another wall has a blown-up and framed black and white photograph of Isaac cutting down the net when Ottawa won the state championship a few months ago, Miles grabbing at the net, looking up at Isaac who is looking somewhere else. "The place is nice," says Isaac.

"It's okay," Miles says. "Two bedrooms, but one of them is for the studio. You got the basement, bro. It's all concrete, but the rent's free until you get on your feet." Miles leads Isaac down a set of wooden stairs, dark brown paint peeling off them. The room is a cement box. Drywall sheets are piled under the stairs. An air mattress sits atop a slab of shag carpet. "It ain't much," says Miles.

"No, it's cool, Miles. This is fine."

Isaac takes in his new home: Cement floor. Cement walls. Floor boards for a ceiling. The consistent coldness of a jail. Isaac's clothes are in three garbage bags heaped next to the air mattress. His bookshelf is leaning against the wall, a few books: Don DeLillo's *Underworld*, Colum McCann's *Let the Great World Spin*, John Updike's *Rabbit Redux* are unpacked and on the top shelf while six moving boxes are stacked containing the rest of the books, like Miles had begun unpacking for Isaac and then changed his mind.

Isaac walks over to his boxes and pulls out a book: Phillip Roth's *The Human Stain*. He smells the pages, enjoying the dead-leaf scent. He smiles, remembering the Christmas of 2012, the Christmas that Mae broke Jackson's nose. The Christmas that all he received was books. Books and socks and boxers. And this big ass bookshelf that Jackson helped him put together. "Reading is a writer's weight room," says Isaac.

"Huh?"

"Reading is a writer's weight room," says Isaac. "That's what Mae used to tell me." Isaac puts the book back on the shelf. "Have you heard from her?"

"Yeah," Miles says. "She's been asking about you."

"She knows?"

"Yeah. You should call her," Miles says. "Let her know you're home. Let her know what your plans are."

"I'm not ready," Isaac says.

"Okay," says Miles. "But what *is* the plan, Isaac? I told you don't come home without a plan. What's the plan? Maybe you should just stay close to home. Go play ball for Grand Valley or something?"

"I'm done with basketball, Miles."

"What the fuck are you on, Zick? For real. Tell me something. I mean really tell me something. I deserve more than this vague bullshit you keep giving me."

"I used to think basketball was the only way I could survive my life," Isaac says. "But then I survived."

"Explain that."

"My dad had a drug problem. He was abusive. My next-door neighbor," Isaac starts, "the one who was murdered—he taught me how to play basketball . . ."

"Isaac, I know all this."

"I know. Just let me get this out. You asked, I'm trying to explain it to you."

"Okay."

"Anyways, basketball was a distraction. It helped me deal with all the shit going on in my life. My dad, my mom being gone all the time. But when Joey was murdered some kind of switch got flipped inside me. I became obsessed. Like basketball was all I had. It kept me from breaking down, you know. It kept me sane. But it was mine then. You know what I'm saying? Mine. The recruiters, the cameras, the circus— at some point it stopped being mine."

"Okay," Miles says. "That makes sense."

"But, it's like . . . I spent my life pretending, you know? I have all this shit in me, Miles. I have all these memories. All these words."

"Okay," says Miles. "But the question still remains . . . what are you going to do?"

"I want to record a song."

Miles takes a deep breath. "Zick, man, I'm trying real hard to support you. I am. But you're talking crazy. You don't just become a rapper. That's like me waking up one day and saying, hmm, I think I want to go to the NBA. It's disrespectful to the craft, bro. I been at this since I was a shorty."

"Look, I'm not trying to be a rapper, Miles. I just need to get these words out of me. Off the page and in the air, you know? I've been writing raps since we were kids. I just never showed them to anybody. I want you to hear what I put down on the page. You don't like it, cool. I'll leave you alone. But if you like it, I want you to help me put together an album."

Miles shakes his head.

"I know this sounds crazy, Miles. I know I sound crazy. I just feel strongly about this, about writing."

"Then write, shit! Mae's been shoving that Writing Program at Grand Valley down your your throat all year. Go to Grand Valley. Write until your heart's content. Rapping ain't writing. You gotta have swagger, bravado. Attitude. Your mysterious white boy in the hoodie persona—niggas ain't gonna feel that shit. Even Eminem has swag."

"Like I said: I'm not trying to be a rapper. I just feel like I need to do this. To get it off my chest. One song, Miles. You don't like it I'll leave you alone."

"The timing is so bad right now, Isaac."

"One song, Miles."

•

Miles sits in his recording studio adjusting knobs while he scrolls through beats. Librarian-like. A large mixing board lies atop a wooden desk that takes up most of a wall, a computer with two monitors sit next to it. Cords stretch across the room and into a closet. That's where the mic is. Miles' forehead bunched in thought, squinting, lips puckered and cocked to the right, concentrating, immersed in his element.

"What kind of beat are you looking for?"

"Something dark and slow."

"Dark and slow? Should have known." Miles clicks the mouse a few times and finds a folder titled "Dungeon Beats." He opens the file. A sixties soul singer whines the blues over a heavy baseline. Violins weave through the beat, spiraling around her voice like they are slow dancing with it. Like the strings and the voice are wrapped around each other. "What about this?"

Isaac bobs his head, whispers his lyrics. Looks at Miles. "That'll work."

"You only heard one beat."

"The mood matches the song."

"Oh lord."

Isaac steps into the closet and closes the door. He turns a knob and the lights dim. He props his lyric sheet on a music stand that leans against the wall. Headphones hang over a stainless steel microphone shielded by a spit guard. Isaac puts them on and waits.

"Can you hear me?" Miles asks him.

"Yeah."

"Okay. We need to get our levels right. Say the first couple lines a few times."

"Good. Good. Alright, Zick, make sure you come in on time. Wait for the intro. When the beat drops lay your vocals over it or the timing is going to be off. Got it?"

"Got it." For a moment there's no noise but static. Then the sixties soul singer is singing. Isaac gets lost in her voice. Then the beat vibrates in his head, surrounds him, as if he's part of the beat, the beat is a part of him. Isaac closes his eyes and goes back to Francis Street, to Nelly lying dead on the carpet, to Frank's menacing eyes, to Joey's body being carted away. And then he lets go.

I was ten when I met him, eleven when he died.
Eleven when I held his little girl and wiped her eyes.
The gunshot that took him, it still echoes in my mind.
That's when I crawled into the concrete and what's left of me survived.
But what's survived, when existing means you're living in your mind?
A prison where what's lost is something you could never find.
And the world keeps on watching, but won't look you in the eyes . . .

•

Miles stares at the computer monitor, squinting, slipped into Miles World, like Isaac isn't even in the room. Isaac looks for the verdict in Miles' face, but sees no signs either way. Miles, a tactician's gaze, the monitor making his face a pale blue mask in the unlit studio. Isaac folds his lyric sheet. Miles tilts his squint toward Isaac and half-cocks his head, a smile creeping across his face. "When you write that?"

"In the brig."

"The infamous Joey Cane, huh?"

"Yeah."

"Don't get all, *I told you so* on me, Zick. Cause I really don't feel like hearing your mouth. But check this out: A few tweaks here and there and I can take this down to the Jungle. Guarantee I can get you spins in two weeks, tops."

"So, it's good?"

"You kinda sound like Em a little. Just your voice, though. You're like a mesh of—of Pac and Nas. Like, passion and word play. It's like nothing out there. Plus, this Joey Cane cat being local—it's a story worth telling. Man, I didn't know you had it in you."

"Told you so." Isaac laughs.

"You been sitting on this all these years, bro? Crazy. I been waiting all this time for the right emcee. Turns out that muh fucka's you."

Isaac doesn't want to tell Miles that he's not. That it is about the writing, the music. He knows the business plan by heart, thanks to his brother: 1. Hit 'em with a hot single. 2. Use the single to promote an album. 3. Start local. Do shows. Gain a following. 4. Attack the college radio stations in the Midwest. 4. Set up a regional tour. 5. Secure regional distribution.

Isaac wants no part of that plan. Isaac does not desire a stage. He's done with the spotlight. Isaac's half-tempted to pull the plug right here and now. But Miles' eyes glisten with his dream. Isaac doesn't have the heart. The headphones are on and Miles is clicking his mouse, bobbing his head, immersed again, entirely in his element.

Kat's looking good tonight. Real good. A tight white T-shirt with Biggy Smalls face on it. Black skinny jeans making her ass pop out a little more. Black lipstick. Those fake eyelashes that look like spider legs, that bring out the light brown tint in her eyes. Torey's here with her, but he's not really here. His cell stays buzzing. Torey stays checking it. Kat playing it cool, trying not to act bothered, but Dee sees all—sees her glancing at Torey everytime his phone vibrates, sees Torey shrug his shoulders like he's telling her *There's nothing I can do,* Torey knows it, Kat knows it, even Dee knows it: there will be no creeping tonight.

And Dee's got his mind on that *good* good. The Isley Brothers *Greatest Hits* CD plays in the smoke-filled basement. Everybody sips something but Dee. An Uncle Slim gathering. Spades and dominoes, no drama, no dumb shit, nine adults just chillin'. Just having a good time. Dee watches Torey walk over to Kat and whisper in her ear. He shows her his phone and she nods. Torey says goodbye to all the adults and fistpounds Dee before he leaves. Dee watches Kat refill her drink and sit on the couch, stare at whatever movie is playing on the TV.

That *good* good. To pen that in a letter to his father. *Hey Pop, Aunties doing fine. Nitty's doing fine. Guess what? I finally got that* good *good!* To go x-rated with it too—describe every detail—paint a picture so vivid he'll show all his boys the letter. But how to get it? His father used to tell him to shoot his shot. All you gotta do is ask for it, D.J. Pull your dick out. Put your cards on the table. Worst she's gonna say is no. But Dee's thinking something crazy. Dee's thinking about Auntie's case of sleeping pills in the cabinet upstairs, he's thinking about crushing a few up and waiting until Kat's not looking, mixing it into her drink, letting her pass out on the couch, wait until Uncle Slim's asleep and everyone's gone home. But that wouldn't make him a man.

Now Nitty's pulling on his arm telling him to come upstairs. Dee picks up his sister and says she shouldn't be down here. Says there's too much smoke. Nitty tells him that Auntie sent her down to get him. That there's a man here to see him. Dee holds Nitty against his chest and begins to work out an escape route, thinking it's the police, wishing there were a door downstairs so he could take off running.

But it's not the police waiting for him upstairs. It's the man with the dreads, from that night at Miss Tracy's, and he's standing in the doorway talking to Auntie. "No, no, D.J.'s not in trouble, Miss Netta. I just need to borrow him for a minute. Five minutes tops." Auntie sits in her chair smoking a Salem. She looks at Dee like she's watching him die. Like she's seen his end coming from a great distance, and now that distance has been closed, like this whole time she's been readying herself for it and now it's arrived. "Go on then, D.J." says Auntie. Dee sets Nitty down and follows Dreads outside.

Dreads lights a Black and Mild. He hits it twice and offers it to Dee. Dee declines. "You made the news, D.J." Dreads tells him. "And you're real lucky no one saw you too. Real lucky neither of those pigs were shot or killed." He hits the Black and Mild again. "You need to lay low for a couple weeks, you understand me?" Dee nods, but Dreads doesn't see him do it. "Nigga, are you listening to me? You want to do grown man shit you need to start acting like a man."

"I hear you," says Dee. Wondering why Dreads is here, watching him pull a small clear plastic bag out of a pocket in his jacket. The bag is packed with another twenty or thirty twisted and tied smaller bags, full of pale yellow rocks that look like chipped-off and rotted chunks of teeth.

"Stuff that in your pants," Dreads tells him.

Dee does what he's told.

"Division and Cherry," Dreads says. "I hear you're posted up anywhere else I'm cutting you off. Tell me you understand me."

"I understand you."

"I collect my money before you spend a dime of it. Tell me you understand me."

"I understand you, but how much . . ."

"Don't worry about how much right now. I'll find you when it's time to find you. And remember. Next two weeks you're laying low."

Dee watches Dreads step off the porch and head toward a large S.U.V., the engine still running, headlights still on, the quiet rumble of bass coming from the back end of it. "Wait," says Dee. "Why? Why you looking out for me?"

Dreads turns. "Your father," he says. "When I was a hungry stupid little nigga like you are, DeMarco did it for me."

Auntie isn't in her chair when Dee steps back into the house. Downstairs he hears a couple people saying their good byes. He walks into his bedroom and locks the door. Pulls the plastic package out of his pants and drops it on the bed. Then he remembers Kat. He remembers his father's words. Dee rips open the package and cups one of the bags in his palm. He stashes the rest of the crack in that old Sunday suit, in the opposite pocket as the weed. Stuffs the bag in his pants pocket, finds a joint in the top drawer of his dresser, then goes downstairs.

Kat's on the couch by herself scrolling through her phone. Bruce Willis is on television waving a gun around with a crazed look on his face. Uncle Slim and three others sit at the table talking and laughing over a domino game. Dee sits beside Kat and she puts away her phone. "Hey, D.J." she says. "How you doing?"

"I'm good," says Dee. "You looked like you could use some company."

"Ha! Damn, baby. I look that sad, huh?"

"I didn't mean it like that." He shows her the joint. "You want to go out to the garage?"

Kat smiles. There's a smear of black lipstick on her left front tooth. "I'd love to."

Dee glances at Uncle Slim to see if he's watching. He isn't. Uncle Slim's got his back to them, slamming down a domino, laughing loud saying "Thirty, Motherfuckers!" Dee leads Kat upstairs, out the front door, and into the garage. He finds his ashtray and his lighter. Turns and sees Kat getting comfortable on the couch. That's when the nerves get the best of him. His hand shakes a little when he lights the joint, hits it once, and passes it to her.

He settles into the couch beside her. Their thighs touching. His dick already starting to get hard. Should he put his hand on her leg? Should he put his arm around her? Should he do what his father told him, just pull out his dick, and ask her for some pussy? Or should he just get high? Let Kat get high. Maybe Torey has her feeling lonely enough tonight to try something. Maybe she'll read between the lines, maybe she'll read Dee's mind and make it easy for him, mercy fuck him, do it because she's bored and he's there. Maybe.

But now the joint's almost gone. What if she leaves? What if she thanks him for the high and walks out the door? Shit. He's blowing it. Dee, do something. Stop being a punk. He puts his hand high on her thigh but doesn't look at her. He waits. She doesn't move his hand. She puts hers on top of it and laughs, settles deeper into the couch. "What you doing, D.J.?" she asks.

I'm trying to fuck, he's thinking. But he can't make himself say the words. "What do you mean?" He looks at her. Takes his hand off of her thigh. Her head rests against the back of the couch and she's smiling at him.

"What are you trying to do?" Kat asks him.

Can we fuck? "What do you mean?" He asks.

"You're so cute," Kat tells him. "Damn, D.J." says Kat. "This is some good shit. I'm so high. This is just what I needed tonight." Kat stands and begins her way across the garage floor.

Dee watches her ass, watches his chance for that *good* good slipping away. He reaches into his pocket and pulls out the small plastic bag. The last card, the only card he has to play. "Wait," says Dee. "I got something else."

Kat turns. Still smiling.

"Come here," Dee tells her. He shows her the rock.

"Where'd you get that?"

"Don't matter. I got it." Kat isn't smiling anymore. He hasn't thought this through. Is she supposed to fuck him for a rock? Is he really supposed to ask her that? She's clean. She's been clean. For how long, he isn't sure. "Do you want it?"

"I don't smoke," Kat tells him. "Not anymore." Her tone sounds like she's trying to convince herself. She watches Dee set the rock on the table. "Why are you doing this?"

"You don't know?" He rubs his dick through his jeans, but doesn't take it out. The change in her demeanor gives him confidence. Makes him feel like he's the one in control. "Kat," says Dee. "I'm trying to fuck. I'ma give you the rock. But first I'm trying to fuck."

Kat glances at the rock. Then at Dee. "You're just a boy," she says.

"I ain't no boy."

"You're just a boy," Kat says. Quieter this time. She shakes her head and walks over to the table. She doesn't look at Dee when she palms the rock. And then she's gone. The rock gone with her.

Jackson sits at the kitchen table staring at an unopened bottle of Hennessy. He's freezing but his forehead is hot. He's sweating. His hands shake. His heart does gymnastics in his chest. Maybe a nip or two from the bottle, he's thinking. Maybe cold turkey was not the best way to slay this thing. He keeps hearing Mae's voice. He keeps hearing her bitching. He's checked the driveway for her Camry four times tonight. He's checked the bedroom, the basement. He's called out to her, cussed at her. Begged her to show herself. He keeps telling himself it isn't real. It's withdrawal. This madness is a part of the process.

Jackson grabs the Hennessey bottle and brings it close to his face. "Fuck you," he whispers, and then hurls it against the wall. The glass seems to shatter for hours. The sound filling the house, the noise just below a hum. The spilled Hennessey filling the kitchen like a pool until Jackson is treading in it, lifting his head toward the ceiling trying not to let a single drop touch his tongue. Because if one drop touches his tongue he knows he's a goner. Jackson closes his eyes and when he opens them the madness is done. Everything but the cold sweats. The shakes in his hands.

He picks up the phone and dials Mae's cousin's number.

"This is Jackson Carter. Will you please put my wife on the phone?"

"Yes. I know it's late. I just need to talk to Mae."

"I know. I'm sorry I yelled at you last time. I am. Will you please just put her on the phone?"

"Okay. Alright. Uh huh. But can you do me one favor . . ."

"Will you tell her I love her?"

"Bitch," Jackson whispers after she hangs up the phone. Jackson walks out of the kitchen and into the basement. He mummies his fists in black Everlast hand wraps, slides into a pair of ancient bag gloves, and tightens the Velcro band across his wrists with his teeth. Jackson scowls at a duct-taped heavy bag and jabs. He one-two's and dust clouds the bag when his right hand thuds against it. Jackson hooks to the ribs of the thing and the bag sways. He continues until his chest is on fire. Until his knuckles throb. Until his brain is quiet enough to take a stab at sleep.

"Day three," says Jackson. "Day three."

Isaac feels the walls tonight. The furnace breathes. The duplex rattles against the wind. He lies on his back, fingers interlocked behind his head. Colum McCann's *Let the Great World Spin* lies open on his chest. Reading is a writer's weight room. A line from McCann's novel is stuck in his head, "The world spins. We stumble on. It is enough." Is stumbling on really enough though? Isaac isn't sure. He's been devouring books. One after another. But McCann. McCann's *Let the Great World Spin*. The language, the way he portrays the human experience, finds beauty in the ugliness—he has Isaac ready to read every word the man has written.

Over socked feet Isaac stares into a small square of the world. Through a grass-level window he can see the headlights of cars on late night journeys through the quiet pulse of Kentwood. He imagines the pilots of these cars. These night crawlers. Teens sneaking out their parents' houses, stealing keys off kitchen counters, putting a car in neutral, letting it coast down the street out of hearing range before starting the engine. Booty calls texted for last-resort companionship, the third or fourth option, the only one that replied to the drunken words *wat u doin???????* Factory workers coming or going, night shifters with either a 24-ounce beer or a 24-ounce gas station coffee between their legs. Drunk drivers coming home from clubbing, a sick friend vomiting out of a passenger side window, maybe they're sitting next to a one-night stand, he or she rubbing on his or her thigh.

Night crawlers: Those who thrive when night becomes morning, when people with busy minds toss and turn, or give up sleeping like Isaac has. He's been thinking about Myra since he's been home. Wondering how things landed with her and Mike. If the marriage has been rekindled. If she misses Isaac, thinks about him sometimes. Isaac hasn't heard from her since that last hotel night, the night of the State Championship game. Did she walk away with no remorse, no guilt? Was he really no more than payback sex to her? Does it really matter? What he using her too? Was Myra just a distraction for him, something to do besides make a decision—or something else: mature, big breasts, light brown skin—was Isaac taking something from Myra, satisfying some primitive need that he was never able to fulfill.

Miles has been going on constantly about blowing up, getting rich, shaking the world. But what Isaac loves about writing is the empty wreckage of the act—the way the release comforts the mind. To package it, market it, sell it, taints its beauty, or maybe not? Maybe that part isn't what bothers him? To give your words to the world and have them received could be okay. It's the spotlight that bothers him. Isaac left the concrete for the darkness. Where he could look into his life and learn. And Miles is promising to put a spotlight on that darkness. And bring back the gaze of the world that chased him there.

Isaac finds his laptop at his feet and powers it on. He toggles around on the Grand Valley State University website. Enrolling in classes might be a good start. How long will the $2,000 graduation gift from Jackson last him? He needs a job, a plan. He slips into his Nike sandals and walks up the stairs. Goes to wake Miles and ask for his car keys, but the slow jams are playing on low, which means he has some chick with him, which means knocking on the door is not an option. Isaac's heard the cock blocking speech twice already in the two weeks he's been home. He walks into the living room and finds Miles' Impala keys hanging from a coat rack mounted to the wall.

Isaac's song is playing when he starts the car. Miles burned a disc after James mastered it and had since been bumping it nonstop while he drives. Isaac finds it strange hearing his own voice, his but not his, somehow distorted. He remembers writing the words in his mind on the plane to San Diego, marching across the concrete in boot camp. Penciling them in his pad at the Camp Pendleton Base Brig. Writing to no beat but the thump of his pulse.

He turns off the CD player and rides in silence. Too much too soon. Miles' ambition dwarfing his: Miles wants to conquer the world; Isaac only hoping to conquer himself. He's only ever wanted solace. To thrive in the crevices of existence, slip into the dark cracks of life and avoid the noise. But the noise finds him, the chaos—it's persistent beckoning toward a path that is not his own. Can never be his own. He needs seclusion. Yet every tangible ability he has requires an audience.

Sleepless on the southeast side. Sweat pants and a beater. Couch lounging. Leaning against propped pillows. Sportscenter on but the TV volume is low. One hand holds a beer mug filled with ice water. The other hand is stashed in his pants fondling his balls. Jackson's only been home one day and already he fiends for the road, where at least he's in motion. Here he's taunted by the house's whispers, by Mae's absence, her voice, her scent still lingering in the bedding, her recliner, his mind.

Headlights in the driveway. Jackson limps over to the blinds and peeks out into the night. Miles, no, Isaac, steps out of the car and approaches the porch, hood cloaked, stubble across his jaw line. Jackson opens the door. Isaac looks the same as he did the day Jackson met him: a stone statue of a boy, nothing alive but his eyes. "Where's your key?" Jackson asks.

"Dunno." Isaac doesn't enter the house. He just stands there looking at Jackson like he needs an invitation to come inside.

Jackson leaves the door open and walks back to the couch. He takes a sip of his water. "Bolt the door behind you." Jackson moves his pile of pillows. Sits in his recliner.

Isaac steps inside and kicks off his sandals. He looks around the place like he's never been here before, though his own accolades cover the walls: Framed newspaper articles. A large wooden medal holder with a glass cover and a velvet backdrop, all-conference medals pinned to it, all-area medals, all-state medals. His achievements. His house. Yet Isaac wears an expression like he's wandered into a museum. Like he's seeing somebody else's history. Or trespassing on someone else's memories.

Isaac flips down his hood and walks across the room. He settles into the Jackson-sized imprint on the couch. They had words the day Isaac left for the Marines. Loud words. Spit flying words. Isaac saying *You're not my dad. My dad's dead.* Jackson saying *Closest thing you got. The only thing you got left.* Jackson and Miles had cornered Isaac for an intervention, tried to bully him with reason: Go to school. Get your education. See what happens with basketball. The military is for people without options. You have options.

"Have you heard from Mae?" Isaac asks.

"No." Jackson doesn't mention the letters or the phone calls to her cousin's house. Her location given reluctantly by Mae's father, Hank, only after Jackson broke down into tears, the laughter in Hank's voice turning fatherly toward the end of the conversation, like he was talking Jackson off of the edge of a building, saying, "Jackson, you two just weren't right for each other. Was only a matter of time before she came to her senses." Hank said she accepted a teaching position down there. That she was moving on. Not even considering coming home. He said that Mae was starting a new life. Told Jackson to go ahead and call, make his apologies, do his begging. And when all that was done, Hank told him, and Mae stays in Mississippi, then you move on. "Mae doesn't want to talk to me."

"You think she's gone for good?"

"I don't know ... Look, I'm sorry about what I said. I'm sorry about how you left."

"It's okay," Isaac says. "You were right. I never should have gone. Soon as that plane took off and the city got smaller, I knew I made a mistake." Isaac's eyes pierce through Jackson until Jackson looks away.

Jackson finds his water and sips. He turns back to Isaac and finds his eyes still on him. "Have you ever dealt with it, Son?" Jackson asks him. "Have you ever dealt with the past? Confronted it?"

"Every day, Jackson. Every day of my life."

"Listen, Isaac. All that shit you've been through. That's what you came from; that's not who you are," Jackson says. "Your history doesn't define you; it creates you."

Isaac nods. His eyes soften a little. Jackson wonders what Isaac sees, what he's thinking. A father figure, a friend, the Big Bad Wolf who chased Mae out of this house and out of his life. A drunk. Still weak for it, longing for the buzz. Sipping ice water constantly because he's so used to sipping. Punching the heavy bag to kill the shakes in his hands. He starts to tell Isaac about his sobriety, but something stops him. Like if he speaks the words aloud he'll jinx it. Like he'll piss his demons off and they'll come lurking about, reenergized, and give him another beating.

"I need your advice," Isaac tells him. "I'm thinking about going to Grand Valley. I'm thinking about the Writing Program. Do you think that's a smart move?"

"According to Mae it is," Jackson says. "Have you called her since you've been home? I know she'd like to hear your voice. She'd be able to tell you all about the program, maybe even speed the application process up for you."

Isaac's demeanor changes. Like he's become uncomfortable in his skin. He stands. Walks over to the bookshelf. "You think she'd mind if I borrowed a couple books?"

"No. Of course she wouldn't."

Isaac runs his finger across the second row and takes two books from the shelf. "Colum McCann," Isaac says to Jackson. "He's a beast." Isaac flips his hood over his head. Jackson watches him walk across the room and slip back into his sandals.

"You should call her, Isaac."

286 • THE CONCRETE

"I'm not calling her."

"This is my fault," Jackson tells him. "It's my fault she left."

"Everybody I ever loved has left me," Isaac says. "You have any idea how that feels?"

Jackson goes to speak, but can't find any words worth saying. Isaac's eyes are locked on him, waiting for some healing truth that Jackson can't muster.

"Everybody," says Isaac. He steps out of the house and shuts the door.

"I'm still here," Jackson says. He walks over to the window and watches Isaac from the blinds. "I'm still here," he says again, watching Isaac peel out of the driveway and into the belly of the southeast side.

T wo Ecstasy pills and a pint of Courvoisier: the cocktail to survive these nights, these wolves, these men. It doesn't matter the age, creed, or color—you get them together, you get a young girl taking off her clothes—when that blood crawls into their cocks they go back to the stone age, where it was socially acceptable to grab a bitch by the hair, drag her into your cave, and fuck her in any hole you can find.

Tonight's party is mild though. These East Grand Rapids white boys ain't got shit on those southeast side thugs—you're always dodging cocks—that's part of the game, but at an East Grand Rapids White Boy party that's all you're dodging. At a southeast side party, on a bad night, you might be dodging bullets.

Lyric works the room, topless, but wearing a thong. The party's in a Marriott suite overlooking the river. There's a table of older guys playing poker, disinterested in her unless she steps into their space, then they want to squeeze her ass to get a laugh out of their buddies. The best man is wasted but the groom isn't drinking. They sit together on what they're calling the "Party Couch" getting lap dances from the other two girls, both blonde, both skinny, neither willing to do more than dance. Legally speaking, at these kinds of parties no touching is allowed.

Lyric's not concerned with legal. She's looking for the white boy in the room who likes brown sugar, and when she finds him she's gonna make him feel like he's God. Let the blonde skinny bitches make their rounds, let them stash their dollars in their g-strings. Lyric has other plans. When she finds her white boy she's gonna give him all her time. And it doesn't take long to find him either, long-limbed and baby-faced, Indiana Pacers hat cocked sideways, Pacers T-shirt, white Chuck Taylors, baggie jeans. His eyes are glued to her ass—that's how she can tell—she's got too much ass for most white boys, but not this one, she can see his mind working, thinking of all the nasty things he'd like to do to it.

"Hey, baby," Lyric says. She doesn't ask if he wants a dance. She asks if he's bored, asks if he's staying in the hotel. He says he was until now, and he is, a few doors down from here. She doesn't ask his name, doesn't tell him hers, doesn't tell him anything. She lets him talk. She stares into his eyes when he tells her he's a Sports Marketing major at U of M, that he's interning with the Pacers right now and back home for his buddy's wedding.

"I never do this but . . ." she says, lets the 'but' hang there for a moment, then says, "I want to give you a free lap dance. You're just so fucking adorable." And when she dances for him, and here's the key . . . when she dances for him she drops her big juicy black ass on his white boy dick, and she grinds until she feels him get hard, and she takes his hand and guides it down the front of her panties, and she presses his fingers inside her, and then she turns and she whispers "$500 to fuck" and she smiles, and she gets off his white boy dick, and she walks out of the room and into the hallway, and leans against the wall and waits, because she knows he's right behind her.

And when he joins her, fidgety, nervous, because maybe he's never paid for pussy, or maybe because he's never been with a black girl, she reassures him, kisses him, takes his hands and puts them on her big juicy black ass. She lets him lead her to his room and the moment he closes and bolts the door she reminds him, $500, and watches him reach into his back pocket and pull out his wallet, and say, *Shit, I don't have any cash on me.* And when she mentions the ATM in the lobby, her white boy smiles and he turns on the radio, and it's the DJ Blaze Show, and he turns the volume up a little too loud, and then his white fist is breaking her nose, she's being thrown to the floor, her thong ripped off.

She blacks out because she's face-first in the carpet and there's so much blood, and no one has ever taken the pussy from her, ever, every nasty, despicable, degrading thing that Lyric has ever done in her life has been her choice, and she never imagined tonight when she scoped out this white boy, when she chose him, that he'd be the one to take it, and she's dizzy and confused and her head throbs, so she leaves her body, it's no longer hers, but it isn't his either, it's lost somewhere between them. It's like she's floating inside of herself, in the dark, and whatever hasn't already emptied inside her is emptying now, and the radio is so fucking loud, and DJ Blaze is saying, "This is a local cat. Ya'll might recognize the name: Isaac Page." And she thinks she imagines it but then Blaze says, "He's dedicating this song to the late, great Joey Cane. Rest in peace, Joey. This is Grand Rapids' own, Isaac Page, with "The Concrete.""

T he clouds hang thick and bleak over Garfield Park, but the artwork of the sky marries Isaac's mood. In the field next to the basketball court a father and son attempt to fly a kite on this windless day. The father runs, hoping to catch a pocket of air; the son watches, smiling, and Isaac is reminded of Frank Page in those video game days, those puzzle days, those pre-crack days when Frank was a father and Isaac was a son. Isaac smiles when the kite plummets into the grass.

A rich-looking white guy instructs hood youths on the nuances of tennis. The rarely-used courts are busy with kids climbing the tall fence, hurdling over nets, whacking balls out into the field, competing to hit cars driving down Burton Street.

The long-dried-out wading pool babysits a few kids, hoisted over the locked fence by their parents or caregivers. A toddler pulls off his shitty diaper and hangs it on a fence post. He runs around the cement box laughing. He falls down on his bare butt and begins to cry. His teen-age mother flirts with a grown man, sitting on a bench, letting the boy cry until finally turning and saying, "Shut your ass up! Damn!"

Isaac rode the number four bus down here from Kentwood. He rested his head on the window and watched Eastern Avenue. He watched the suburbs become city; the green become gray; manicured lawns become unkempt and twisted with weeds. The southeast side hasn't changed. This gray. This gloom. This concrete pocked with small islands of faded grass.

Flick. Snap.

He's going to have to talk to Miles. Isaac asked for it: the beat, the studio time, but Isaac never really believed anyone would hear the music but him. He had it in his mind that he'd create the album as more of a project, music more of a hobby than a career. He's already applied to Grand Valley. Maybe there's a way he can do both? Maybe Miles has a way to promote an album without going on tour, without Isaac being on a stage.

The song wasn't supposed to hit like it did. This wasn't supposed to happen so fast. "The Concrete" is getting spins on the Blaze show, and the city's buzzing, and Miles's dream is happening for him. And with Isaac not on board that dream will be put on pause. And Miles isn't talking small. The thought of those late nights, the club scene, the stages—it's just not going to work. Not for Isaac.

Flick. Snap.

A young boy is on the opposite end of the court shooting jump shots. A mixed kid, maybe nine or ten years old. The boy does push-ups every time he misses. He's wearing tattered Nikes and dirt-stained shorts. He's shirtless. Another kid sacrificing himself to the concrete. Isaac wonders if their demons know each other. He wants to walk over to him, tell him, there is no escape from this life. Hide in your mind and the world still finds you. Instead he nods when their eyes meet. Flame recognize flame.

Flick. Snap.

Isaac retrieves the ball. The young boy has been watching him. "What's up, little man?" Isaac asks. It sends an earie chill through him. Filled with the ghost of Joey Cane. When Isaac thinks of Joey he sees a sweat-stained shirt. Chain-smoking cigarettes. The way the basketball seemed to hang in the air before it snapped the net inside out.

Isaac rolls his ball off of the court and into the grass. "Let me rebound for you," he says to the boy. Isaac tries to remember the way Joey had taught him to shoot. With the toe and the elbow and the follow through. But the kid steps back to the three-point arc and lets the ball go before Isaac can speak.

Flick. Snap.

"Damn," says Isaac. "Nice shot." Isaac tosses him the ball. The kid drains two more before missing.

"You're Isaac Page," the kid says. "I saw you play against Creston last year. You had like forty points that night."

"Thirty-seven."

"My dad says you could have gone to college. Said you could have played anywhere you wanted."

"Yeah." Just as he realizes who the boy is, remembering him from the picture hanging in Mike Goslett's kitchen, Isaac sees Myra walking up the sidewalk. Mike is holding her hand. A little mixed boy is running ahead of them, on a b-line toward the swings. Isaac can't tell if he feels guilty or jealous, but the feeling, gathering in his chest, stings. Myra sees Isaac before Mike does.

"What happened?" asks the kid.

He longs for Mae, for her hugs and her cheek kisses, her scolding glances, her love. He tries to imagine Mississippi, but can't. He sees Mae in front of a classroom, giving thirty faceless strangers all the love she should be giving him. Isaac looks down at Myra's son. "Life happened." He lets the words soar over the kid's head. He leaves his basketball lying off in the grass and heads toward the sidewalk.

Mike Goslett phonies a smile as Isaac approaches. Myra looks away, off at her little one, already pumping his feet on the swings. "Isaac fuck-ing Page," says Mike. He doesn't offer his hand. Isaac doesn't offer his. Myra glances at Isaac, then at her feet, then back at her son. Isaac's heart flutters and retreats, twists in on itself. The ball echoes off the concrete. Isaac turns toward the court. Myra's son drains another three. Isaac starts to apologize to Mike, but for what? Instead he looks at Myra. She meets his eyes and looks away. Her son drains another three. "The kid," Isaac says to Mike. "He has skills."

What family was ever perfect? What person? Isaac thinks of Jackson. His wife fed up and gone. Jackson waiting in vain for her to come back home. In spite of all that love. Jackson and Mae Carter had that in abundance. After all the yelling and screaming—at the end of the day they still had love. And maybe Mike and Myra have that. Maybe Isaac's just a mistake Myra made. Maybe she confessed to it and Mike forgave her, calling things even. Maybe Isaac was a fling that happened in the short space of a separation, maybe he's a secret, maybe there was nothing to forgive. Either way, Mike and Myra are some version of together here, now, and for Isaac that is enough to emotionally close the door. "I gotta catch the four," says Isaac, to no one in particular. He flips his hood over his head. "I wish you both nothing but the best." Isaac turns and walks away.

D ee dresses like a college student. A button-down shirt and kakis. Navy blue Vans. Nietzsche's *Thus Spoke Zarathustra* in his left hand. He sits and glimpses at it from time to time, during a slow moment or two, getting lost in the language but still feeling smarter somehow just by looking at the words. The Ruger's stashed in his pocket, hidden beneath his untucked shirt. The dope stays in his backpack, all but the bag cupped in his palm. He only comes down here during daylight, before the GRPD triples their patrol efforts, before the spot gets too hot.

Dee leans against a pillar at Pekich Park, a small gathering of benches, surrounded by a floor of red brick and casually landscaped woodchips and plants. It's located on the corner of Division and Cherry right next to Ascentcare, an injury-rehab center or some shit, Dee isn't sure. There's a large mural on the Ascentcare wall that faces the park. An ode to the city's Dutch founders. A beautiful painting of white men in suspenders, overcoats, and hats, chopping down trees, discussing their plans to bring the lumber industry to Grand Rapids by way of the Grand River.

Three black junkies sit on a bench beneath the mural sharing a cigarette.

When Kat walks up to him, he doesn't recognize her at first. She's not gone yet, but she's well on her way, with her tattered clothes and her unbrushed hair. It's her gap that gives her away, when she smiles and asks him how Uncle Slim is doing. She leans in to hug him and he lets her. She tries to kiss him on the mouth and he turns so her lips land on his cheek instead. She has a strange scent to her, something like food on the verge of going bad. What's cupped in his palm is what she's after and she's got that look in her eyes like she has no money, like she wants to walk him down Cherry Street, past Commerce, and under the overpass. Like she wants to give Dee the only thing she has left to offer.

"Where you been?" Dee asks her. His dick getting hard. He hadn't seen her since that night in the garage and he suspected this was why. He almost feels guilty. Almost. But what was it his father used to always say? A junkie is a junkie is a junkie. Up is a temporary state of being. They all fall back down.

"I been around, D.J. I just been around."

Dee watches Kat scratch her arm. Look over her shoulder. Down the street.

"You got something for me?" Dee asks her.

"Maybe," says Kat. "That night," she says. "What you asked me for . . . you still want that?"

"Am I a man now, Kat? Is that what you're saying. I'm not just a boy no more?"

"You're a man, D.J."

"Hmm. Okay. Way I see it though, is you owe already. You took something from me that night and gave me nothing in return."

"We can go for a walk, D.J." Kat says. "We can figure something out."

Dee might have followed her down Cherry Street . . . The past month every time he jerked off he was picturing Kat—wishing things that night would have played out differently—that unattainable *good* good right here in front of him now, willing—he might have followed her down Cherry Street, but he won't, he can't, because he can't get past her smell. "Nah," says Dee. "Not today. I'm gonna come find you though. Real soon. Shake my hand, Kat. It was good seeing you."

Dee watches Kat walk away then slides into the park and finds a free bench to sit on. The junkies know he's holding, but know better than to walk up on him. One wears a zipperless gray winter coat. A black beanie rests on his head, so loosely that the smallest gust of wind would blow it off. The man has a trimmed white beard and a gold tooth. The place where his eyes should be white are just a few shades paler than the gold. He nods at Dee and Dee smiles.

Dee gets his kicks off of making them wait. Tweaking. Itching to get that fix. Dee looks away. He reaches into his backpack and pulls out a letter from his father. Read Nietzsche, his father tells him in the letter, it will change your life. But the fucking words make no sense. Dee keeps it on him though. He keeps trying. Just to feel a little closer to his father. Dee folds the letter and stashes it in the book. Puts the book in the backpack. Zips it.

He stands and uses his hand as a visor against the sun. Across the street from Ascentcare a taupe Cadillac is parked. Cesar Bolden feeds the meter while his son Miles and this scrawny white boy step out of the car and walk over to a white man in a business suit, who stands with a briefcase at the front door of the building that used to be DeGage Ministries. "Motherfucker," says Dee. He straps the backpack over his shoulders. Tries to cool the rage building in him. Looks to the sky for some kind of sign. It's the shade of periwinkle with huge cotton clouds.

"Unc!" Dee yells at Cesar from across the street. Cesar doesn't smile when he sees him. He's got an expression like Dee had dragged himself out of a grave. Like that $50,000 bribe was goodbye. Little does this nigga know, Dee's thinking, and he's back on his game. He crosses the street and shows Cesar love. He daps him, half-hugs him, and tries some version of small talk. Auntie's doing okay. Getting old, but doing okay. Yeah, for sure, I'll give her your best. Apparently this nigga's starting a record label with his son. His son and the goofy white boy with him. Apparently they're buying the building and turning what used to be DeGage Ministries into a recording studio. Dee's smiling in Cesar's face while he listens to him. He nods and shows interest, but Dee's imagining some quiet weeknight, Cesar leaving this building alone—he's imagining Cesar's lips wrapped around the Ruger, begging for his life like the bitch that he is. The time is near, Dee's thinking, as Cesar rushes out of the conversation and into the building, chirping his car locked before he closes the door.

A bright sun stretches across the cool basement. It's early morning, but no birds are chirping. The only sound is loud knocks on the duplex door. Wake up the world knocks. Knocks like the house is on fire. Isaac knows Miles is gone. He's always gone first thing, going who-knows-where, making deals with who-knows-who, aggressive in all of his pursuits. Even if he's up late, Miles is out of the house by 7:00 a.m.

That leaves Isaac to roll off the air mattress and drag himself up the steps to answer the door. He peeks through the blinds and sees, of all people, Cesar Bolden, holding two gas station coffees, glancing around the duplex neighborhood like he's someone that doesn't belong here.

"Miles isn't here," Isaac says when he opens the door.

"Wasn't Miles I came here for." Cesar hands Isaac a coffee. "Wanted to invite you to take a ride with me."

"Ride where?" asks Isaac, realizing he accepted the coffee, pissed at himself because he did.

"Nowhere in particular. All these years, Isaac, and we ain't ever gotten to know each other. I think today's as good a day as any for a conversation."

Isaac wants to tell Cesar to fuck off. But Cesar Bolden's demeanor is an authority of moments, talking in the calm kind of way that says a storm's coming if you don't do what he asks you. So Isaac just nods. He sips the coffee and feels a pang of weakness.

The same Cadillac from all those years ago, preserved just like Cesar's preserved, timeless, beautiful. Yes, beautiful. What the man has inside him is disguised by a physical charm that could fool the world into thinking whatever he is saying is truth. Even knowing better, you go along with it.

"I know you don't like me, Isaac." Cesar pulls onto US 131, going north toward Grand Rapids. "I know you don't trust me. But you're safe. The only thing I love on this earth is my son. And my son loves you. You understand me?"

Isaac sips his coffee.

"You know why I let Jackson Carter raise him?" Cesar doesn't take his eyes off the road. He guides the Cadillac with one hand and sips his coffee with the other. Eyes hidden beneath black Ray Bans. He's in no rush at all. Cesar talks smooth and slow, the car coasting five miles below the seventy miles-per-hour speed limit, barely a soul on the road. "Cause hustlers ain't got no business raising kids. Last thing I wanted was for my boy to end up like me."

There was something real in Cesar's voice when he said it. Something not scripted and sly. And for that, Isaac drops his guard a little, tolerates Cesar's words. The Cadillac coasts past the Thirty-sixth Street exit. Isaac sips his coffee. Cesar sips his.

"My mother killed herself when I was ten," says Cesar. "Razor blade across the wrist. I found her naked in the bathtub when I got home from school. Thought she was fucking with me. Her eyes were dead black and I thought she was fucking with me. One arm hanging out of the tub, the other laying across her body. I kept shaking her. My clothes were soaking wet. Bathroom floor covered with blood and water. I just kept shaking her."

"Why are you telling me this?" Isaac asks.

"Shit, I don't know. Just figured the way things are going, you and I need to have an understanding. I don't expect you to like me," says Cesar. "But I want you to understand me."

The way things are going?

Cesar gets off on Business Exit 84B and hooks a right onto Cherry Street, eases the Cadillac down to twenty-five, past a man holding a cardboard sign saying: Three Kids. No job. Anything Helps. God bless!!! Further down the road a man on a ten-speed bicycle carries two garbage bags in one hand, holding them over his shoulder, his other hand guiding the bike down the road.

"I lived with my daddy after my mother died. But I basically raised myself." Same cool tone, no emotion, each word sliding off his tongue and into the air. "In an ugly world. To survive out here you have to get your hands dirty. Miles didn't have to see none of that. Drop him a few dollars, help him out when he needs it—"

And let Jackson do the hard part, Isaac's thinking, but he doesn't say it. Just waits for it: the bottom line. What does Cesar Bolden want from him? That's the question. Why is he on this ride listening to the history of a man he cannot stand? Isaac braces himself for the bottom line as Cesar hooks a left on Division and parks at a meter.

"I heard the song, Isaac. Shit, everybody heard the song. And everybody knows what's coming next. Miles has given his whole life to this shit. And I know you love him like he's your own brother. He *is* your brother." Cesar sips his coffee and leans back in his seat. "It shouldn't surprise you that he asked me to get involved. Asked me to help speed up the process."

"He what?"

"Look," says Cesar. He nods at the building they're parked in front of. A bronze plaque-looking money-green sign flanks the glass front door. The sign says *Get Green Records*. "I bought the building," Cesar says. "Built the studio. I'm one-third owner of Get Green Records. Me,

Miles, and James. We begin recording your album today. Miles wanted to surprise you."

Isaac sips his coffee. He hesitates a moment before stepping out of the car. Cesar's smiling. Not arrogant, not cocky—Cesar's smiling a real smile, something Isaac's never seen the man do before in the handful of times their paths have crossed. He seems changed, happy even, like he has arrived at a place he's been trying to get to for a long time.

Isaac follows Cesar into the building, past a simple reception area, cluttered with construction materials. He steps over a few boards and a can of paint, into a dark hallway that leads to a thick wooden door with a glass window. Cesar opens the door for Isaac and Isaac steps inside.

The room has a red tint to it. Fluorescent lights that look a lot like lasers run across the border of the ceiling and walls. The wood floors shine. A long brown leather couch sits elevated off the floor, against the far wall, a small bar beside it, a television mounted to the wall above the bar. James sits at a massive mixing board facing a large window where the sound booth is, headphones on, working the knobs. Miles stands smiling, shaking his head, looking at Isaac. His arms upturned like he's asking Isaac, "Can you believe this shit?"

Isaac can't believe it. Can't believe Miles involved Cesar without asking him first. Cannot believe the deal has already been made, and the excuse—the excuse is that it's a fucking surprise. Miles knows exactly how Isaac feels about Cesar. How many conversations—Miles making Isaac swear to keep secrets from Jackson—until Isaac finally said he's done, don't bring him up, Miles, I don't want to know. And Miles hasn't. But does he really believe that Isaac's opinion has changed? "Miles," says Isaac. "Can we step outside for a minute?" He doesn't wait for Miles to answer. He walks out the studio, down the hallway, and out the door. He shoves Miles against the wall when Miles gets outside. "This is bullshit!" Isaac tells him.

"What?"

"You know damn well what. You know how I feel about that man."

"That man is my father. Let go of my shirt. Shit, bro. Chill out."

Isaac lets go. He hadn't even realized he'd grabbed him.

"Listen," Miles says. "I'm sorry I blindsided you. But this has been in the works for a long time. Cesar's always been involved. It was me telling him to wait . . . to wait for this. This was always going to happen when I found my emcee. All these years, Zick. Every time I bring up Cesar you get all negative and shit."

"So you go behind my back? Just make the decision for both of us? You don't even tell me; you just pull the trigger . . ."

"You judge out of ignorance. You don't know him. Not like I do. I know he's no traditional father. I know that. But he's had my back. This whole time he's had my back and I trust him."

"That's you, Miles. What gives you the right to make that decision for me?"

"All I'm asking is you give him a chance. I'm not even asking you to trust him. I'm asking you to trust me."

Isaac takes a breath. He wouldn't be wrong for walking, he wouldn't. But in spite of the dreadful pit in Isaac's stomach, in spite of his better judgment, for Miles sake he has to see this thing through. "Listen," says Isaac. "I've been thinking . . . is there some other way we can do this thing. I mean, I want to do the album, Miles. I do. And I want you to make some money off it—that's not the problem."

"What's the problem, Isaac? Seriously. You asked me to record the song with you. Practically begged me to do it. You listened to the plan. You must have heard the plan a hundred times. Now you're trying to pull the plug? You're going to play me? Me? Because of Cesar you're going to play *me*?"

"No, that's not what I'm saying. Cesar's a separate issue. I'm not saying pull the plug. I'm just asking can we do things differently."

"Like what? What are you saying?"

"The tour. The stage. It's too much for me, man. I'm tired of being in the spotlight."

"So what's *your* plan, then? How do *you* want to do this?"

"I don't have one . . . I'm asking is there another way? YouTube? iTunes. I don't know."

"What are you afraid of?"

"Nothing, Miles. I'm not afraid. It's not that. Shit's just happening too fast. That's all. And I'm thinking about going to school. Is there a way to do both?"

"Now you're going to school?" Miles laughs. But he's not really laughing. "Wow. Really? You're something else, Isaac." Miles takes a deep breath and looks at the ski. "Listen, we can figure out something that will work for both of us. Let's just record the album and see what happens."

"Okay," Isaac says. "Okay. But what about Cesar?"

"Shit, man. Now we're back on Cesar?"

"Yeah. I just thought about Jackson. He's going to be pissed," says Isaac. "You better not blindside him like you blindsided me," Isaac says. "Or Jackson's gonna hurt that man."

The machine spits out parts at a reckless pace and Tara's expected to keep up. If she doesn't the machine shuts down, an alarm sounds, and a grouchy, mannish-looking supervisor named Lisa comes over and bitches at her. Tara's armed with a box cutter. She trims flash off plastic door panels, inspects them for flaws, and then drops them in a bin. It's boring, but boring never felt so good. Nostalgic in a way too, knowing Joey used to grind in this same factory, come home with the same sore body, the same calloused and cut hands.

Iggy's Place is finally behind her. A closed chapter. A pride-swallowing means to a tolerable end. Her dignity bruised but healing. Her soul still belonging to God. She feels accomplished. She followed through with her plan. Didn't get addicted to the money of the flesh game like most of them do. She got out when she said she was getting out. And in her mind that stands for *something*.

People are sweeping their areas. The shift must be coming to a close. She shuts off her machine and checks her cell-phone. Nothing from Lyric. No texts. No missed calls. Tara's been calling her for weeks.

Texting her. She even left a note at Iggy's Place for her, thinking maybe she'd turn up there. No response. Nothing. She hasn't been by Tara's mother's house either. Tara's beginning to worry. She wipes off her work station with a rag. Sweeps up her mess. Sets her phone on her purse.

This is the worst part of her night. Punching out. The men here aren't shy. Not with their mouths or their eyes. And this walk across the factory to the time clock—Tara feels more naked than she did in that damn glass cage. She could wear sweatpants. Khakis. Jeans. There's just no hiding a big fat ass. They have all night to find excuses to walk by her station and they don't even bother being nonchalant about it. They let Tara see them, they nod and raise an eyebrow at her, they give their approval. It's like they're congratulating her on it.

But whatever. She'll make this walk for the next 20 years if she has to. Anything's better than the alternative. She ignores them, even the polite ones, the ones who keep their eyes to themselves and their comments friendly. She slides her clear safety glasses on top of her head, eyes forward, punches out and leaves. Tonight someone is bold enough to follow her out to the Olds. Joey's Olds. She keeps the oil changed, never lets the brake pads get too thin—she treats it like Joey used to treat it. No matter what their money was ever like Joey Cane took care of his car.

"Tara," this man says. Creepy. Stalker all over him. Eyes like he's hiding something. Like he might have a formaldehyde rag in his pocket, or he might sneak into the breakroom fridge and slip a Mickey into your Diet Coke when you're not looking, and then you wake up chained to a bed in his basement. His type frequent Iggy's Place and Tara scoped his creepy ass out night one on the job: Davis Shaw, six foot something and slim, well-groomed African American male, no wedding ring, ten years on the job, and no one ever invites him out to drinks. "You dropped your phone," he says, extending his hand.

Tara already has the pepper spray out of her purse, cupped in her left hand. She accepts the phone with her right and watches Davis Shaw walk away. False alarm, but you can never be too careful. Tara checks her phone again when she gets in the car. Nothing. She calls Lyric and gets her voicemail. She texts her, *Baby plz come home.*

Tara starts the Olds. All these years and the engine still purrs. Next winter she's going to need a truck though, or something with four-wheel drive. A Delta 88 isn't built for the snow. The Blaze Show is on the radio. "We're back with Miles Davis Green and Isaac Page," Blaze says. The name doesn't register at first. But then she sees that hooded white boy in the driveway. She remembers watching him from the bed-room window that very first time. Early in the morning. She and Joey made love right after.

"Miles," says Blaze. "You've been doing your thing for a minute. I mean the production is dope. Last couple years. Any local act worth his salt has spit to one of your beats. But, Isaac, man, you came out of nowhere. The song: man! But what else can we expect from you?"

"I don't know," says the voice of Isaac Page.

"An album," says the voice of Miles Davis Green. "We're in the pre-production stage right now. Getting the studio up and running. When we lay down something new you'll be the first to know."

"Cool. Cool," Blaze says. "So, Isaac. This Joey Cane cat. He was your mentor?"

Tara grips the steering wheel. Her foot pressed down hard on the brake. The car is still in park.

"He was my friend," says Isaac.

"The song," says Miles Davis Green, "is about overcoming your past. It's about growing up in the southeast side . . ."

"Alright," says Blaze. "Alright, Grand Rapids. Once again this is Miles Davis Green and Isaac Page, a man of few words, and they're hanging out at the Blaze Show. Here it is again. Miles is calling it a southeast side anthem. Here's Isaac Page with The Concrete."

Jackson sits dragging on a Newport, leaned back in a barstool at Iggy's Place. Iggy has two glasses of Hennessy in front of him, the one he's sipping from, and the one Jackson has refused. Iggy is still smoking a cigar in spite of the lymphoma that's eating his chest. Black strands no longer mingle with his silver curls, they've aged. The chemo has corroded his teeth and gums, has thinned his face, has left him a mere shell of his former self.

Seeing his uncle now, for the first time in years, Jackson feels a bit guilty for never checking in on him. How he got to and from all the doctor's appointments, Jackson isn't sure. Who loved Iggy through it, Jackson cannot fathom. So many inconsequential women had come and gone from Iggy's life. So many of them loved Iggy. He returned none of the love.

The club has aged with him. The glass stripper cage is tinted with smoke. The wood floor is soft in places, sighing, complaining beneath Jackson's weight when he walked across it and followed his uncle upstairs. Iggy's Place is nothing like it was in those golden months of Joy Green. When the entrance line wrapped around the block and Iggy got away with charging twenty bucks at the door.

"It's good to see you, Jackie. It's good to see you dry. You alright?"

"I'm trying to be."

"When I called, I didn't think you'd come."

Jackson looks at his uncle. The one with sense in his family. His drunk dad. His wayward aunts. Coming and going; creeping and crawling through the southeast side, no pot to piss in and no back door to throw it out of. In spite of his faults Iggy has always had Jackson's back. Always. But there was something about the way Joy Green was found floating in the river so close to Iggy's Place, naked as when she worked the cage, body swollen with water, nibbled on by creatures, that made Jackson place the blame on his uncle. And he hadn't spoken to him since.

"Word was eventually gonna get back to you," says Iggy, "I figured I'd give you the heads up."

"Heads up?"

"Your boys are doing business with Cesar Bolden."

"Cesar Bolden?"

"He bought that building on Division and Cherry. Built a studio. They're putting out the white boy's album."

"Album."

"Yeah."

"You mean Miles. Not Isaac."

"No, Isaac. The white boy does the rapping. The black boy makes the beats. Shit, Jackie, you don't know? They been playing that song on the radio for weeks—the song about the white boy's friend dying, about his daddy being on drugs."

Jackson glances at the neglected glass of Hennessy. The first real urge he's had in weeks to take a swig. He feels robbed of something. All these years guiding his boys along a path. The path somehow leading to the very thing he was leading them away from. All these years. That same Cadillac. Prowling through the southeast side like a shark. Hiding behind window tint. Hiding behind a gun.

"You got that look in your eyes, Jackie."

Jackson knew it would eventually come to this. He and Cesar have been squaring off for years, with glances, gestures, occasionally words—only once did it come to blows, when he caught Cesar parked on Griggs talking to Miles, when he snatched Cesar out the window of his Caddy while he was trying to pull away, car in gear, coasting against the curb, Jackson beating Cesar bloody before Mae came out the house screaming. Cesar left that day threatening to kill Jackson. But he never came back.

Iggy reaches from behind the bar and sets a pistol in front of Jackson. "Take it," he says. "That man won't let you give him another ass whooping."

Jackson pushes the pistol away. "I don't have violence on my mind, Unc. I think it's about time me and Cesar Bolden have a talk. Man to man."

Why tonight Isaac's thinking about Lyric Cane, he isn't sure. But he's thinking about her. Wondering where she ended up, what her life became, remembering that summer on Francis Street, the summer when everything changed. All that death at once and then that

numb road to the Carter's house, via police station, via group home, via
silver Cavalier driven by a social worker named Doreen.

Isaac finds his laptop on his dresser and sits on the air mattress,
stacks pillows against the wall to lean against. He powers up the laptop and then he logs into Facebook. Types Lyric Cane in the search bar
and hits enter. In her profile pic she wears a hoodie, her curls tumbling
down her cheeks, middle finger pressed against her forehead, fucking
the world. Her background pic is an all-white poster with bold black letters that read *Niggas Ain't Shit!!!* She's listed as single. Her occupation
says *Noneya Damn Business.* Isaac clicks on a photo. She wears black
yoga pants. She sits on the edge of a bed. Her back is arched and her ass
is out. Her phone has a camouflage cover. She wears pink lipstick and
pink nail polish. A TV in the background shows Alex Trebek's face. A
beach towel is draped over a lamp shade next to the TV. The lamp is on.
The towel looks like a glowworm.

Isaac's cursor dangles over the *Add Friend* icon. But what would
he say to her after all these years? Remember me? I was there the night
your dad was murdered. You want to grab some coffee? He moves his
cursor back to her photos. Begins scrolling through them. She'd be
beautiful if she knew it. Instead she's something else. In one picture she
wears a white sports bra. He can see the outline of her pierced nipples
through the nylon. In another she smokes a blunt, blows smoke into the
camera. She's got that southeast side in her. That unapologetically gutter quality that Isaac's never quite understood.

He sets the laptop down and paces. The floor is cold beneath his
socked feet. *That's when I crawled into the concrete and what's left of me survived. But what's survived when existing means you're living in your mind. And
the world keeps on watching but won't look you in the eyes.* Who was Isaac
before he met Joey Cane? He was a kid filling journals with words. Even
before it all went to hell Isaac was writing. Who is he now? A man filling journals with words. Tragedy, considers Isaac, either derails you from
your path or makes you more intent upon it. For him it did both. The boy
in him needed to be derailed. The boy in him needed to be distracted

by basketball. The boy crawled into the concrete so the man could survive. And when the man began to emerge the distraction was no longer needed, the man could do more than peek into the past through spread fingers—the man could face it, learn from it—the man could grow.

Isaac returns to the laptop and clicks the *Add Friend* icon. Then he x's out of Facebook without logging off. He walks over to his bookshelf and finds *This Side of Brightness* by Colum McCann, one of two McCann novels he borrowed from Mae. He tosses the book on the air mattress and then texts her, *Mae, I just wanted to let you know that I'm reading.*

She texts back. *That makes me happy, Isaac* ☺

Moments later she texts again. *Are you ready to talk yet?*

Soon.

Okay, baby. I love you.

I love you too.

Isaac returns to the laptop and searches *Busty Asian*. Scrolls through a few thumbnails but finds nothing of interest. He searches *Busty Latina*. He watches about thirty seconds of a clip before he gets bored. He searches *Busty Ebony*. He scrolls through the thumbnails. Sees the headlines: *Busty Black Teen First Time Anal. Ebony MILF Rides White Cock.* He clicks: A pimply white kid sits on what's supposed to be his friend's mom's couch. The friend isn't home from school yet. The mom, busty as advertised, is braless in a tank top and finding excuses to lean over the boy and drop her boobs in front of his face. Isaac skips the plot and fast forwards to the sex. He loses interest about a minute into the mom giving the pimply boy a blow job.

Isaac exits out of the movie and scrolls on. That's when he sees it. *The Tragedy of Joy Green.* Isaac doesn't want to open the thumbnail, but he has to. That Miles' mother did porn is legend. Isaac knows. Miles knows. But it's not something that's talked about. Not something that's sought out, looked for. It's not something that's actually real. And now he has to see it. It's too late—his cursor hovered over the thumbnail a moment too long, Isaac saw too much and now he has to see more.

A young Joy Green sings about boys. She wears a yellow halter top and stone-washed jeans. Two long pigtails bounce on her shoulders as she moves through the set of her video, clips of her recording the song, clips of her at a park where teenagers break-dance and skateboard, clips of all these different boys trying to get a date with her, Joy playing hard to get. Then the video fades out and Joy's sitting at a table. A cigarette is in her mouth and she's looking away from the camera. "All I ever wanted to do is sing," she says. She isn't crying, but she has been, her eyes look like she made the cameraman wait, like she wanted to get herself together before being interviewed. "I was living the dream," she says. "And then I fucked up. Life started moving too fast for me and I fucked up."

"What do you mean?" It's the unmistakable voice of Cesar Bolden.

"You know what I mean,_____, shit." Cesar's name had been spoken, but had been bleeped out."

Joy looks at the camera now. "I started living that fast life. Drugs, alcohol . . ."

"Then what?"

"Motown dropped me."

"Then what?"

Joy shakes her head and looks away from the camera.

"Can this be over?" Joy asks. The camera focuses in on her hands. Her press-on nails are bitten down to nubs. A vague hint of polish clings to what remains. Then the camera retreats slowly, first revealing her breasts, her neck, and then it finds her eyes.

"Just a few more questions," says Cesar's voice.

"Okay."

"What are you willing to do?" he asks. "What are you willing to do to get high?"

She shakes her head. The cigarette has died. She relights it. Pulls in smoke. Looks away and exhales.

"What are you willing to do to get high?"

"Anything," she says. "Okay, nigga? You happy? Anything."

That's when the sex begins. This is Miles' mother. It's hard for Isaac to wrap his mind around that fact, but he cannot look away—this isn't porn, it's a car crash, or a train wreck, or someone on Wall Street throwing herself off a building. And the clips keep coming, scene after scene until Isaac sees it, sees him—his hands shake on the mouse when he pauses the movie, when he scrolls back to the frame and sees the man hovering over Miles' mother, those unmistakable crackhead eyes, his enormous dick between her breasts, and Isaac tries to scream for Miles, but his mouth has no words, there is no air in his lungs, his heart beating so fast he cannot breathe.

"Miles," Isaac musters a whisper. Then finds the strength to scream, "Miles!"

The house on Francis Street is vacant. Bagged newspapers are scattered across the porch. The front window is busted and boarded. Lyric slides her battered old Creston high school student ID card through the doorjamb. On the second swipe the metal tongue gives and she eases open the door. She puts the ID in her purse and steps inside.

The house is rotting. Mildewed carpet and decaying floorboards. No signs saying it's been lived in since she and her mother left. The place is ransacked and gutted. Robbed of its hot water heater and appliances. She walks up the stairs and into her parent's old bedroom. She stands in front of the window. Blinds hang half-open, caked with dust. She runs her thumb across the flimsy surface and bends it. Blows dust off her finger. Pulls the cord and jumps when the blinds come loose from their socket and land in a pile on the floor. She lights a Marlboro and leaves it pressed between her lips when she opens the window.

Lyric kneels and sets her purse on the floor, rests her elbows on the sill. Chipped white paint. Her name carved in the wood, + *Isaac* carved beside it, a lopsided heart pocket-knifed around their names. She remembers hiding behind the blinds, watching Isaac mourn her father, hiding in his hoodie, the basketball echoing off the concrete, the net half-attached to the bent rim, her father two-weeks dead and not there to buy Isaac a new one. Lyric blows smoke out her nose and watches it float off into the night.

Lyric takes her mother's note out of her back pocket. *Baby, come home.* What home? That two-bedroom apartment where her childhood was stolen from her. Her dead father's pictures all over the walls, his pretty blue eyes seeing everything, watching it all go down. Lyric rubs her broken nose. The little girl who loved her father more than anything in the world is gone. Who survived has survived wolves.

She flicks the dying Marlboro into the driveway, finds a bag of weed in her purse. Then she guts a Cigarillo, wets it with her tongue, twists it in her fingers. She kisses it when she's finished. Lights it. The sweet stink of erb fills the room. She takes a water bottle and two pill cases full of Vicodin from her purse and sets them on the sill. Eighteen to end it. That's what Google told her. She might feel a little pain or she might pass out. She might just slip quietly into death. Cutting her wrists was never an option. She can't even do needles. She could get her hands on a pistol no problem. But could she pull the trigger? And if she did pull the trigger, what if she survived?

Lyric stares across the driveway to the house next door. The window across from hers is shattered. Jagged edges of glass looking like a shark's mouth, like the house is trying to take a bite out of the night. She hits the blunt hard and chokes. A dog barks. Sirens ride the air a few blocks away. She opens the first case of pills and swallows them with a large swig of water. Opens the second and does the same.

Lyric opens her eyes and she's on the floor. How much time has passed she isn't sure. The room pulses. The moon is full. She can see it through the open window. It appears to be resting on Isaac Page's roof. Then she's walking through a dream she once had. Where she's standing on a black marble path surrounded by trees made of bone. The eagle dream with the glass leaves. The dream where her father was an eagle. Only this time she feels like an eagle too. Like if she could only get to the window she could fly away. But she's so heavy. It's like she's pinned to the floor. She holds her hand in front of her face and she wiggles her fingers. She sits and the moon whirls in wide circles over Isaac's house and then lands in her palm. She kisses the moon before setting it free. Reaches for the window sill and pulls herself to her knees and closes her eyes.

She hears a basketball echoing off the concrete. She hears her father's voice. Pictures him, a cigarette in his mouth, one behind his ear, wearing sandals with long white socks. Isaac Page is young again, hiding beneath a hood and clinging to every word her father says. But when she opens her eyes no one is there. She's tired.

She feels no pain.

She rests her head on the window sill.

Lyric stares down onto the empty driveway.

Only on the rare occasion will Cesar drink, but tonight he sips a Leroy Burgundy alone, standing at the window of his apartment watching an orange cat paw through his neighbor's trash. The woman sleeping on his couch is fully clothed, a Puerto Rican bank manager and graduate student named Angie who Cesar met a few weeks back. She's thirty with no kids. She has nothing to do with the flesh game. With this one Cesar's taking his time.

Cesar closes the blinds. He lets Angie sleep. He hasn't decided if he'll lay down with her yet. Because right now she's perfect. Her slender neck. Her death-black short-cropped hair. The way her ass curves out from the small of her back and steals two inches off the length of any skirt she wears. And Cesar knows himself all too well. He knows she'll have to conquer his heart before he conquers her body—knows that if he sleeps with her too soon they'll have no chance of lasting.

His lifestyle has changed considerably. Life has slowed down. He no longer fears the sirens, his door being kicked in by the police, a bullet in the head by somebody he's wronged. He's found some version of peace while navigating his forties, leaving the drug game clean, and the flesh game cold turkey, that night at the Holiday Inn, watching Little Thunderbooty, barely of age, that carnage was the end of it, all he could stomach. He paid her but never released the movie. He shut down the website. That night was the end.

He's accepted there are some wrongs he can never right. He can never give Joy her life back. Cannot give Isaac Page back his family. So many lives he's affected. Generations of lives. Families broken or destroyed. One day Cesar will have to answer to God. But tomorrow is Sunday. Tomorrow he'll go down to the river, look out at the water, and make his peace with Joy Green. He'll say his apology to the wind. Then he'll close that door and move on.

A fist pounds Cesar's door. His cell phone vibrates on the kitchen counter. It's Miles. Angie looks up from the couch. She rubs her eyes and then lies back down. Cesar sets his half-drank wine glass on the counter. He walks over to the door and checks the peephole. Unbolts the door. Miles is dressed like he got dressed in a hurry. His shirt is buttoned off-track and his collar isn't folded down. His shoes aren't tied.

"Shh," Cesar says. "She's sleeping."

"You think I give a fuck about that bitch on your couch?"

"Whoa. Whoa," Cesar says. "Kill that noise. What's on your mind, Miles. What happened?"

"I trusted you," Miles says. His fists are clenched. He's rocking back and forth on his feet like he's trying to decide whether or not to swing.

"Miles, what happened?"

"The Tragedy of Joy Green," Miles says. "It's online. I saw, Cesar. I heard your voice. I saw what you made her do."

"You don't understand . . ."

"Understand? You degraded my mom. You filmed it. And Isaac's dad? You knew this whole goddamn time and never said a thing. Got the nerve to go in business with us like none of that shit ever happened. I bet you had something to do with his dad's death too, didn't you,"

Miles says. "Aw, shit." Miles grips his head. "You did, didn't you? Man, I see it in your eyes."

"Miles, I'm sorry about your mom. I am. I mean that."

"Sorry? Keep your sorry. And stay the fuck away from me too. We're done, Cesar. The music. Everything. I don't want to hear from you. We're through."

Miles slams the door on his way out. Cesar follows him. "Wait! Miles, wait."

"Nigga, I said we're through!"

"At least let me explain."

Miles turns. "Explain? That's my mom, Cesar. What can you say?"

"The truth," Cesar says. "All I can say the truth."

"Who's truth? Yours?"

"The truth."

Miles says nothing. He stands there with his arms crossed. Cesar says, "I loved her, Miles, but your mom had that beast in her. She was a junkie. There was nothing I could do."

"If you loved her you would have gotten her some help. If you loved her, you would've put her in rehab."

"She was too far gone."

"You couldn't try?"

"I should have. Look, Miles. I can't do anything about the past but apologize. I'm sorry about your Mom. I'm sorry you had to find out the way you did."

"Sorry isn't good enough, Cesar. I thought I knew you. I trusted you."

"You do know me, Son."

"No," says Miles. "I don't."

Then he's gone. Driving away in his green Chevy Impala.

"Cesar," says Angie. When Cesar gets back inside. "Who was that?"

"The neighbor," Cesar tells her. "He was mad cause I parked in his spot.

"Oh," she says, standing now. "What time is it?"

"It's late."

"Can we go to bed?"

She doesn't wait for Cesar to answer. He watches her walk through the living room and turn down the hallway. He follows. Stands on the threshold of the room, watches Angie turn on his bedside lamp and slip out of her clothes. Each butt cheek has a dimple. A tattoo that says Antonio makes a rainbow across the small of her back. He could ask Angie to get dressed.

He could tell her to leave.

But tonight he doesn't want to be alone.

Tonight Cesar Bolden has never been more alone.

Dee's dressed in a black Burberry suit with gray pinstripes. The Ruger lies barrel-down in his breast pocket. A Victoria's Secret bag sits on the seat beside him. Today could be his last day breathing free air, or his last day breathing—Dee's ready for either—but first he needs to close a chapter, to die or go to Jackson State Penitentiary with no regrets.

The limousine pulls up to the corner of Cherry and Division and Dee rolls down the window. Kat wanders like she always wanders these days: from car to car, corner to corner. This morning she's dressed in sweatpants and heels, in a pink crewneck sweatshirt with the state of Michigan outlined in green. *Mitten Made,* the sweatshirt says. Kat smiles and walks over. "Get in on the other side," Dee tells her, showing her a one-hundred-dollar bill, then rolling up the window.

"The Grand Plaza or the Marriott. You choose," he tells her. She glances at the Ruger. Dee smiles. "Don't worry, baby," he says. "That pistol ain't got nothing to do with you."

"The Marriott," Kat says. She crosses her arms over her chest.

They don't speak the rest of the ride.

The room overlooks the river. Dee hands Kat the Victoria Secret bag and tells her to go wash up. Tells her to take her time. Dee stands at the window looking at Iggy's Place, at the river, at the Blue Bridge. Cesar isn't out there yet but the sun is shining. It would be a beautiful day to die. Bathwater runs. After awhile the room is filled with the scent of bath salts and body wash. The smell reminds Dee of spicy peaches. Dee sets the Ruger on a table next to a black duffle bag. The bag holds $50,000 and enough crack for Kat to stay high for weeks. Dee loosens his tie and sits.

A fog of steam follows Kat out the bathroom. Her hair has been washed. It's damp and already beginning to curl. A shear pink teddy clings to her. She walks over to Dee and kneels in front of him. Starts for his zipper. "Not like this," he tells her. "Like you love me." She takes his hand and leads him to the bed. Her breath, her body—she smells like a woman should smell, the crack has been washed away, her need hidden beneath the scent of shampoo and body splash. She kisses him. "I love you, baby," she whispers in his ear. "I love you so much." He believes her. She's barely touched him and he feels like he's going to come. He steps away. Walks over to the window. Cesar still isn't out there.

"What's wrong, baby?" Kat asks him.

"Take it off," Dee tells her. He turns and watches her strip. He'd imagined so much less than what he was seeing—he'd imagined the thickness of a thick aging woman, her body just past ripe and already beginning to go. But Kat is firm. A rose tattoo on her left breast, its stem and thorns twisting around her nipple. Her pussy is shaved bald. It looks pale gray or light purple. It's beautiful.

"Come here, baby," Kat says.

He's worried he'll bust his nut the moment she touches him. He's worried he'll die without knowing what a grown woman's pussy feels like. She kisses his cheek. His lips. Unzips his pants. Takes him in her mouth. It's crawling through him. He's got a minute at most. "Wait," Dee says. "Shit, wait a minute."

"We have all day, baby," Kat tells him. But they don't. Today is the day. Dee didn't see a sign in the sky, there was no message from God. He just woke up this morning to the voices, to the whispers, something in his bones saying today is the day. Today is the day Cesar Bolden has to die. *Kill him, Dee,* the voice whispered, continues to whisper. *Do it for your daddy.* He just has to do this one thing first. This one thing. He has to know what it feels like.

Dee takes his dick in his hand. "Can we just skip the foreplay?"

"This is your show, baby."

Dee watches Kat scoot to the edge of the bed and lie on her back. Spread her legs. He hikes his slacks down a little and buries his dick in her as deep as he can. He doesn't stroke, doesn't move, he just stops fighting the throb and lets go. Kat lies there rubbing his back. Dee closes his eyes. The *good* good. No matter how this day goes, there's this. Now there will always be this.

"Baby," Kat says. "You okay?"

"I came."

"Don't worry about it. Take some time to recover. We can do it again."

Dee leaves her lying in the bed. He zips his pants and walks over to the window. Cesar's out there now looking down at the water. Dee unzips the duffle bag and empties the crack on the table. Kat sits on the edge of the bed. "The room is yours," Dee tells her. The Ruger is back in the breast pocket. The duffle back is zipped and strapped over his shoulder. His tie is tightened.

"If anybody asks," Dee says. "I did it for my daddy."

The shooter, a young black male, fires twice at Jackson when he sees him, and then runs the opposite direction, into the city, where moments later he is chased by a chorus of sirens. Cesar Bolden could be Jesus falling from the cross. The way his arms are spread, his body limp, landing face-first on a mound of earth poking out of the low river. Money floats down behind Cesar in slow swooping arcs. Jackson finds a hundred-dollar bill pinned to the bridge railing by the wind. He drops the bill over the bridge and looks down at Cesar's body.

Iggy's outside now. Lighting a cigar and walking toward Jackson. The sirens are so loud it's hard to decipher which direction they come from. Since his sobriety Jackson's been thinking a lot about forgiveness. Apologies owed and apologies owed to him. Jackson's decided you have to forgive yourself for the wrongs that you've done. That's the only way to change. You have to forgive those who have wronged you even if they don't ask for forgiveness. He'd come down here to forgive Cesar. To free himself from years of animosity. He'd come down here ask Cesar to leave the boys alone, to let them find their own way. And now looking down at Cesar Bolden's body what Jackson feels is pity. How many will mourn this man? Who really understood the root behind his choices? We all have a story. Who will understand Cesar Bolden's story?

"Put your hands behind your head!" Officers come from both sides of the bridge. Their guns are drawn. They walk in assault formation. Jackson interlocks his fingers behind his head. The breeze feels great today. The memories Jackson has on this river. So much love and so much pain. So much history. How many Newport ashes live in this water, how many butts flicked off the edge of the railing at Iggy's Place, remembering Joy Green and loving her and wishing she'd love him in return. How many afternoons with Mae? Holding hands and feeling this same breeze. Jackson remembers the exact moment he fell in love with her. Walking the boardwalk, getting bit up by mosquitoes and Mae kept slapping those mosquitoes off of him and when Jackson glanced her way he noticed Mae was covered with them. She was covered with mosquitoes but was taking care of Jackson instead. The most selfless person he's ever known. And all Mae ever asked for was sobriety.

They used to walk this river and Mae would talk of all her plans to travel. They vowed to take a trip a year. Rome, Costa Rica, Africa. They'd get passports and no matter what life became, no matter how busy it made them, each year they'd choose a location and they'd go there. All these years. No passports. No flights. No vacations. All those broken promises and Mae never said a word about it. And sometimes

Jackson would remember those promises and in his mind he'd plan a surprise vacation for her, but those plans never left his mind. He was a drunk. All of his ideas stayed ideas. Nothing was ever done.

He owes Mae a marriage. He owes Mae the life he stole from her. He owes her sobriety. Jackson knows what needs to be done. Even if she makes him beg, he's no longer accepting no for an answer. Mae might believe their love is dead, but Jackson knows better. Love knows no grave. Real love can rise from the ashes. Mae's home is here. With Isaac. With Miles. Hank McCoy is wrong; Mae's place is with Jackson. This marriage isn't over. She saw something in him that no one else saw. He couldn't even see it in himself. He's ready to be that man. He sees the open road, windows down in the F150, the southeast side of Grand Rapids, Michigan, at his back.

"On your knees!"

He's going to Mississippi.

Jackson's going to Mississippi and he's not taking no for an answer. He's not coming home without her.

The number four bus bullies its way down Eastern Avenue. Hydraulics handling the potholes, the driver tailgates the sedan in front of her, holds down her horn and almost rear-ends the car when it brakes abruptly. Isaac leans against the window, hooded, his breath fogging the glass. A bouquet of pink carnations sits beside him. A backpack between his feet.

A young couple sit a few rows in front of Isaac. A black boy and a white girl. The boy holds a sleeping baby against his chest, kissing its cheek every so often. The girl strokes the boy's thigh and watches the outside world. Her worried expression morphs into a smile when the boy reaches for her hand.

Isaac lifts the flowers and smells them. After DeMarco Payne's son lost a gunfight with the police, DeMarco Payne talked. He told it all.

About his involvement in Cesar Bolden's crack empire, about the accidental death of Joy Green, about getting paid $10,000 to murder Frank Page and Terrell Lewis and bury them on Punk Island.

DeMarco was featured on *60 Minutes*. The story had the city in an uproar. When they returned from Mississippi the press was staked out on Griggs Street. Jackson parked the F150, took a deep breath, and dealt with the reporters while Isaac watched from the living room window, Mae rubbing his head. Miles put his headphones on and went upstairs, to their old bedroom, a man of few words since the day his father died.

Cesar left Miles millions. How much was crack money and how much was legit money the feds weren't able to sort out. Cesar's books were immaculate. He filed taxes for his porn business. Every cent was accounted for. And with no trial to be had, said Jackson, they had no choice but to let Miles have the money. Cesar also left Miles the studio. Isaac's album on hold, but they left the door open, "Just in case you change your mind," said Miles. Then he used "The Concrete" as the first single on the debut album for his label, a mix tape titled *Death and Taxes*, featuring several local artists, and a few major acts, who Miles paid generously. The album is set to release this winter.

Isaac unzips his backpack and pulls out a folder. A masking tape label is stuck to the red binder, *Intermediate Creative Nonfiction* written on it in black Sharpie. He opens the folder and pulls out an essay by a kid that goes by Sully. A wild-haired sarcastic kid that Isaac considers a friend. He goes over his notes. A combination of praise and criticism for Sully's piece about fathers and sons and guilt and religion. Satisfied with his comments, Isaac puts the folder away.

Isaac pulls the bell cord and the bus chimes loud as his stop approaches. He grabs his backpack and the flowers before he stands. He exits the bus from the side door, walks across Eastern, and begins his trek through green grass littered with dead leaves. The November air has teeth. Isaac zips his hoodie and navigates through tombstones of varying sizes. He's at ease among the dead. Some graves with flowers, some without.

Joey Cane's grave is marked with a concrete headstone with black

Acknowledgments

I thank God for the gift, the path, and the courage to walk it.

To my wife and children: I owe an apology. For spending three and a half years with one foot in the real world and one foot in the world of THE CONCRETE. For being preoccupied and unavailable. For being moody and often unpleasant to be around. I cannot give you those three and a half years back, but I promise to be better and more aware on future projects.

I owe thanks to the many people who have contributed to the creation of this work:

Garrett Dennert, for always being available and honest and armed with a red pen when I need a second set of eyes.

Jesse Davila, for his friendship and for sharing this journey with me.

My teachers: Sean Prentiss, who preached a blue-collar approach to revision, which has become the backbone of my writing process; Caitlin Horrocks, for her great influence on my early development as a writer; Dominic Stansberry, who saw past my circus of sentences and unapologetically told me I didn't know $#%& about plot; Ellen Lesser, for putting on scrubs and white gloves and taking a scalpel to the early, sludgy drafts of THE CONCRETE; Connie May Fowler, who went way beyond her job description, who treated my work with great passion and tenacity, and refused to accept average. ·

My agent, Sarah Levitt, for her vision, her relentlessness, and her keen editing eye.

My editor, Robert Lasner, for recognizing the beauty in the ugly world of THE CONCRETE and for taking a chance on me.

My family, who probably thinks I'm crazy, and has no idea what it is that I do, yet love and support me anyway.

THE CONCRETE is in the world largely because of all of you.